If It Makes You Happy

If It Makes You Happy

CLAIRE KANN

SQUARE
FISH

Swoon Reads

New York

SQUARE FISH

An imprint of Macmillan Publishing Group, LLC
120 Broadway, New York, NY 10271
fiercereads.com

Square Fish and the Square Fish logo are trademarks of Macmillan and are used
by Swoon Reads under license from Macmillan.

Our books may be purchased in bulk for promotional, educational, or business use. Please
contact your local bookseller or the Macmillan Corporate and Premium Sales Department at
(800) 221-7945 ext. 5442 or by email at MacmillanSpecialMarkets@macmillan.com.

Library of Congress Cataloging-in-Publication Data is available.

Originally published in the United States by Swoon Reads
First Square Fish edition, 2021
Book designed by Liz Dresner

Square Fish logo designed by Filomena Tuosto

ISBN 978-1-250-25087-2 (paperback)

10 9 8 7 6 5 4 3 2 1

For my troubles and my sorrow

One

My heart stuttered as thick gray smoke billowed into the air, rapidly filling Goldeen's small kitchen. Angry reddish-orange flames licked the sides of the formerly pristine stainless-steel oven, singeing it a sooty black.

Rage snarled bright and furious inside me. I had spent a whole hour last night polishing that oven!

Running on autopilot, I hit the emergency off switch and grabbed the fire extinguisher. "Move out of the way!"

My cousin, Sam, decided somewhere in the depths of her brain that panicking within an inch of her life would somehow magically put the fire out.

Hands shaking, I pulled the pin, aimed the nozzle, and let the life—and business—saving carbon dioxide flow, sweeping it across the base of the fire and into the mouth of the oven until the flames winked out of existence.

"I know what you're going to say." Sam fanned smoke away from her worried face. "So I think we'd be better off without you saying it. I'll just quietly get my bag and exit stage right—"

"Pursued by a furious Winnie. What the hell, Sam?" I slammed the extinguisher on the metal prep table.

Sam flinched. "It was an accident."

Swaddled in her usual black and neon-colored gear—this time a mix of electrifying blue and dazzle-me yellow—with her permed bone-straight hair held back from her forehead with a headband, she nervously picked at her lips. She wore her post-exercise glow like a supermodel lathered in oil and dropped into an ocean to create that maximum shiny yet somehow sexy drowned rat vibe. Rain or shine, that girl got her endorphins in. And judging by the way sweat continued to glisten on her tanned skin and stain her clothes, it must have already been hotter than hell outside.

Don't yell, don't yell, don't yell, don't yell. I pinched the bridge of my nose, silently counting to ten. According to my mom, deep breaths in and out would help control my temper in times of crisis or "severe emotional instability." I would have tried that, too—if I weren't standing in a kitchen full of lingering smoke because the oven had been on fire!

Seven . . . eight . . . nine . . .

Sam's eyes would start to water if someone looked at her funny. Berating her first thing in the morning after a near-death experience would make her unleash a torrential downpour at me.

It probably hadn't been her fault. Maybe. Hard to say. My cousin could not cook. Couldn't even follow a recipe to make toast without it ending in disaster. Goldeen's definitely needed a new oven, which hadn't done Sam any favors.

"I would hope so." A joke formed in my mind, one Sam would appreciate. "I know Granny is in self-righteous mode right now and refuses to buy a new oven, but this is *not* how you scam an insurance company. You set an inconspicuous, untraceable, freak-accident fire, and flee the scene. You don't stand around screaming '*help me.*'"

Sam coughed and let loose a tiny smile. "I would make a terrible criminal."

"The worst. Which is why you are always the alibi."

She raised her right hand. "I accept my role as an eternal getaway driver, capable of convincing anyone of my ability to be in two places at once, and hereby subject myself to your masterminded whims."

"That's all I ask."

"Can I have a hug?" Her pouty, remorseful face was too cute for her own good.

"No. You're all sweaty."

"Okay."

"Yes, you can have a hug. Come here." Sam didn't hesitate, clinging to me like a baby koala in milliseconds. She wrapped her arms around my waist, placing her head on my shoulder, and I perched my chin on the top of her head. The distinct sound of a sniffle made me sigh deeper than I wanted her to hear.

"Why does it smell like barbecued dog hair in here?"

Winston stood at the foot of the stairs that led to the apartment above the diner in his rumpled plaid pajamas, a neutral frown on his face. To be fair, that was his natural state: pseudo-surly and quiet. At fourteen, he'd already grown into a small giant, towering over me at a solid six feet two to my average five feet six, and gave me major attitude when I introduced him as my "baby" brother.

The fact that we didn't look alike burned my biscuits faster than Goldeen's faulty oven. Taller, thinner, with darker, richer skin that he'd inherited from our dad and strong, symmetrical facial features he got from our mom, how else were people supposed to know that he was mine if I didn't tell them every chance I got? No one thought we were related at first glance because we looked like total opposites. I couldn't trust people to just guess one of the most important facts of my life. I was his big sister—his *only* big sister. They needed to *know*.

"It does not," Sam said, letting me go. "If anything, it smells like burnt Cinnamon Toast Crunch." She had the audacity to giggle at her bad joke.

"Obviously." He walked toward the emergency exit that wasn't really an emergency exit because the alarm had been disabled so it could be used as a regular door, but it still had all of the fancy red-striped tape. He pushed it open and set a box of glass preserves jars on the ground to keep it that way. "It's from the movie. I watched it again last night."

We'd watched the original *Ghostbusters* on the two-hour flight to Misty Haven, the small town where our granny owned a diner: Goldeen's. We stayed here every summer, me being the record-holder for twelve straight years, sort of like summer camp, except with less macaroni-and-popsicle-stick art, more family time, and better food.

Also, *small town* meant the smallest. According to Wikipedia—shut up—Misty Haven, with its population of 352, qualified as a village.

Correction: population of 354. The Berkowitz family had twins in April.

"What did you do?" Winston asked.

"Why did you assume it was me?" Sam whined. "It could have been Winnie."

"I heard you screaming. And besides, Winnie knows how to cook"—he peered into the charbroiled mess of an oven—"cinnamon rolls, without it looking like a botched arson job. Goldeen's doesn't need money that bad. Granny will break down and buy a new oven eventually."

"That's exactly what I said. Great minds."

"I thought the kids might like them." Sam didn't work in the diner like Winston and I. Somehow, she became *the* babysitter for Misty Haven. Her phone started ringing the second we crossed the town limits, as if all the desperate parents could sense her presence. They'd probably been staring out the window, waiting to spot Granny's dark blue Cadillac—still in mint condition for such an old car—and lit up the community phone tree like it was Christmas and no one cared about the electricity bill.

"I'm sure they would have," I said. "Next time, ask for help. Please. I'm begging you."

"Fine."

"Winston, can you get me a rag and a bucket?"

"I cannot. My shift doesn't start until ten so I'm going back to bed. I just wanted to be nosy and get my insults in before you tried to make her feel better. Once again, I was too late," he said with a wistful sigh.

"Jerk," Sam said.

"Don't start." I pointed my finger in warning at both of them.

"Blame puberty." Winston shrugged. "I'm supposed to be this way and it's only going to get worse."

"Not in my house."

"Good thing this isn't your house," he said, walking away with a wave.

"He's going to be a demon by the time he turns sixteen. I can feel it." Unsurprising, really. We might not have looked alike, but we certainly made up for it elsewhere. "And he'll make an excellent apprentice." I twirled around. "Okay! Let's get this cleaned up before Aaron gets here and tries to glower you into oblivion."

"Umm," Sam said.

"Oh, no. You are not leaving me alone to clean up your mess."

"I'm sorry. My shift starts in twenty minutes and I still have to shower. You know how Ms. Fellows gets if I'm not on time."

"What's she gonna do? Fire you? No one else is willing to watch her kids."

"That's not their fault. They're good kids. Hence the cinnamon rolls." She inched closer to the stairs.

One, two, three . . .

One day, Sam would stop being so thoughtless and irresponsible.

Four, five, six . . .

One day, I would stop letting her get away with (cinnamon roll) murder.

Seven, eight, nine . . .

One day.

But one day was not that day.

"Go. And know that I hate you," I said.

Sam changed direction, leaping forward and hugging me again. "You're the best."

"The beautiful. The only," I muttered.

She bounded away, happy as a rabbit to once again skate by scot-free, while I covered my face, staring at the ruined mess of an oven through my fingers.

These days, fire and Goldeen's went hand in hand. Kit and caboodle. Peas in a pod. You'd think an established diner would do anything to avoid that whole no open flames in the kitchen next to the full fryer of oil thing, but no, not at Goldeen's. Nothing short of a miracle that the oven didn't explode set at—I squinted at the thermostat—500 degrees?

Yep. Definitely Sam's fault. "How many times do I have to tell you that you cannot bake something at double the temperature to make it cook twice as fast?!" I yelled up the stairs, for the sake of doing it.

"I'M SORRY!"

"What in the world happened to my kitchen?"

Aaron—the day, night, always around and available cook—stood at the door, legendary glower already in place. White and tall, something like six feet seven or some unreal height, he had the honor of being one of the few people who actually made Winston look up. He also had dirty blond hair in a military-style cut, only wore white

T-shirts and dark blue jeans, and had a wicked scar on his left cheek. Nadiya, the mid-shift waitress, might or might not have been slightly obsessed with him. Said he resembled an actor who played a Viking vampire.

But, as far as I knew, and I knew more than most when it came to Top Secret Agent Aaron, he wasn't interested in anyone. Ever.

"Murphy's Law," I answered.

Samantha Murphy-Woodson. Winston had come up with the catchall explanation. With Sam at the helm, whatever could go wrong would. And then probably spontaneously combusted. Metaphorically and literally.

"We open in thirty minutes! Why did you let her anywhere near my kitchen?"

"Me? I didn't!"

I'd been upstairs, minding my merry, magical Black-girl business, getting ready for my morning shift. This summer I'd volunteered to work the shifts nobody wanted or that everyone wanted a break from: Crack of Dawn A.M. Rush, Midnight Oil Solo Burn, and I Dream of Deliveries.

Goldeen's had the best uniforms. Total fifties-style hoopskirts and button-up tops with rolled-up short sleeves in mellow mint-green and black. Instead of a poodle, a cluster of unicorn seahorses had been sown onto the fabric of the skirt in the front. And the best part? They were custom-made by a retired seamstress in town. I never had to worry about not being able to fit my uniform after a school year away or having to order a new one every summer. Miss Jepson, said seamstress who operated a costume shop, altered it for me, no questions asked.

"I ran downstairs when she started screaming," I said. "'*Oh my God, it's on fire. Help. Someone help me.*' Somehow it didn't cross her mind to pick up the fire extinguisher."

"That child is an absolute disaster."

"That she is. But she's my disaster, and so I take full responsibility."

Aaron side-eyed me, blue eyes narrowing into harsh slits that made me bare my teeth at him in a warped version of a smile.

"Nobody asked you to do that."

"Some things don't need to be asked." I shrugged.

Sam's mom died when she was four. After the funeral, she and her dad, my uncle Mark, moved in with my family—a short-term arrangement that lasted two years. When my parents wanted to buy a house, they came with us. She wasn't my sister, but we've been together for a good chunk of our respective existences. I didn't know a life without Sam in it every waking moment. Could barely even remember it.

Aaron raised his hand like he wanted to touch the top of my head, but stopped himself, arm returning to his side. "You're a good kid."

"I prefer almost-adult, but thank you." I poked him in the side.

Physical affection was my jam, everyone knew that, but I didn't really like it when people touched my hair without asking, so the fact that he stopped made me happier than if he would have actually done it.

Using a pot holder, he exhumed the charred remains of what should have been lightly browned, flaky deliciousness, soon to be topped with Goldeen's secret-recipe cream-cheese icing cinnamon rolls.

"I'll get this cleaned up. You handle the opening?"

"Deal." I smiled at him, a real one. "Thanks."

Goldeen's stayed open twenty hours a day, closing from two a.m. to six a.m. because those were "druggie and serial killer" hours, as Granny had put it.

Meanwhile in Misty Haven reality, that's when the cleaning crew showed up to polish the diner to a brilliant shine.

Out front I booted up the registers, cashed in, and prepared the bank deposit, then leaped from booth to booth to open the blinds and left a message for Frank, the oven repair guy, to have him on standby.

Twelve whole summers of working and practically living in Goldeen's and I'd only been officially on the payroll for three of them—this summer being the most important one yet.

Co-Assistant Manager. Printed on my new shiny name tag and everything.

My family's business, our legacy, Goldeen's had stood strong and proud and profitable hundreds of miles away from me for almost fifteen years. She opened her doors right before my fourth birthday, right before Winston had been born, right before my family packed up and moved to the Bay Area.

When Granny had bought the building, she'd decided to keep the original Formica-topped bar and round stools in front of the kitchen, and the booths on the opposite side against the front windows. My dad had picked out the sea-green upholstery and the coral-reef-inspired tiles for the floor. My mom had decorated the walls: starfish, pearls, netting, paintings of mermaids and sirens, old boats and ship's wheels. And then, there was me, in all of my three-year-old, gap-toothed glory, given the most important job of all. I got to pick the name.

"Gowdeens."

I couldn't even say the name right, but it was my favorite Pokémon. Luckily, my mom spoke fluent Toddler!Winnie and knew exactly what I'd meant.

My parents had their careers, an English professor and a welder slash artist. Sam's dad had his, an exceptional carpentry business. Sam herself knew she wanted to be a nutritionist and kinesiologist, and Winston hadn't figured anything out yet.

Personally, I'd always thought about my future in possibilities.

Maybe I'd go to college evolved into maybe I'd major in hospitality to maybe I'd be a diner owner someday. And maybe that diner would be Goldeen's.

Juggling the large key ring in my hand until I found the right one, I walked to the front door. Two cars were already waiting in the parking lot, and a third—a large white van—was pulling into the accessible parking spot. Customers ready and waiting before we opened usually meant it would be a good day, and a good day meant lots of profits, and lots of profits meant a happy Granny. Nothing made her happier than a nice bank deposit.

I unlocked the door at the same exact time as the all too familiar *whomp* of a fire starting erupted out of the kitchen, followed by startled shouts from Aaron.

"*Oh damn it*," I said, already running. "I'M COMING."

Two

There's an old movie about a girl dying from cancer who wished to be in two places at once, among other more pertinent things. And so, the boy who loved her, in true Prince Charming of the high school variety fashion, drove her to the state line. They stood together, straddling that metaphysical border, metaphorically making her wish come true, and subsequently ruining the real lives and standards of romantics everywhere.

Like mine.

Anyway, that's how the town lines between Misty Haven and its sister city had been set up. Cross a street and boom: WELCOME TO MERRY HAVEN. POPULATION 478.

Together, they were known as Haven Central, but both town mayors had enough ego to put up back-to-back signs, depending which side of the street you were on.

THANK YOU FOR VISITING . . .

WELCOME TO . . .

I made the right turn out of Misty and into Merry, driving down Main Street—one long strip lined with shops on either side. Merry had tried its best but definitely lacked the idyllic beauty that Misty possessed. But the houses?

Visitors would hop off the freeway, drive through Merry, and ogle the homes. They'd also stop at a few of the shops because why not, and eat at a diner because might as well. Cheaper than going to the movies and an excellent opportunity for pee breaks on road trips.

Most of the houses slanted toward becoming historical landmarks. Old enough to be considered too important to tear down, but sturdy enough to be lived in with some slight renovations. According to ye olde Mayor Way, any remodeling required city approval and usually excluded any "extravagant" exterior work. That's how most of the houses became a quirky mishmash of the past and the future. On the outside you'd think you'd find a house full of Puritans ready to hang some witches, or witches ready to bake some kids, but inside you'd swear someone let Steven Spielberg have at it to create a futuristic domestic wonderland.

The Meyers, the most (in)famous family in Merry, had the distinct honor of being my first delivery of the day. I'd been to their house dozens of times last summer on official Goldeen's business but had never gotten past their kitchen, which kept things disappointingly normal for the most part. Chrome with black trim everywhere and a hardwood floor that probably killed their heating bill in the winter. Or they wore a lot of socks and flannel to keep warm. That's what my family did anyway.

I slid the gigantic tray of deviled eggs onto the counter before heading back out to the car for the array of pretentious-yet-delicious finger sandwiches, multicolored macarons, and mini egg-and-bacon quiches with the finest chops of green onions. Aaron always sent a list of typed-up instructions for how to reheat the food if they wanted, so I placed that on top of one of the lids, in plain sight.

"Hey! Delivery lady who no one thought to help carry the trays needs a signature!"

A familiar voice replied, "Do you always yell in people's houses so early in the morning?" Dallas Meyer. The bane of my romantic existence.

Distracted and trying to find the delivery paper, I said, "Only if they're special." I looked up—a startled gasp ripped out of me. My hand slapped over my mouth on reflex.

Dallas had shaved his head! All of those soft, natural curls—gone. Just gone! I moved my hand long enough to whisper, "You're bald! Oh my God, you're bald!" before putting it right back over my mouth.

"Not quite." He laughed.

The remaining shorn hair made his light brown skin, which he took amazing care of, seem brighter.

Ordering Korean beauty products and using face masks a minimum of twice a week kind of amazing. He even had his eyebrows professionally done once a month. Anyone who spent more than two minutes watching YouTube videos could tell that was not a natural arch. Not that he kept his beauty routine a secret or anything. In Haven Central, secrets of any kind never lasted.

Dallas walked toward me, still smiling. My inability to stop making an overdramatic fool of myself must have been amusing. He stood on the other side of the kitchen island, kitty-corner to me.

Me, who couldn't stop staring at the top of his head.

He leaned forward into my space. Mint and some kind of sweet-smelling cologne washed over me. He'd already put in his contacts. Clear ones because he didn't need to enhance his already freakishly lovely blue-green hybrid color.

I planted my feet, waiting, looking him in the eye, but blinking far too often. He probably thought I'd developed a twitch in the last thirty seconds. Eye contact made me nervous sometimes, but I wanted to do this. I wanted to be there in that moment, so I pushed myself to be strong.

"Dallas?"

"Hmm?"

I'd had dreams about touching those curls. Long, detailed dreams that I would *never* confess to, not even to save my life. It was just hair. It would grow back. But still—"Why did you cut off your hair?"

He smiled wider, squinty and cute with his stupid button nose, and rubbed the top of his head. "Kind of just decided to do it and then did it. My mom screamed when she saw me. Do you like it?"

"I don't dislike it," I admitted before grinding my teeth at my stupidity.

His hand seemed to move in slow motion. Before I took my next breath, I knew where his hand was headed . . . and I waited. I waited for him to touch my braids. His fingers wrapped around a cluster of them, holding them loosely in his open palm. "These look nice on you. I like the little gold clips." He kept on staring at my braids while I shamelessly stared at his bow-shaped lips.

A swirl of infatuation and self-loathing curdled in my stomach, made my palms sweat, and my heart beat fast enough to register some kind of arrest—until I stomped a mudhole in it, forcing it down, down, down for the millionth time. It was never going to happen. Never. Boys like him didn't date girls like me. The End. No need for a sequel. No need to waste my emotional energy.

A small voice in my head, which sounded suspiciously exactly like my mom's, screamed something about *self-rejection*, but I ignored it. I always did.

Taking a half step back, I angled my torso away from him as my braids slid out of his hand. He looked up at me, eyebrows slightly raised.

"No touching without permission." I winked at him and smiled. It would have been nice if he had asked first, but I wasn't mad. I would've stopped him if I truly wanted to. So.

"Ah, sorry." The tiniest bit of redness flooded his apple cheeks as he cleared his throat. He righted himself before saying, "I'm surprised Goldeen's sent you."

"It's my family's diner. I sent myself."

"I doubt it. When have you ever voluntarily made deliveries?"

"Never." The summer I got my license, actually. I drove *everywhere* but pretended like I hated it to earn some martyr points with Granny. It didn't work. "But I decided to make a change this summer. Like the song."

"I think he was talking about things a bit more serious than making deliveries."

"Everyone's gotta start somewhere." I shrugged. He smiled. And my knees turned to jelly when he laughed softly.

"I see you haven't actually changed, though."

"Why would I? I'm practically perfect in every way," I said, regretting it immediately. Playing Quota-Pun-Looza with Sam, Winston, and Kara all the time had *ruined* me and any hope I had for normal interactions with other people. "I don't mean that. I mean, it was a quote-joke. It's from *Mary Poppins*."

"I know," he said, still smiling, perfect eyebrows still raised. They had to be tired by now, right?

I gestured with my chin, keeping my mouth shut before I embarrassed myself again, sliding the delivery paper forward.

He plucked a pen from a silver cup near the fridge. "In a rush?" Instead of signing, like he should have been doing, he used the pen to tap a steady rhythm out on the counter.

"A little bit."

"More deliveries?"

"Why?"

"Just wondering." He signed the slip, a fast scribble where the only discernible letter was *D*. "Are you going to the street fair tomorrow?"

"Probably? I dunno. The HSR always makes me feel weird."

"How come?"

Some towns had annual beauty pageants for Little Miss Milkmaid Haybelle of the Year. Others put on plays where the prize positions were (a) the director or (b) the leads. It always had to be something good and wholesome before things somehow always went awry.

Chaos—and bigotry, depending on the story you were in—came home to roost. There would be (first) kisses, temporary heartbreak, inspirational transformations, and a healthy dose of comeuppance for those that deserved it.

In the 1970s, Haven Central had decided to skip all of that only to replace it with something equally sinister.

Haven. Summer. Royalty. A sham of a matchmaking system.

Anyone who had their hearts set on becoming Haven Summer Royalty put their names in a giant, glittering fishbowl made of dreams and glass. Someone got picked, they stood on stage, and then the mayor called for volunteers to be their counterpart. The resulting pair would wear crowns and sashes, be in the parade, kiss babies, pose for pictures, put ribbons on animal cages, judge contests, and *blah blah blah*.

Problem was, there usually ended up being more than one volunteer. The more popular and prettier the person was, the more volunteers they racked up. Haven Central went full-on medieval court affair after that, and then things got *really* weird. Extremely so.

"I don't know," I said. "It just seems so antiquated. It's like an unofficial beauty pageant hell-bent on pretending it's not a popularity contest merged with arranged marriage minus licensing. It's weird."

He laughed. "I don't think I've ever heard it described that way."

"But am I wrong?"

"Everyone has to volunteer, so kind of?" He closed one eye, openly judging me. "I don't know. I'm not convinced. I don't think I can give this one to you."

"Oh, come on! With the dates? And the games? Don't even get me started on the tiebreakers."

His face morphed into a serious frown. "Tiebreakers are definitely weird, yeah."

"Thank you." I picked up the delivery slip, sliding it into my front pocket. "I would never enter that contest. *Never.*"

"But you're still going to watch, right? It's like reality TV in person. Everyone loves that."

What he *said* didn't make me look at him, but rather his *tone* did. Unsure and breathy, as if he wanted to laugh to cover something up. His smile seemed a bit stiff, too. Strange.

Talking with Dallas had always been easy, *too* easy—turns out, steadfastly denying that you had feelings for someone did wonders for your conversational skills—but our paths had never crossed much. He had his friends and I had mine. And I was also sort of maybe obsessed with Goldeen's and very rarely left it, preferring to work my life away instead of running wild with Haven kidfolk.

"FYI, I don't love it," I said. "But Kara does. If she goes, maybe I'll be there. Maybe."

His smile relaxed into a grin full of perfect teeth made possible by what had to be painful years of braces. "Well, maybe I'll see you there, then. Maybe."

Three

After leaving Dallas's house, I deserved a break.

Admittedly, *deserve* was a strong word, but I was taking one anyway.

The stoplight turned green, and I made the turn back into Misty Haven. Main Street turned into Main Circle—a giant roundabout with a memorial gazebo erected in Misty Haven's honor at the center.

I drove past the ice-cream shop, Meltdown Scoops, which always had a reserve of praline ripple just for me; the coffee bar, the Traveling Cruz, which supplied Goldeen's with freshly roasted beans in exchange for advertising space on the diner's menus; the dance studio, Day and Night, where I made it through six summer-school lessons before breaking my ankle and never going back; the twenty-four-hour grocery and convenience store, Nina's, where I'd worked the overnight shift after the diner closed for a few weeks last summer with my partner, Kara, to earn money for a new Cuisinart-something that Kara absolutely had to have but her parents refused to buy for her; and the joint post office/town hall/government building across from the gazebo.

Every second, every scene and sidewalk and side alley, every inch held a memory. My heart would always belong here.

At a stop sign, Mrs. Pantoja awkwardly tried to wave as she crossed the street, hands full of leashes for the ten dogs she walked. She'd worked at the local shelter for as long as I had known her. The scene looked a bit like a picture you'd randomly see online.

A digital painting of a lady walking too many dogs on a breezy day in the middle of a quaint town that made you smile and get all warm and fuzzy.

Summer in Misty Haven had that kind of artistic, frozen feel to it.

Almost like it could make you believe time didn't exist and everything would be perfect forever. Plentiful trees, flowering bushes, green grass full of picket signs asking people to not walk on it, little kids with scraped knees running around and yelling because they had nothing better to do.

A place where you'd be just as likely to be eaten alive by mosquitos, born and bred in the swampy parts of the man-made lake at the west edge of town, as you would be to have a hate-to-love romance with a cutie-with-a-booty who had moved to Misty during the spring and had a supernatural affinity for math and working out, and also adored kids.

I pulled into an empty parking spot in front of Winter Wonderland Books. The door chimed as I entered, but no one greeted me. No one at the front desk meant Kara was on duty and had abandoned her post to go bake something.

Easily fixable.

"DO LIBRARY RULES APPLY IN THIS PLACE? I HAVE A LOUD SPEAKING VOICE BUT REQUIRE RECOMMENDATIONS FOR BOOKS."

One.

Two.

Three.

A scream shattered the silence of the bookshop moments before Kara appeared. She ran at a full sprint, arms outstretched as she launched herself straight into my waiting arms.

In the five years I had known Kara, she'd barely changed. She still had the same super curly, auburn-colored hair; face full of the same-colored freckles; and the same olive-toned skin. She always wore the same rectangular deep-purply-red glasses and a shrewd, calculating look on her face at all times. She hadn't even grown a single inch, still clocking in at an impressive five feet zero, with the same slightly chubby build and penchant for wearing jumpsuits.

And my heart still thumped extra hard against my rib cage every time I saw her. Truth be told, I wasn't always sequestered away in Goldeen's. Winter Wonderland Books took third place on the where-to-find-Winnie list. Second place? Kara's room upstairs.

"You didn't tell me you were coming over, punk!" She let go, slapping my arm.

"I like it when you scream for me. Makes me feel special and wanted, and also kind of scared. Keeps me on my toes."

Kara laughed. "Working?"

"Eternally."

"Figured. How long you got?"

"Not very. Just wanted to see your face."

"I like it when you make good life choices. Come on." She didn't wait, grasping my wrist and leading me forward. "I just finished making waffles."

"Scratch or Eggo?"

"Girl, please." Kara gave me a withering look.

The tiny kitchen with its rounded retro teal refrigerator and oven/stove combo looked and smelled like the single greatest bakery disaster area in the history of explosions. Collateral damage included flour *everywhere*; a fleet of similar-sized bowls dripping sticky glaze onto the counters; piles of unfrosted cupcakes arranged haphazardly on cooling racks; baking sheets stacked with a multitude of cookies; a seven-layer rainbow cake practically screaming for fondant, pearls, and sprinkles; and icing stuck to the cabinet doors like she had flung it to check its consistency.

I'd actually seen her do that last one once. Kara baking in the kitchen was An Experience™, but she ignored it all, not attempting to explain, apologize, or make excuses for the mess. Instead, she marched to the wooden table in the center of the room, where a red Belgian waffle iron steamed and hissed with urgency, and pulled out a chair for me.

"Why does it smell like brownies? You said waffles." I sat down. Above the scents of sweetened cream cheese, irrepressible vanilla everything, German chocolate heavy on the coconut, powdered sugar delightfulness, chocolate with that slightly burnt smell that never stopped it from still being delicious, cinnamon, and graham crackers, I caught a whiff of something cooking that didn't quite make sense.

"It's the best of both worlds." Kara grinned with feverish pride as she lifted the lid. "My two-hour-old secret recipe for crisp brownie waffles. Toppings pending, but I'm leaning toward ice cream, whipped cream, and/or fruit to give it that familiar funnel-cake vibe." She inhaled. "Doesn't it smell *amazing*?"

It did. Truly. But it was unfortunately off-limits, as were just about all of the baked goods in the kitchen. A severe gluten intolerance was nothing to mess with. I had finally been diagnosed a year ago, after enduring a solid two years of mysterious and at times debilitating pain. Not even the most delicious looking and smelling brownie waffle would be enough to tempt me to try it. That pain aimed to jack up your whole life. Enduring that was not worth even a single second of delectable happiness.

Not even if Kara made it.

"I got the idea from s'mores," Kara continued. "I used a combination of marshmallows in my scratch chocolate-chunk brownie batter recipe that I came up with last year to give it that magnificent sticky-gooey crunch. The heat and steam from the waffle iron keeps the white-chocolate Chex mix from getting soggy, but only if you place them just right. Oh, *and* I'm working on a gluten-free version exclusively for that special someone in my life."

"You're too good to me," I said, voice slipping into that everlasting-awe tone reserved solely for when Kara immersed herself in her craft and allowed me inside her world.

"It's what you deserve." Kara grinned at her quote-joke, and the world got that much brighter. "I've been testing out potential entries for the Sana Starlight contest."

"*Sana Starlight?*" I choked on air, sputtering in disbelief. "*The* Sana Starlight? Cooking show, bestselling books, and national tours, Sana Starlight? What the *what?*"

"She's filming a pilot for a new show here." Kara removed a bright orange piece of paper held to the fridge by a giant seashell magnet. "*Small Town Spotlight with Sana Starlight.*"

I managed to stop myself from being a complete heathen and didn't snatch the flyer out of her hands.

Sana Starlight, the next big foodie mogul, and her crew planned to film the pilot episode of her show, calling it "My Sweet and Savory Haven." Her inspiration for the theme came from the dual towns' history, with *sweet* representing Misty and *savory* representing Merry. A preliminary round to narrow down the contestants to ten per category would be held first, followed by the final competition and taping taking place at the annual M&M Carnival. There'd be three winners, one for both categories, and a grand prize overall.

"They started filming B-roll about two weeks ago." She sat in the seat next to me. "The camera crews are gone now, but they're supposed to come back for town events. Shelley gave them a schedule, I think. Everyone's saying they'll be here tomorrow to get some shots of the HSR."

I frowned at Kara. "How long have you known about this and why didn't you tell me?"

Since when did she keep secrets from me? Especially ones that the entire town knew about? Oversharing was our brand. We knew each other and the minutiae of our lives inside and out, backward and forward.

Got an A on a test? Texted Kara.

Saw a rabbit while driving? Called Kara.

Fell down the stairs and cracked two ribs? GOTTA TELL KARA. Who needs an ambulance anyway?

"Because there's an issue," Kara said. "Granny's not entering Goldeen's."

A beat passed. I blinked at her. "Excuse me, what? I don't think I heard you correctly. Did you just say my granny's not entering a contest with a wicked grand prize that she's a shoo-in to win? Literally no one could stand against us."

"I asked her about it, and she said the meetings and prep would be too much for her, so she couldn't. And since she's the business owner, Goldeen's is out." Kara shrugged. "I'm entering the sweet competition, but since I'm not eighteen yet, my dad had to do all of the entrant requirement stuff with me."

Those brownie waffles weren't even close to their final form. Like clockwork, Kara would find something wrong with them and knock some sense into that recipe until it acted right—if that was even what she'd choose to enter. My girl came up with recipes in her sleep. Something bigger, better, bolder could come along at any moment. Her empire would be frosted in twenty-four-karat gold icing. Nothing would stop her from becoming the immensely successful love child of Betty Crocker and Rachael Ray.

"My condolences to your competitors," I said, only half joking. "May their pride rest in peace."

She laughed. "Julia dropped out when the judges agreed to let my dad be my proxy."

"Seriously?"

"Yep. At first they said I couldn't enter but my dad talked them into it. You know how he is," she said with an affectionate eye roll. "And then after the announcement, Sanjay told me Julia said something like, 'I'm not going to let a kid beat me on national TV.'"

"Wise woman. Her cupcakes are terrible and she knows it."

"Winnie!" She cackled behind her hand.

"What?! *She knows it.* If you ask her, she'll tell you. I don't know why she sells them."

"Because tourists don't know any better. It's not like we're going to warn them. Havens over everyone else."

I nodded in agreement before staring at the flyer again. "I can't believe Granny didn't enter. We'd dominate savory, because obviously we wouldn't enter sweet. No offense, but we probably could have won overall, too."

"I have no shame in admitting I'd lose against Aaron, that experienced and talented jerk." Kara tore off a piece of cooled waffle and ate it. "Damn, I'm good," she said still chewing. "I'm pretty sure Colin threw a party when he heard Goldeen's wasn't in."

Colin owned Archie's, the Goldeen's equivalent in Merry. I'd never eaten there, but rumor had it that while his food was better than average, it couldn't hold a candle to Goldeen's.

"And I guess it's too late to enter."

"Why would you? You don't cook."

"But Aaron does."

"And Aaron works at Goldeen's."

"Yes," I said, thinking it through. "Granny doesn't want to enter. I could do it for her. Be her—young proxy."

"No."

Damn. She didn't even give me a chance. "I could! And then use the prize money to buy Goldeen's a new oven."

"There you go."

I almost laughed at her disapproving tone. "*What?*"

She narrowed her eyes. "If your granny really, truly wanted a new oven, don't you think she'd buy it herself?"

"Maybe. But that thing keeps exploding! She's not in the kitchen! She's barely in the diner now that Nadiya has ascended into Granny's good graces. She really trusts her," I said, fire dwindling out of me. "If I won, I could use the money to buy it for her. It could be a functional present."

"She's doesn't need you to do that."

"It's not about need. It's about want. What I want. And I want to do this for her."

"Okay. Fair." Kara sat back in her seat, raising her left leg and holding her knee to her chest. "But just because you want to do something doesn't mean you should. *Or* can even do it. Did you miss the part where it said TV show? TV as in cameras and interviews."

My weird feelings weren't the only reason why I'd never volunteer to be Haven Summer Royalty. I might have had just a tad bit of trouble coping with public speaking. And being the center of attention. And people looking at me.

The thought of talking on camera, knowing anybody anywhere in the world would be able to watch it and I would be powerless to stop it, almost made me start dry heaving.

"I-I-I can handle it." *God*, how were my hands sweating *already*?

Kara scoffed.

"I can! It's different when it's not about me. This is for Granny," I said and would keep saying until I could trick my brain into believing it. "I can do it if it's for someone else. I think. I'm at least willing to try! And if I fail, then—I fail. I guess. I hate losing, so maybe that will overpower the fear?" Kara wasn't convinced. Lucky for me I knew exactly what to say to get her on my side. "Besides, it could be something we do together."

Secret weapon deployed, I let the moment stand as Kara's eyes slowly lit up, as a smile crept across her lips.

Long-distance relationships of any kind sucked. They're hard and stupid, and I hated everything about them. But choosing to be together had been the right choice for us. We stood by that and did the work. Commitment. Dedication. Communication. None of that came easy.

So when something that *was* easy came along? We both jumped at the chance.

"If we're going to do this," she said, "we have to do it right. There's still a few weeks of casting calls. They hold them every Friday for an hour or two."

"Casting?"

Kara nodded. "Pretty much everyone who signs up gets to compete in the preliminary round, but only a select handful of entrants from that pool will appear on the show. Including yours truly."

"Shut up. I mean, I'm not surprised, because look at you, but shut up."

"Oh, and that's not the best part. I'm not only cast, but I'm being *featured*. Think like a TV producer: an underage prolific baker who dominates school bake sales already accepted to a university with a prestigious adjunct culinary school on a merit scholarship and the dad that fought for her to enter the contest. Of course they let me in, and they'll do the same for you. A Black-owned family business beloved by all and the granddaughter determined to keep her family's dream alive, so much so that she's tied her entire collegiate future into it? That is ratings gold."

"Why you gotta play the race card like that?" I joked.

"Because they'd use it against you if they could. Might as well play it up and shove it in their faces."

"You're absolutely vicious with this kind of stuff," I said. "I love it. You're amazing."

"Naturally."

Unlike hers, my story for TV wasn't entirely true. Goldeen's was Granny's dream. My dad and uncle weren't exactly all that jazzed about the family business—they'd already tried, more than once, to get Granny to sell Goldeen's and move in with us so they could take better care of her, but she refused. Her exact words were, "*No. And stay out of my business!*" Also? My collegiate future didn't really have much to do with Goldeen's. It actually had more to do with Kara than anyone else.

But the casting producers, or whatever they're called, didn't need to know all that.

"Think you can convince Granny to let you enter on her behalf?"

I chewed on my lip, thinking. Granny could have the last unpolluted water tank in existence during the end of days under her care and say no to someone dying of thirst on the street because of an inconsequential slight from forty years ago. She had a memory like an elephant and a will made of pure iron. If she didn't want to do something, there wasn't a force alive that could make her change her mind.

"Maybe. We could really win, though," I said. "Wouldn't it be kind of weird if we both win? Ungirlfriends, going to the same college, all set to be roommates . . ." I trailed off.

Ungirlfriend: a curious step after friendship. A knowing jump beyond best friends. A leap of faith into an abyss of commitment that didn't have a name that we liked yet. And I quote, *"I'll be damned if I let anyone refer to me as zucchini."*

So Kara had given it a new name and then gave it to me.

"Coincidences make amazing reality TV." She walked over to the fridge, returning with bright blue Tupperware. "Besides, we don't have to tell them *everything* about us. Just the pertinent bits. Here, I made you cupcakes."

Chocolate and buttercream, Funfetti and pink cream cheese, red velvet, bare-faced vanilla—"But you didn't know I was coming by?"

"I always make you cupcakes." She leaned against a chair, hand on her jutting hip. "The extra freezer is filled with them."

Four

The next day, I decided to make my move. Time, essence, all that good stuff.

Watching Goldeen's come alive during the midday rush launched me into the oddest state of slo-mo euphoria. The sea green shone, the pearls caught the light just right to sparkle, and there was a good chance I'd entered hallucination territory at this point, but the mermaids seemed more playful and the sirens much more murderous. Every meal, every dish, as tempting as an apple—or a pomegranate, if you were into historical biblical accuracy—in Eden, snake and all.

The enduring charm of Goldeen's could never be embellished. One sniff, one bite, and you'd become a regular for life.

Between Granny's recipes and Aaron's preternatural cooking skill, magic happened in that kitchen. The smoky bacon, seared hashed browns, and freshly baked biscuits slathered with homemade organic jam bought from a local farmer two towns over would have stomachs rumbling in one millisecond flat. Sweet, fluffy pancakes with crispy edges drenched in honey butter, because syrup was outlawed in the diner, made the patrons groan in anticipation. Tangy seasoning, fresh lettuce, delectable tomatoes and salsa, and warming corn tortillas made customers pout because that gastronomic goodness existed for me and me alone.

A little thing I liked to call Proprietor's Progeny Perks.

Another of said perks? The music. I sat in my usual sunlit corner booth during my lunch break, tapping the tabletop with my fingers and bouncing in my seat as I waited for my tacos. I tried to keep it family friendly when I took a spin as Goldeen's DJ. A solid mix of pop, R&B, and funk from across the decades—a little something for everyone. Every now and then, I'd slide in some '90s New Jack Swing, in honor of my dad, or some K-pop for Layla.

Which just got turned off.

"Winnie." Granny appeared beside my table just as the music started up again. Back to Motown Goldeen's went. "What did I tell you about touching my music?"

"You told me that I could—" It's not like I didn't include her music, too. I totally did. "—not."

"So why did you change it to that mess?"

"It is not *mess*. It's music, which the patrons were enjoying, thank you very much."

Granny had on her favorite tracksuit—the one she owned in nine different colors because when Granny liked a style, she stuck with it. Color of the day? Royal blue with her white tennis shoes, and her giant tan-and-gold purse hanging from the crook of her elbow. She had slicked back her pressed gray hair into a low bun and dappled on the tiniest bit of makeup. "Just enough to make 'em wonder," she had said once.

Truth be told, makeup or not, no one could ever guess Granny's real age.

"I don't care. My diner, my rules. Don't make me tell you again."

Don't touch the music. The customer is always right. Goldeen's never closes early. *Ugh*. All the other rules followed common sense laws, but I always seemed to struggle with those three for some reason.

I puckered my lips and puffed out my cheeks. Tantrums, no matter how cute or mild they were, didn't go far with Granny. But it was enough to make her lean over and kiss my forehead.

"Your hair smells like smoke."

"Three fires in one morning will do that." After the last blaze, we had to upgrade—up the stairs to use the oven in the apartment. Frank had finally shuffled into the diner twenty minutes later, declared all was not lost, and fixed it.

Bless him and his bald head.

"That damn oven. Not worth the money I paid for it, but I'm gonna squeeze every last dime out of it."

"Fire hazards be damned."

Granny snapped her fingers, lips shriveling until they barely moved as she said, "Cussing in my house, you must have lost your last mind."

"Sorry." I held back my smile and my comeback that Granny had also just cussed. Double standards could be such a thing of humorous beauty.

"I don't know what your daddy is down there teaching you, but you better watch your mouth up here."

"Yes, ma'am."

"And your mama called. Your school sent an email about your vaccinations not being good enough."

"No they didn't."

I pulled out my phone, opening the email I'd specifically created for applying to schools. Lo and behold, an email did exist, already opened. It seemed the offspring of anti-vaxxers had grown up safely to cause measles outbreaks on a few college campuses. All incoming students had to get a blood test to prove immunity or get a brand-spanking-new rubella inoculation.

"Mom."

"Mm-hmm." Granny pretended to rummage in her bag. "I see she hasn't changed."

A side-eye would've earned me a quick smack upside the head, so I frowned instead.

Rejection and I don't get along. I applied to ten schools, gave my mom a list of my top five, and had her check for me when acceptance/rejection emails started rolling in. Lucky for me, my top choice said yes and accepted my college fund as a dowry.

The other nine shall forever remain a mystery—my mom deleted them all before I could see them.

"I gave her the password," I said. "She was helping me field rejections."

"Any school that wouldn't accept you clearly don't know what they're doing and they don't deserve you anyway." She smiled. "I made an appointment for you on Friday to get the test done."

"Oh joy."

"Stop it."

"I hate doctor's offices. But thank you. I appreciate you."

She held me softly by the chin. "You want anything while I'm out? I'm going to the bank and out to Beliveau Farms to renew the contract. I'll be back before they do that royalty thing in town."

Almost all of Goldeen's food and supplies came from local vendors. Beliveau supplied the diner with dairy, beef, and pork, but another farm had contacted Granny boasting cheaper prices. It wasn't the first time this had happened—Beliveau always matched the new offer or, if they couldn't, included a boon for loyalty during contract renewal.

I sopped up every bit of knowledge I could glean from Granny's dealings. Being a diner owner wasn't just working the floor or the kitchens or ensuring the books balanced every month. I would have to work with farmers, vendors, and grocery stores. Learn how to read and write contracts, maybe even vet a good lawyer to help. Study advertising and the market to make sure I didn't get swindled.

When it came to business, people saw old Black lady and dollar signs appeared in their eyes. When they saw me coming, those dollar signs would probably quadruple. But Granny had been born shrewd and no-nonsense.

I had that same blood in me.

"No, I'm good. But, um, I was wondering about something else." I placed the flyer on top of the table. "Kara told me about this contest."

"What about it?"

"Well, I was thinking Goldeen's should enter. Making it to the finals guarantees we'll be on TV, which would be amazing, and the prize money could buy a new oven."

"I don't have time for that, baby. I know all about it—meetings, interviews, preliminary rounds, and jumping through six hoops on Sundays no less. No."

"That's the cool thing. Kara couldn't enter without her dad's help so we thought that maybe the judges would bend that same rule, only backward. You don't have time, but I do. Pitch it as a family thing."

"You? On TV? In front of a camera?"

"Why does everyone keep saying that? I'll be *fine*."

Her skeptical look pinned me into almost telling the truth.

"I can do it. No sweat." Lots of sweat, actually.

"Mm-hmm. I heard about your little laryngitis stunt."

I cringed so hard, I'm pretty sure I cracked a tooth.

Once, I had to make an oral presentation in history class. Begging, pleading, *crying*—nothing would convince my teacher to give me an alternative assignment. Desperation took over, and two days before my turn to present, I pretended to have laryngitis to get out of it. For two solid weeks, I didn't even speak at home. Winston knew the truth, willingly playing along while simultaneously tormenting me to force me to break. As expected.

My parents had gotten so worried they nearly forced me to go to the doctor. Magically, my voice had returned at a strained whisper the day of my appointment—a true Christmas Miracle! Except that pretty much gave me away. They'd figured out I had faked the whole thing.

It was a shitty thing to do, I knew that. But I'd gotten to write an essay instead. Yay for positive reinforcement for bad behavior!

"That was different," I said. "And before. I'm much better. I've been working on it. You know, a personal goal. Getting over my fear. And stuff."

"And what about your shifts?"

"I wouldn't miss those. Not a single one."

"That's a lot, baby. Staying up until two a.m., getting up at five, skulking around my diner all day because you refuse to go *outside*—when are you going to have fun?"

"I have fun! This is f-f-fun for me." I couldn't even lie straight. Winston would have thought that was hilarious. "And honestly, high school really isn't how you remember it. It's way more intense than this. If I can get through that without having a nervous breakdown, I can work and enter the contest. I can handle it."

"And that's why you're supposed to relax in the summer," Granny said. "I know exactly how hard you work. You come here to relax and earn some spending money for yourself." She shook her head. "No."

"But—"

"I said *no*."

And that was that.

I watched her leave, frowning at the slight limp she'd developed. Her Dr. Skinner–ordered cane must have been collecting dust somewhere in the back of a closet.

When Granny said no, it left zero room for negotiation space—no light, no hope, like a black hole sucking the joy out of life.

~

Kara (Kara Kara Kara Kara) Chameleon

Kara: Hey babycakes! How did it go?

                     Winnie: I'm certain I have no idea
                               what you're talking about

Kara: Yikes. That bad? Want me to stop by this afternoon during your split? We could brainstorm before going to the HSR

                  Winnie: Stop by? Always. Brainstorm?
                         Ehhhh. Demoralized. I am it.

Kara: I get it, but you know . . . I told you so. You know I told you so, right? Because I told you so.

                     Winnie: We're breaking up.

Kara: Aww! But I already tattooed your name on my shoulder! Don't make me go get a rose cover-up. Please love me again?

                                 Winnie: Ha!

                Winnie: Did you really want to go to HSR?

Kara: YES.

Kara: Pack your bags and tell the kids.

Five

The Haven Central Wednesday Night Street Faire started and ended, and vice versa, at Misty's gazebo and Merry's statue.

That stretch of crowded ground was packed with craft vendors selling customizable flower crowns and spray-painted street art. Food trucks had rolled in from out of town to coexist with the local restaurants and specialty shops, front doors wide open and decorated in brilliant window-marker designs. As part of their fundraiser, the sheriff's department sold sparklers, party poppers, and the kind of fireworks that were loud and did almost nothing. Dance music from the '80s, heavy on the synth, floated around us, because according to Shelley Way, the mayor's wife, that decade had the best music. Even fireflies appeared out of nowhere to twinkle and show off after all the other hell-spawn insects retired to their crawl spaces of evil for the night.

And Kara had been right. Two camera people from Sana Starlight's team, dressed all in black, weaved in and out of the crowd, recording everything. A silver curlicue S shimmered on the backs of their shirts as they moved.

For as packed as it was, I thought I'd see more unfamiliar faces, but had only spotted a few here and there. Part of me wanted to mingle. Maybe say hello to some of the people I hadn't seen in a year. Like Jenny Randall, the manager at Nina's, and her new husband. They had commandeered a prime spot on a bench close to the gazebo. Her mouth seemed too busy to say hello, unfortunately. Aloof suited me better than social butterfly anyway. Besides, if they wanted to come talk to me, they could.

Sam, Kara, Winston, and I hung around the fringes of the fair, sitting atop the short stone wall in front of the library. Far enough away to look like we didn't care about the goings-on, as was the Murphy-Woodson-Alviar way, but also in the perfect location to witness everything that would go down. Because once the sun set and the dreamy town lampposts turned on, both mayors of Haven Central would stand in Misty's gazebo together.

Granny almost never sat with us. She either stuck with the other grannies—I dubbed them the Hell's Belles—or with Mr. Livingston. Kara had told me about it of course, that she'd seen Granny around town with him more often than not and guessed Cupid had gotten trigger-happy. I never really thought I'd see the day when my granny canoodled with anyone, but the two of them next to the shaved ice cart had proved me wrong.

Grampy—pretty sure that's what I'd call him—didn't exist, and if he did, no one ever talked about him.

I looked for Dallas, too. His usual group of friends had clustered close to Penny's Antiques, but he wasn't with them. It took a bit of squint-searching—because I really needed to get some glasses—and neck craning, but I finally spotted him sitting with his parents on a picnic blanket near the memorial willow tree. I only knew surface-level basics about them. His mom, Madeleine, a quasi-famous Parisian singer. His dad, Rob, a retired but easily recognizable

American football star that had chosen Merry Haven as the place to settle down. They loved their only son.

Madeleine threw her head back, laughing at something Rob said. Turns out a laugh could be both booming and elegant. Interesting. Dallas shook his head in that omg my parents are so embarrassing kind of way, but his entire face turned a wonderful shade of ruddy peach from trying not to laugh. I guess I knew one more thing, too: he loved his parents.

Even from where I sat, I could see it. You didn't look at people the way he looked at his parents unless you loved them. You didn't sit with your parents, fully present and engaged with them, when your friends were fifty feet away, unless you wanted to.

I struggled with that sometimes. A lot of the people I hung out with back home didn't like their families for whatever reason. One person, who shall remain nameless, said, "Stop trying to make everyone jealous. We get it. Y'all are the Black Brady Bunch. No one cares."

It felt good to see Dallas with his family like that. Validating, even.

I wish my parents could have come up this year. My mom would have loved this fair.

Something about Haven Central made me want to believe it might be okay to relax and be my honest self. Might be safe to give whimsy a chance, have a good old-fashioned magical time. Not quite distressed enough to make a deal with a sea witch, but also not in a position to say no to a beggar who would ask me to enter a mysterious cave in exchange for money.

As long as I didn't have to ask Granny for permission.

"I mean, I really don't know what you expected her to say." Winston had lined up a row of small pebbles next to him, flicking them into the crowd, one by one. "Obviously, she knew about it. If she wanted you to enter for her, she would have told you to."

"It never hurts to ask." I hated when he got like that. Baby brothers were not supposed to be more pragmatic than their big sisters. That's exactly why I didn't tell him about it beforehand. Both he and Kara belonged to the no-chill brigade when it came to rubbing in *I told you so.*

"And she really wouldn't say why?" Sam asked, around a mouthful of ice cream. Earlier, at Meltdown Scoops, she'd made Sascha smash six scoops of cookies-and-cream into a standard-size waffle cone.

"When does she ever explain herself?" His hardcore frown at Sam gave way to an irritated eye roll. Another one of his pebbles shot forward, nicking Joseph Neddleton in the back of the leg. He leaned down, brushing at nothing before turning back to his cotton candy.

"I just meant that that's how it is with my dad," Sam continued. "If he has to tell me no, he always says why. To make it fair."

"Good for you."

"All right." Kara hopped down off the wall, standing in front of Winston with her arms crossed. "What's your problem, space cadet? You've been in a shitty mood all night."

I'd noticed it, too. Usually, Winston's snapping-turtle tendencies were laced with wry laughter and mischievous eye smiles. He liked to ride that line between biting wit and being a straight-up asshole, never choosing one side or the other unless he got mad.

Winston stared at Kara, his unique brand of unreadable anger out in full force. "I don't have a problem." He said it like a warning.

The music stopped. Feedback whining from a microphone pierced the air as Mayor Way tapped it and said, "Is this thing on?" His voice echoed through the speakers. "Excellent."

Mayor Iero had claimed the center spot in the gazebo—the perfect angle for photo ops—and Rush Ballard, the *Haven Herald* photographer, squatted on the steps below, camera slung around his neck.

Both mayors had the same stocky build, same sallow skin, same thinning dark brown hair, and faces that resembled the other so much they could have been brothers. They were also Haven Legacy, like Kara's family, and people had been swearing scandal their entire lives.

A giant glass fishbowl filled with red half-slips of paper had been set up on a column in the gazebo.

The tension between Kara and Winston dragged on, neither one willing to back down, but the center had gotten quiet enough that people would hear anything else they said.

Sam stepped up. "I bribed Ms. Wendy with two hours of free babysitting for a last-minute entry."

Winston took the bait. "Aww, how cute and totally unexpected." His gaze rolled in her direction. To her credit, Sam didn't flinch when his war-stare landed on her. "I never would have pegged you as the Summer Queen type. That's just so unlike you." He returned to focusing on lining up a new row of pebbles.

"It's a shock to us all," I said with a full smile to soften Winston's harsh teasing. "You'd be perfect, really. They'd waste no time getting your pictures on the website and printing new brochures. No one should be as photogenic as you are."

"They'll probably put you on the postcards, too," Kara said, jumping back onto the wall next to me.

"You think so?" Pretty as she was, Sam still needed me to say yes, because that was the way of things. So I did.

"Yeah. Absolutely."

"Better be careful what you wish for. The curse might get you," Winston warned. "Married at eighteen with a baby on the way? Yeah, your dad would love that."

As with all great things in Haven Central, the HSR came with a fantastical upside—or downside. The first HSR couple ended up dating, and later, getting married. So did the second. And the third.

After the fourth go-round, the people of Haven Central accepted what the universe was clearly attempting to tell them. They'd struck divine matchmaking gold.

Side note: nobody talked about how the seventh go-round blew all the way up.

Mayor Way plunged his hand into the fishbowl. He took his time, shuffling and swirling the red strips of paper. Dramatic music kicked in—that was new and probably Shelley's doing to impress the Starlight crew.

"And so it begins." Kara laughed. She hated romance for herself, but could never resist a good somebody-else's love story.

I leaned toward Sam and whispered, "May the odds be ever in your favor," and got a sly grin in return.

Thing was, I could totally see it. Mayor Way would read the slip and nod in approval before passing it to Mayor Iero, who would shout Sam's name into the microphone because that would be just oh so necessary.

Sam would then look at me, mouthing, "Me?" for confirmation because that's what she always did. The clapping would start, followed by whoops and aws and more than a few disappointed death stares. Sam would blink away her surprise, hand Kara her ice cream, wipe her hands on her cut-off shorts, and bound toward the gazebo, hair bouncing in a metaphorical manifestation of her internal giddiness. Her strangely familiar amethyst sunflower earrings would catch the spotlights just right.

Winston would say something snarky. Kara would halfway agree but smooth it over somehow. Sam's bright smile would light up the night. And I would sit, split into warring parts—happy for Sam and ready to cause bodily harm to any inappropriate volunteers wishing to be paired with my sixteen-year-old cousin—and concealing it all under a blanket of *whatever, it's cool.*

Haven Central had a tendency to look the other way. I sure as hell didn't. Neither did Granny or Winston. We'd burn this place to the ground for Sam if anyone tried anything.

"Winnie Woodson?"

My head snapped toward the stage as the crowd began to turn. Searching for, and then finding, me.

ſix

e.
m Not Sam, who wanted this. Not one of the people who had been looking forward to this all year. Nor anyone else who had voluntarily written their name on that small slip of red paper.

I did not enter the HSR. I did not write my name down. I did not hand my slip to Shelley to place in the bowl. Mayor Iero got it wrong. He read it wrong. It wasn't *me*.

It couldn't be.

Mayor Iero cleared the question from his voice. "Winnie Woodson." He used his hand like a visor to cover his eyes, searching the crowd. "Is she here?"

"But I didn't enter," I whispered, unmoving. "I didn't." The words, stuck in my chest, escaped when I exhaled. Awake and breathing, but too much and too fast. The dreamy summer lights became harsher, sharper, searing into my eyes.

Kara jumped up and down in front of me. *"Why didn't you tell me!?"*

"What am I supposed to do?"

"Go up there," Sam said, at my side. She tugged on my hands, urging me to stand up before turning and yelling, "She's here! She's coming!"

"*No.*"

I stood up to make Sam stop before she pulled my arm out of its socket.

My heartbeat vibrated in my throat and in my head. My lungs would start flirting with hyperventilation, and any second I'd start wheezing. I could *feel* them staring at me. Boring holes into my skin, muscles, organs, and soul with judgment. And disgust. *Everyone* would start talking about me in barely disguised whispers and bold proclamations. To my face.

They would say, "Oh."

"*Ew.*"

"Not her."

They would be silent. No one would volunteer for me.

They would giggle and laugh and point and—

"Come on." Winston placed a hand on the middle of my back, between my shoulder blades.

My eyes were hurting—burning, dry, and scratchy—and I realized I hadn't been blinking. I'd felt the tears forming and had been holding them in by sheer force of unconscious will. "*I can't.*"

"You can."

I wasn't like my brother—cool, calm, confident. I flailed, lied, and hid my way through life, shrinking myself down to fit in the smallest of spaces that thrived behind the scenes. He *knew* how hard things like this were for me. How frantic and desperate to run they made me.

That traitor pushed me forward anyway and I almost tripped over my feet.

Almost falling jump-started my self-preservation mode, forcing me to take an unsteady step. I refused to fall. On top of everything else, I didn't need them to see me collapse so they could *really* point and laugh at me.

Winston stayed by my side as the crowd parted to let us through. No one cheered. No one clapped. My stomach revolted, churning my dinner and threatening to send it back up.

Before my next exhale, a camera appeared on my left, matching our promenade pace.

I swallowed hard, acid burning all the way back down.

A high-pitched whine filled up all of the extra space in between my ears that hadn't already been taken over by the voice shouting, *Run! Run! Run! Get out now!* I focused on the ground, hand reaching out and finding the hem of Winston's shirt, squeezing it for dear life.

All too soon, the white gazebo stairs that led straight to my doom appeared.

"Ah, what a gentleman!" Mayor Way said. "Escorting your sister, definitely a welcome first!"

I scooched closer to Winston, shoulders hunched against the outside world, turning into his loose embrace.

Winston nudged me again. One step on autopilot led to another and another, until I made it to the center of the gazebo, slowly turning to face the crowd. My brother hadn't moved. He stood tall and perfect in my line of sight like a bodyguard, arms crossed and feet planted. The tiniest of tiny smiles ticked at one corner of his mouth.

Rush glared at him. Winston was ruining his shot. Shelley's outstretched hands reaching for my head made me jump to the left, fists ready to punch the next thing that got too close to me.

The tiara. Shelley smiled at me, holding up the tiara, saying, "It's okay. Don't be so nervous, dear."

My tiara.

Because this was happening. Awareness slammed into me—the people, the smells, the *sounds*.

Clapping. Cheering. Polite and not at all enthusiastic, but it existed! And farther back, I heard the irrepressible shouts of Sam and Kara, chanting my name, louder and prouder than any two people should have been.

Shelley's momlike laugh drew my attention back to her. The kind of laugh that said, *You're ridiculous and I love it.* She motioned for me to lower my head. The tiara weighed almost nothing. I touched the cool metal and jewels to make sure I wasn't imagining any of this.

I'd really just been crowned Misty's Summer Queen. That was a thing that happened, was still happening, with the vast majority of Haven Central watching me—the dizzy spell struck me upside the head, and I had just enough time to brace myself so I wouldn't sway into a full-on faint.

"And now that the queen has been crowned," Mayor Way said, stepping into the limelight, "do we have any volunteers to rule by her side?"

A heartbeat of silence. I squeezed my eyes shut.

"ME! OH, ME! MOVE OUT OF MY WAY! MOVE, DAMN IT!"

I should have known. How could I have ever worried for one second that I would be alone?

Kara pushed her way toward the front, yelling the whole time. She took the steps two at a time and pushed Mayor Way to the side when she got to the top. "Hi! It's me! I'm Kara, but y'all know that. She's mine, though, and you *didn't* know that, so ha!" She spoke rapid fire to the crowd, beaming as they laughed. "I'm ready! Give me my crown. Where's my Merry crown? Gimme, gimme, gimme—"

Mayor Way adjusted his clothes. "Well, you certainly get an A for enthusiasm, but we have to finish the ceremony, so if you'll stand to the side here"—he gestured to the right of me, and Kara leaped into place—"we'll make the next call for volunteers."

Kara hopped from foot to foot, clasping her hands together. "Look how cute you look with your tiara, oh my God, I'm gonna *die*." And then she lowered her voice so only I could hear as the crowd laughed. "Don't worry. I got you. This is going to be *so* epic."

My lungs loosened up. The tension curling inside my shoulders straightened out, letting me slouch into my normal relaxed posture. Kara had no problem falling on the proverbial spotlight sword in the most dramatic way possible to protect me. To give me a chance to breathe and stop my bearings from rolling away.

There'd been two queens before. Two kings as well. There'd even been two kings *and* a queen one year—one of the wildest summers I've ever had in Haven Central. A veritable all-you-can-eat, I'm nosy as hell and don't know how to mind my business buffet. Good old polyamory had won that summer.

People would be disappointed that there wouldn't be a romance to follow this year, but whatever. We would make up for that with . . . antics.

If Kara was by my side, I could perform *in public*. We could totally be entertaining. We could let them into our world for a summer. No problem.

Kara smiled at me, practically vibrating with energy. Between the Starlight competition and becoming the Merry Haven Summer Queen, she had to be overdosing on happiness.

We hadn't bothered to try to explain our relationship to anyone besides our families. I knew Kara. She wouldn't want to bother with it now either. But we could probably even pretend to be lovey-dovey if we had to. Now *that* would be hilarious and so, so over the top. Right up Kara's alley.

"Going once," Mayor Iero said.

"Going twice," Mayor Way said.

"And the contest is cl—"

"Wait! I do," a voice said from the right.

"Excuse me!?" Kara snapped.

"I volunteer," he said again, and I forgot how to breathe.

I must have been hallucinating from lack of oxygen over being picked to be queen of a contest I'd never entered. Because no way on God's good green with a lot of brown thanks to climate change Earth did Dallas just volunteer while standing under the willow tree.

Or step forward.

Or walk through the crowd.

Or climb the gazebo steps.

"Hey, Winnie," he said.

"H-h-hi," I whispered. "What are you doing?"

"That's what *I'd* like to know." Kara whispered, too.

"I'm volunteering," Dallas answered, voice low, eyes focused on my face. He moved into position, standing on my left. And then, he took my hand in his—slender fingers wrapping around the back of my hand, warm palm pressing against mine—and gave it a firm squeeze.

"But why?" I asked, unable to comprehend the fact that Dallas had also voluntarily decided to hold my hand.

His resulting smile grew in luxurious slow motion.

No more volunteers stepped up.

Mayor Iero had started speaking again, gesturing at us—Kara fuming, Dallas smiling, and me confused as all get-out.

Me. Misty Summer Queen.

Kara had volunteered. Dallas had also volunteered.

They'd have to compete in a tiebreaker.

That did not compute so hard, my brain short-circuited around the thought, making my eye twitch.

The hand-holding continued on. I didn't feel like I had completely returned to my body after mentally floating through the ether of despair and panic, but historically speaking, my palms should have been slick with sweat by now. That had to be gross. *I* didn't even like the feel of it.

Without looking at him, I flexed my fingers out, like I wanted to let go. He squeezed again, twice, in rapid succession.

Why was he doing this? Did he feel sorry for me or something? Because he'd been way off. Maybe if I told him I wanted to be queen with Kara, he'd back out.

I watched him watching the mayors banter back and forth, engaged and laughing when necessary. Maybe the hand-holding was all for show—a boy could be interested in me, I didn't need my *friend* to rescue me.

A familiar anger began to bubble up inside of me. I didn't need or want him to try to swoop in and save me like some misguided knight fighting a dragon. He and his pity could go somewhere bright and fiery for all eternity. I refused to be anyone's charity queen.

"Um, why are you holding *my* queen's hand?" Kara demanded, standing in front of me and Dallas. The mayors had finished whatever comedic set they had planned for this year and had left without me realizing it.

"She looked like she needed it," Dallas said with a shrug. "You okay? You looked like you were going to pass out for a second there."

"I'm fine." I sounded it, too. Calm and monotone. And suspicious.

The anger hadn't left. A wariness settled under my skin. People were *mean*. Especially to fat girls. There was no guard to let down, because I stayed at attention.

He nodded. "Good." And then let go of my hand. "I'll see you at the tiebreaker." And then walked away. Just like that.

"Is there something you want to tell me?" Kara asked through her teeth, looking around.

The crowd had begun to drift away, along with the cameras, but if she yelled they would hear, and she definitely wanted to. Her cheeks bloomed into spots of soft red, and she stared at me with harsh eyes.

"No?" One of us had to stay calm. In the short time between my name being called and now, my mood had fluctuated violently across the board. Some residuals of the anger I began to feel toward Dallas held on, but I couldn't take that out on her. If we fought, we would both regret it. I had to let her have this moment.

"Then why did *he* volunteer?"

"I don't know! How am I supposed to know? It's not like I could ask him."

"You should've told me," she insisted, crossing her arms over her chest. I could read Kara like a book—in a matter of seconds, anger had begun to give way to hurt. "I can't believe you would keep something like this from me."

We didn't have secrets between us. We made three unbreakable rules, and that's number one.

"I didn't tell you because there's nothing to tell." I looked her in the eye. She needed to know I meant every word I said. "I do not keep secrets from you. *Ever.* How could you even think something like that?"

"Because you always get weird about stuff."

"Weird?" I asked, taken aback. "What the hell is that supposed to mean?"

"Con-gra-tu-lations!" Sam sang, appearing with Winston. "I cannot believe that happened!"

Winston poked me in the side, a wry grin already in place.

They hadn't heard us fighting. Was that even a real fight? Kara and I never fought, so I didn't even know.

"It was like a movie," Sam kept going. "When Dallas volunteered, you could hear a pin drop. I swear Lacey almost fainted."

Lacey. Last I had heard, Dallas and Lacey had broken up after prom. Both Kara *and* Granny had told me, which meant everyone in Haven Central had to be talking about it. I didn't know the specifics of the breakup, no one did apparently. Dallas volunteering must have been a huge shock to everyone, not just Kara.

"Are we gonna get out of here or what? Everyone's leaving," Winston said.

"Yeah," I said, eyes still on Kara, who made a show of not looking at me even though she knew I wanted her to. "Let's go."

Seven

Being a newly crowned queen did not come with a get-out-of-your-shift-free card.

Granny had smiled that smile I love most in the world—the one that said, *I am both thrilled and confused by this but you're my baby and I love you*—tried on my tiara, but then promptly gave it back and reminded me that I had to work in two hours and should probably take a nap.

"When did you get new menus?" one of the two customers sitting in the booth asked. We made eye contact and my brain went blank for a second. East Asian with perfectly tousled hair, a perfectly symmetrical face, and a stare that made you fall in love at first sight, maniacally giggling the whole way down. People who looked like him got scouted to be models in random public places like malls and banks.

"We didn't. This is the special Midnight Oil menu. Limited selection and such." I tried not to stare, but did I know these people? Both were obviously Very Beautiful™ and not from Haven Central. But if they were familiar enough with the menus to notice the day/night change, they must have been regulars.

"Oh," the other customer said. Her braids looked like mine except shorter, stopping just above her shoulders, and her skin color resembled Winston's. She didn't have physical facial perfection down pat like her friend did, but damn she was cute. Her smile alone could warm and charm the coldest of hearts. "We really just wanted milkshakes and fries."

"She wanted that," he said. "I'm here against my will."

"We agreed: I would go on this little road trip of yours as long as we ate proper road trip food. You promised." Her smile could also dazzle me into committing whatever crime she wanted, Jesus Christ. Talk about a power couple. "We want these ones." She pointed to the menu. He didn't object again, sighing dramatically and turning away—before turning back to her with a beautiful and resigned smile I recognized from watching hours upon endless hours of rom-coms. His fate was sealed. She was it for him.

Before I could get all weepy because *why not meeeee????* I collected their menus and headed to the kitchen. Fries in the basket. Basket in the oil. Set the timer. Milkshakes: two scoops of chocolate ice cream, half a cup of whole milk, chocolate chips, Marshmallow Fluff, and secret sauce. Blend.

After making sure the customers had plenty of salt and ketchup, I flounced back to my podium.

"There are people here," Sam whispered. She'd been wearing my tiara since Granny handed it to her.

"Yeah, they do show up now and again." I sat next to her and she linked our arms together, resting her head on my shoulder.

"Go to sleep. I'll be up in an hour."

"No." She looked like if she blinked too hard, she'd fall off her stool and into a deep slumber for the next hundred years.

"Why?"

"I miss you."

I snorted before I could stop myself. Sam's "sensitivity" often meant she took things the wrong way. I had a strong dislike for that word. Her dad disagreed that it was anything more than that, but I knew Sam. I was almost positive she wasn't just *sensitive*.

"You see me every day."

"But we don't have a thing."

"What?"

"You know." She raised her head, eyes half closed and bleary, bottom lip jutting out slightly. "You and Winston have Win-Win movie night. You and Kara have, um, well *everything*. And now you're gonna spend all of your free time with whoever wins the tiebreaker. What about me? We don't have anything. We should have a thing."

Back at home, Sam, Winston, and I never really hung out together at school.

I'd already said good-bye to most of my high school friends. The vast majority of my friendships existed out of necessity. I saw them five days a week and we fell into a routine. Nothing wrong with that or going our separate ways after graduation. I'm sure we'd keep in touch online, but that'd probably be it.

Winston was one of those kids who had found a group in kindergarten and stuck with them. Casey, Henry, Ethan, and Winston— the Chew Crew, a walking pack of snarky human garbage disposals doused in AXE body spray, with hearts of gold buried way, way, way down underneath all of their unstable hormones.

I liked them. Most of the time.

Sam, however, didn't seem to have anyone. I knew she mostly hung out with her cheer squad, who hung out with the football team because they seemed determined to be a stereotype, but I didn't think she had someone she would consider a best friend. She never mentioned any of her squad members at home. After her last relationship ended, she flat out refused to date anymore.

I'd thought that maybe she was the kind of person who naturally preferred being alone—she *liked* cheerleading as a sport and tolerated the social part of it because she had to—but lately, I wasn't so sure.

It was kind of weird, because kids ten and under practically worshipped her, followed her around like a beloved general who earned every ounce of their respect. Adults *adored* her. She charmed them senseless and became their shining example of everything a teenager should be. But in between those two age ranges? Things got dicey.

There'd been a couple of incidents where a few girls on her squad stole from her. Another time with a different group, from her AP biology class, who decided it would be a great idea to drive to Canada without telling anyone. We thought she'd been kidnapped because she left her phone at home. And I heard her crying more than once in her room because of stuff people said about her online. It even happened with Winston. I knew he didn't hate her, but sometimes, he said things that really made me wonder if I was wrong about that.

"Is that why you're sitting down here with me?"

"It's why I'm here at all. Me and Winston only come here because you want to." She nodded—I had to look away. Her earnestness always burrowed straight into my soul. Her happiness was my happiness and vice versa to cover any and all vagueness.

Everyone had that one truth that fueled them. Mine was this: my family. My life revolved and lived and breathed around being that one person everyone could count on.

If Sam needed something, I usually got it done.

My baby cousin, both a delight and a wreck waiting to happen, knew she could count on me.

"We can have a thing," I agreed.

"Can I pick it?"

"Ehhhh . . ." When it came to *things*, our interests didn't overlap.

At all. "I guess. But it can't be this. You do too much to try and stay up late with me. There's only room for one superhero in this family."

"There could be two."

"Yeah, no. Competition would turn me into a supervillain faster than a speeding bullet. It's for the greater good that I remain unchallenged. Truly."

She laughed, sleepy and snorty. "Do you promise?"

"I promise we can talk about it later. But what we *can* talk about now is Winston. Help me out. What's up with him?" Winston's foul mood had returned the second we pulled into Goldeen's parking lot.

"How should I know?" She shrugged. "It's not like he ever tells me anything."

Sam had been my one and only hope of figuring out Winston without actually asking him. "Damage control it is, then."

~

Later, upstairs, when Goldeen's and the house had stilled and Sam's chainsaw snores in the top bunk threatened to knock down the walls of our shared room, I allowed myself five sleepy minutes to be happy and not worry about anything.

FAM-BAM-MAJAMA

Winnie: MOOOOOOM! I'm the QUEEN!
Winnie: They pulled my name and
I'm the Misty Summer Queen! I HAVE
A TIARA! And! Kara volunteered!
Winnie: Dad, yes, there might be a king. His
name is Dallas and he also volunteered.
Winnie: He's really nice. Winston will tell you.

Winston: no. i won't.

I switched chat windows.

WINSTON (Zeddemore)

> **Winnie:** Unless you're going to tell
> me what's up GO TO BED

I waited for his response but it never came.

WINSTON (Zeddemore)

> **Winnie:** Thanks for walking with me
> to the gazebo. I kind of froze.

Winston: /kind of?/
Winston: [picture message]

I covered my mouth with my hand to muffle my laugh. Winston had the absolute best mock-shocked face. Instead of sending GIFs like everyone else, he always sent pictures of his actual reactions. He had such an expressive face that he hid from everyone except for me.

Restarting my five sleepy minutes felt like a wonderfully brilliant idea, because in every universe eight minutes of indulgence out-matched a measly five. I turned onto my side, snuggling down farther under my soft sheets with the wickedly high thread count. When it came to little things like that—bedding, shoes, lotions—Granny didn't mess around "with the cheap stuff," as she put it. "Your body deserves to feel good even if you're struggling. *You* gotta take care of *you.*"

Indeed. I wiggled my toes, rubbed my freshly shaven bare legs along the fabric, sighing in happiness.

Queen Winnie.

Dallas had stood poised and glorious, smiling the whole time. And he had had such warm hands! I squeezed my hand into a fist, trying to remember that first moment when he had grabbed it. The feeling felt buried under the pressure to remain calm, trapped under the fight to stay present and not collapse. I couldn't reach it. Yet another memory lost to panic because I couldn't get my shit together and be brave and not care what anyone thought about me. Because I was too busy trying to figure out *why* everything was happening instead of experiencing the moment. *My* moment. No matter what else happened, I'd always regret missing out on that first sensation, that first touch in its purest first form. My regret came through stronger than the memory of holding Dallas's hand had. It twisted inside of my mind, maliciously whispering, *"that's all you'll ever get"* and *"it's over"* and *"you blew it"* while punching me in the heart.

I'll always remember the first time I had held Kara's small soft hand in mine, because my heart thumped so hard I thought my body would split in half. Crack straight down the middle without a single regret because I had died happy.

But Kara *wasn't* happy. She always texted me to say good night, but I didn't have any messages from her yet. It seemed so stupid—how could she possibly think I had anything to do with Dallas volunteering?

I needed to know why. I needed to be able to give Kara a definitive answer and fix this before it was too late.

Eight

My summer, my perfect, fun, and stress-free summer, had been thrown to the Haven wolves. Kara's radio silence, Dallas's disappearing act, Winston's grouchiness, Sam and her surprise-attack *thing* we'd soon have to share, the impending tiebreaker—no more surprises were allowed. None!

On top of that, I should have been at Goldeen's, twirling happily around the floor while taking orders, serenading customers with some surprisingly pleasant off-key renditions of whatever song played and impressing them with my ability to shimmy while holding four plates full of food, two on each arm.

Instead I had been doomed to endure the unnatural stillness of Dr. Skinner's waiting room. Only the ticking of the analog clock meant time continued to pass and we hadn't been transported to some accursed Langoliers dimension.

Winston made me watch that movie during a random Netflix binge session.

Nightmares. For weeks.

Too short to elegantly tap my toes on the floor, and thighs too big to comfortably cross my legs at the knee to do that fidget thing with my foot like my mom did, I sat slumped in my seat. Shoulders raised near my ears. Flicking my fingernails. Just *miserable*.

Granny tapped my arm. "Don't slouch. Sit up."

"Winnie Woodson?" the nurse called.

I shot to my feet, ready to skulk across the room. Granny stood, too. "Are you going to the bathroom?"

"I'm coming with you." She placed a hand on my lower back.

"Uh, no? I mean, I'm okay. It's just a quick test."

"I want to ask the doctor some questions. Come on. We're wasting Nurse Nicole's time."

"I doubt it. There's no one else here."

Granny pinched the skin above my elbow with pursed lips.

"Hi," Nicole said, cheerier than any human had any right to be. "I've heard so much about you. It's nice to finally meet."

"Likewise."

Notwise. Or whatever the reverse of that word was.

Naturally, I had already heard the lowdown about Nurse Nicole Winters since Granny made weekly trips to the doctor for her asthma and arthritis pain management. Recent graduate, top of her class, couldn't get a job in the saturated nursing field until nepotism kicked in and got her the gig in Misty. No kids. No spouse. No roommate. "Pretty as could be"—Granny's words—"and had that Michael Jackson thing but didn't cover it up with makeup."

Vitiligo. Every time I had to explain to Granny that it wasn't a *thing*, had a proper name, and didn't need to be covered up, my temper shortened another inch.

Nicole walked us to the back, stopping at Dr. Death's way station in front of a short hallway with four doors, two on each side. She smiled. "I'm going to take your blood pressure and temperature. Have a seat here."

I sat, trying to remain motionless and calm while the machine inflated the cuff that squeezed the life out of my arm, and returned her smile. Sort of. It might have been a grimace—like I had a stomachache I wanted to hide, which, coincidentally, I did.

"Excellent." Nicole sounded surprised as she jotted down the numbers in the manila file. I narrowed my eyes, watching her. "And if I can get you to step on the scale."

The metal base of the scale gleamed in the light.

"No, thanks."

Nicole blinked at me. "It'll only take a moment."

I held in my initial reply, a superb and snarky one, instead choosing to say, "I'll keep my moment, thank you."

"But I have to."

"But you don't, actually." I aimed for pleasant. Conversational. "You're not legally required to weigh me and I am within my right to say no, so no, thank you."

"Winnie," Granny said, voice a decibel away from a hiss. "Stop it."

"What? I was *nice.*"

"I'm sorry, baby," Granny said to an increasingly flustered Nicole. "She can be so hardheaded sometimes. Stubborn just like her daddy."

I picked my battles with care. Denying Granny anything often came with the unwelcome side effects of silent treatments, disappointed sighs, nagging, and an abundance of newly created chores. But hospitals and medical clinics and even a tiny doctor's office in a small village could be an active war zone for fat people. I'd read the stories online of fat people not getting the treatment they needed because the magical catchall cure for them was to lose weight. Not even suspected cancer stood a chance against weight loss!

I wasn't ashamed of the way I looked. I weighed what I weighed and that was that. Everybody *else* seemed unable to comprehend that memo. The second Dr. Skinner saw the number, my appointment would turn into a lecture meant to "help." It wouldn't be my first fat-shaming rodeo. I knew that script, and nope. Not happening.

"Stop making Nurse Nicole's job difficult. Get on the scale so we can get on with your appointment. I want to inspect that shipment of strawberries before the driver leaves this time. Come on, now." She waved me toward the scale. Nudged me in that direction, tapping my behind.

I knew what I needed, a blood test and a possible shot, and that it didn't require me to get weighed. This battle? Worth it? Defiance in the name of self-preservation.

Twisting away, I walked past both of them. "Which room am I in? Eeny, meeny, miny, mo?"

Granny's eyebrows hit her hairline. She tucked in her chin, lips formed to make the "*Tuh!*" sound.

"Um, number two." Nicole hurried to open the door and escorted us in.

I jumped onto the exam table, legs swinging.

Granny followed, settling into the chair in the corner.

Nicole placed my chart in the inbox for Dr. Skinner.

I eyed Granny. Her physical cues of indignation rose like a thermometer stuck in boiling water. Any second now . . .

Granny placed her bag on the small counter because it was bad luck to set it on the floor.

Nicole excused herself.

The door clicked shut.

"So I guess you grown now?" Rain or shine, the Vexation Express was always on time. Granny sat back, hands laced together on her lap, staring at me with enough wrath to make Khan bow down. "I'm talking to you. Answer me."

"I didn't want to be weighed today. That's all. I wasn't disrespectful."

"But what did I tell you to do? Out here acting like . . ."

Well. That conversation had ended. Anything I said from that point on during Granny's tirade could and would be used against me in the Black Parental Court of Law. The right to remain silent didn't exist. Once the rhetorical questions started, the tirade would turn into a trap of *Faerie Queene* proportions.

If I answered, I was screwed.

If I stayed silent, I was royally screwed.

". . . you look at me when I'm talking to you!"

"Knock, knock," Dr. Skinner greeted as the door opened. Granny shut up mid-sentence, mouth snapping closed. "How are you, Winfrey? Or should I say *Queen* Winfrey."

"Ha. Ha." I smiled until the urge of wanting to kick him in the back of the knee and watch him roll down a hill passed. Usage of my real name was punishable by bodily harm.

Most people assumed Winnie had been shortened from Winifred. My full government name was Winfrey Diane Woodson. Yes, *that* Winfrey. My mom loved Oprah. Loved her to the point of worship.

My mom had given birth to yours truly, had wanted to name her darling newborn daughter Oprah, and then my dad threatened to divorce his glowing and exhausted wife on the spot. She had settled for Winfrey. He had called me Winnie. History had been made.

No one called me Winfrey. Skinner knew that but insisted on using my real name every chance he got because that's the kind of guy he was.

He placed the stethoscope pods in his ears and did all of the normal doctor checker-upper things—listened to my heart and lungs, looked in my eyes and ears, made my knee kick like a possessed donkey, and made my ankles twitch.

"So what's this about you not wanting to be weighed?"

Granny's head swiveled in my direction, an expectant look on her face.

"It's not illegal to say no." *One . . . two . . . three . . .*

"That's true," Skinner confirmed. "But in order to give you a complete health assessment, I need to know how much you weigh."

Four . . . five . . . six . . . Maybe if I smiled he would just do what I wanted. "Mmmm, that's not why I'm here. I have a primary already. Thanks."

Skinner exhaled, leaning back against the small counter. "I don't have access to your file, so I need to collect information to help me help you. Do you understand that?"

"Do I—understand? Ooookay." I felt that familiar indignant, self-righteous pull, the speech already locked, loaded, and eager to go. Half the time I didn't even have to *think* of what I wanted to say because my mind stayed ready. "I *understand* that you know my weight is irrelevant to the task at hand. And I *understand* that you are not listening to *me*. Can you *please* give me the blood test so I can leave?"

Another exhale with a headshake on top of it. "I'm not the enemy here, Winnie. I want to help you—"

"Then give me the blood test." *Seven . . . eight . . . nine . . .*

Dr. Skinner began rattling off a litany of ailments, conditions I could look forward to if I didn't lose weight.

Osteoarthritis. Gout. Hypertension.

I sat there, taking it, letting the words wash over me. It wasn't like it was Brand! New! Information! I'd heard the same preachy speeches for what felt like forever.

Infertility. Sleep apnea. Depression.

But with each new potential prognosis, Granny's face fell a little lower.

Stroke. Sudden cardiac arrest. Death.

"—but she's not *that big*. It's just baby fat," Granny protested.

The sadness in her voice broke my heart, and rage flooded the cracks.

Ten.

I tried.

I really, really did.

"You know what?" I looked him dead in the eye. "We all have to go sometime. And evidence has shown that the universe doesn't care if you're skinny or not. Otherwise, mass shootings wouldn't happen in schools. Don't even get me started on genocide.

"*I'm* paying *you* out of pocket because my insurance doesn't cover any kind of service here at your little Podunk practice. So do the job I'm *paying* you to do and stop trying to use me being here as a chance to flex and make my granny upset. You don't know the first thing about me, but oh, I know *all* about you, and I know you have way bigger problems than a fat girl in your office, Dr. I Cheated on My Wife with Her Sister. Learn to worry about yourself."

nine

my temper landed me in more trouble than I would have liked. No trouble would have been great, but actions had consequences, and I accepted that fact of life. *But.* If people would just chill out and listen to me, I wouldn't be forced to snap so often and hurt their little feelings.

And honestly? My parents told me that I'd straight up inherited that trait from Granny, so it was pretty amazingly hypocritical of her to get mad when my sass showed up to party.

And punishment number one of the forthcoming eleventy billion? One-hundred percent unfair.

Instead of letting me spend the afternoon shadowing Nadiya to finish learning my managerial duties like I'd planned to, Granny kicked me out.

"Go outside and get some air. Take a nap. Do something. I don't want you or your attitude in here."

That cut me deep. Right to the bone. Nothing could have *possibly* hurt me more than being banished from Goldeen's.

Also, for the record? Air was everywhere. That made zero sense, but even my parents said it.

I walked to the Sugar Shoppe on Second Street even though the weather could be described using the words *muggy*, *hot*, and *balls*, with a few conjunctions thrown in for clarity. Kara loved chocolate-covered walnuts and red whips, so I bought those and some jawbreakers for Winston because he hated them. Sweetening Kara up and irritating Winston would at least open the communication door.

Granny was mad at me. That overrode everything else. I needed my people back on my side and talking to me. She would get over it eventually, but I wasn't above playing the victim card to gain sympathy points from my people until that happened.

After buying the candy, I wandered through Misty Haven, saying hi and catching up with everyone.

That lasted like twenty minutes.

Granny had kept me up to speed throughout the year. I already knew everything about Miss Shin's new online store, Sunshine Cross-Stitch; the automotive shop's expansion into the tow-truck business; the day care that opened up last fall and was currently really pissed off at Sam for taking some of their business; how the floral boutique Forget-Me-Nots had reached their first million-dollar revenue milestone after thirty years. . . .

All of it so wonderful.

All of it so boring and not what I wanted to be doing.

I ended up at the park, sitting on a bench, with a cup of praline ripple ice cream. Not even Sam could save me from my boredom. Her shift babysitting the Honey Bunches of Kids didn't end until five.

Side note: I really needed to make more friends in HC.

I could've moved on to Merry, but thanks to Kara I knew all about the happenings over there, too. Move-ins, babies, foreclosures—all of it started to bleed together after a while.

The indelible charm of Haven Central tended to suck people in until, when you thought about it, only one pervasive whimsical feeling stuck out. Nothing felt unique or exceptional about it. It was a place to live, just like any other.

"Winnie."

Butterflies, birds, bees, name a winged creature, and it flapped inside of my stomach at the sight of Dallas. That initial gut reaction from seeing him always took me by surprise.

Having a type was a strange, strange thing. So far, I knew I liked pretty boys and beautiful girls, and thought that love at first sight was a myth on par with the Loch Ness Monster. Maybe it was real in a prehistoric, tale-as-old-as-time kind of way. But maybe it was a fantastical hoax created to uphold unreal romantic expectations, because there was no way that's all there was to it.

Right then, all I knew for sure was that I really, *really* liked Dallas's face.

And that two days ago, he had volunteered to be my king and would have to compete against Kara to win that title.

He stood next to my bench, holding a reusable canvas bag stuffed with—I squinted for a second—books.

"Oh. Hey," I said, setting my ice cream down. I was cool with eating in public alone as long as I didn't feel like someone was watching. But if someone had joined me and they weren't eating? I had to stop.

"You know, they only sell that flavor in the summer when you're here." He gestured to my ice cream. "Sascha told me. People don't even know what it's called. They just go in and ask for Winnie's ice cream."

"They are rather fond of me."

"Most of the people here are. When you're not biting their heads off anyway." He smirked. "Skinner's already lit up the phone tree."

"So much for doctor-patient confidentiality. I'm convinced the devil created group texts."

"Probably. And doubled down on the evil by creating the ones you can't opt out of."

I laughed, but it sounded like a humorous, drawn-out growl. "This is going to haunt me for the rest of the summer. I can feel it."

"Not gonna lie, I was pretty shocked when I heard about it at the library just now," he said, gaze drifting off to the side. The muscles in his jaw worked as he shook his head, a quick frown settling then disappearing on his features. Whatever he had just thought of in that briefest of seconds irritated him. "It didn't seem like something you would do, insult him and stuff. You're always so nice."

Sometimes, I didn't want to be *nice*. I didn't think I was a bad person, but that niceness felt like a burden I had to endure because of my Blackness. Doubly so because I was a girl. Triply so because I was fat. How come I wasn't allowed to have that space where my attitude could be less than? I was a person, human, too. People weren't always nice. Neither was I—I just hid it until the breathing and the counting failed me.

"Well," he continued hastily. "Maybe not *nice*, but you're not that kind of *mean*."

My face must have given something away for him to change his mind. Unsurprising.

"I did what I had to do," I said.

"I'm sure. Dude's an asshole." He gave me an approving look. "If you say you had a good reason, I believe you."

I . . . wasn't expecting that. He believed me? "Thanks," I said, softer than I intended, while looking at him. "Usually, people don't give me the benefit of the doubt."

He nodded as if to say *you're welcome*. "So what are you up to? Just enjoying the view of screaming, happy kids terrorizing their wooden playground empire?"

"It's been *fascinating*." I pointed at a pair of kids. "The one in the red shirt pushed the one in the blue shirt down the slide because he was taking too long. Blue was super scared, and, I mean, look at the height on that thing—I'd be scared, too. Anyway, Red pushed him, and Blue *howled* for his dad the whole way down, poor kid. But then he gets to the bottom with Red trailing behind him, right, and then he turns around and slaps Red dead in the face. I heard the smack from way over here. I was shocked! *Shocked!* Five minutes later, they're holding hands running for the seesaw like nothing happened. Truly riveting stuff."

Dallas chuckled. "If only that worked the same way for verbal slaps."

"Kids, man. They don't know how easy they got it. My granny is mad at me about the Skinner thing. She kicked me out. Temporarily. I think. I'll see what happens when I go home."

"Yikes," he said. "So you want to get out of here or what?"

Ten

Dallas had a long stride, walking faster than I did, but after a few minutes he slowed down without me having to ask. The park behind us, we headed toward Merry's Main Street in comfortable silence.

Semi-comfortable. I'd been burning to ask him why he had volunteered at the HSR. After he had brought up Skinner, I didn't want to just blurt it out and change the subject.

Other than the people at the park, very few others braved the Haven Central heat, so the streets were fairly empty. There'd be an event that night—something usually went on every night in the summer thanks to Shelley, and people would willingly leave their air conditioners then.

"I've been meaning to call you," he said.

"Call? Like on the phone?" I didn't bother trying to hide the repulsion in my tone.

"No, I was going to stand in front of my window at sunrise and yodel your name until you answered. I'm pretty good at it." He tapped his stomach. "Strong diaphragm. Good lungs. Nice tone. It's genetic."

I jokingly frowned at him. He could be slick if he wanted to be, his comebacks almost as good as mine. While I loved a good smart-ass as much as the next snarky girl looking for a challenge, he didn't need to know that.

"I meant call as opposed to texting."

"I don't like texting."

"Excuse me, what?"

"I like talking on the phone. It feels better. I'm guessing you don't like it?"

I thought about it. "What I like are shortcuts. I'll talk if I have to, but texting and emailing are faster. I only really willingly talk on the phone with Kara. Or my parents."

"Kara." He said her name so low, I didn't think he meant for me to hear him. Another frown appeared, quick as the first, and another headshake.

He must have had a terrible poker face.

"Why did you volunteer anyway? Kara wanted to do it."

"Did she? Oh. I couldn't tell."

Sarcasm. Nice. "Then why?"

He grinned, eyes on his feet. "It's kind of obvious, isn't it?"

"No. It's not. I need you to tell me why."

"Because I wanted to be king."

"So it wouldn't have mattered whose name was pulled? You would've volunteered?"

"I didn't say that."

Between Dallas and the sun, my sweatiness barreled toward an unbearable saturation point. I could feel my skin getting darker by the second. My shirt had three-quarter-length sleeves and I had on ankle socks. Wasn't really in the mood to have to navigate contrasting skin tone lines until my skin faded back to its natural warm brown color. Most of the Main Street shops had canopies over their front entrances and as soon as we hit that sidewalk, I made sure he knew that was the end of our walk.

Deonna's Joint advertised itself as a mixed bar. They sold drinks like standard and imported sodas, milkshakes, some cool craft beers, and super syrupy alcoholic drinks that I swear I have never, ever tried while no one was looking. I waved at Deonna through the window before we sat under one of the umbrella tables on the patio. The shade felt brilliant.

I started to fan myself with one of the menus. "Look. I need you to be level with me so I can talk to Kara. She's upset because she thinks you volunteering means I'm keeping secrets from her, which I'm not. Help me out here."

"I think I followed that." He gestured between us, pointing to himself, then me and back again. "She thinks there's something going on between us? That I volunteered specifically to be with you?"

A hot flash of embarrassment surged through me. *No, I did not think that, why would he even say it like that, Jesus, be an ice cube, God.*

"I don't know what she thinks other than she's upset." This was about *Kara* not me. I didn't want him to think he—*whatever.* I needed to focus. And stop overheating. "I don't like it when *Kara* is like this, so I'm just going to preemptively apologize, but in order to do that I need information. So spill it. Why?"

The heat, and our conversation, didn't seem to be affecting him. A light sheen of sweat covered his face and exposed arms, but he sat infuriatingly unagitated across from me like he didn't have a single problem worth stressing about.

"I was thinking about doing it. And when your name got called, I was sure that I would. You can tell her that, if you want. I didn't volunteer for you, but I did volunteer because of you."

"And that's not the same thing?"

"Nope."

"Mmmmmm. She's gonna need a little more than that." And so did I. *Because of me?* It'd be way too easy to assume and be dead wrong in this situation. I wouldn't let myself leapfrog into a full-on face-plant.

"Tell your girlfriend that's all she's gonna get from me. *I* don't owe her anything."

"She's not my girlfriend."

"What? Yes, she is." He said it with an air of *duh* authority, scrunching his face and partially rolling his eyes.

"No, she's not."

His gaze sharpened, confusion slowly settling in. He leaned forward in his seat, body angling across the table to be closer to me. He whispered like he was telling me an important secret. "Yes. She. Is. Everyone knows that."

I matched his posture. The table was small, made for two, and we ended up so close together, I had a split second to marvel at the tiny brown freckles that I didn't know were there, blessing the bridge of his nose.

"No, she's not. I think I would know."

"But everyone says—"

"We don't care what *anyone* says. They don't know us."

He sat back, watching me with a disbelieving look. "So you two really aren't together?"

"I didn't say that." And then I couldn't help myself. "Not so nice, is it? Remember that next time you try that cryptic stuff with me."

"Deal. But only if I can trust you. Can I?"

"Trust me?" Where did that come from?

"Yeah."

"I don't have a reason to lie to you unless you give me one."

"Huh." He tilted his head slightly to the side, eyes never leaving mine. "And if I tell *you* something?"

"I'm not a confessional," I warned. "But I can keep a secret. If it's important."

"I didn't expect you to say that," he muttered, looking away.

The strangest idea like I had just won something he hadn't intended me to popped into my head. "What were you expecting?"

"What I wanted to hear," he said, eyes on mine. "What *you* thought I wanted to hear."

The thrill of making eye contact gave me an immediate adrenaline rush. Talking to him like this—so fast, so close, so candid—made my heart beat at a full gallop. My body moved on its own.

Closer, my body said. *Be close to him again.* I didn't fight it. Neither did Dallas. Close enough to whisper. Close enough to kiss.

"I don't know you well enough to even kind of guess that," I said, meaning it.

"You don't need to know someone to do that. Our conversation could have led you to what I expected you to say."

"What?" I scrolled back through the last five minutes, remembering. "Yes? You expected me to just say yes to you?"

"You want to know why I volunteered. I want to know about you and Kara. Pretty straightforward."

Except it wasn't. Why would he expect me to give him an unconditional yes to something so broad? "Can I trust you?" I spat back at him.

He smiled. "No."

"So you would lie to me? Tell all my secrets?"

"Also no."

I frowned at him, not liking where this was heading. It reeked of a word game. A riddle I had to figure out. Some kind of test he wanted me to pass. But just because I didn't like it didn't mean I wasn't about to own his ass.

"You don't trust yourself. I'm right, aren't I? You couldn't answer me honestly without lying, so you said no."

"Damn it," he muttered.

"You're like a troll under a drawbridge. Don't play games with me."

"It's not a game. Not to me."

"Then why can't you just tell me?"

"I did tell you! It's not my fault that wasn't enough for you."

"But there's obviously more to it."

"Which I obviously don't want to tell you!"

Don't assume.

Don't assume.

Don't assume.

The secret to my success had always been to keep my expectations in check. It would be so, so easy to let myself believe the obvious, simplest answer staring me in the face was the right one. The blurred line between fact and wishes all but disappeared with every cryptic word Dallas said. It wasn't impossible that it could be true. Just—highly unlikely. Improbable. It didn't make sense that this would come out of nowhere suddenly. The most time we'd ever spent together added up to a handful of hours, the culmination of all the deliveries I made last summer to his house.

I knew what I liked about him. Besides his face, I mean. People talked about the Meyer family. Not exactly gossip—even banal details spread about him. Through everything that I'd heard and seen firsthand, more than anything else I'd always thought he was kind. Genuine and funny. Dedicated to his family and sports.

But I didn't know everything. And I didn't think Dallas knew anything substantial about me either.

I wasn't so down on myself that I believed no one could ever be physically attracted to me. It wasn't impossible—again, just highly unlikely. I guess.

Damn it. I balled my hands into fists under the table.

I did not need those thoughts running through my head. I did not need to tumble down that rabbit hole. I did not need to believe for one second that I was unworthy of *anything*, never mind a boy thinking I was pretty and wanting me.

"Hey, guys." Dana, Deonna's twin sister, stood next to our table. "I don't mean to interrupt, but I wanted to see if I could get y'all anything? If y'all just wanna sit, that's okay, too. Just checking."

"Oh, sorry. Do you want a drink?" Dallas asked me.

I shook my head. I knew I should buy something, regardless of what she said, but I wanted her to leave and not come back more than I wanted to be a decent customer.

"I guess we're fine," Dallas said. "I gotta get going soon anyway."

I wanted to know the rest. For Kara and myself. I wanted to know and I was running out of time. He wasn't obligated to tell me anything by any stretch of the imagination. But maybe . . .

Maybe a good-faith payment could convince him to. Trust mattered to him. And I had a guess that fairness did, too. Maybe if I opened that door, started off with something honest, maybe he would follow suit.

I had surprised him before. I would do that again.

Dana left us alone. I waited, counting to ten to center my temper in advance, and said, "Kara's not my girlfriend." I sounded colder than I intended. When I talked about us, my natural state had turned defensive out of necessity. I had to protect her. "She's my partner."

"There's a difference? I'm not trying to be rude." He held up his hands in surrender. "But my friend calls his girlfriend *partner*, too, and there's no difference for him. You two are together, right?"

I pulled on the thin gold chain hiding under my shirt, showing him the gold band with a single glittering blue stone. "I never show this to anyone. And I never take it off. It's a promise ring. Kara cried the day she gave this to me, and if you know her at all, you'd understand how important that is."

He scoff-laughed, looking away quickly and then back to me. "I have an idea."

Dallas and Kara were the same age. Lived in Haven Central all their lives. Went to the same school, had been in the same classes, graduated at the same time. He got to see her every day for months at a time, while I only ever had the summer. He knew her in a way I never had. But it was hard to imagine someone, anyone not liking Kara. And yet, all signs kept pointing to the fact that for some reason, Dallas didn't. I took another deep breath, holding on to that nonsensical thought before continuing.

"Kara's parents let her fly down for my birthday a few years ago. After dinner, she waited until we were alone and said she wasn't sure how to explain everything she felt but wanted to try anyway. She asked me to be her ungirlfriend because being with me felt like falling headfirst into wonderland and she never wanted to leave. But then when she tried to put the ring on my finger, it didn't fit. She just burst into tears. Full-on uncontrollable sobbing." I put my ring back in its place, laughing. "I still tease her about how red she got and how much snot leaked out of her. Amazing."

"Ungirlfriend?" Dallas asked. "Like unbirthday?"

"People dismiss friendship. They think of it as not being nearly as important as romance. Instead of having one special day like Valentine's Day for couples, we have every day. To us, every day gets to be special because we're together. And if people can't understand that, then—" I shrugged.

His lips twitched like he wanted to smile but wasn't quite sure if he should.

"It's not any different from what other people who date and decide to be in a relationship do. We want to have a future together, so we are."

"So," he said, "it's a non-romantic open relationship?"

Kara and I both knew the all-encompassing thing between us had to be wrangled into submission. It screamed at us to be defined, to be shaped into a word, to be freed. But we had to find the word we wanted before we could share it with anyone else.

Non-romantic open relationship? No. Absolutely not. It made sense, those words, in that order, but that wasn't *for us*. It didn't make us happy. Queerplatonic worked sometimes—if we were willing to explain, to sit there and be interrogated. Those conversations usually ended with Kara getting frustrated and saying, *"Fucking Google it. We're not a damn dictionary or lesson for you to learn."*

"If you must," I conceded. "If we want to date other people, too, as in 'in addition to' us being together, we can. We made rules and stuff. She doesn't want to, though." I shrugged again, running out of words. Eventually, it would sink in for him that I didn't care if he understood. "*We* just *are*."

"*Who*. Are. *You*," he said, imitating the caterpillar from Disney.

"Now you're getting it."

"I think I do, actually." His triumphant grin could make the sun give up the ghost and implode.

"We still say ungirlfriend, but mostly use partner now when explaining us to other people. You got the behind-the-scenes bonus feature explanation. Feel special."

"I do," he said, standing up. "Thank you. For sharing that. It's pretty cool."

I stood up, too, pushing in my chair. "I shouldn't have to say this, but thank you for not laughing or calling us weird or something like that."

He nodded, stepping out from under the umbrella. I hung back, reluctant to leave my shade sanctuary. With the sun behind him, it made it hard to see his face clearly.

"Kara gets really excited when we get to do things together, and I think she's really looking forward to being queen with me."

"Oh. Right."

"Right," I confirmed, shielding my eyes so I could see him better. It barely worked. "So now that you *understand*, if you dropped out of the HSR, I'd really appreciate that, too."

"Yeah. Right," he said again. "Umm, when you talk to Kara, please tell her I'm sorry—"

"Oh, you don't have to apologize, we—"

"No, Winnie," he said. "Tell her I'm sorry because I'm still going to win the tiebreaker."

Eleven

genuinely didn't know how long I'd been kicked out for. Granny hadn't made a joke or a false threat. "Get out" truly meant *leave*.

It would've been stupid to waltz through Goldeen's front door. Granny was most likely down there, in the office or filling in. Instead I slunk around back, taking the old cement stairs two at a time. I held my breath as I unlocked what was technically the front door to Granny's apartment and pushed it open just a crack, listening.

Silence.

Winston's shift didn't end until six. Sam tended to randomly show up when no one was looking because nobody could ever remember her hectic schedule. I slipped inside, closing the door behind me, pausing to breathe and listen with my back flat against the wall.

Empty. Thank God.

Granny wasn't the easiest person to love or even get along with. I loved that old joke: if you open up a dictionary, this person's picture would be next to this word. Granny's beautifully classic, black-and-white photo would be next to *cantankerous*.

My uncle always made excuses like "she's set in her ways." My mom gave Granny space because "she refuses to progress with the times." And my dad, well he's told me more than once, "You're just like her. Watch out."

I was the first grandbaby on the block. I've always known that made a difference in what she expected from me versus the lax attitude she had with Sam and Winston. I never took it personally.

Finally, in my room, I flopped facedown on my bed before turning over and lightly kicking the top bunk planks with the bottom of my foot in a steady rhythm.

Stupid Dallas.

I'd bared my soul for *nothing*.

Fine, okay, *sure*, he wasn't obligated to help me out.

And it was a trash move to expect him to open up to me just because I did it first.

But that didn't mean I had to *like* it. Sometimes, I just wanted everything to be the other person's fault so I could rage in guilt-free peace. Being *rational* sucked.

I curled onto my side, facing the wall. Someone had taped a piece of paper, folded into a yellow heart, near my pillow. Carefully, I unstuck it—on the back the words *READ ME* had been written in a neat, tight print and inside the words *Hoping this makes you smile. It'll be okay. I love you* did just that.

Sam.

So cute. So corny.

She'd probably heard about the Dr. Skinner Debacle. Sam was a rapid-fire texter—meaning for every message I sent, she sent about five or six in return. But instead of doing that, she took time out of her day, probably while on break between babysitting jobs, to make the heart and leave it for me. These little notes from her always made me feel special. Loved.

My phone rang—one of the few personalized ringtones I had bothered to program.

"Mom!" I never knew why I shouted like that. Every time she called, I turned five years old again after my first day of kindergarten, excited to see her, go home, and tell her all about my day. I sat up, situating the phone on its stand so I would be in frame. "Hello, *Mothaaaa*."

I also tended to use accents when I talked to her. Making her laugh made me feel good. A buoyant shot of dopamine straight to my brain cells. But she didn't laugh. She stared at me with her *you got me fucked up* face.

"Uh-oh." My upper body began to curl inward, a reflexive move to brace myself for the incoming tirade.

"You haven't even been there two weeks. What are you doing?"

I winced and let out a high-pitched whine. Nothing made me squirm faster than my mom could when she used that tone. Shame, nothing but *shame*, as far as the soul could feel. "You see, what had happened was—"

"I know *exactly* what happened. There are better ways to get your point across than insulting people. You promised to stop being so hostile when you disagree with someone."

"I didn't insult him. Why is everyone saying that?"

"Stop lying," she said, voice tight. "His 'little Podunk practice'? Really? And that thing about *his wife*? God help me, you always go straight for the jugular."

A laugh bubbled in the back of my throat. I pressed my lips together, cowering while trying to hold it back and look contrite. "I do not recall saying that. Lots of words were said in various sentences and I didn't, I mean I may have, but I don't think—"

"Why do you always have to go straight to ether mode?"

According to my mom, because she likes to make sense of things by placing them in pretty little boxes with pretty little labels, I have three modes.

Saint.

Combat.

Ether.

In that order.

"You have such a beautiful, giving heart," she continued. "I don't understand where that nastiness comes from."

It's a statement, but she's asking. She's asked it before and I knew she'd ask it again. I wanted to say, *This is just how I am! I'm not a fairy! I can have more than one emotion at a time!* but she'd never accept that. I think she convinced herself that I was hiding some irreparable hurt or trauma and it was her job to dig it out of me. Maybe I did have something like that—I thought most of my generation did. We've gone through a lot of traumatic shit and it had to end up somewhere, I guess. But right then, I didn't have an answer that would make her happy, so I did what I always did in that situation: deflect.

"Hey, well, you know, I'm just doing what Dad said. He told me not to let anybody punk me, so I don't."

"I did what?"

"Oh, Dad! Hi! You're here, too." I looked off into the distance. "Oh, this is happening. Oh God." Both of my parents present meant I had reached the ultimate levels of deep shit. When I dragged my gaze back to my phone, they were sitting together.

"I taught you to talk back to adults?"

"I, too, am an adult."

"You are a child."

"Almost-adult," I countered, nearly under my breath, but they heard me.

"Winnie." I hated when they said my name in unison like that. A united front against their unruly daughter.

"Sorry," I said. "I just don't think being an adult means you automatically get my respect. I don't care how old you are. If you act out of pocket, Imma put you back in it."

My dad laughed, covering his mouth and shaking his head.

"Charles! Don't encourage her." My mom's glare could shatter windows. "That's your daughter. Do you see? Do you see what I'm talking about?"

"Imma be real: I don't give a shit what you said to that doctor. I really don't," my dad said. "But what you not gone do is disrespect my mother. Your grandma doesn't have to *earn* your respect. You are in her house, which means you respect her rules, and you know exactly what that means. Is that clear?"

"Yes, Dad." I did know. It meant unconditional obedience for me.

"How many times are we going to have to do this with you?" Mom sighed, angry and weary at the same time. Watching her strain to keep her temper under control made my shame intensify.

My mom and I almost never fought, because when we did it turned into Apocalypse Now: Woodson Edition. We both refused to back down, screaming at each other until my dad stepped in to separate us.

So far I've been metaphorically kicked out three times and actually packed my bags once for dramatic effect, been on punishment more times than I could count, had my phone taken away twice—but given right back because the *unthinkable* could happen, and had my car—that I bought with my own money—my car use restricted to school trips only.

Punishments never stuck because my mom was too good. She always apologized later, vowing to be a "better mom." I can admit I probably deserved at least a smooth ninety-five percent of my mom's wrath at any given time, but her apologies never felt less than genuine. It wasn't some parental manipulation tactic to make me feel bad and promise-lie to do no wrong ever again. She felt bad for failing to shape *me* into a decent human being. She took on that burden. Lead by example meant something to her.

My mom took three deep breaths with her eyes closed. I did the same, eyes open, and decided to cut her some emotional slack.

"I don't like it when people talk down to me." I spoke through my teeth, hands digging into my thighs. Those feelings belonged inside of me, not out in the open where anyone could hear them. "It—*upsets* me when people don't listen. But I was fine. I was in control. Everything was fine until Granny got upset, and then I just lost it."

I could practically see the light bulb click on behind my mom's eyes. My dad swore under his breath. "Now, *that's* your daughter," he said.

Wholly inappropriate considering the death-drop mood, but them doing that had always made me laugh. They each pushed off the "worst" parts of me onto the other, and neither could deny where it had come from.

I had a powerful voice because I was my father's daughter.

I stood up for others because I was my mother's daughter.

They might have been mad, disappointed in me, but I never stopped being theirs.

"It might not seem like it, but everyone feels that way." Her soft tone soothed the wound that telling the truth ripped in me. "I know you meant well, but the way you express those feelings? It doesn't just push people away—it launches them into the next dimension. It's okay to be honest with people. It's okay to let them know how you feel, how you *really* feel. If you're upset or hurt, it's okay to say that. You don't have to be so cold and hard all the time."

I knew what to say to make her happy. "Okay. You're right."

Because she wasn't completely wrong. That did work for some people if they looked a certain way, like her or Sam or Kara.

My mom understood the rules were different for my dad, my uncle, and Winston. But she didn't understand that the rules were different for people like me—who looked like me and sounded like me, moving through a world like ours.

When you're too soft and expose your underbelly, people would see that weakness and choose to slice you to shreds because they could. Physically. Emotionally. Mentally. In all the ways that mattered.

So I fought hard. I fought dirty.

That part was all me.

~

Kara (Kara Kara Kara Kara) Chameleon

Winnie: I talked to Dallas.

Kara: So?

Winnie: Must you continue to be like this? It's been two days! Forty-eight whole hours! I'm going through constant contact withdrawals

Winnie: I swear I didn't put my name in the Goblet of Fire. He entered because he wanted to be king. Not for me.

Winnie: [picture message]

Winnie: This is Ron. Don't be like Ron. I know gingers have to stick together but COME ON

Kara: I'll give you points for the A+ reference but that's all

Winnie: I bought you candy

Kara: extra credit awarded

Winnie: I also talked to my parents.

Winnie: Well, they talked at me. The Shame Talk

Winnie: And Granny's not talking to me at all.

Winnie: She (temporarily) kicked me out

Kara: woman what did you do!?

Winnie: SEE WHAT HAPPENS WHEN YOU LEAVE ME???? EVERYTHING IS IN SHAMBLES TAKE ME BACK I'LL DO ANYTHING

Kara: you give me gray hair I swear

Kara: I'm on my way

Kara: I'm still mad so it better be GOOD candy

Twelve

Sam had agreed to watch Nadiya's kid, Malachi, while she worked her evening shift downstairs. We sat on the floor with him, teething toys and stuffed animals spread around him in a semicircle to trick him into crawling.

Kara had walked in a few minutes ago, sitting next to me without a word, but with her hands out.

"Are we okay? I swear I didn't have anything to do with Dallas volunteering."

"We're not *not* okay. That's all you get pending the tiebreaker."

The tiebreaker Dallas planned to win. Not telling her things gave me instant heartburn. "You're lucky I'm desperate."

After I paid up as promised, she asked, "So what's up? Your granny seemed upset when she answered the door. I was expecting *Reign of Fire*, not *The Mopening*."

Granny's mood had finally downgraded from furious to unbearably sad.

"You don't know?" Sam asked.

"Obviously not," Winston said, lying on my bed with one earbud in as he watched a movie on his phone. I still didn't know what he was so mad about, but he hadn't been upset enough to sit in his room alone, scowling and raging against the machine, so that was a good sign.

"Mrs. Lemon came home completely scandalized." Sam pitched her voice, clutching her neckline. "What is *wrong* with Winnie? I almost don't believe *she* said something like that. You three have never been like those—*others*."

"Oh joy," I said. Racism in Misty loved to pop up like a jump scare in a horror film—the whole time you're on edge waiting for it to happen, and yet it somehow always happens when you least expect it.

"She seriously said that?" Kara's mouth hung open in shock. "To your face?"

"Yeah, and for some reason"—she pitched her voice again—"Sam is mysteriously no longer available to watch my kids this summer. It's just *so* strange. Is someone paying her double again? We agreed no one was allowed to do that."

I grinned at my cousin. Unlike me, Sam never caused a scene. Her job had always been to smooth things over, because adults loved her. She smiled, and Aphrodite herself descended from Olympus to bestow an enchanted flower crown on her head as a tribute. We started calling her "the Goddess" after the time Kara thought it'd be a good idea to convince one of the church deacons to let us "borrow" a bottle of wine and get drunk with the other Sunday school kids. Granny yelled about "sacrilegious shame" for about an hour, until Sam did her goddess thing, even though she'd been just as drunk and guilty at the time.

Kara tapped my foot with her own. "Tell me." Once I finished she said, "Well, damn. Remind me to key his car."

"Is it weird how much the thought of you committing acts of vandalism on my behalf warms my heart?"

"That's called love." Kara shot me with a finger gun. "Embrace it."

"She'd probably get away with it, too. Do white kids get prosecuted for that kind of thing?" Winston asked.

"Probably not," Kara admitted. "Definitely not here. All I'd have to do is cry and Sheriff Mills would probably fall over himself to make me feel better."

"That's messed up," Winston said.

Kara shrugged. "At least I don't deny it."

"No cookies for you."

"I make my own. Baker, remember?" she joked, then turned to me. "So that's it? Granny's upset because you put Dr. Wannabe Know-It-All in his place?"

Winston said, "And our parents are mad because she's hardheaded."

"Only a little bit." I lowered my voice and added, "I think she wants me to lose weight."

Present company, while loved, weren't exactly the people I wanted to have that particular conversation with. I trusted them not to laugh, but not a single one of them had ever been fat in their lives. Winston got all the beanpole genes. Sam had the body of someone Granny would call "this big" while holding up her pinky finger. And Kara had what the internet declared to be the acceptable slim-thick shape, with curves in all the right places. *Fat* and *thick* weren't the same thing—one had arbitrary superiority. Chances of them, my people, truly understanding my side?

Slim to none.

"Do you want to lose weight?" Sam asked.

"No."

Kara turned, eyes tracking from my head down to my legs and back again. I didn't care what anyone thought. Not really. But. Like.

An adrenaline rush hit me anyway.

You could see someone every day without actually seeing them. A sense of familiarity took over once you got used to the way they looked. They became a vague *insert-person's-name-here*-shaped thing that could be spotted at a distance from a quick glance out of the corner of your eye. Tiny changes didn't register, but maybe a new hairstyle did.

Had I changed since last summer? Did I look older? Better? Worse?

"You're fine. Strong," Kara said. "Not that my opinion matters."

Fine.

What kind of fine? Fine as in okay? Fine as in fine? Why did she have to use such a loaded word?

"It does to me. I mean, you'd tell me if I didn't look okay, right?"

"No, because that makes zero sense," Kara said. "What you're asking is absolutely not the same as you wearing a tacky outfit and embarrassing all of the fashion gods, forcing me to be the person to tell you about yourself." She poked me in the thigh.

"Although," Sam said, "if you're worried about your health, that's a different conversation, too. You'd be surprised how many people with 'perfect bodies' can't even walk up a flight of stairs without getting winded, but no one cares about that because they 'look okay.'"

Malachi wiggled, happy and drooling, until he turned himself around and promptly tried to eat my big toe. "Come here, you little cutie." I snatched him up, helping him stand on my thighs, and made him dance to a song I made up on the spot.

Everyone loved a fat baby. The internet lost their collective shit over pictures of fat cats and dogs, and God help their feels if a chubby-cheeked rodent graced their timelines. But fat people? Fat kids and fat girls, especially? It might as well have been open season on our right to exist.

"I don't think you're unhealthy," Sam continued. "No one who can lift sacks of rice or run around Goldeen's the way you do needs to be worried about cardiovascular disease right now. But you do kind of have a high percentage of body fat."

And things had been going so well.

Sam had been in a committed long-term relationship with fitness for years. Someday they'd have babies in the form of expensive pieces of paper called diplomas.

"Uh, thanks? For the first part anyway?" *I love my cousin. I love my cousin. I. Love. My. Cousin. Yes. I do.*

Breathe.

"I'm not saying that to be mean!" Sam whined a little. "This is why I didn't want to say anything. I'm not saying fat as in *you're* fat and there's something wrong with you, but like you have extra fat you could get rid of if you wanted to. Does that make sense?"

"Kind of." I exchanged a look with Kara, who treated Sam the same way I did—protective and tolerant except with oven mitts and the occasional soft pat on the head.

Murphy's Law didn't only apply to early morning cinnamon roll massacres. Nine times out of ten, Sam trying to be helpful, or even thoughtful, twisted itself into something supremely ugly.

I was the only one who took Sam head on, for better and for worse. She didn't have anyone else.

"We talked about this in one of my online AP classes. There's this worldwide problem of understanding the difference between *being* fat, which is seen as a negative, versus *having* fat, which is something that's a part of the body. The professor was really amazing."

"Okay."

Sam sighed. "I'm messing this up, aren't I?"

"No, it's cool. I get it," I said. "I have extra fat, which makes me fat."

"It sounds so bad when you say it like that."

Maybe Sam should have paid better attention in class. Clearly, she still didn't understand either—I wasn't insulting myself.

"The good thing is, it's easily fixable. The weight would fall right off if you started to exercise."

Kara turned her head, whispering, "My God" into my shoulder.

"W-what?" Sam asked. "I'm just saying—"

"And *Winnie just said* she didn't want to lose weight. It's like it's impossible for you to listen to anyone except for yourself," Winston added. "I like the way you look. You look like my sister. That's good enough."

"That's not true," Sam said quietly. "I listen."

"We know that," I said before Winston *really* opened fire and made her cry. I didn't want them to fight because of me since I'd end up being the one to fix them later anyway. Besides, I didn't need Winston standing up for me. I appreciated it but I didn't need it, not when I understood what Sam *thought* she was doing. "And you"—I pointed at Winston—"no taking your bad mood out on Sam."

"I'm not in a bad mood."

"Come on, Sam," Kara said, climbing to her feet and then picking Malachi up. "I want ice cream."

Sam locked eyes with me—I nodded for her to go—and then followed Kara out of the room, closing the door.

"What's your malfunction?"

"I don't have one."

Arguing and prying, going back and forth until I browbeat the answer out of him, never worked on Winston.

I sat on the bed next to him.

And stared—still as stone, blank as a mannequin, unblinking as if he were a weeping angel.

"Stop," he said.

I didn't.

I had figured out how to aggressively stare at someone after he made me watch a horror movie where the supernatural killer seemed to do the most boring thing of all time:

Walk. Slowly. Everywhere.

A full-on leisurely stroll that turned out to be surprisingly effective: four of the six teens got murdered, and not just in a convenient for the plot kind of way. I'd looked it up later and found out about persistence hunting. Doing the bare minimum to outlast your target worked. Using their own body chemistry against them made sense. I knew firsthand how staring could unnerve someone, so I only used my ability in dire situations.

Side note: I wasn't kidding about becoming a supervillain.

Eventually, he'd get tired of me.

Two minutes and counting . . .

The longest he had lasted against me was five minutes. He'd break any second now . . .

"Why did you have to go and ask her?" he exploded. "You don't care! You don't even *cook*!"

"Ask her what? Who is her?"

"Granny," he fumed. "About the contest."

"Um." Of all the things he could have possibly said, that didn't rank on my list. "I thought it would be a good opportunity—"

"For who? Granny doesn't need your help. And again, you don't cook, so why? Why would you even care?"

"I thought I could lead it. You know, be the spokesperson and let Aaron do the cooking."

"You have a panic attack if someone even points a camera in your direction—"

"No, I don't!"

"Yes. You. Do. But you thought you'd magically be able to *talk in front of one*?"

"*Fine!* I'll admit that was a tiny kink in my plan, but I would've gotten over it! I wanted to use the prize money to help Granny buy a new oven and get some good exposure for Goldeen's. I can do certain things for *other* people." I huffed, frowning. "So that's why you're mad? Because I don't cook and I asked and *oh*"—I paused, sure that the answer had popped in my head, but I didn't quite believe it—"*you* wanted to enter?"

Winston had unofficially begun apprenticing under Aaron last summer. At home, I did kind of notice he'd been in the kitchen more with Dad. I'd thought it was like a bonding thing, like how I helped Mom with her garden in the backyard.

"Dad said he would sign the form, but I still needed someone on-site to enter with me. I was going to ask Aaron because I can trust him, but since you asked, now he can't," he said. "Granny won't let him help me, because she doesn't want *Goldeen's* to have anything to do with it, because she doesn't want *you* to do it. If I ask her again, she's going to think you're making me do it so you can get your way."

Winston had planned to ask Granny on his own. And I *ruined* it.

"Maybe—maybe we could talk to her again? I'll promise to stay out of it."

"*We?* Oh, now you want to include *me* in my own plan. Thanks *so* much."

"Oh, I'm sorry." The right thing to say wouldn't fix the wrong done at all.

"Whatever." He rolled onto his side, away from me.

Thirteen

Damn it.

Damn it *damn it* DAMN IT.

I rubbed the heel of my hand into my eye. Stress wore me out. *Feeling* made me tired. If I could, I'd burrow under my super soft blankets and not come out again until college move-in day.

Granny: upset, twitchy, and somehow able to make me feel like I'd done something wrong for being fat.

Winston: also upset and surlier than normal *at me*.

Sam: plotting and leaving me on constant high alert for a worst-case scenario Thing she wanted to do.

Dallas: just him in general.

Kara: so cute and supportive, as always.

A perfect potion for sleeping the summer away.

"Hey, sorry I'm late." Layla, the day waitress, rushed behind the counter. She'd managed to subdue her massive amounts of curly hair into a messy yet perfect topknot. "Getting Calvin settled into day camp has been a nightmare."

She gave me a quick hug. The top of her head barely reached

my shoulder and the smell of coconut suntan lotion covered every inch of her. Layla had the palest skin—the exact type the sun had a personal vendetta against.

Ruder-than-average customers would ask her, "What are you? An albino?" To which Layla snapped in the only way that wouldn't result in her getting fired, "I'm a human being. Would you like to hear about today's specials?"

Granny refused to budge on that customer is always right rule. We weren't allowed to talk back to customers. Period.

"He bite anyone this time?" I asked, untying the triple knot from my apron. I had the signature Woodson beanpole shape, too—no hips, no butt, just straight up and down—but the fat version, and my apron refused to stay put without some extra knotting measures.

"Thank God, no." Layla stashed her purse in the small locker under the counter. "All he did was cry and howl and kick and scream."

"He could always hang here. You know that."

"I do." She smiled. "But he needs to be around kids, not truck drivers who teach him phrases like 'let 'er drift' and 'scary as fuck.'"

My cackle drew some curious stares from customers. I winked at them and waved.

"I need a favor," Layla said. "JR's baby girl has whooping cough and an appointment with Dr. Skinner tomorrow. Mind putting in overtime in the kitchen?"

JR had been Goldeen's prestigious dishwasher for almost two years. Without him, business pretty much came to a standstill. No dishes, no glasses, no utensils? No service. He also helped with janitorial; prepped the big jobs for the cleaning crew, like draining the fryer when needed; and worked as the host during the dinner rush every now and again.

"Sure. Is she okay?" I asked.

"Yeah. They think it's winding down, but the poor thing got banned from day care until it's gone."

"We should send him something. If Aaron whips up some feel-good food magic, I can stop by with a parental care package."

"You are so sweet."

"Only when I want something. I figure I could trade the food for a future favor."

"Right. I forgot Opportunist is your middle name."

In the kitchen, Winston and Aaron cooked on opposite ends—one doing cold prep and the other at the stove. The walk-in refrigerator door had been propped open. I peeked around the wall to find Granny inside, reorganizing. We hadn't really talked since Skinner. I had planned to lob an empty apology at her to smooth things over—it was just easier to deal with her that way—but that was before she'd called my parents.

Traitor. Everyone knew that what happened in Haven Central, stayed in Haven Central.

If it was bad anyway.

"Cindy is sick so JR is out," I told her. "I'm going to fill in for him."

She didn't pause or stop or look up. She waved one hand dismissively at me, meaning, *I heard you. Go on, now. I'm busy.*

Whatever.

When I turned around, Winston stood staring at me from across the prep table. He shook his head, eyes cutting to the fridge and back to me. I shrugged and kept it moving toward the sink to start washing the dishes from the morning rush.

"Don't let her do that," Winston whispered, towering over me. His grudges never lasted long. Chances were good he was still mad about not being able to enter the Starlight competition, but saying it out loud, actively blaming me for what happened, made him feel better. I didn't mind—I mean, technically, it was my fault. I'd find a way to make it up to him.

I always wanted him to feel like he could come to me about anything, even if he just needed to blow off steam or cry without having to say anything about it. I'd heard him talk with his friends—those conversations could make a wrong turn and head straight into toxic masculinity in a terrifying heartbeat. I'd be damned if I ended up with a little brother chock-full of aggression and misogyny because no one would listen to him talk about his feelings.

I grabbed the hose and blasted a pile of dishes with water to remove food bits. "Do what?"

"Treat you like that," he said. "Manipulate you."

Aaron had picked that exact moment to place a single spatula in the sink—his not-so-subtle pathway into eavesdropping.

"She isn't."

"You can't see it because it's happening to you," Winston said, oblivious to Aaron's intimidating presence. "You didn't do anything wrong. Remember that."

"I don't know. I might have gone too far this time."

"If she doesn't like what you did, then she doesn't like you, because you've always acted like that."

"Harsh." After scraping the dishes that the water couldn't get clean, I loaded the full tray into the dual washer-sanitizer.

"It's the truth. You don't have to like someone to love them." He looked over his shoulder at the refrigerator. "She thinks she can control you. But you're not her clone and she hates that. It's only going to get worse if you don't stop her."

Aaron really wasn't heading back to the stove. We could trust him. He wasn't Granny's spy or anything, but she did sign his paychecks.

"You know, it's really annoying when someone whose diapers I helped change tries to be all grown-up and give me advice."

"And you know I'm right."

Aaron walked away with a parting *hmph*. As if he agreed with Winston.

Did I know that?

Deep down, I think I did.

There'd always been this fine line between disrespect and growing pains with me and Granny. I messed up *a lot*. Trying people's patience was my unintentional theme song. But sometimes—sometimes, it really felt like she wanted me to be ten years old and wholeheartedly obedient forever.

In Skinner's office, she had physically pushed me toward the scale after I had said no. Focusing on Skinner had been easier than acknowledging what she did, too.

Was still easier.

"Sam said something the other day," I said, kind of scared to ask. "Do you really only come here because of me?"

"She talks too much." Winston clicked his tongue, exhaling as a hiss. "I don't hate it here or anything. I'd just rather stay home."

"Then why come?"

"I go where you go." He said it as if that's all there was to it, but then added, "I really don't like the way she treats you."

"Granny."

"Sam, too. I get why she's like that, though. I don't like it, but I get it. I have like the tiniest, microscopic shred of hope for her," he said. "Anyway, it's not like you come here just for Granny. I like Goldeen's, too. I like Kara. It's fine."

I leaned to the side until—oops!—I hugged him. "You're a jerk and I love you."

"I know."

"I'll talk to her," I promised him. "Eventually."

We could be in the middle of the Sibling War: Volume 1861, but if someone else did me dirty? Winston *always* had my back. "I'm the only one who gets to be an asshole to you," he had told me once. "You got that? *Me*."

"Don't swear," I had said, smiling. "You're eleven. Act like you got some sense."

UNKNOWN NUMBER

Unknown Number: Hi, Winnie. It's Shelley.

Unknown Number: I've scheduled an appointment for you with Miss Jepson for your costume. The committee has decided on a tiebreaker :)

Unknown Number: Please don't be late!

~

Kara (Kara Kara Kara Kara) Chameleon

Kara: DID SHELLEY TEXT YOU

Kara: She picked pearl diving on purpose!!!!

Kara: I'm gonna murder her

Winnie: IT'S PEARL DIVING!? She only told me about my costume appointment

Kara: She asked me if I knew how to swim and like an absolute tourist I said yes I CANNOT BELIEVE

Kara: I am so stressed HOW AM I SUPPOSED TO WIN AGAINST THAT LONG-LIMBED BASTARD NOW

Winnie: We'll figure something out. I'm sorry.

Winnie: Family dinner time. Text you in an hour

Fourteen

Back at home, my mom got just as angry as Granny did when I texted at the dinner table, so I was used to being cut off from Kara for about an hour per day. I put my phone in my pocket before sliding into my usual seat in between Sam and Winston at the small round dining table.

However, unlike back at home, we didn't have family dinner every night with Granny—only on Sundays.

"How was your day?" Granny asked no one in particular, but I knew she wasn't talking to me. Winston didn't answer either.

"One of my families, the Castillos, are on vacation this week, and I told anyone who asked that I filled those openings," Sam said, saving the day. "I got to relax a little. Alone. With no kids."

Granny said, "You're such a hard worker, just like your daddy. Always so busy running around. It's good you can recognize when you need to rest."

"Resting is for the weak," Winston muttered.

"What was that?" Granny asked.

"I said the sink has a leak. Downstairs. One of the pipes underneath it has a huge crack in it."

"JR is handling it," Granny said. "I already know."

Silence descended around us again. Usually, our dinners had way more life to them. Me, cracking jokes. Granny, laughing. Winston and Sam, tormenting each other in plain sight. One more round for me: tactical diffusion.

I set down my fork. "About the other day—"

"So I have an idea," Sam said at the same time as me, turning to Granny. "We were all sitting around talking and I had this great idea. I figured out how I can help."

Help? Help what? I didn't remember anyone asking for help. Winston and I exchanged a look—he didn't know what she was talking about either.

"A lot of people don't realize that health doesn't necessarily equal weight loss. Even doctors sometimes," Sam said. "Winnie is really fit. Dr. Skinner shouldn't have said those things to her."

Oh no. Oh nooooo.

"Is that right?" Granny said coolly.

"Yes," Sam said, enthusiastically nodding and turning to me. "Which is where I come in. You could go jogging with me in the mornings."

"No," I said, easy as can be. Winston cough-laughed behind his hand.

"And why not?" The first words Granny had said to me in days. *Really?*

"Because I don't like running."

Visions of me wheezing before succumbing to death by embarrassment danced like svelte sugar plum fairies in my head. I was not *fit*. I had never been athletic. My mile time in PE had always sucked. Every year.

"Not running. Jogging," Sam said.

One day, I really would roll my eyes so hard they'd get stuck in the back of my head, fulfilling the prophecy told by Black elders everywhere.

"I'm not training for anything right now, so we could do this plan I read about. It's designed to help future baby runners get started over seven weeks."

"Nope. Baby runner, I am not."

"Oh, come on!" Sam said with complete earnestness. Murphy's Law back at it again. "It's a good idea. You might like it. And it could be *our thing*. Wink wink."

"Saying *wink wink* defeats the purpose. You just do it," Winston said. "Oh, right. You can't."

Sam couldn't wink. When she tried, both eyes always closed.

"I'll think about it." Whenever my dad said that, the answer was no. He needed a cover sentence to buy himself some time and me some perspective. Sam wasn't going to let it go today, but she might another day.

"Well, I think it's a great idea," Granny said, eyes locked on mine. "You should go."

"Oh, I see," I said. "I'm too busy to help *Winston* enter the Starlight competition, but I have just enough free time to go running every morning. Cool. Got it. Makes total sense."

"Jogging," Sam said quietly.

"You've had a bad attitude since you got here and I'm tired of it," Granny said. "If my rules are such a problem for you, why do you even come?"

"So that's a rule now, too? Go *jogging* with Sam because you say so? Even though I said I hate it?"

"How do you know you hate something if you've never tried it?"

"I'm not even going to point out how flawed that question is. Really? *That's* your argument?"

"It was just a suggestion." Sam's wide eyes had already filled with tears. "Please don't fight."

"We're not fighting." Granny placed a hand on Sam's wrist. "I don't fight with children."

The first shot. My age. Every time. I could be in my fifties and going through menopause while supporting my three kids in college, and she'd still find a way to call me a child.

She continued, "Every time someone tries to help you, you always act like this."

"I don't need help."

"No, you *think* you don't need help, which you can't know because you never listen. In one ear and out the other with you. What's it gonna hurt for you to go with your cousin, huh? Keep her company, keep her safe while she's out there by herself so early in the morning. She wants you to go with her, but all you can think about is yourself."

Winston said, "Told you so," while pushing the food around his plate.

"Told who what?" Granny asked.

He kept silent, but gave me a quick glare out of the corner of his eye. *Don't do it,* the glare said.

I wasn't stupid. I saw it—the way she flipped the conversation, using Sam to manipulate me into doing what she wanted. She couldn't order me into the wild blue jogging yonder. I just wouldn't go. But she could guilt-trip me into it. Because that was what I did: put everyone else's feelings before my own. And when I tried to put myself first? Everyone hated the way it looked. Everyone hated the way it sounded. Everyone seemed to hate me for it.

Sam placed her hands in her lap. She kept her eyes on her plate, shoulders hunched, bottom lip sucked into her mouth to stop it from trembling.

I sighed, resigned to rescuing Sam again. "What time?"

"May I be excused?" Winston asked. "I'm done."

Fifteen

SA(RU)M(ON)

Sam: Meet me at Rogerson Pond in thirty minutes!

Sam: Wake UPPPPPPPPPP and pay

attention to meeeeeeeee

Sam: It's such a nice day!

Sam: Come onnnnn

Sam: [Attached voice note]

Sam: WOMAN 20 mins and counting

Sam: Don't make me pull you out of bed. You won't like it

        Winnie: CALM THE HELL DOWN

               OR I'M NOT DOING THIS

Sam: . . . you don't have to yell

If my phone hadn't been so expensive, I would've launched the thing out the window. Thinking about running made a headache appear right between my eyes. Or it could have been the screen from my phone turned up too high and burning holes in my still-sleeping retinas.

Whatever.

Sam had printed the outline for the plan, rudely taping it to our shared vanity mirror. I'd seen it after I had finished taking a bath, where I complained to Kara for a solid hour on the phone, until my cosmic-swirl bath-bombed water got cold.

We'd be on flat land but with intervals. Even the word sounded painful, like it belonged to the family of stabbing motions—Lunge! Riposte! Interval! A deliberate reminder of the relentless pain I'd soon feel in my side.

They were called running stitches for a reason.

Reluctantly, I threw off my blankets and half rolled the few feet to the floor, because there was always time for dramatics even if no one watched me. Sitting in front of the dresser—I'd been given the bottom two drawers, while Sam had the top—I surveyed my lack of options.

The only thing I owned that could be considered Workout Clothes™ was my high school PE uniform, which I'd already thrown away back at home. Bright yellow and in a size that fit by the grace of God and the skin on her teeth, every time my compulsive need for good grades forced me to wear it, I flashed back to the first day of school when some douche canoe had called me Big Bird. And then another person joined in. And then another. And another—until the name began to spread.

But they messed up when they started calling Sam Elmo by association and because of her laugh.

If we had to live on Sesame Street, so did everyone else.

I bought a pair of striped pink leggings to wear under my shorts and refused to use anyone's actual first name.

Mikayla? Oh, no, she was Snuffleupagus because of her shaggy brown hair.

Chris? Oh, you mean Grover because of his too-wide mouth.

Jim and Aiden? Bert and Ernie.

Turns out, it wasn't as funny when the fat girl joined in or when *their* new nicknames began to stick. That particular group never messed with me, or Sam, again.

The best I could do for the impending jog was an old T-shirt and a pair of leggings with holes in the knees. After changing, I pulled my braids back into a ponytail.

Dallas liked them.

The memory hit me like a hot flash. Him, inches from me, eyes downcast and soft, staring at my braids like he'd never seen something so great before. My cheeks and ears began to feel especially hot.

I had liked being that close to him. Even if I was kind of mad at him now, it didn't change that fact.

"You ready?" Winston stood in the doorway in a pair of sweats and a T-shirt.

"For?"

"This stupid run thing. Oh wait—*jogging*. Sorry."

"It's supposed to be our *thing*," I said, slide-dancing to him. "A Winnie and Sam Limited Edition Engagement."

"So? She comes to movie night. It's your *thing* while I'm there."

"True." I nudged him out the door. "Fair."

Granny stood in the kitchen wearing her signature plush red bathrobe and matching satin scarf. It made the tiny space come alive with reflective warmth in the morning sunlight. The apartment had amazing lighting. With two huge windows in the living room, a good-sized one in the kitchen, and a skylight in the hall, we almost never had to use the lamps in the house. Even the moon got in on that window action, making things bright enough to see in the dead of night.

I hated how happy she looked.

"I asked Aaron to cover for the opening in case we're not back in time," I said.

"Oh, no. I'll take care of it."

I almost protested, mouth and stance ready to argue her down. Granny despised being told what to do, even if it was doctor's orders of "taking it easy" and "learning how to rest." The irony wasn't lost on me there.

While I hadn't exactly conspired to give Granny the boot out of the diner for the summer, on paper, in a court of law, that's exactly what it looked like. Guilty as charged.

I'd be gone an hour. At most.

Not worth it.

"I'll have breakfast ready for you when you get back." Granny wiped her hands on a towel and left the sink, shuffling to her room.

"Guess that meant we're supposed to eat afterward?" Winston asked.

"I—I guess so?"

"Alrighty then."

❦

I parked the car, said a silent prayer to baby Jesus, and marched, slightly annoyed by how good Sam looked. She sat cross-legged and grumpy, left foot kicking out in irritation while she waited. The Marshes' family dog, a German shorthaired pointer named Mabel, spun in circles next to her while barking up a storm. They paid Sam to walk her every morning.

Excess sweat always gave Sam a radiant, dewy glow. Meanwhile, I planned to duck and weave to avoid any and all mirrors until after I could hit a bathroom and get cleaned up. There's this word I liked: *bedraggled.* That would be me after this *jog.*

Bedraggled as all hell.

"They're here. I'll call you later," she said before hanging up.

"Good God, do you have to look so sporty? Is that spandex?"

"It's Lululemon."

Mabel yipped and whined. Well-trained enough to not jump on people, but refusing to be denied, she could whine the most stringent dog-hater into submission for a quick rub behind the ears.

"Good morning, Miss Mabel. Beautiful as ever, as expected." I kneeled down, maneuvering away from the assault of dog breath and saliva trying to make contact with my face while I petted her. "Did you run here?"

"Yeah. I wanted to get some miles in."

"Of course you did."

"Oh, stop. Here." She passed us a reusable water bottle each. "I figured you two didn't think to bring water."

I stood up, taking it. "Right you are." Sam had written our names on the side in her perfect cursive that could have passed for straight-up calligraphy.

"Nothing too extreme today, but I wanted you to start getting used to your heart and lungs working a bit harder. I picked this spot because it has random patches of incline."

"I'm going home," I said, straight-faced, before walking away.

"Why?"

"You lied. You said flat land. I hear *incline*, which rhymes with *bedtime*, so GOOD NIGHT."

Sam grabbed the crook of my elbow, spinning me back around. "You would be up running around the diner anyway. Might as well do this." She wrapped her arms around me from behind, forcing our legs to move at the same time, inching us forward. "I'm with you. You'll be great!"

"I'm not with me. That's the most important part." I hooked my hands on Sam's forearms, hoping to find some comfort or strength in that brief touch.

"Nah. That's just what they want you to think."

"They?"

"The government. Aliens. *Cosmopolitan*. Choose your poisonous mind-set." She let go, replacing the back hug with a handhold. "We'll go as slow as you need. Right, Winston?"

He cocked a mighty eyebrow. "I like how you assumed I'll be good at this. We come from the same gene pool. I'm as athletically challenged as she is. I'm probably going to die."

"My God, you two are dramatic. It'll be fine."

Five. Two. Five.

Walk. Jog. Walk.

My hands shook thinking about it as Sam led us through basic stretches. I would either surprise myself or it would be the longest twelve minutes of my life if I couldn't hack a two-minute jog.

Hack. Cough up a lung. Suffer a thousand embarrassments.

Sam started the timer and set our walking pace. Three steps in, I pegged it as being faster than a normal walk.

Speed walking: the unholy offspring of languor and effort. Hands in position as if we were about to run, hips working overtime, knees pretty much straight, we circled a rarely used trail that surrounded a pond—stagnant, stank, and full of geese.

No one went there, because the geese attacked anything that moved. Some geese waddled behind us and another gaggle drifted in the water. Watching. Plotting.

"You okay?" Sam asked me.

"Yep. We're just walking. But are you sure this place is a good idea?"

Sam nodded to Mabel, happily trotting along. "We come here all the time. I think the myth of her legend has spread amongst them. There's an uneasy truce in these parts." She laughed.

A goose honked. Loudly.

"Then why are they following us?" I asked.

"Probably because you two are here. New humans, new rules." Sam burst out laughing. "Don't look so scared! If one gets too close, just punt it."

"I don't want to punt a goose! Jesus Christ, Sam."

She kept laughing. "Then let Mabel handle it. She won't let them get you."

Another jarring *HONK* echoed around us.

Mabel barked and growled.

A sinister beep sounded from Sam's arm.

One-minute warning.

At this rate, from all of the adrenaline, sudden cardiac arrest was becoming a real possibility. If I were alone, I wouldn't be this keyed up. I also wouldn't have chosen this place. Pretty sure one of those murderous birds had flashed a shank at me.

"I'm still fine, too," Winston said. "Thanks for remembering me long enough to ask."

"Of course you are," Sam said in an offhanded kind of way. "I'll set the pace. I'm going to move a little bit faster because you're both taller than me. It'll look like I'm running, so don't copy what my body is doing. Just keep up with my pace."

The second beep sounded, accompanied by upbeat music.

Sam began to run.

Mabel increased the speed of her trot.

Winston stayed by my side.

"Don't hold your breath," Sam said with an air of authority. "In through the nose, out through the mouth."

"I'm doing that." I wasn't. Each new step increased my worry about wheezing and sounding like a dying walrus out loud. After every inhale, I held it for a beat, swallowing it down and exhaling through my nose as quietly as possible.

I hadn't exercised in, well, ever. Not on purpose anyway. Exercise had always seemed like a thing you'd meant to do. You had to make an active choice to get up and say, "AH, YES, I FEEL LIKE SWEATING AND GETTING MY HEART RATE UP TODAY."

But then there were those people who wore those step-counter things. They did their normal everyday stuff and got to say, "I walked ten thousand steps today! Woo-hoo!" That was exercise to *them*, so it must have counted, too. Right?

It confused the hell out of me, to be honest.

I'd never thought of myself as out of shape. These tiny hills were nothing to scoff at, but Christ Almighty, it took all of my willpower to not look at my chest in shock. I almost didn't believe how hard a time I was having. The weather probably didn't help. The remaining wafts of night air still felt too dry, and breathing it felt like someone rubbing sandpaper inside of my nasal cavity.

"Howmuchlonger?" Winston asked, voice strained. His deep, deep frown and halting breaths through his mouth almost made me trip.

Sam said, "Thirty seconds. Almost there!"

"Do you need to stop?" I asked.

Winston shook his head. "I—can—do—it."

Just as I was about to tell Sam to stop, she shouted, "And done! Walk it out!"

Winston bent over immediately, hands on his knees, slightly wheezing. "I'm—definitely—out—of—shape."

I was a little light-headed, but my breathing had already begun to slow. I rubbed his back while Sam repeated, "In through the nose, out through the mouth."

"I heard you—the first—seven times." He looked at me. "My chest—hurts—a little."

"It's better if we keep moving. Let's walk, come on."

"Give him a minute," I snapped.

Sam took a step back, a wounded look on her face.

First and foremost in life, I was a sister—Winston's big sister. I lost all semblance of civility and loyalty at even the slightest hint of my brother in distress.

He stood up straight, closing his eyes and placing a hand on his side. "Okay. I'm okay." He draped an arm over my shoulder. "I'm okay," he said. "At ease, Ranger." And then he did something he almost never did—smiled, happy and brighter than the blazing summer sun getting ready to start the day.

When we returned to the diner, Aaron stood behind the front counter. He lived in the kitchen and only voluntarily came to the front for emergencies.

"Hey, how was it?" I asked.

"Your grandmother has commandeered my kitchen." He stared at Mabel, who wagged her tail, pleased by even the grouchiest of attention because it was such a dog thing to do.

"What kind of evil person hates dogs?" Sam whispered as he walked away.

"He doesn't hate them. He just doesn't want them in the diner if they're not service animals," Winston said.

Granny popped her head out the window. "Oh!" Moments later, she appeared with a plate on each arm. Granny could cook almost as well as Aaron, but this? The smallest and most cheese-less of spinach omelets and microscopic bowls of fruit, as if she counted out exactly how many pieces were inside.

"Oh, good, I'm starving," Sam said. "I was hoping for pancakes, but this works, too."

Granny's eyes darted to me before she smiled at Sam. "Next time. I'll come up with something."

Well. Guess that meant I was supposed to be on a diet. I was too tired to get mad. No, that's not true. I *was* mad, but too worn out and weary to show it—my legs felt a bit too jellylike to hold up my steel spine anyway.

"I'm more tired than hungry," I lied. "I'm gonna head up."

"You need to eat," Sam said, popping a strawberry into her mouth. "That's not optional."

"I never said it was and I will."

Someone shoving a plate of food in front of me didn't make me obligated to eat it. Yes, yes, I knew I shouldn't waste food. My parents had laid that guilt trip on nice and thick, and I probably had some kind of deep-seated complex because of it. But what if I didn't *want* to eat *that*? Shouldn't that matter, too?

I didn't look at food as fuel or some sinful indulgence. I wouldn't have liked eating a dry can of tuna. I wouldn't have liked eating chocolate cake every single day. When you're fat, everyone always has something to say about what you should and shouldn't be eating. Helpful things like, "Maybe you should get a salad," and, "You're gluten intolerant? You must eat really healthy now, huh? You're going to lose so much weight!" They put food in categories for you, like good and bad, healthy and junk.

It was simply food to me, and I had worked *hard* to see it that way.

Balance mattered. Enjoyment mattered. But most important, choice mattered. And I didn't want anyone choosing what went inside of my body except for me.

"I'll eat after I take a shower. I feel gross and sweaty."

"Me too," Winston said. "I'm just going to get some juice and lie down. My back is starting to hurt." He looked at me. "Before you say anything, I'm fine. I just need a nap. I woke up too early."

Upstairs, I changed my mind and decided to take a bath. Sure, a meadow-scented bath bomb, rose bubbles, and candles seemed indulgent at six thirty a.m. on a weekday, but who was gonna stop me?

I twirled my ponytail into a massive bun, undressed, and took my sweet delightful time sinking into the giant tub in Granny's bathroom until the water reached my neck. Last year Granny had fallen and broken her hip. My parents and my uncle had her bathroom renovated to make the tub wider, with a door and handles for accessibility.

The water covered my mouth, stopping just under my nose. Somehow, I avoided snorting water when I breathed in the smell of fake grass and roses while blowing raspberries with my lips. Then I lifted one leg into the air, flexing my foot and wiggling my bright-peach-colored painted toes.

I wasn't sure why I loved myself as much as I did. Never really questioned it.

Of course, my self-confidence could be a flighty bee whenever it felt like it. I had good days where I could twirl around the diner singing to customers in my pretty uniform. I had bad days where I hated shopping in stores for clothes because I always ended up crying in the dressing room. Days when I felt like too much, too wide, and too loud. Moments when I second-guessed whether or not I was allowed to wear a crop top or if my skirt was too short.

But I *loved* myself. I knew and felt it deep in my bones. Even on downswing days when living and being happy in my skin felt impossible, I knew I could rely on my true self to come back around to save that struggling version of me.

Why couldn't knowing I was happy with myself be good enough for Granny?

Reaching out of the tub, I shook out my hands, called Kara, and put it on speakerphone.

I loved the way Kara sounded on the phone.

Well, I loved almost everything about Kara, but Phone Voice definitely made top five. She didn't sound too different—her signature husky and measured tone, the same throaty laugh, and the same staccato wordless sounds of agreement when I said something: "Mmmm . . . mmm-hmmm," or "accccccckkk," her duck noise of displeasure and disagreement.

During our months apart, her voice became one of my favorite sounds, because not being able to see her changed the game. I imagined the way her lips formed around her words, the animated way she gestured with her hands for emphasis, and the absolute radiant joy in her eyes as she laughed. Absence didn't make the heart grow fonder—that sneaky mastermind imagination hosted that show.

Kara answered, not bothering to say hello. "I have been WAITING all morning. I need updates!"

"The walk-sort-of-run went okay. I didn't die."

"Woo!"

"But I think Granny thinks it's cool to try and put me on a diet."

"Boo!"

"I know. Trying to figure out what to do about that."

"Talking is usually the best answer."

"Whose side are you on?"

"Hers. Bottling up until you explode is no bueno for anyone. I like my Winnie at DEFCON Five and smiling, thanks."

"I don't explode."

"Uh-huh."

"Whatever."

God, I needed that.

ſixteen

iss Jepson didn't have a shop in the Misty roundabout. She operated her business out of the den in her house in the third section. On Misty's side, Mayor Iero couldn't be bothered to police historical house reconstruction and let homeowners do whatever.

First section: the occupational district, filled with the people who lived in the apartments above their businesses, like Granny and Kara's family.

Second section: the closest Misty got to suburbia. The houses didn't look alike but were built with little space between them and had front lawns, neighborly rules, and exclusive block parties where they barbecued and ordered side dishes from Goldeen's and desserts from Meltdown. It was also the place where you'd be most likely to meet Ned Flanders reincarnated.

Third section: mostly spaced-out ranch-style houses. Small farms; pools or ponds galore; and almost everyone had animals, pets or livestock.

Miss Jepson looked after a feral cat colony that lived behind her house and rescued rabbits. No one knew why, but it worked for her.

I walked up her front steps, knocking on the painted green wood panel of the screen door. A calico cat slept unbothered on the porch swing. Two tuxedo cats stared at me from inside the house. None of them actually belonged to Miss Jepson. The feral cats kept their distance, but random strays never stopped showing up for food; snuggles; and a comfortable, safe place to sleep.

"Yo," I said, knocking again and ignoring my potential new friends. I didn't dislike cats, just knew all of their tricks. You had to act disinterested to get them to take an interest in you. A long con worth waiting for.

"Coming, dear! Coming!" Miss Jepson called. Canadian by birth, she'd missed Old Hollywood by several thousand miles and decades, but I'd never heard her speak without her signature Katharine Hepburn accent.

The indoor cats turned tail and met her as she stomped toward the front door. She'd always walked hard, like she was used to wearing heavy shoes but had forgotten she'd taken them off.

"Hi, Miss Jepson."

"Winnie! Darling! Prompt as ever."

I stepped back to give the screen door space to swing open, and Miss Jepson joined me on the porch, giving me a huge hug, rocking me back and forth and everything.

She always smelled like lemons.

"Oh, let me look at you," she said, pulling back but still holding me at the shoulders. Her warm brown eyes looked tired. A few more lines had settled in around her mouth. She hadn't bothered to dye the patches of gray hair rooting around her edges this summer, and her warm brown skin looked as radiant, and moisturized, as ever. "Ah! Such a beauty. Your mother must be beside herself with pride."

I laughed, holding back an eye roll. "Sure."

"Well come in, come in!"

And in we went.

When I was little, before Sam and Winston joined me in Haven Central and when Granny was busy, this was where I'd end up—hanging out with Miss Jepson, the cats, and the rabbits. She was the only person Granny trusted enough to watch me. Which was probably my fault. I've been hardheaded my whole life and went through a pretty intense daredevil phase for a while.

I liked to jump off of things for fun. Porches, chairs, stairs, balconies—the higher the better. It took dislocating my shoulder during a botched roof-to-pool leap of faith to make me give up my adrenaline-junkie ways.

Miss Jepson had hovered and fussed over me while at the hospital until Granny arrived and said, "Betcha won't do that again, will you?"

Nope. Mortality *was* real and scared the hell out of me.

Miss Jepson led the way down the short hall toward the back of her house to her office. Fabrics of all kinds and colors decorated the room, along with sewing busts, ancient-looking treasure chests, a multitude of sewing machines, a burgundy love seat, and a good-sized wooden worktable stationed just below the one window in the room.

"Let's see." She turned the pages of the familiar leather-bound book, saying my name with each flick of her fingers and the page. "Winnie, ah, there you are. Have your measurements changed since last year, dear?"

"My uniform still fits, so probably not." I stood in the doorway, leaning against the doorjamb. One of the tuxedo cats eyeballed me from a few feet away, tail flicking with curiosity.

"How do you feel about mermaids? Too cliché?"

"Well, it's pearl diving, so I guess not."

"Mm-hmm. I can't imagine you with a mermaid-style dress,

though. I just *can't* see it." She clapped her hands together. "I've got it! Water nymph—no! A summer beach goddess! A tight bodice—"

"*Tight?*"

"Reasonably so. Nothing too revealing up top; I know how you are. Flowing skirts, liquid pearls, jewels, yes. You'll look like you belong on a wall in Goldeen's." She laughed, delighted by her idea. "And I have just the fabric for this. I've been saving it for a special occasion."

She held out her hands. I took them and she spun me in a small circle to bring me to the center of the room. "By the time I am done with you, that boy will fall head over heels in love at first sight."

"I dunno if I want him to do that. Maybe we can tone that down a little."

"You don't?"

"I have two volunteers remember? Two. Gotta keep my options open," I joked.

She didn't laugh as she walked over to one of the chests. "But it's pearl diving."

"Yeah. I know."

The likelihood of Kara not winning made me nervous.

She wasn't a particularly strong swimmer. The only reason I knew how to swim was because my mom made it a point to make sure I learned. I remember in elementary school on Mondays and Wednesdays in the spring, my mom would pick me up early from school for lessons at the community center every year. I hadn't swam in a while, but I felt confident in my ability to not drown as soon as I hit the water.

And *I* was a better swimmer than Kara.

"You want her to win?"

"She wants to win. I think that's more important."

Miss Jepson stopped rifling through the dark blue chest in the corner of the room. Slowly, she turned her head and gave me that *mm-hmm* look. "I see the divine matchmaker is already working its magic. You like him."

Under oath and in a court of law, I would never admit to being a believer in something as nebulous as divine matchmaking. Unfortunately, the *what-ifs* had me by the heartstrings. Honestly, it had to be a mixture of both. Real things like chemistry and desire holding hands with timing and luck. All of the past royal couples who had partnered up had to want to be together. The M&M fishbowl pressure cooker had just as much potential to drive us apart as it did to steer us together.

"I definitely don't dislike him."

"That's hardly the same thing." She smiled at me. "He's cute."

"That he is." I cleared my throat.

"Oh."

"Please don't. I'm embarrassed enough on my own, thanks."

"Why?"

"Being cute isn't enough of a reason to like someone."

"Says who?"

"People," I mumbled. "Because it's shallow."

"No, it is not. Cut that out." She turned back around. "It's only shallow if that's *all* there is. You're not that kind of person."

"And! *And* I don't know what he wants. I asked him why he volunteered, but he wouldn't tell me."

"Of course he didn't." She laughed. "What fun would that be?"

"Fun?"

"Yes. *Fun.* If you liked someone and had the perfect romantic opportunity to win their heart handed to you, would you just blurt out the truth? Or would you play the game?"

If *I* looked like Dallas? The truth. All the way. "But he doesn't like me. Romantically. I'm sure he finds me delightful and thinks I'm funny, because I am, but that's kind of it."

"And you know that how? Did you ask him?"

"No."

"Did he tell you?"

"No."

"Well?"

"Well, that doesn't make you right. He hasn't given me a clue in either direction. He could like me, he could also want to be friends, and I'd rather be wrong than read too much into something that doesn't exist."

Liking liking Dallas would forever be an absolute waste of emotional energy that I would forever expend in private on the nights when the stomping didn't work and I let myself have five minutes of *what-ifs*.

"What am I going to do with you?" She found the fabric—velvet in golden yellow with peach undertones. After standing up, she held it out for me, tilting it toward the sun. "I'll add a little extra something so it really catches the light. You'll sparkle like water on a crystal-clear day."

"Pretty, but won't it be too hot for that?"

"Not if it's done right." She set the fabric down on the worktable. "Arms out—yes or no?"

"No."

"Legs?"

"Shorter the better." I grinned.

"I'll do you one better: strategic slits. When you walk, the gown will ripple and part like water and show off a touch of thigh and those killer calves of yours. Heels?"

"Nope."

"Wedges?"

"Possibly. Not too high."

"Excellent." She pulled out the chair, wheeling it around so she could begin. "Shouldn't take me more than a couple of hours."

"Can I hang out here? I'll go sit with the rabbits if you want to work alone."

"Have a seat. Put your feet up. Relax." She pointed to the love seat in the corner. I wasn't even sitting three minutes before the cat jumped up and joined me, draping half of its body across my lap.

Miss Jepson said, "I'm thinking of calling him Simon. He feels like a *Simon* to me."

Giving the cats real names—not just generic ones like sweetie or grumpyface—meant things had gotten serious. Simon must have decided to live here.

"How long?"

"Six months and counting. He likes to sleep on my ankles at night."

Yep. Definitely serious. Strays weren't allowed in her bedroom.

"Welcome to the family, Simon Jepson." I scratched him behind his ears and got purrs in return. With my other hand, I started replying to Kara's texts, sending her my signature Dealing with a Sibling Who Refuses to Admit They're Dead Wrong advice, patent pending, because she was in the middle of a fight with her sister, Junie.

Miss Jepson hummed to herself as she worked. Sketching, measuring, tracing, cutting, and assembling. It amazed me how she turned a few swaths of fabric into incredible clothing.

I wished I could take her home. I wished I had enough money to pay her to create an entire wardrobe. Clothes always interested me. Not enough to become a designer or anything, but I wished I could be one of those girls who could wear mix-matched designs, slouchy shirts, and look perfectly thrown together with just the right amount of careless flair to pull it off.

I tried it once and a relative told me I looked "slovenly." *Slovenly.*

She actually used that word. "Big girls need to look put together. Like you care about yourself."

Whatever.

Miss Jepson asked, "Have you thought about how you want to wear your hair?"

"A top bun. I think it'll look good with my tiara."

"Never thought I'd see you in braids, by the way. They look good."

I had braided my hair on my own. My first successful set since deciding to give up relaxers. My mom couldn't help, so YouTube University it was, until it wasn't. Most of the YouTubers I followed didn't have hair like mine. My first wash-n-go turned into a wash-n-no. Then the heavens parted; the sky cracked open and rained blessings down upon me: Jasmine Rose and Franchesca Ramsey made loc maintenance and hairstyling videos. My braids were a stopgap measure until my natural hair grew out enough to start locs in college.

"Thanks. I did them myself." And then, because I like pain, I said, "He complimented them, too."

"I bet he did." Her sly know-it-all look made me laugh.

There's this phenomenon that happens when you have a crush and make the mistake of telling someone about it, intentionally or not. Everything is cool. You have all of your feelings under control. A slight undercurrent of butterflies. A fantasy here or there. But nothing too extreme.

But then, that someone starts pointing out all of the ambiguous things you intentionally, and rationally, overlooked. You start thinking your crush is trying to tell you something without actually telling you. You start seeing and believing in signs that don't exist so your feelings get completely ahead of themselves.

If I told Miss Jepson what Dallas had said about winning, she'd really start rubbing it in.

Audience participation. The last thing I needed.

I hadn't talked to anyone about this on purpose. Ignoring the fact that I didn't have anyone in the first place—Granny didn't care, Winston's lip would curl, my mom would definitely talk me through it but we'd barely closed Skinner-gate, and Sam was terrible at keeping my secrets—I didn't want anyone hyping me up about it.

The only thing that mattered were facts.

Dallas kept information sparse about his decision to be king other than admitting that I had been a deciding factor. A solid non-hopeful, educated guess could be that he wouldn't have minded spending time with me, easily putting us in the friendship column.

That made sense. If he wanted to get to know me and be friends, HSR made it super simple for him.

But if that were true, why did Kara react the way she did? Her gut reaction had been to assume Dallas and I had planned the whole thing, not that he wanted to be my friend. My own gut screamed *pity*, and she didn't consider that either.

She assumed I—we—had kept a secret from her.

She proclaimed that I got "weird" about "stuff." Educated guess: *stuff* meant our relationship because I fully planned to date people *in addition to* her someday and she didn't.

When it came to crushes, I had no problem declaring myself a full-blown polygamist. I flitted around wherever my heart led, fell in like at first sight, the drop of a hat, turn of a page, and wink of an eye. But they never lasted longer than a week. Why involve her if I didn't have to?

If the crush wasn't leading to anything real, she didn't need to know.

I never told her about my crush on Dallas that definitely did not exist. So why would she know—unless he had told her something.

Dallas had thought Kara was my girlfriend. Then, I corrected him, told him the truth. And he told me he planned to win.

Could Miss Jepson have been right after all?

Wait—wait a minute. Oh my God.

Did Kara *know* that Dallas liked me?

Seventeen

Over twenty years of designing and costuming experience had given me an incredible dress. A one of a kind, a Miss Jepson original, made specifically to fit my body like a perfect velvet glove.

Fashion runway in Paris perfect. Two-page haute-couture spread in a magazine perfect. I would have never been able to find something like it in a store. If I searched online long enough and had it altered once it arrived, I might have gotten close.

Tears sprang into my eyes when I saw it, but I didn't cry until Miss Jepson began to button and cinch the bodice closed, because it fit. On the first try.

Hands down, the single most beautiful thing I owned, and I had to wear it to the Haven Central public pool.

Irony had died a brutal death.

In the locker room, I slipped off my flats. We'd decided against the wedges. Barefoot looked better while I practiced walking in it to test out the slits. As promised, the bottom half of my dress parted and flowed while I walked, the soft strips swirling around my legs.

Oddly enough, the sleeves made my heart sing almost more than any other part. They had a similar design to the slits, elegantly draped around the length of my arms (only with less space between them), and the ends had been sown into a cuff. She'd decorated each one with clear teardrop jewels. Light, airy, and relatively modest—exactly how I liked it.

I checked my reflection one last time. Dress? Amazing. Tiara? Centered with my bun. Makeup? Subtle, my usual no-makeup make-up look. My promise ring hung around my neck, fully visible.

Kara would smile when she saw it.

Outside, she was waiting for me. Unfortunately, so was everyone else.

My stomach roiled, already ready to revolt. I pressed my hand against it, breathing in and out. I could do it. Walk out there and own it. Miss Jepson didn't spend hours working on this work of art for me to throw up all over it. This dress had been made to be seen. Designed to make me look like a summer beach goddess. I hesitated one extra second before turning the corner at the brick wall and walking outside.

People gasped when they saw me. Grabbed the person next to them so they would turn around and stare at me too with widened eyes. The bleachers were bursting with spectators on both sides. The overflow stood along the sides and sat on picnic blankets on the ground crowding the cement. No professional cameras, thank God. Sana's crew must not have been interested, because I'm sure Shelley invited them.

"Winnie, my goodness!"

Speak of the devil. "Hi, Shelley."

"I knew Miss Jepson had some skill, but this is—"

"Too much?"

"No, just unexpected and not at all what my notes said to do." Ah, so the mermaid look had been Shelley's request. "This way."

An ostentatious throne of thick curlicue gold pieces and purple velvet cushions sat under a canopy at the deep end of the pool. At least I wouldn't have to sit in the sun. Kara stood on one side of the throne. Dallas on the other—distinctly not looking at me.

Funny. Everyone else was watching me, but not him.

I speed-walked, leaving Shelley behind. Another stomach gurgle. Another hard swallow. I struggled to keep my head held high when all of my instincts urged me to lower it, to hide myself.

Kara met me halfway there, turning and keeping stride. She walked on her tiptoes to whisper, "Breathe. Remember, I got you."

My stomach didn't calm down, but my mind did. Having her there felt like being wrapped in cotton, insulated against hyperfocused, prying eyes. A protective shield to keep me from feeling too much.

I'm not sure how, but being with Kara always helped me remember how to be myself while in the thick of it.

Someone in the crowd wolf-whistled.

"HEY!" Kara stared in the general direction of where the sound came from. "YOU DARE DISRESPECT YOUR QUEEN WITH CRUDE WHISTLES? I WILL FIGHT YOU!"

"It was a compliment!" I knew that voice. Melodic and powerful, it could only be Shane Brisbane, the vocal pride of Merry Haven. His parents owned a music shop in Merry. They sold instruments and had a side business that employed music teachers. Dallas's mom had been the one to teach him how to sing.

We reached the throne, and as I sat, Dallas said, "You're taking this way too seriously."

Kara narrowed her eyes. "Damn right I am. I'm winning this thing. I'm not above cheating, so you better watch out."

"Cheating means you get disqualified." His voice sounded bored. Lifeless.

"Maybe when peasants do it." She flipped her hair over her shoulder and said, "Watch this." Raising her hand in the air, she stepped away from me. "I WOULD LIKE TO MAKE A FORMAL COMPLAINT."

"Excuse me?" Shelley sounded scandalized, like how dare Kara do whatever it was she was about to do even though she had no idea what it was.

"Pearl diving is biased and unfair." She raised her voice, shouting now. "I'm four feet and ten inches short. That giant over there is six foot infinity. All volunteers are supposed to have an equal shot of winning the tiebreaker, but he can cover twice the distance I can in the same amount of time."

Kara wasn't *actually* that short, but she correctly guessed no one would break out a measuring tape to challenge her.

In the grand scheme of tiebreakers, pearl diving resided firmly in the mild middle. Right in between sonnet recitals and jousting.

The first person to swim from the shallow end to the deep end of the pool, dive the thirteen feet for a treasure, and present said treasure to yours truly would be declared the winner.

The problem wasn't only that Kara was short.

Dallas had been the Haven High swim team captain. Shelley and her "council" had very obviously wanted him to win.

"That is super unfair." Sam stood up—she sat in the front row of the bleachers directly to my right—and hit Winston in the shoulder.

"Yeah," he said, standing. "Something should be done to level the playing field." He said it like a bad actor reading their lines in an infomercial.

"I agree!" Kara's older sister, Junie, stood with her boyfriend on the other side of the bleachers. Junie and Kara looked alike for the most part, except Junie didn't wear glasses and was taller. "My sister deserves a fair chance to win!" She started chanting Kara's name and waving her hands to get the crowd to join in with her.

"You see?" Kara said to Shelley. "The people have spoken!"

When had she become the crowd favorite? *Everyone* joined in with chanting her name. Maybe it was like the wave thing they do at sporting events, where once it starts you go along with it for no other reason than groupthink.

My little revolutionary in her black-and-white polka-dot tankini.

"*Your* people have spoken," Dallas said. "I like your dress."

I whipped around, realizing he was talking to me. It had happened so fast, but my face found just enough time to heat up. "Uh, thanks."

"You look beautiful."

My face shot straight past feeling flushed to inferno. *Beautiful!?* I met his eyes; shock had to be plain on my face, mouth hanging open and everything.

Truly, I was a dignified queen.

But he smiled at me with his head tilted to the side as if I were a painting worth being appreciated in a museum. My heart pounded in my ears while the rest of me forgot how to move.

"I WILL FIGHT YOU, TOO." Kara charged toward him, but Shelley stepped in between them.

"Enough. Kara, while loud and wholly inappropriate, you do have a point. The council did not take your height into consideration when making our selection."

"Thank you." She continued glaring at Dallas, who went back to looking bored.

"How about a head start? One minute—"

"Three."

"Two. Two minutes and that's final."

"Done."

Shelley nodded, walking away toward the shallow end. "Now that that brief interruption is over, we'll get started." The woman didn't even need a megaphone. "Per tradition, the queen will have up to one minute to show favor, if she so chooses."

I hated this part. Whoever got that minute would be dubbed the Queen's Champion—the one I wanted to win.

I picked Kara.

The way Dallas looked at me after I chose made me feel like I should've said something to him, good luck maybe, but it was against the rules. I watched him go, walking to the shallow end to stand in position. His swim trunks were the same shade of yellow as my dress.

Kara tapped me twice on the collarbone on the left side of my chest. Our signal.

"Glasses?" I held out my hand and she handed them to me.

Volunteers weren't allowed to wear goggles under the water. I've seen pearl diving take up to an hour because no one could find the treasure. Thanks to that failure of a year, there'd been a rule change: more than one treasure would be available—the number of participants plus one.

"Nervous?"

"I don't get nervous. I win."

"I know."

Did I want Kara to win? I wanted her to be happy. If winning would do that, then yeah, I did. As queen, with my summer (and heart, if you believed in it) on the line, I'd be happy with her.

If Miss Jepson had asked me what I wanted, instead of asking if I had wanted Kara to win, my answer would have been different.

The HSR equaled romance. Every year, it almost always had the same outcome. This year was my year. This year was my chance to spend time with someone that I've been in denial about wanting, someone who might want me back.

To Kara, romance was a thing for other people. A hardcore shipper, she wanted what her faves wanted, and if that was another person, or two, she was all for it to the extreme and back again. "I'm happiest when the people I love are happy," she had said once. "It's not hard to figure out."

"Other people" included me. And more than anything, I wanted a chance. A chance for the *what-ifs* to be *mine*.

The absolute surety of that wish nearly knocked the wind out of me. I hadn't really thought about what would happen to Kara and me when we reached this crossroad. We had made easy promises, like I would never date someone she didn't like and she would always give whoever I chose three fair chances to mess up before declaring them dead to her. It sounded so simple while we whispered the rules between us, writing them down in our *Ungirlfriend Book*. Kara might not mind someone else in the future, but she had a big problem with Dallas right now.

Could I have told Kara that I wanted Dallas to win? Yeah. But I knew, felt in the darkest corners of my heart, that she wouldn't have been okay with it. Making a rule and having to accept it when the time came were two very different things.

Kara touched the bodice of my dress. "This is really pretty. She definitely went all out this year."

"It's okay if you don't win." I tried to keep my voice even. "They set you up to fail. I won't be disappointed or anything."

My hands started shaking—from the betrayal or from keeping a secret, I didn't know. She wrapped her hands around my wrists, looking up at me. Her entire body was a constellation of freckles. I stared at her shoulders, down her arms, to her hands.

"It's okay. If I don't win, I'll still go to all of your events. I'll be right there, every time. Concentrate on me and we'll get through it."

Oh Jesus. She wanted to win for me. She wanted to win to help me and would spend her whole summer following me around during Royal Engagements just in case I needed her. I bit my lip, and my face started to hurt from trying to not cry because I was selfish and terrible and a liar.

I had to tell her. I had to.

"See you on the other side." Kara skipped all the way to her spot, playing the part. Her way of boasting about being chosen as my champion. Even from where I stood, I could see the smug smile she aimed directly at Dallas.

I sat on my ostentatious throne of lies. Shelley handed me an air horn and stopwatch.

"Count down and press here." She explained it as if I had never seen either one before. "Whenever you're ready. Remember to project, and it's only a two-minute head start. No cheating."

I did it quickly to get people to stop looking at me. Kara jumped in while the crowd cheered her on. She had just made it to the deep end, treading water to catch her breath, when the stopwatch beeped. I blew the horn for a second time.

Dallas didn't move. He continued sitting at the edge of the pool.

The crowd began to rumble in confusion, not knowing who to watch, him or Kara. What was happening? Had he changed his mind about winning?

Disappointment sliced through me, quick and vicious. Had I been wrong? Was he upset that I'd picked Kara to be my champion? I explained everything to him. He should have known I would! It shouldn't have been a surprise.

"What is he doing?" Shelley asked me as if I would know.

"Why does everyone keep assuming I know what's going on with him?"

"Is he dropping out?"

"I don't know!"

He didn't speak to anyone or look anywhere in particular. Why bother to show up if he didn't plan to compete? My jaw began to hurt from clamping it shut to combat my nerves. Was this just some elaborate prank to get my hopes up so people would laugh at me, make fun of me later? Dallas was *kind*. He wouldn't. He would not do that to me.

"Blow it again." Shelley snatched it out of my hand because I didn't move fast enough and did it herself.

Dallas held up a hand, but remained sitting.

Shelley would burst a vein if she didn't calm down soon. "Why isn't he participating?"

"Woman, if you ask me one more time."

Kara held on to the wall, breathing hard. The swimming, the diving, and the searching had already worn her out. Thirteen feet was a long way down for someone not used to it. Had she been able to make it to the bottom at all?

I couldn't help Kara. I didn't know what Dallas was doing. Overwhelmed, I stared at my hands. The white stopwatch had continued to count the seconds and minutes because I had forgotten to press the button. A single minute had barely passed.

A minute. My hope bloomed back to life. Dallas was waiting an extra minute before starting. He was giving Kara the three-minute head start she'd originally asked for! Sure enough, at three minutes and one second, he dropped his hand and dove into the pool. He cut through the water effortlessly, all clean lines and smooth strokes.

Dallas dove and surfaced a few times before clinging to the wall himself to take a break. He turned back, staring at Kara just as she dove back in. He matched her, diving as well.

A few people in the crowd stood up to see better. I couldn't help it—I did, too. A flash of red and yellow seemed to cluster together under the water—her hair and his shorts.

Kara broke the surface, gasping and turning and swimming to me. My heart leaped into my throat—she'd found a treasure! The crowd exploded with noise, standing up and shouting, telling her to hurry and swim faster, chanting her name.

Not a single drop of disappointment touched me. I wanted Dallas to win—even wallowing in hope and shame, I could admit that—but Kara would never be some second-rate consolation prize. I tried to run to the edge to meet her, but Shelley held me back.

"You have to sit! She has to come to you!"

I glared at her, but did what she said. My hands squeezed the arms of the chair so tight I could feel the fake gold remolding around my grip. I didn't dare blink or take my eyes off of Kara.

"There he is!" Shelley damn near shouted next to my ear. I would throw up on her if she didn't get away from me soon.

Dallas hadn't surfaced, but a bright spot of yellow trailed Kara under the water, dangerously close to passing her.

Kara tried to lift herself out of the pool—and failed. Arms too short and body too tired, she fell back into the water. She didn't try again, instead turning and swimming for the stairs not too far away.

"Oh no." I gasped. "Oh no, oh no, oh no."

Dallas had no such problem. In one smooth move, he pulled himself up and out of the water. He didn't run, reaching me five seconds before Kara did, and presented his treasure to me: a fake pearl bracelet with a weighted bright red plastic heart attached to it.

~

FAM-BAM-MAJAMA

Winnie: Update: Kara lost.

Mom: Oh no! Is she okay? I know how much she hates losing.

Winnie: Shelley tried to make them shake hands after I crowned Dallas and Kara kicked him instead so I'd say she's a little upset. Just a little.

Mom: !!!!!!

Dad: Do I need to come down there?

Winnie: It's not like that Dad.

Dad: If Kara doesn't like him there must be something wrong with him.

Winnie: ... I never said Kara didn't like him.

Dad: She's all mouth same as you. You said she kicked him. He must have done something. Or will do something.

Dad: Send me his parents' number

Winnie: DAD NO

Dad: I'll get it from my mom. Don't test me child

Mom: Charles calm down. If something was wrong Winston would tell us.

Winston: call his parents

Winnie: DON'T LISTEN TO HIM

Mom: Winnie. Phone number. Now.

Winnie: WHY ARE Y'ALL LIKE THIS

Eighteen

The lighting in megastores always creeped me out. Maybe it had to be brighter than the wattage the Creator of the Universe intended for the sun so customers could see all of the discount slashes on price tags. Or lack of slashes in my case. I wasn't cheap. I was practical—fiscally conservative minus the Republican agenda. I knew the value of a dollar and how far I could stretch that into one hundred pennies.

The day was for Kara anyway. She placed a toaster, a waffle iron, a hand mixer, and a set of mixing bowls in the cart. "I decided just to go on and get new stuff, so I don't have to worry about packing and shipping my babies."

"How practical." Retail therapy wasn't a myth. Whenever Kara's emotions got the better of her, she shopped. Or I shopped and mailed her presents.

I had a photo shoot coming up soon with Dallas—the symbolic kickoff to Royal Engagements—and I didn't want Kara to feel left out. Whenever I had to spend time with Dallas, I'd make sure to spend time with her first. On the same day. No excuses. The perfect primer for my impending confession.

Nothing would change between Kara and me. I'd show her that before she could even think it. Perfect plan was perfect and not for me. At all. I didn't need convincing that this could work out between the three of us. Nope.

"This is a pretty lamp." Granny held it up, admiring the refracted crystal surface. She had declared a cease-fire on the silent treatment. It wouldn't last, which hurt more than I wanted to admit. Her joy stemmed from the running, from the dieting, and one of those was about to go soon.

Well, soonish.

I wasn't quite ready to willingly give up her smile.

"Pretty expensive," I said. "I'm sure the dorm will have built-in lights. The pictures on the website had them."

Kara and I had been assigned to the brand-spanking-new student tower funded by the hundreds of extra dollars slid into student fees all of the students who had attended before me had been forced to pay. "Renovations," they had called it. "Suites" replaced dorms.

I could see why they were trying to sugarcoat the reality that housing (rent) alone would cost $10,000 a year per person, when we'd be shacking up with two other girls. Between the four of us, that was enough money for a down payment on a nice house.

Whatever.

We hadn't met our future roomies yet, but knew their names and student emails.

Emily Quan.

Shahera Rose.

"I told you to stop worrying about that. You only get to do this once, so get whatever you want." She smiled, admiring the lamp's kaleidoscopic shimmer. "It'll look beautiful next to your bed."

"Technically, I'll get to do it eight times."

Granny cut her eyes at me.

I placed the lamp in the basket. "Beautiful. Thank you." My college had provided a move-in checklist, and there were fifty-eleven articles on the internet in case they hadn't. Back at home, my mom had gotten:

Two sets of XL twin sheet sets—blackity black and polka-dot green/black

One comforter—also black

One throw blanket—green

Requisite plastic fare—a drawer set with wheels, four cubes, and a shoe rack

A complete flatware set

Two sets of bath towels

A rolling laundry basket

Floating shelves

Fairy lights

With Granny, I had gotten: a fancy lamp.

Granny pushed the basket as we walked to the next aisle—actual school supplies. Binders, paper, folders, pens, and pencils. Office supplies galore. Holy God—sparkly purple gel pens! I hadn't seen those since elementary school.

"I need these." I also needed the things that worked well for my study system. Ooh! Neon mini Post-its! Several of those went into the cart. "Feeling better yet?" I asked Kara.

"Nope. Still punchy." Kara stared at the perfect stacks of composition notebooks. The ones that looked like they'd been covered in TV static were her favorite.

I picked up matching notebooks and folders. Five different colored sets—one for each class. "Did something happen between you and Dallas?"

Kara's face revealed nothing. "Like what?"

Last night, unable to sleep, I had revised and simplified my facts:

Kara had a secret history and an ongoing problem with Dallas that she didn't want to tell me about.

Dallas had an ulterior motive in volunteering to be HSR King that he also didn't want to tell me about.

I had been trapped in the middle of a feud between my ungirlfriend and my newly crowned king. And I was pretty sure I had figured out why.

"Like maybe he told you something important that upset you, something you should probably get around to telling me." I tried to keep my tone neutral. Far from accusatory and even farther away from hope. My educated guess—that Dallas liked me and told Kara—could still be wrong.

Her brow furrowed as she stared at me. "What makes you think that's what happened?"

"So something did happen?"

"Maybe." She turned away, picking through the folder selection.

That meant yes. Kara didn't deal in maybes. That was my job. Kara lived in absolutes. We would be together. She would win the Starlight contest.

A *maybe* from her meant that she'd almost lied to me. A *maybe* from her meant she caught herself last minute. A *maybe* from her meant she didn't want to tell me.

More secrets.

My initial gut reaction, anger, made my mouth snap shut before I said something I would no doubt regret.

One . . . two . . . three . . .

Even a simple tease or a reminder, "Since when do we keep secrets from each other," could come out laced with venom. I couldn't be honest with her if she refused to be honest with me, but that wasn't how our relationship was supposed to work.

Four . . . five . . . six . . .

Kara was the only absolute I had. The only thing I could believe in and actually feel the weight, the truth, of it. I held on to that tighter than I should have, cherished it, hoarded it, and defended its honor. Breaking our rules wasn't allowed.

Seven . . . eight . . . nine . . .

Lashing out would make things worse.

"Got it," I said. "No pressure, but is there something I need to know right now? I have to see him later for the photo shoot."

Kara didn't answer immediately.

I had watched my tone again because I didn't want her to figure out how much I was looking forward to seeing Dallas. We hadn't talked at all since he had won. And I was eager to— stupidly so. The second he clasped that pearl bracelet around my wrist and looked into my eyes, I was done for. Gone. My heart would have burst out of my chest and straight into his if that were physically possible. He had wanted to win. And he did . . . to be with me.

I would tell Kara the truth. Soon. Just not yet. It wasn't fair for me to have to be the one to lay all my cards on the table while she got to continue being so standoffish. I hated thinking that way, reducing our relationship to a scale where everything had to be perfect and balanced before we could move forward. That wasn't us, but there we were.

"If you like him," Kara said, already starting to walk away, "then like him."

People seemed determined to be cryptic with me. I had to stop taking it personally before holding back my temper burst a blood vessel in my eye. I'd get to the bottom of this eventually.

Miraculously, I let it go. For now.

Granny continued to lead the way, heading straight to electronics for a projector. Easier than hauling a TV, it would also save space, since we could hook it up to our laptops and use a blank wall to watch whatever we wanted.

Feeling a little antsy, I started to sing along to the song blasting through the store, twirling and two-stepping around the cart.

"If you don't stop." Granny laughed anyway. "Don't embarrass me in this store, missy."

My spirit did its usual happy dance, overjoyed to see Granny laugh and to be the one who caused it. I stood next to her, singing and moving my shoulders—the "deep shoulder action" move I'd learned from watching *What's Love Got to Do with It*. For longer than I should probably admit to, I had thought Angela Bassett *was* Tina Turner. She was that good.

I shimmied again, did a *Five Heartbeats* pivot and turn, and began shuffling like I'd seen in *The Jacksons: An American Dream*.

Side note: that's how I had figured out Angela Bassett was an actress and not Tina—because she also played Katherine Jackson. I'd also learned about those old movies because they were Granny's favorites that she'd shared with me and Winston.

Granny and Kara laughed that time, beaming at me, and for a quick second, everything felt exactly like it was supposed to.

As we passed the clothes section, Granny turned sharp and with purpose. "Baby, let's get you a new outfit. You need to look nice on your first day of class."

"I only have one class for ninety minutes."

"We'll get you two, then. And some pajamas. Can't have you

running around in those holey stretch pants you refuse to throw away. And some underwear." She poked my back fat. "And a good bra."

"Hey!" I twisted away, stomach cramping with instant anxiousness.

"Well, you need 'em. Don't you *hey* me."

"Fine, but not from here." I lowered my voice. "I don't think anything will fit."

"Won't know until we try. Come on."

Kara busied herself with a row of piggy banks, pretending not to listen. We operated under the same game plan when it came to Granny. She picked her battles, too, and backed me up when I picked mine. Her distance signaled she was waiting for me to choose.

Shopping for jeans would make me cry. T-shirts could be touch and go depending on the neck style. Button-up shirts were out, thanks to the boob gap in between buttons my shirts always ended up with. Trying to put together an outfit? Next to impossible, unless the store made an active effort to give fat people some semblance of a fashionable life. We didn't all want to wear shapeless floral patterned designs with weird shoulder cutouts and *ruffles*.

Granny led us to the junior section—"Kara baby, pick out some clothes for yourself and meet us over there when you're done"—and then past the women, to the plus sizes.

"This is beautiful." Granny held up a floral maxi dress. "It's long enough and the color complements your skin."

I ignored that "long enough" jab. Above the knee was the way to be in my book.

"Do you want to try it on?"

"Definitely not." I took it from her, folding the hanger downward and holding it near my chin, tugging it around the waist. "It'll fit. Do they have any more?" Summer maxi dresses: the holy savior of average-to-tall fat girls everywhere.

"Mm-hmm. Look. See, I told you it was fine. Always thinking you know best. Listen to me when I tell you something."

The dresses had been a pure stroke of luck, which I took full advantage of, placing five of them in the cart. Blessings didn't last—if I came back to get more, they'd probably all be gone.

I convinced Granny to hold off on the bras but lost the pajama fight. She tried to buy a year's worth of long sleep shirts, shorts, and socks.

"A couple is fine. I don't need all of these!"

"You don't like to do laundry."

"Kara does." I shrugged. "I'll just throw my stuff in with hers."

"Already treating me like your wife. I love it." Kara returned, having found two pantsuits and several pairs of sunglasses. "It's true, though. I love that kind of stuff. I can't wait to put domestic technician on my resume to mess with people."

Nineteen

My hands clenched into fists as I walked into the portrait studio. I had decided to wear a solid black dress à la Wednesday Addams and a silver sweater that looked good with my tiara, already sitting in its place of honor in front of my top bun.

Shelley and Rush stood together next to a camera set up on a tripod. She was saying something about the lighting. He replied that whatever she wanted had to wait until I arrived, because my skin was darker than Dallas's. He wanted us both to look good.

Rush mentioning that, let alone caring about it, nearly stopped me in my tracks with surprise.

For the shoot, silver tulle had been placed on the ground like mist against a matte dark blue background. "Floating" flower-filled orbs hung in the air like bubbles, and two podiums had been wrapped in fairy lights with the fishbowl brought back into action. Tacky in a way that somehow worked, it had Shelley written all over it.

Dallas stood off to the side in his crown, arms crossed and waiting.

He spotted me before the other two did. A relieved grin that part of me desperately wanted to trust brightened everything about him.

"You're late." He frowned but the judgment slid from his face almost as soon as it appeared, smile returning.

"Two minutes."

"Still late. You're supposed to be on time for our Royal Engagements."

"I plead the Fashionable Fifth."

He stepped back, giving me a once-over. My face burned in embarrassment, throat locking up.

"The court finds that plea acceptable. Very cute."

Cute. Cute was *good.* Cute was *great.* It was a considerable down-grade from beautiful, but I'd take it any day and say, *Please, sir, can I have some more.* I relaxed, tension leaving me like a charley horse cramp *finally* letting go.

"Thanks. You too. I guess."

"You guess? Wow, okay. And here I thought I could impress you with my psychic powers." He laughed, pointing from himself to me and back again. "Nobody told us to both wear black and silver. Behold my power."

"Oh." I hadn't even noticed, not really, not beyond my normal (irritating) reaction of thinking he looked good. His dress shirt and slacks had been ironed—the crisp creases would cut me if I touched him—and his silver tie had reflective threads woven into it, catching the light just right to make them shine. "You must promise to never use your aesthetic powers for evil."

"Eh, evil is relative. Power and perspective are what you really have to watch out for."

"Fair. I'm evil, though."

"I know. It's why I like you." He winked and a smile jumped out of me before I could catch it. "You try so, so hard to be good, but we both know you're only going to succumb to the dark side."

"Finally. Someone gets me. I might cry." My smile kicked into overdrive—the gummy one that showed off the overbite I refused to get fixed.

"'The darkest paths are best walked with a friend to hold the light.' I read that somewhere."

"Kara's my light. It's dimming because she's just as bad as I am, but we make it work." Nothing about him changed when I mentioned Kara—no flinching or looking away or frowning.

"Room for one more?" He held out his arm, gazing down at me with a soft, amused smile that turned my heart to mush.

That smile would be the end of me. "If they're special, sure." I linked our arms together.

"I'm psychic, so obviously I qualify."

"Obviously." I laughed as he escorted me to the photo shoot setup. "How long have you been waiting?"

"Longer than I would've liked," he said, voice lowered. We were within earshot of Shelley and Rush now. "I hate it, but I still agreed to be here."

He knew what kind of over-the-top obligations came with the crown and had volunteered for them. And then doubled down on his decision by not letting Kara win.

"Do you really?" I stared at him, hoping to read his body language for an unconscious clue.

"Not because of you or anything." His eyes widened as he spoke too fast.

"I—that wasn't where I was going with that."

"Winnie!" Shelley shouted. "I had no idea you arrived. Why didn't you say something?" She beckoned us over as if we hadn't already been walking toward her.

With no preamble, Shelley maneuvered us into the middle of the scene and adjusted the floaters to look like a frame.

"This shouldn't take too long," Rush said, face downturned as he fiddled with his camera settings. "We need a couple of shots for the website, the town hall, the newspaper, and a few promotional posters, and you'll be free to go. I'm going to take some tests shots."

That seemed like . . . a lot.

The flash popped and the lighting flickered a bit, making me jump. "Perfectly normal noises." Rush used an odd tone, almost like he was counting down to zero with words instead of numbers. "Perfectly normal! Almost done and got it!" He grinned. "See, not too bad?"

"Says you." Standing still felt wrong. I needed to be moving, running, fleeing from that awful, awful place.

Unlike Sam, I was not blessed with the gift of being photogenic. I'd learned how to smile in pictures by practicing in the mirror and how to pose from watching hours of old episodes of *America's Next Top Model*. Cameras, and the people with social media accounts who wielded them, *never* caught me off guard. I'd made sure of it.

But right then, I was too on edge to deploy my skills. I'd mess up, channeling deer in the headlights with beaver teeth and a shocking amount of human infant gums, a chimeric monstrosity that would forever be immortalized in the *Haven Herald*.

And the worst part? I couldn't make it stop.

"Okay, kids," Rush said. "Be natural. Stand close together and smile. Uh, Winnie, do you need a moment?"

"I'm fine. Let's get this over with."

I rolled my shoulders, taking a deep breath, trying to sink into a happy place and paste my Tyra-taught smile and smize on my face. I'd run right the hell on out of there if I had to. If I so much as sensed the familiar twinges of an oncoming panic attack, there'd be literal cartoon dust in my wake. They'd never catch me panicking on camera again.

A few moments later, Shelley called, "Winnie, keep your head straight but turn your body toward Dallas."

That earned a side-eye from Rush, who said nothing but clearly didn't like having a co-director. I tried to do as she asked. My cheeks had begun to hurt from holding my smile in place. It looked good in pictures but as far from natural as artificial sweeteners.

Diet Winnie: calorie free and optimized for public consumption.

"Like this?" Every inch of me felt tense, tightly coiled like a spring under too much pressure.

"Perfect! Get the shot, Rush." Several snaps later, Shelley called out, "Dallas, put your arm around her."

He reached—I flinched away from him like I was scared of being hit.

His face didn't betray anything other than a question I couldn't interpret. He kept his stance open, arms at his side, as we looked at each other. I opened my mouth, inhaled, and knew if I tried to talk only garbled word-goop would come out. I wanted to tell him that it wasn't *him*. If anyone had tried to touch me right then, I would have had the same instinctive reaction. I stretched my eyes wide, trying to keep my tears at bay, willing him to understand. Why did my words always abandon me like this when I needed them most?

"Go on, Dallas," Shelley urged, oblivious.

"No." He turned away from me.

"Oh, please? It'll look adorable. You'll thank me later."

Dallas huffed through his nose, mouth set in a grim line. That was the most irritated I'd ever seen him. "I seriously doubt it."

"Woman! Please! I'm trying to work." Rush placed his hands on his hips, face turning red. "Winnie doesn't want him to touch her."

"Don't be ridiculous. Of course she does." Shelley's matter-of-fact tone made me want to die. "They're already together. Everyone saw them the other day."

"No, we're not." Dallas sounded *appalled*. "Did you get pictures you could use?"

Was it possible to die twice? Sign me up.

Rush sighed, straightening up. "We'll have to make do." He cast a harsh glance at Shelley. "The mood's ruined now."

"Let's get out of here." Dallas didn't touch me—his hand hovered near my elbow instead.

Shelley called for us to wait.

"Don't." He moved behind me when I looked back.

I nodded, concentrating on moving one foot after the other as we exited the studio.

Twenty

I hated thinking about things that I had no control over.

I really hated thinking about things that I had no control over after midnight, because while everyone I cared about slept, I was still at work in Goldeen's, suffering through my mental anguish alone at my podium, staring out the front window and waiting in vain for customers that never showed up on Sunday nights.

Time machines didn't exist (yet). I couldn't change what had happened and my brain refused to let it go, replaying the photo shoot over and over. It had been great at first, talking to Dallas, who had decided to forsake his living puzzle-box ways, and then it got awkward. Outside, Dallas hadn't said anything to me. Clearly mad, but again unwilling to tell me why.

Had it been the photo shoot?

Me recoiling when he tried to touch me?

Shelley assuming we were dating?

Oh, he really didn't like that last one. What stuck out the most and replayed in vivid Technicolor with nary a way to change the channel? The way he had said, *"No."*

Sure, if someone had rudely assumed I had started dating some-one, I'd get upset, too, if it wasn't true. On some level that made sense to the rational parts of my brain, but those parts had been regulated to the corner, nose against the wall, the same way Sam tried to discipline the kids she watched.

Because boys like Dallas didn't date fat girls. For a second there, I had truly lost my romantic mind. No matter what my mom said or might say in the future, it would never erase what I'd seen firsthand at school.

Valentine's Day: War in the Time of Commercial Romance.

A certain population of people had become notorious for send-ing fake proposals through the school-sanctioned flower-giving spectacle.

Meet me after school behind the gym. . . .

I've had a crush on you forever. . . .

Text me, please. I want to get to know you. . . .

The innocent carnations with cards attached had been used as humiliating weapons of mass emotional and romantic destruction. No one could be trusted. I had made it out unscathed. Not a single fake flower had ever been sent to me.

But one of my friends had gotten one. Two years in a row.

That had been my initial thought when Dallas had volunteered—it was for a joke. But I'd dismissed it quickly because I at least trusted him enough to not be *that* kind of douchebag.

But more to the point, according to Nadiya, who heard it from Michelle, who heard it from Megan, who saw a text from Lacey, Dallas didn't date Black girls. Which, okay, hurt. A lot. A special kind of hurt right in my metaphysical jugular that I didn't want to poke at or examine too closely. Admittedly, that rumor was a few years old now, and people could change, but.

I'd already lived through that in school, too, and the opposite:

whenever someone transferred, there would be literally zero point in getting a crush.

It started like this: "Oh. They're really cute."

And then common sense donkey-kicked its way through the front door: "He probably doesn't like Black girls."

Again, the rational part of my brain knew everyone couldn't possibly think like that, but man. Hear it enough, see it enough on the internet, and that stuff starts to sink in after a while. Rom-coms were fantasy—the real dating playing field was sloped and ravaged by weeds, doubt, stereotypes, and unavoidable Eurocentric beauty standards.

But it was cool. Whatever. I'd meet a lot of different kinds of people with different mind-sets in college.

Hopefully.

I'd be happy if Dallas wanted to be friends. I *wanted* to have that with him. Funny. Snarky. Kind. Perceptive. Nice to look at, which probably shouldn't be on this list, but whatever, here we are.

A car pulled into Goldeen's parking lot, the engine roaring even as it idled before the driver cut it. Standing up, I stretched to wake up and shake myself out of my brain fog of escalating and borderline irrational worry.

You would think watching Dallas get out of the car, walk toward the door, enter the diner, and make his way to the podium would be enough time for me to prepare some kind of witty greeting to counteract the obscene levels of surprise pelting my brain cells. But no it wasn't.

I stared at him. That's all. Didn't move. Didn't speak. Just stared.

"Can I sit?" He gestured to a table.

"Are you going to order something?" Did it matter, Jesus, *really*?

"Sure."

"Okay." I grabbed a single Midnight Oil menu and led him to the second booth from the door.

He sat down. "What do you recommend to eat?"

I could have handed him the menu, like a normal waitress who knew how to do her job, but no, I clutched it to my chest. "Depends on how you're feeling."

He looked relieved. "Pretty shitty, actually. Will you get in trouble if you sit with me?"

"Probably not." I slid into the booth across from him.

"Please don't make fun of me for this." He kept his eyes on his hands, folded on top of the table. "I tried to tell some of my friends and they didn't—they were assholes about it. I feel like I can trust you, and I think if we're going to be hanging out all summer we should try to get along, you know?"

"Okay." I didn't even need to think about it. "I won't laugh."

"I've been working on not ignoring the way I feel about things. People." His earnest, slight smile jolted me to the core. I'd never seen him look like that, let alone look at me like that. "I don't want to hide who I am anymore, and I feel like you're someone that would understand me."

"Wait, so, your friends *laughed* at you for that? For wanting to feel your feelings, if I'm understanding that right?"

A memory of Winston popped into my head—him crying, my dad saying, "Cut that out. Men don't cry," and my mom threatening my dad within an inch of his life for belittling Winston and "putting that poison into his head." It made sense.

"Well. I can certainly try to understand you," I added. "No promises or anything, but what I do know about you, I like."

"So about the photo shoot. I want to apologize." His sincere stare pinned me in place. I clutched the menu tighter. "It was a clusterfuck from beginning to end. I was mad before you even got there. Shelley wouldn't stop, and it got to me, even though I tried not to let it. I don't want you to think you had anything to do with that."

"What did she do? Before I got there, I mean."

"Same thing she did while you were there. Making it seem like we were dating because she heard we went for a fucking walk, and how glad she was that I had given you a chance because not everyone would have, and that I was a real man because of it."

"Oh."

In those kind of moments, the less I said, the better. I had only said something because I felt like I had to. A tiny acknowledgment to let him know I had understood his words, his anger, and Shelley's meaning.

"It was so fucked up. I kept telling her we were only friends, but she brushed it off, like I wanted to keep it a secret because it was too soon or something. I don't know. Rush kept trying to distract her, but she kept finding a way to bring it up again."

Elation and disappointment rolled together in a writhing mass, crushing me from the inside out. Both feelings blended together until I couldn't tell them apart. Perfectly equal. Perfectly awful.

Friendship was the bee's fucking knees. Great, wonderful, amazing, spectacular. And dating friends felt like an honor straight from on high. It's why things with Kara had always been so magical. "We're a recipe made with all the best, most expensive, and rarest ingredients," she had said once.

I had tried so hard to keep my hopes in check, secreted away in a lockbox and buried so deep down not even Pandora and her twitchy disobedient hands could find it. In a matter of days, my resolve had shattered, and I let myself think it was okay to truly want something. Someone. Him. That I had a chance.

Dallas wasn't required to like me. I knew that. Divine matchmaking or not, he didn't owe me anything.

But at some point, *only* being seen as a friend had stopped feeling like an everyday, average part of life, and more like a targeted part of my existence. I'd seen plenty of movies and countless shows where *funny fat friend* morphed into *always a bridesmaid, never a bride*. I didn't know how to explain that without sounding like an entitled broseph complaining about the mythical friend zone.

"No offense, but it sounds like it has a lot to do with me."

"I meant I wasn't mad because of you. You didn't do anything. You were just an innocent bystander." He wrestled with what he wanted to say next. "And it's like that keeps happening. Kara and I don't really get along."

"You don't say."

"That's not about *you* either. Well." His eyes rolled up to the ceiling, face scrunched up in thought. "Not exactly."

"Are you going to explain that, or are we playing more word games? Because I really don't like those."

"She hasn't told you? Anything?"

"Obviously not."

"I don't want to make it worse, but"—he paused—"she wants me to stay away from you."

"She said that? When?"

He nodded. "A while ago."

Well, that wasn't true. Not a chance. I decided to humor him anyway. "And did she say why?"

"It's been a standing agreement between us that I kind of broke when I volunteered."

"Okay, but why? She wouldn't just ask you to do that out of nowhere. Make this make sense."

"That's *why* I thought she was your girlfriend, but like you said, she's not, and it *didn't* make sense anymore, so I decided I wanted to win."

"Rewind, rewind. You didn't know she was my ungirlfriend until *after* you volunteered. Why did you do it if your agreement was intact?"

"I wanted to be king. I'm not really friends with my friends right now. I broke up with Lacey. I wanted someone to hang out with before I moved away instead of spending all of my time alone in my room." He began to wring his hands. "And then it was you, and it felt like my last chance."

Looking at him felt like the equivalent of Superman voluntarily swallowing kryptonite. "Chance for what?"

"I've always liked you. I like the way you don't ignore your brother. I like the way you're always helping people. I like your jokes and your laugh and the way you look at people like you can cut straight through them when you know they're bullshitting you. But then I made that deal with Kara, so I've always just stayed out of your way. I figured if *you* wanted me around, you'd come get me. Swoop me under your wing like you did with Kara."

And there it was.

Dallas *had* noticed me. So much so that he could list out all of his favorite things. I exhaled in a hard, shocked huff. And he wanted to be like Kara—well maybe not that intense, but he wanted *me* to choose *him*. He'd been waiting. For me.

The last time I had felt this special, Kara had been the cause.

"I dive-bombed that girl." Still stunned, my voice sounded too soft. "You wouldn't have wanted me to."

"Yeah. I would have and she knew that."

"I'm gonna talk to her. It's just you can't really push her, you know? She has to be ready to tell you something or she'll shut down." I nodded, willing myself to believe in it, in this moment. "If we're all going to be friends, I want her to be on board."

"Friends."

"Thank you for being honest with me. I like you, too—I don't know why I didn't say that earlier, because I do." I covered half of my face with my hand, half embarrassed but too happy to care. "I want to be able to put whatever happened between you two behind us."

Dallas's smile faded as I spoke, until it disappeared completely. "I don't think it's going to be that easy. I want it to be, but"—he shook his head, eyes sad—"you really need to talk to her."

~

Kara (Kara Kara Kara Kara) Chameleon

> **Winnie:** We need to talk.

Kara: What did he tell you?

> **Winnie:** Why would you assume it's about that?

Kara: What /else/ would it be about?

Twenty-One

The Twilight Zone was a real place. I would know, because somehow I had ended up there.

Lying on my bed, and ignoring the alarm Sam had set for me, everything looked normal. The room—immaculately clean and decorated in shades of white, slate gray, and deep blue—began to warm up as the sun rose. My sheets still felt soft and smelled like Granny's favorite fabric softener. The goldfish swam in their bubbling tank.

But talking candidly with Dallas, the recurring fights with Granny, Kara keeping secrets, agreeing to run with Sam? Nothing about any of that could be considered normal. My world had begun to shift in strange, parallel-universe ways.

Summer in Haven Central had always felt like one long slog of time. Days blurred into midnights. Weeks and months were interchangeable words. I'd arrive one evening, and a blink later it'd be time to go home again. It had never been like this, where each day felt a thousand years long, punctuated by some life-altering event.

I'd have to handle the situation with Kara delicately. That more than any of the rest sat at the forefront of my brain, demanding that I fix it.

"Are we quitting yet?" Winston asked from the doorway.

I sighed. Then got up to start getting ready.

Five. Three. Five.

Walk. Jog. Walk.

In the last Harry Potter movie, Winston's favorite character said dying was "quicker and easier than falling asleep." That's how I convinced myself the extra minute wouldn't be the death of me—it wasn't quick, it wasn't easy, but *man*, did I need a nap. Rolling over and running after only three hours of sleep would get really old, really fast.

"Good job, today." Sam held up her hand for a high five as we walked back to the car.

"No."

"Oh, don't be like that." She lowered her hand, placing it on the small of my back. "You're doing fine."

"I'm sweaty. Don't touch me."

"I hate this." Winston's singsong voice sounded out of place amongst all of the agitated goose-honking. "Everything hurts. My legs, my back, my chest—everything. Why do people voluntarily do this? How do they do this without their bodies falling apart?"

"Sheer force of will, probably." I eyed Sam for an answer.

"You're not completely wrong."

"Masochists." Winston clutched his side. "I don't feel good. I never feel good after this. I was promised endorphins. Exercise gives you endorphins. Endorphins make you happy."

"Happy people don't kill their cousins. They just don't."

Sam frowned. "Y'all are so weird."

When we got back to the diner, I had the bright idea to ditch the other two, who walked in through the front door. Too tired and too cranky to wiggle out of another one of Granny's Special Breakfasts, I took the coward's way out and crept up the back stairs to the apartment. I had a date with a bathtub, my bed, and some unused sick time collecting dust in my employee coffers.

Exhaustion, thy name was Winnie.

And it was only day two.

I woke up several hours later, stomach rumbling and dying of thirst. Halfway to the kitchen, I nearly jumped out of my skin when Granny called my name from the living room. She was sitting in her recliner, knitting, and I hadn't seen her. Tunnel vision for the refrigerator would do that.

"I just woke up." My code for *please don't talk to me yet*. Which she never cared about. I poured a cup of water from the refrigerated filter jug, gulping it down before going back for seconds. A dehydration headache pulsated rudely in between my eyes.

"There's some oatmeal in there. Put a little water on it and cover it with a paper towel before you microwave it."

"No, thanks."

"What are you going to eat?"

"Not that." I rubbed my forehead. Pain made my temper nonexistent. But if I didn't answer her, that would set her off, and I just—

Why couldn't she just leave me alone?

"Stop being ridiculous." The clicking from her knitting needles sounded like nails on a chalkboard. "Have a yogurt, too. They're on the refrigerator door." So, so close to letting it go and giving up, my hand in mid-reach for that damn yogurt, she just had to add, "But *only* have one. They're not fat free."

I slammed the refrigerator door shut, turning away and staring out the window. My hands perched like claws on the sink's edge. Eyes closed, I tried breathing and counting and breathing and counting. I didn't want my food to be measured, calculated, and monitored. My body, my rules. If I wanted to eat dry, lumpy oatmeal with extra flax seeds and fat-free yogurt, then *I* would do that, but it would be *my* choice—same as if I wanted to eat gluten-free pizza and ice cream.

Maybe Winston, bless his baby brother heart, had been right. Granny did want to control me. Both of us, actually. The Starlight contest: the one thing he had ever wanted to do, the only thing he had ever asked her for, and she wouldn't let him.

My thought process shifted like a train switching tracks and barreling through a tunnel. Purpose filled me as I walked across the room, moving quickly before I lost my nerve. Unsure of what I'd say before I said it, I trusted myself to find the heart of what needed saying before long.

"Can I talk to you about something?"

Granny glanced at me over the rims of her reading glasses. "About what?"

I sat on the ottoman in front of her. "About the contest." Start small. Work my way up to potential devastation.

"Contest? That Starlight thing?"

"Yeah."

"I said no."

"Yes. No to me. But Winston—"

"No."

"Can't you just—"

"I already know about Winston. He's too young. People in that competition have been cooking for years. He isn't going to win. No point in putting him through that. There'll be plenty of opportunities for him when he's older and more experienced."

"But I've been watching him lately. I think he has—"

"Mind. Your. Business. The answer is no."

My temper swelled to a frothing boil. Jaw clenched, I took breaths that were not fucking working. How could she doubt him like that? Her own grandson!? He was *my* brother. He could do anything he wanted and be successful. My hands shook at my sides, balled into fists, and it took every last ounce of love I had for Granny to not explode. I thought of Winston, of making it worse, of fighting his battles anyway even when he told me not to. "Fine." Teeth still clenched, the word, the lie, vibrated in my mouth. "Let's talk about me, then."

I was the oldest. Everything began with me. If I could get her to see how unfair she was being to me, I could convince her to cut Winston the same slack. We weren't babies.

"What about you?"

Deep breath. In and out. In and out. Let go of the anger.

Anger and hurt tended to blend together inside of me, with anger surrounding the hurt in a ferocious, protective ball so no one could ever reach it. Not even me. But I needed it.

I would try my mom's method. Starting here with someone I loved, someone who loved me back, someone who was supposed to understand.

"About what happened in Dr. Skinner's office. I'm not sorry." Granny scoffed and I held up my trembling hands. "I know that sounds terrible, and I know I probably could have handled that better, but like, everyone hates fat people. At least it feels that way. They might not admit it, or consciously think about it, but at one point or another, a fat person will piss them off and that's the first thing they go for when they retaliate."

"Winnie." Granny used her stern *and that's final* voice. "You are *not* fat."

"But I am. It's not a bad word to me at all. I get what you hear when I'm saying it: I'm calling myself ugly or unlovable or it's *the* horrendous state of slovenly being. That's not what I'm saying, and it's not my fault that almost everyone has been conditioned to think that way. I just don't see it like that. I don't know why I don't. I don't know why the word *fat* as an adjective, as an insult, doesn't hurt me. It just doesn't. But what does hurt me is the way people treat me because of what I am. So—I get defensive. Sometimes preemptively."

"He wanted to help you. You don't behave like that when people are being nice."

"He *wasn't*." I closed my eyes and breathed. It wasn't about Skinner. I couldn't let him ruin this for me. *Let go of the anger. Speak the truth.* "Being fat changes the rules for me because . . . being nice? Being helpful? All of that becomes an act. Saying things that he thinks could happen to me because I'm fat wasn't nice. It wasn't kind. It was dehumanizing."

"You don't honestly think that."

"Yeah. I do." I nodded, finding the steady pulse of confidence that would carry me through this conversation. "Look at it like this: I may have snapped but only because he had all of the power. He's a doctor. He has degrees and experience and science, and so by default it's assumed he knows better than I do, right? He didn't look at my chart to see my blood pressure is stellar. He didn't call my doctor and ask to see my records and blood tests and everything else. He saw me, a Black fat girl, and assumed diabetes and hypertension and death by thirty-five from a heart attack. Those same exact things could be just as true for Sam as they are for me, and the only difference is he looked at me and with no evidence other than my weight deemed me more likely to be the one to go through that."

I paused to breathe again. Granny sat still as stone, lips pressed together, eyes judging and weighing what her next step would be, regardless of how long that took.

"That's what I have to fight against all the time." My voice softened against my will. "They see me and refuse to hear me. And it's not just doctors. So no, I'm not sorry for sticking up for myself, but I am sorry for the way I handled it. I knew what I was doing would make you upset and I chose to do it anyway."

Everyone always said I had Granny's eyes. Deep set, dark brown, and could cut through anything with a single look. They'd skipped a generation and jumped straight into her grandbaby instead of her son. She even took a deep breath before deciding to talk, too.

"I'm not going to live forever. Some days I wake up and the pain is so bad, I don't know how much longer I can take it."

"Granny—"

"Don't." She held up a gnarled finger. "I listened to you, now you listen to me. I'm old. It happens. But I've lived my life. I have two wonderful alive and free sons who went to college, met their beautiful wives, and gave me three beautiful grandchildren. I'm spending my retirement living my last dream—owning my own business. My own restaurant. You're still young, Winnie. You have your whole life ahead of you. You are so, so blessed that you can do and go and be just about anything, but you have to think about your health."

There'd be no point in repeating that fat didn't mean unhealthy. Or mentioning that even if it did, it wouldn't automatically disqualify me from deserving a dignified life. "I can live my life and be fat. If I want to lose weight, I will, but I don't."

"Life will only get harder for you."

"Then that's the path I'll walk."

"If you don't care, then why did you go running with Sam?"

"Deciding to do that doesn't mean you were *right*. I'm not doing it for you. That's about Sam. She wanted to do something together, just us, and that's what she picked. So you don't have to make me special diet food. I'd super prefer if you didn't."

"Baby, I hear you but I can't just do nothing. I talked to your mom."

"Yeah." I flirted with danger for one hot second and narrowed my eyes at Granny. "Feel free to not do that either."

"Winnie."

"Sorry, but don't bring my parents into this. They've never done stuff like this."

If my parents cared, they never showed it. The only time my mom had ever said anything about my weight was when she asked, "Do the kids at school bully you?"

It got hard at times when my friends, not just my fat friends, would cry about the way their parents restricted their food. I'd sat through lunches of them eating carrot sticks, not because they liked them but because they were being *good*, chugging protein shakes and tearing protein bars into smaller and smaller portions to make them last, while staring at hamburgers because they had to make weight. I never judged. Never said anything. But I watched and I listened.

They would say things to me like, "It's nice to talk to someone who understands." Thing was, I actually didn't. I could empathize. I believed them. People had messed-up thoughts about food and weight and took it out on their kids who took it out on one another.

I knew I was lucky. Lucky that I was being raised by two rebel unicorns who wanted to be different than their parents had been. I never took that for granted—on God, I loved my family so, so much.

"I love you. Your mama loves you." She shook her head and breathed again. "I can understand how you would think Dr. Skinner wasn't trying to help. I don't judge, but that man sins Monday through Saturday and is in the front pew in church on Sunday. We want what's best for you and it would be wrong if we didn't do something to help."

I almost laughed.

"Help me with what? Medical problems that I don't have? If that's the case, why aren't you talking to Winston? He doesn't exercise, eats more than I do, and considers Pepsi and Doritos to be major food groups, but he's skinny so I guess it's fine. Don't you see what you're doing? How unfair it is?"

"We're not talking about Winston. We're talking about how we can help you to—"

"Right." I stood up. The shift in my mood hit me like an adrenaline rush—heart pounding, hands shaking, and an added hot flash for rage-tinted funsies. Being soft, being open and honest hadn't worked. I'd wasted all of that time being vulnerable only to go back to square one. "Okay, I can feel this isn't going to end well right now, so I'm going to go. I love you. Thanks for listening."

"Don't walk away from me. Sit down."

"No. I don't want to yell at you, but I'm frustrated and I'm going to lose my temper if you keep on. Just let me chill for a minute. Please."

Twenty-Two

My fury refused to leave.

I locked myself in my room, hands fisted in my top blanket, staring at the slats underneath the top bunk until my eyes unfocused and crossed. I had to stay still and stay away from everyone. I'd attack the first thing to look at me. Tear into them with unrepentant glee. I hated that about myself almost as much as I loved it. The ballooning feeling of my anger. The way it fit and molded itself into every nook and cranny I had inside of me.

Not even Kara would be safe.

Winston knocked on the door about an hour into my self-imposed isolation, asking if I was still taking the deliveries.

"No."

I had never missed a shift at Goldeen's. Even in the summer, if I had caught a cold, I had sat in the back office doing paperwork to help out in some way. Today I had missed not one, but two.

Winston didn't ask why or if I was okay. But he did knock three times on the door—our code for when one of us had passed the point of all sibling help.

I'm. With. You.

I didn't want to move. I didn't want to leave.

Unfortunately, when six thirty rolled around, my crown and I had somewhere to be.

Second Street Food and Wine Tasting. Our first Royal Engagement.

Dallas took one look at me before pulling me to the side. "Are you okay?"

"No."

He nodded, eyes never leaving my face. He had the deepest wrinkle of concern between his perfect eyebrows. "Tonight is really easy. I'll do all of the talking; you can stand there and be pretty. Maybe a little less ragey? I think there might be a few children out there."

I scoffed. "No promises."

"Understandable." He smiled, tilting his head to the side—his art appreciation stance. "Your angry face is actually pretty cute. I like it."

"Are you trying to make me laugh?"

"Not a chance." He winked. "You okay with touching?"

He remembered. Surprise slashed straight through my turbulent anger. When he had come to the diner, he had steered the conversation. I never got to explain my side of what happened at the photo shoot.

But he remembered *and* he asked. I wanted to thank him, to show him how much I appreciated his thoughtfulness, but all I could manage was, "I don't know," because I still didn't trust my mouth to be civil.

"We'll keep it PG, then." He stood next to me, one hand hovering near my lower back, leaned in close, and whispered, "Five minutes. Not a millisecond more. I promise."

We walked together to the small stage, where a band had already set up. He stood directly in front of the mic, me slightly off to the side. His crown glinted in the rapidly dwindling sunlight. He looked like the kind of king that would star in a racebent historical drama. Unfit for the throne because of a glut of kindness, but eager and ready to learn how to rule.

"Can I have your attention please? Hello?"

The small crowd near the stage quieted, but he didn't have the attention of everyone present.

"Hi. I'm Dallas. The Merry Summer King." He turned to me. "And this incandescent beauty, Winnie, first of her name, courageous and unchallenged, quick in thought and sly of tongue, holder of a laugh that can make the angels weep in envy, is my Misty Summer Queen."

"You showboating jackhole." The words, ugly and unwarranted, ripped out of me before I could stop them. But the crowd laughed and so did he.

"She's a bit more reserved with her compliments for me." He nudged me closer. "Needless to say, my queen and I have been getting along brilliantly. Communicating, playfully insulting each other, plotting world domination, conducting interrogations masquerading as twenty questions, as is the way. Tonight is pretty special. It's our first official date—ah, please, applause isn't necessary—and we decided to share our night with you. There are a few rules for the Food and Wine Tasting, of course. Number one being leave us the hell alone."

The crowd laughed again. Dallas continued, "Vultures all of you." More laughter. "Second rule, please do not provide alcohol to minors unless they're your own children, in which case they will need to remain with you at all times and you will then be responsible for their hangovers."

Dallas continued on, listing each rule he must have memorized, his jokes landing every time. Watching him, I'd almost forgotten about my anger. He knew I would snap at his over-the-top introduction and everyone would laugh. He had called them vultures and probably meant it, but they thought he didn't. The crowd, which had grown substantially in less than two minutes, was loving every second of this.

Speech ended, we walked off the stage. "Have I impressed you yet?"

"You are diabolical. I like it."

"I thought you might. How do you feel about pizza?" A few steps to our right, a vendor sold fresh slices.

"I feel just fine about it. Can't eat it. I'm gluten intolerant."

"For real? That sucks. Almost everything here is wheat-based." He scanned the carts. "Gelato?"

"Sure."

We picked the same flavor, lavender, for the same reason: to see if it was as gross as it sounded and to suffer through an entire cup together if it was.

"Holy God, this is amazing." He looked to me for confirmation. I waited to try it, letting him go first. "I honestly expected it to taste like perfume."

"I did, too. That was exactly what popped into my head when I saw it."

The crowd thinned out toward the end of the street, so we headed that way. According to the Royalty Rules, we were supposed to mingle and take pictures with everyone. People said hi to us, smiled, and shouted congrats, but no one stopped us per Dallas's decree.

"Do you want to talk about why you were so mad? I'm a good listener if you need one."

"Just stuff with my granny."

"Are you two close?"

"Relatively." I snapped my fingers into a finger-gun aimed at him. "Pun point for me."

He laughed. "Cute."

"It's a game me and my friends play. It's kind of like that old show *Whose Line?* where the points don't matter."

"Cool."

A wild bench appeared. The same one he'd found me at a few days ago. My subconscious must have led me to it whenever I was mad at Granny.

Behind us, the band began to play soft rock, the singer crooning with his voice the same way Kenny G did with his various saxophones. My uncle loved Kenny G and always played his music in the car. I think he must have grown up constantly defending why he liked Kenny G so much, because he always said, "That white boy can *play*. I'm telling you, he got soul. Respect him" when I tried to change the music.

I needed to talk to my parents. I'm sure Granny had already called them again, telling on me for being *combative* again. They'd probably take something away from me this time. After leaving Haven Central, I'd have two weeks at home before moving for school. I'd most likely have to spend all of that time in the house on punishment.

Dallas gently pressed his index finger against the back of my hand, drawing my attention. "You zoned out there for a second."

"That happens. I've got a lot on my mind."

"Is it me?" He sounded playful, flirty. Fitting, since he had dubbed the night our first date.

I smiled at him, unmoved by his charming grin. "You're in there. Like way, way in the back. A distant speck on the horizon of my consciousness."

"*Ouch.* I'm sitting right here."

"Guess you're not nearly as captivating as you think you are."

He didn't answer right away, but when he did the smile was gone and his voice had gone deeper. "Give me time."

"No." I didn't like games like this either. Flirting for sport wasn't fun to me.

"If I can't have time, then what can I have?"

"Nothing. Why should I let you have anything?"

Dallas turned his body to face me. He leaned on one arm, draped across the back of the bench. "Because you want to."

"And what makes you think you know what I want?"

"Because I want the same thing. Like attracts like."

"Oh, is that how that works? I had no idea. So what is it that *we* want? Enlighten me."

"Easy. To talk. To get to know each other—find out what we have in common, what we don't." He paused so long I thought he'd finished, but then he added, "To be friends."

My smile froze in response to his astounding confidence. "And here I thought your psychic powers were only fashion-related."

"I'm a man of many talents. Let me be your confessional tonight. I want to help."

"Why do you even care? It's nothing."

"Because I like you."

"You already said that."

"And I'm saying it again because it feels like you don't believe me."

"I believe you." But did I trust him? What happened with Granny wasn't a small thing. Baring my soul to him, on technically our second night of friendship, didn't feel like a good idea.

"How about this? You only tell me the parts you're comfortable with me knowing and skim over the rest. You could also vaguely summarize what happened so I'll only get the gist of it. Just enough to help."

That didn't sound too bad. "We need a code first. Since we're still bright and shiny, we should have something we can say that means it's private. It stays between us."

"Do you have a code with Kara?"

"I know her well enough to not need one."

"Ah. Okay then. How about *gelato*? In honor of tonight."

"Gelato." I nodded, taking another bite of mine. I hadn't eaten all day, but my stupid emotions were in control of things they shouldn't have been, so I still didn't feel hungry. "Do you ever feel like people don't listen to you on purpose? My granny does that. It's like she refuses to."

Someone like Dallas probably wouldn't understand. People loved him. He was a boy. He was good looking. He was popular. He could call a town meeting solely to read the *Haven Herald* from cover to cover and people would line up to see him.

I knew I shouldn't have judged him like that, but there wasn't exactly any evidence pointing to an alternative. It wasn't his fault that his voice and face and gender would always be valued more than mine, but a good-sized chunk of me resented him for it anyway.

"Refuses as in you're a kid and she's an adult, or refuses as in she doesn't *want* to hear you?"

"Both. I might get frustrated or angry, but I'm pretty good at getting my point across. And yet when I start talking, it's like people suddenly lose all of their comprehension skills. Then they start talking, repeating their point that I'd already refuted, like saying it again is going to make me change my mind. It drives me up a wall when people do that. We go in circles for no reason. I wish there was a way I could just make them *listen* and *understand* before they push me too far and I snap."

"They hear us." Dallas stressed the last word. "But they don't want to acknowledge it, because they're right and we're wrong. They're older and they know better. Do it their way, wait and see, everything will be perfect because they know what's best for us."

I nodded, eagerly turning toward him now, speaking too fast. "She was being completely unfair, refused to admit it, *and* still kept trying to push what she wanted onto me. I was literally shaking, I was so mad."

"I don't even get mad anymore when my dad gets like that. I shut down. I don't feel anything." He tapped his chest. "Completely dead in there."

"For real? That's harsh."

"No." But his sardonic smile said otherwise.

"I definitely don't feel dead inside, but I did get really sad for a while. I didn't have anybody to talk to about what happened because then I'd have to explain, and I just feel it in my bones that they would agree with her and I super could not deal with hearing it. The anger swooped right back on in after that."

"I get it. We handle the same problem differently, but I definitely get it. We react the way we do because otherwise we would feel helpless. Being angry, feeling nothing has to be better than that, right? Because if they see us give up or be too vulnerable, then they'll think they've won and keep doing it until they break us down."

"Yes. *Yes.* We're fighting for them to hear and see us, but they don't think it's a fight. It's us being disobedient or hardheaded."

"And we deserved to be punished for it. Yeah."

I hadn't been able to relate to someone this quickly since—since Kara, if I'm being honest. I felt so seen, *wow.* He understood as if we shared a brain. My ego had limits. I knew when to admit I was wrong.

"Thank you. I honestly never would've thought that you'd gone through something like this, too." I smiled at him. "Oh, and I'm sorry I called you a showboating jackhole. I didn't mean it."

"Apology accepted." He smiled back. "I'd ask why you thought that, but I don't want to know. Wanna keep you perfect for as long as I can."

"That's not alarming or anything."

"It'll pass. I'm sure the real you is better than the idea I've been holding on to for three years."

Three years!? He'd wanted to be friends for three years?

He raised his gelato cup. "I know you have Kara but you can have me to, if you want. You can call me whenever."

"Call. *Ehhhh.*"

"I mean it. I'm a dial tone away. If you use a landline, which you probably wouldn't, so never mind."

I laughed, feeling good for the first time that day, and clinked my cup against his.

Twenty-Three

Having a bonfire on a bookstore rooftop didn't seem like the brightest idea. But the Alviar family had done it for years, and according to Kara, they had an amazing insurance policy.

The trick to an epic rooftop barbecue was in the ratio of lighter fluid and wood to summer sunset. Hopefully the sun, bathing the cloudless sky in bright oranges with hints of deep purples, would take the unbearably hot weather along for the ride as it set, because it was still too hot to get close to the fire.

Cookouts required marshmallow roasting. It was the law and I didn't make the rules. I selectively chose which ones I followed. Like that one.

I lounged on a deck chair under the divine shade of a beach umbrella angled just right. I didn't really care about looking at sunsets. Seen one, seen them all, really. Junie sat next to me, a huge bag of all-pink Starbursts on her stomach for easier access, while her boyfriend sat near her feet reading a book. Sam had claimed my other side, wearing my crown again. She kept taking selfies of herself, asking me to help pick the best ones, which I did because that was the way of things.

Winston stood at the grill with Kara's parents. "Supervising," he said. Wanting to take over was more like it. My Young Chef had been getting bolder by the day, making me so proud it almost covered up my embarrassment at missing his passion for cooking in the first place. Pretty soon he'd start asking for shifts *without* Aaron.

Only Kara sat alone, sitting on a bench off in the corner. I'd been trying to work up enough nerve to go talk to her. I'd never had to do that before. Not even when we'd first met.

Five years ago, I wished on a star.

Not for anything special—just a total kid move of wasting the universe's time by asking for a boyfriend because Sam had one. The day after I made that wish, Kara had walked into Goldeen's. I liked remembering that moment because I felt like the universe took it upon itself to look deep inside me, yell, "SURPRISE! YOU'RE QUEER!" and granted my wish in an unexpected way.

Side note: my parents really did not like the word *queer*. My dad had said, "Don't say that." My mom had said, "What does that mean? I don't like that word."

I didn't fit in one perfect little box. Boys? Check. Girls? Check. Did gender really matter to me? Eh, probably not. Calling myself queer felt like standing under a kind stranger's umbrella in an unexpected rainstorm. I might not use it forever, but at the moment, it was exactly what I needed.

I swung my legs to the side, standing up.

"Be brave, Chicken Little." Junie's way of being supportive. She must have known why Kara had chosen to mope in the corner instead of hanging out with us. But if Kara had told *Junie*, she must have been desperate for someone to talk to.

This was bad. Catastrophic and soul-destroying bad. She never told Junie *anything*.

I sat down next to Kara on the wooden bench with the peeling and faded hot-pink paint. She didn't say anything, didn't even look at me. The corner we were in provided one of the best views in Misty Haven. Everything perfectly circular and laid out.

"Not to be that person, but silent treatments are against our rules."

We had three unbreakable rules: no secrets, no hiding, and no overwrought miscommunication plotlines.

"I'm not giving you a silent treatment. I'm just sad. I'm allowed to be sad." Her voice sounded raw and tender like she'd been crying. But her eyes and face weren't as red as they normally got when she was upset.

"Do you want to talk about it?"

"No." She chewed on her lip, face contorted into a frown so full of sorrow, I began to panic. "I feel like I have to, though."

"You don't. Not right now or ever—I would hope one day you would trust me enough to tell me, but I'd understand. I get sad like that, too, sometimes, where I feel like I should tell someone but I can't."

I needed to know. I wanted to know so badly, I'd probably sell my soul. I had to fix it. I had to make whatever was hurting her stop. We sat so close, thighs and arms and shoulders touching, whispering around the hurt that had driven itself between us. But the most important thing? Be there for Kara in the ways that *she* wanted and needed.

Deciding to be with Kara had been the most adult thing I'd ever done so far. It wasn't some fragile commitment built on hopes and dreams and rainbows. Or false high school promises that would break once we graduated. No, when we decided to do this, I made a commitment to her and to myself. I decided I *was* emotionally mature enough to be in a committed relationship with my friend. When my heart said one thing and my brain said another, both sentences ended with the same name: *Kara*.

That was enough for me to say yes.

We would talk, be honest about our feelings, plan our future, and not let it be weird. We wouldn't tolerate outsiders judging us and trying to mold us into what they wanted to see, what they thought we should be.

Kara inhaled, a deep, shuddering breath, and lifted her face toward the sky. She closed her eyes. "It wasn't supposed to be like this."

"What wasn't?" I whispered, looking over our shoulders. No one paid attention to us, and if they were, they hid it well. "Whatever it is, I swear you can tell me, Kara." I took her hand. "We come first."

"Do we?" She turned her burning gaze on me.

"Yes. That's the rule."

Whatever the truth was, no matter how angry or sad it made me, I would give her a chance. We would work through it because that was the promise we made to each other.

"What did he tell you?"

Dallas. "Did you really ask him to stay away from me?"

"Yes."

"*Why?* When?" His personality fit mine well. Kara and I tended to like the same people. From everything I'd learned about him so far, he would fit right in with us. It didn't make any sense.

"He owed me a future favor. Lacey likes to take things that don't belong to her. I recorded her shoplifting in Nina's, and instead of turning her in, we made a deal."

"You made a deal with Lacey?"

"And Dallas. He was there." She wiped at her face, at tears that hadn't fallen.

"What did you do with the video?"

Surprisingly, she laughed. "You would care about that."

I smiled back. "Hey, a deal's a deal."

"I didn't do anything with it. I never planned to. I was just messing with them." Her somber mood returned. "I think it must have started last year when his mom had those weekly parties leading up to her fortieth birthday and kept ordering food from Goldeen's."

"I did most of those deliveries," I said, understanding what she meant.

"After you left, that school year he started asking me about you. How you were. Things you liked. The exact date you were coming back. If he could have your phone number. So I used my future favor and he dropped it."

What. The. Fuck.

I had to stay calm. I had to breathe. Calm. Breathe. COUNT.

I promised. I promised that no matter what it was I wouldn't react . . .

. . . but I never thought it would be that! Dallas wasn't lying! She really did try to blackmail him into staying away from me. That's like Abuser 101.

Breathe. Count. Breathe. Count.

I nodded as I processed my next words, because I would keep my goddamn promise even if what I said next wasn't the whole uncensored truth. "So, just for the sake of saying it, because I'm sure you've realized this by now, but blackmailing people to keep them away from me is wrong and extremely fucked up. If you *ever* do some shit like that again, we're going to have a serious problem."

"I know." She bowed her head.

"Like we will *break up* serious problem. We don't treat each other like that. *Ever.*"

"I don't know what I was thinking. I just—but then, this year, right before you got here, out of nowhere, he asked me if I'd been serious that day. And I told him I was, but then he volunteered anyway, and then I knew you would find out what I did and you would hate me."

"I don't hate you. I'm not happy and that is the *mildest* way I can put that right now."

"I know."

"But I know you and I don't think you would've done that without a good reason. So, in the spirit of moving forward because I'm *choosing* that that's where we're at right now, is there something wrong with him? Some reason why you don't want him around me?"

She looked at me, eyes full of remorse—and something else. "You didn't even look for me, did you?"

"What?"

"At the wine tasting. I was there like I said I would be."

I sucked in a horrified breath. "*Oh my God I am so sorry.*"

"Thought so."

"I didn't—I mean, I wasn't thinking at all. I got into another fight with Granny and I was so mad, I just wanted to get through it, and then Dallas—"

"Yes, please tell me more about him, that's exactly what I want to hear right now."

Holy God, how had I messed up so badly? I hadn't just forgotten about her—I spent time with the one person she tried to keep away from me *while* forgetting that she promised to show up somewhere to support *me*. I'd never done anything like this to her. I'd always been so careful and aware of her and us. And how could I have let that happen?

What Kara had done was borderline unforgivable, but if this

wasn't the greatest example of two wrongs not making anything close to right, I didn't know what else could possibly top it.

"I'm sorry. I am so deeply and intensely sorry, Kara. I don't have any excuses for what I did. You told me you would be there, I forgot, and I am sorry."

"I hate your apologies. They're always too good."

"Because I mean them. I did a stupid, terrible thing and I shouldn't have."

Tears filled her eyes. "I don't deserve you" was all she said.

Twenty-Four

I loved clocking in at Goldeen's. Granny still used an old-fashioned punch card system. My name had been printed in purple ink on the long edge of the beige card. You pushed the entire card into the top slot, then waited for it to make a whirring noise and a beep before removing it. The time stamps used blue ink.

Winston zipped past me, carrying two heads of cabbage. "Three trips today. Car is loaded up for the first one. Kara is out front."

My afternoon deliveries wouldn't take longer than an hour, maybe two. Kara joined me every now and then, wearing what she dubbed her unofficial Goldeen's uniform. We weren't okay. I still couldn't believe that she'd done something so extreme over something so trivial. It honestly scared the hell out of me. I didn't want to be afraid of Kara, nervous of making and having friends besides her, terrified to hell her I'd found someone *in addition to*.

Would she be able to handle it?

I'd thought about it after I'd gone home. Everyone made mistakes in relationships—marriage counseling was a billion-dollar industry according to Google. Even my parents went to counseling regularly.

On my end, I had to decide if what she'd done had been unforgivable because I realized she never actually apologized to me. Was she sorry?

Would she do it again?

My heart said no, of course not, it's Kara.

My brain said . . . maybe, but it's Kara.

Kara.

We needed to spend more time together. We needed to heal. For us that meant close proximity. It meant talking about things out loud, as soon as we felt them.

She had broken our unbreakable rules. I was willing to try to reforge them together.

"Thanks." I triple-knot tied my apron while walking to the main floor.

Kara stood near the front door with Sam, Granny, and Mr. Livingston. Her dress with horizontal rainbow stripes shimmered in the light even as she stood still. Miss Jepson had offered to make a knock-off Goldeen's dress for her, but she preferred to always wear that one and an apron.

I wanted to yell for her to meet me out back. Anything over walking toward that group.

"Good afternoon, Miss Winnie." Mr. Livingston said everything at a rumble. It was like the bass dropped inside of him and kept on falling. He looked handsome, in an old-guy grandpa sort of way, with his navy suit, shiny brown shoes, and hair slicked into waves. I had bought him the plaid tie he wore, greenish-blue with hints of brown, as a peace offering for possibly maybe reacting like a brat when he started dating Granny.

"Hey."

They all stared at us—me looking at nothing and everything.

Granny fiddling with her bracelet. She'd stopped talking to me again. And while my anger decided to take a catnap, my mouth refused to even form the word "apologize" because I had *nothing* to apologize for. I was tired of being the one who always had to compromise and try to make it "right" so she'd be happy. If she never talked to me again, then that was her problem.

"So." Sam's optimistic tone refused to read the room. "Are you guys going to the boat thingy today?"

Mr. Livingston laughed. "Yes, we're going to watch the Sailors' Promenade."

"Don't keep her out too late, and if she doesn't come back with salt-smelling, windswept hair and a giant smile on her face, you answer to me."

"*Sam.*" Granny playfully swatted her arm. "Behave, young lady."

"I am. I'm doing my granddaughterly duty." She winked at me quickly, proud to fill the role I'd left vacant, because that was 100 percent something I would've said. But it was cute when she did it, earning a smile and a surprise laugh from Granny.

Funny how my jokes and my snarky punchlines were suddenly okay when they came out of Sam's mouth. Granny would have told me, "Mind your business."

"Geraldine, we should get on the road or we won't get good seats."

"All right. Don't rush me, now." She swatted at him, too. "I'll be back after dinner. I told Aaron to make you something—"

"We can fend for ourselves, you know." Sam smiled.

"All right, all right. Call me if you need anything."

I resisted the urge to roll my eyes, because I knew if I had said that, she would have never let it slide.

After they were in the car, pulling out of the parking lot, Kara said, "I love the smell of unfair treatment in the afternoon."

"I think that went well." Of course Sam did. Of course. "You guys didn't fight or anything."

"But they didn't talk either. Not a hello or a good-bye." Kara hugged me at the waist, staring up at me. "I think it's time for a karaoke party."

Granny knew I touched her precious radio and changed the music on a daily basis. She probably still didn't know about the karaoke parties. I turned the music up super loud and worked the floor like I was in the middle of a number from a Broadway musical—lip-syncing and using the song's original choreography—while still doing my job. Customers loved it. Everyone on shift sans Aaron usually joined in.

I had gotten the idea from that diner in New York where all the staff sings. At best, I could warble on key but I had the singing spirit. One day, maybe, when I owned my own diner, it'd probably have a theme built around my karaoke parties.

"Or not." Sam's eyes widened. "Or really, really not. She's already mad, and if someone tells her—"

"It'll be fine." Kara waved her away. "We should have time for one song, right? Yes or yes?"

I grinned down at her. "Yes."

In about six hours, I would intensely regret watching movies instead of taking a nap. Sam, Kara, Winston, and I lay around the living room after dinner. I had stood up, ready to pass out, but then Kara made puppy-dog eyes at me.

I was trash for Kara's puppy-dog eyes and pouty lips. Even when I wasn't sure what would become of us.

Granny came home when the movie was about half over. She took one look at us, laughed affectionately, and then went to bed. She never joined us. When I tried to convince Kara to keep the party going and hang out with me during my shift, she ditched me.

"I love you, but I also love not being grounded because I didn't tell my parents I was here. Rain check?"

So I ended up alone with a running day staring me down in five hours.

Why did I volunteer to do this again?

I knew I was strong, conditioned to handle more than most, but times like these I felt stretched too thin. Shifts to work, people to please, silent-treatment wars to fight, crowns to uphold, laps to *jog*, ungirlfriend relationships to rebuild—

And for the record, I'd like to point out that the Starlight competition would not have been *too* much. Apart from shopping and experimenting with different recipes, Kara hadn't done jack else for that contest.

My phone buzzed. An unknown number appeared on the screen. I'd sooner poke myself in the eyes than voluntarily answer my phone if I didn't know who it was, but it had a Haven Central area code.

"Um, hello?"

"Hi."

Hearing his voice made my heart stutter. "*Hi.*" I tried to clear away the squeak that I'd suddenly developed, to say something else. He beat me to it.

"Is this a bad time? Or too late? I figured you might be working."

Oh my God. He didn't do that thing when the caller asked for you even though they recognized your voice. Or said their name even though you knew it was them thanks to caller ID.

"No, no, it's fine. Guess you weren't kidding about that no texting thing, huh?"

"I could try. This feels more comfortable for me. Is it okay?" Dallas's phone voice had quickly scaled the mountain of my favorite sounds. Less than a mile below Kara on the phone now. "Also, I kind of wanted to hear your voice."

I giggled. *Giggled.* Jesus, just take me out to pasture. "Uh, sorry. Aaron just made a face at me as he was leaving. Hold on." I was so alone in the empty diner, I could make it echo if I wanted. I pretended to place him on mute and waited ten seconds to regain my dignity. "So. Hi."

He laughed. "So. You're at work."

"I am."

"I was going to visit instead of calling. Coincidentally, I also kind of missed your face, but I didn't know if you worked every night or not."

"Um, is there a reason why you keep saying stuff like that?"

"It's not okay to say I missed you?"

"It is. It's just—I don't know. It's fine. I'm being weird."

"I won't say it if it makes you uncomfortable."

"No, it's fine. Friends can totally miss friends and tell them so."

"Cool." He exhaled loud enough for me to hear it. "Anyway, I also called because we didn't go over our Royal Engagement schedule. I wanted to show it to you, but you were upset and that seemed more important."

"Only the tiniest bit."

"I'll send the calendar to you. We're supposed to make a sincere effort. *Sincere effort.* Shelley said that like five times. Pretty sure if we don't show up in our crowns, she'll hunt us down like Liam Neeson in one of his movies, and drag us there kicking and screaming."

My phone beeped in my ear. Incoming message. I placed him on speakerphone to open the file. "Whoa." The PDF calendar had all the activities each town would have for the next two months laid out in color-coordinated glory. "*Have Fun With Your Phone?* What the hell even is that? I'm not going to that."

"It's not set in stone. If one of us has to work or something important comes up, we don't have to go to the event. When do you work? Do you cook at Goldeen's?"

"No, that's Winston. He lives in the kitchen. I work the floor, so anything before noon is out for me. I also work a couple of hours at midnight, like now, six days a week, and I like to take a nap at some point during the day. My deliveries are flexible. JR could always take them for me. You?"

"Tutoring in the morning. That's my only actual obligation."

"You're a tutor?" I wished I could have hidden how shocked I had sounded.

"Yep. Math."

During his silence, I got the distinct feeling that my reaction was all too common. "Is it a volunteer thing? Something to make your college apps look better and then you got stuck doing it?"

"No. They pay me. I don't work for free."

My surprised bark-laugh did indeed echo in the diner.

"Any conflicts with the schedule for tomorrow?"

I checked. "Don't think so."

"See you then?"

"Yep. With crowns on. Yeah, that pun didn't work."

He laughed. "Or I could see you now. Up for company?"

"You don't have to. I mean, if you *want* to you can. But you don't have to."

The line went silent. I held my breath to hear better, which was kind of ridiculous, and yet.

"I'll be there in fifteen."

Twenty-Five

Five. Five. Five.

Walk. Jog. Walk.

There was a pizza slogan somewhere in there. Whoever had made the running program must have had a sense of humor.

And was also a probable sadist, because my legs hurt something fierce.

Every time I squatted to get something out of the fridge, freezer, lower shelves, I had zero idea if I'd be able to stand back up until I did it. Sam's plan should have come with warnings.

Stretching before probably won't help you.

Surprise! Your knee is going to pop!

The floor is gonna be your new bff :)

"Winnie, what are you doing in here?" Granny asked.

In one heaving move, I pulled myself to an upright position and stretched my lips into what I hoped was a smile to hide all of the internal screaming going on.

"I've been sent to retrieve beets—nature's dirt candy." Nothing against beets, but they really did taste like sweetened dirt.

"I want you in the kitchen. Winston is demanding a turn to cook on his own without Aaron, so I want you to watch him. He gets one hour alone. Not a second more, you hear me?"

"Where's Aaron going to be?"

"Home, I presume. He thinks Winston can handle it."

"And you don't?"

She gave me a withering look. "He's still fourteen."

Right. Never mind the fact that when I was fourteen, I could do every single job this diner had to offer blindfolded.

"I'll watch him."

"Thank you." She adjusted her purse on her arm. "I'm off. The girls and I are gonna head up to the outlets. Maybe check out that new seafood restaurant while we're up there."

Even while on an unofficial staycation, Granny always kept an eye on the competition.

I collected my beets into green grocer bags for easier transport and dumped them on the prep table before dragging a stool over to sit on. "*Yello*, little brother." Sitting down, I rested my chin in my hands.

"I don't need to be watched." He kept his back to me as he flipped five of the sizzling burgers on the grill. As always with hamburgers, the kitchen began to fill with smoke from the grease popping in the fire. Goldeen's didn't microwave or fry them on a stove top. It had taken an Act of Aaron to finally get Granny to agree to switch from charcoal to propane earlier in the year.

"I'm not watching. I'm here for reinforcements if a large order comes through."

He glared at me over his shoulder. "I'm shocked she even asked you."

I shrugged. "Time was up." If the silent treatment didn't escalate within a certain time frame, let's say under seventy-two hours, by either me apologizing or doing something worse, her grudge weakened. She might not talk to me right away, like today, but she'd get around to it.

Goldeen's had transitioned from passing paper tickets through the kitchen window to digital orders two summers ago. I had spearheaded the project. The servers entered the orders on one of two tablets behind the counter. Winston received them on one screen and marked them as up on another through the kitchen tablets. He favored using his pinky for the screens, which was just too adorable.

"When were you going to tell me you liked cooking?"

He moved seamlessly through the kitchen, from the window to the screen to the cooking area. "Later, I guess."

"Is it something you like to do for fun or is it more serious than that?"

"Why?"

"Just asking. I always thought you'd go into film and someday we would make Win-Win Productions. That's all."

That earned me a rare smile. "We still can. We don't have to do just one thing."

"Very true."

He placed each cooked burger on their respective plates, carefully and efficiently piling the chosen toppings into a picturesque tower. "Now, that's a burger."

I laughed. "Don't let Aaron hear you."

He sucked on his teeth. "Two years. Two years and I'll be better than him. Watch."

"I believe it."

It should have been boring watching him. I should have started to nod off, neck bending forward when I lost the fight against consciousness and gravity, eyes drifting closed because I was honest-to-God exhausted. Watching my brother cook was anything but that.

Music played softly and he hummed along to it. He stayed focused and mindful of his hands and cross contamination. The fries were golden and crunchy, never charred and ready to poof into dust; his salads looked like works of art with the food placed in spiraled designs and layered just right; his eggs were fluffy and his milkshakes were the perfect consistency. All of his dishes turned out precise and preternaturally perfect.

If Kara was a mad scientist in the kitchen, then Winston was a brain surgeon. Two sides of the same coin, Dr. Winston Jekyll and Ms. Kara Hyde.

Aaron arrived exactly sixty minutes after he had left. He tried to hide the worried look on his face as he darted through the door, but I saw it. "Everything all right?"

"He did great. You should leave him alone more often."

Another smile from Winston. He briefed Aaron on what he'd done, where he stopped, and then switched places with him for a break.

"Hungry? I'll make you a sandwich." We headed up the stairs together, Winston trailing behind me.

"Sure." He paused. "Would you really go into business with me?"

"The fact that you even have to ask that insults me."

Once in the kitchen, he sat at the table while I got started making his lunch.

"I guess I thought you'd leave me behind once you left for college."

"What made you think a stupid thing like that?"

"Sam. She said you were gonna leave her first then me. I know it's stupid—stop looking at me like that. You're gonna be busy with school and working and Kara, and it made sense that you wouldn't have time for me anymore because you'll be so far away."

"You both are ridiculous. My life is like that now. Have I *ever* left you behind? Excluded you from anything I do?"

"No." He shook his head, tapping the table with his thumb. "I'm sorry I got mad about the Starlight contest. I don't know why I didn't tell you. I should have."

"There'll be other contests, but in the meantime, want to help me help Kara for this one? I'm sure she'd be willing to share some of her expertise with you."

"You think so? I've been thinking about asking her to teach me some stuff."

"Winston, if you did that, it would make her whole life."

"Are you guys okay? It seemed kind of tense between you the other day."

"We're fine." I set the plate down and he gave me a disbelieving look. "We're working on being okay."

"Is it because of that guy?"

"Dallas."

"That guy."

I laughed. "Don't be like that."

"Like what?"

"You know. He's nice. I think you'd like him. Chips?" I held up the bag.

"Yeah. I don't like anyone. Especially not someone you're supposed to marry."

"I am not marrying Dallas!" I flicked him before taking the seat next to him. "And no, it's not *because* of him. It's just something that we have to work through right now. That's all."

❧

This speaking in front of a large crowd thing was getting super old superfast. Once again, Dallas took the lead, this time partially standing in front of me as he introduced the first act for the Haven Central Day Camp Talent Show: Margo and her puppy-lion, Foster!

Summer Saturday nights were not meant to be spent doing this. I had invited Kara to come along, a first step toward building a bridge between her and Dallas so I could stop flailing alone in the water. She had turned me down when I told her it was a talent show.

"Ehhhh, that's not my scene. Rain check?"

Rain check had potential. Rain check meant the answer wasn't no, just later. I fully planned to cash that sucker in soon.

The packed auditorium began to smell a bit too ripe to my nose and ultrasensitive stomach once they closed the doors. Parents had their cameras out. Siblings pouted in their seats. The judges, stationed in the front row, had their clipboards and scoring sheets at the ready. And the event was scheduled to last three hours. We had to stay for the whole thing to host it.

We walked offstage and away from the many eyes watching us, but my lungs wouldn't loosen. My palms tingled something awful, too.

"I really don't like this. Why couldn't we have something like knitting club scheduled?"

"We do. Next week."

"Oh Jesus." I wiped my damp hand across my damp forehead and leaned against the wall, bending as far as I could at the knee before my thighs started to protest. Running in the morning was wreaking havoc on my body. Muscles I didn't even know existed had woken up screaming bloody murder.

"What's going on? Talk to me."

I squinted up at him. "This is as close as I can get to placing my head between my knees. It helps. Somewhat."

He frowned for a moment before looking horrified. "*Oh*. I'll get some water."

The next time I opened my eyes, he knelt next to me, face

inches from mine. The perfect kissing distance at the absolute worst moment. "Is your stage fright really that bad?"

I took the water bottle he offered. "On occasion."

"You seemed fine at the wine tasting."

"Rage will do that." I either had to go up or down—my thigh muscles wouldn't last much longer. The floor looked clean enough, so I sat, legs tucked to the side, and kept my back flush with the wall. Dallas sat next to me, still close and attentive, as if I would pass out any second. "I don't do well with the whole being the center of attention thing if I'm not allegedly yelling. My fight-or-flight response is always turned up to eleven. There is no middle ground with me." I frowned at him. "It hurt to admit that. I'm not doing it again."

"Doing what? Telling the truth?"

"Exposing myself. It's gross."

"I told you, you don't have to tell me anything you don't want to." He must have had a rare gene that turned sincerity into a pheromone. It practically came out of his pores every time he looked at me like that—eyes a combination of amused and understanding. "Just be up front. 'Hey, Dallas. I'm uncomfortable. Can we not?' Simple."

"And you won't ask questions?"

"Maybe one or two. 'Hey, Dallas. I can't tell you what's going on. Please help me.' I'm pretty easygoing." His shoulders touched his ears as he held on to an unreleased shrug, a smile tugging at his lips. "And, you know, I like you. So."

Margo and her amazing puppy-lion had finished their act. The crowd cheered as she bowed.

Dallas squeezed my hand. "Stay here for the next one. I have a surprise for you. I was going to give it to you later but I think it might make you feel better now."

He high-fived Margo, told another joke to the crowd, and introduced the next act: the Lamb Boys, who had decided to form a prepubescent lip-syncing boy band. I watched them, fairly positive they'd win this whole charade because the dancing was rather impressive—I recognized my fellow YouTube University alums when they crossed my path—while Dallas ran off to get his surprise.

Hearing Dallas say that he liked me hadn't lost its shiny newness. I'm not sure why he told me quite so often, and it didn't seem to bother him that I had only said it back one time. I wanted to. I don't think it would've hurt anything for me to say it.

But the words just wouldn't come out anymore. Like they physically weren't allowed to leave my body for whatever reason.

Dallas returned, one hand behind his back. "Close your eyes."

"No."

"Fair enough." He grinned. "I brought you flowers."

Sunflowers. Giant sunflowers wrapped in cool, crinkling plastic.

No one had ever given me flowers before. Holding them turned my insides into heartsick mush. Knowing they'd been bought specifically for me smoothed out the frustrated and unhappy bits that wouldn't stop stressing me out. It felt almost silly how special they made me feel.

Suddenly, I understood why my friend kept falling for the Valentine warfare trick. Receiving flowers was something I didn't know that I wanted until it happened. Getting them from Dallas had immediately tipped me over into soft land.

I shook off those feelings and stamped them down as far as I could. Be strong. Stay in control. I had to be straightforward and keep myself from slipping into that place where my wants would become too different from his.

Ask. Don't assume. "Why?"

"Just because. My mom likes to have flowers in the house, so I went to Forget-Me-Nots and bought her some today."

"You buy your mom flowers? That's oddly sweet."

"It's a small thing I can do that makes her happy. Anyway, while I was there, I saw these and they reminded me of you."

"Hmm. I don't know." I stared into their large brown faces as I pulled them close, touching their yellow petals. They didn't smell like anything, not like how roses could overpower all the everything. And they had a general pleasantness to them—subtle and earthy. Such a stark and surprising contrast to their stunning vibrancy. "I'm not really the sunny type. I think I'm more of a moonflower. Or a tulip."

"Maybe those represent exactly how I see you."

"Maybe you see me wrong and I really am a Technicolor tulip but you want me to be a sunflower."

"That's a good point."

"Not that I trust your floral machinations, but this was kind of you." I couldn't look at him. My joke seemed too harsh even as I said it. "I think."

"You're welcome. I think."

The crowd began clapping again. Dallas raised his eyebrows expectantly. "Ready?"

"Not yet?"

"Sure. Be right back."

He left me and my sunflowers to go back to the stage.

How could Kara not like him?

It *bothered* me so much that she couldn't even give him a chance, because if she did she'd see that he could be perfect for us.

Not just me—*us*.

Sometimes it scared me how forcefully I could desire things. That constantly starving, tender ache thrived in the quietest, deepest parts of me. Parts I was terrified to look at in the light and feel in the dark. The bold audacity of my wishes had the unbidden power to overwhelm everything else that made *sense*. But in those seconds right before sleep, I cracked that door open and let those feelings take center stage in my dreams of *maybe* and *what if?*

When I looked at Dallas, smiling onstage in his crown, making everyone laugh and covering for me, I felt like I might finally be ready for more than five minutes.

I might be tired of waiting and playing it safe.

~

Kara (Kara Kara Kara Kara) Chameleon

Kara: Still not talking to your granny

    Winnie: Not not talking. You know how she is

Kara: I mostly know how you are. Life's too short to hold grudges.

Kara: Especially against family

    Winnie: HA! I know you're not trying to lecture me about familial grudges

Kara: That's different. Sisters are supposed to fight

Kara: SHE DESERVES IT YOU KNOW SHE DOES

    Winnie: LMAOOOOOO

    Winnie: Just checking: this isn't a thinly veiled text to gauge my reaction right? I'm not holding a grudge against you.

Kara: I know <3

    Winnie: I want to call my dad but I dunno. He gets super protective of Granny, you know? It feels like a bad idea

Kara: Call your mom then

Winnie: . . . but I want to talk to my
dad. I need help with a thing

Kara: What kind of thing?

Winnie: Ummmmmmm

Kara: ????????

Winnie: It's not something I want to tell
you over text. Can you call me?

Kara: Oh.

Kara: That.

Kara: No.

Winnie: We can't move forward if you
won't at least try to talk to me about this

Kara: I'm not ready

Winnie: . . . but I am.

Kara: This is new to me too. It's easy for you because
you know what you want. There's no one on my side.

Winnie: I'm on your side! How
can you not know that?

Armed with poster boards, magazines, scissors, markers, and a
crapload of stickers, I headed straight to Kara's house.

She wanted to ignore what was happening. I understood that—
sometimes that felt like the best way to handle things.

Before I came out as queer to my parents, we had that whole
unconditional trust thing going on. Their reaction had shaken that
foundation until only straight-up rubble remained. Parents weren't
perfect at all. They messed up, too, but got to pretend like they did so
in the name of parenting because it "didn't come with an instruction
manual" and they were "doing the best they could."

My parents were supposed to be an instruction manual, a living and breathing one who taught me right from wrong and punished me when I kept choosing wrong. So I decided to punish them back. They had chosen wrong that time. I was angry at them for almost a year after and made sure they knew it. But I refused to talk to them, really sit down and say the words, *"What you did really hurt me. I feel like I can't trust you anymore."* Plain. Simple. Truthful.

And then Kara had come to visit me for my birthday.

My mom had seen Kara give me the ring and thought she had proposed to me. Queer had become lesbian faster than I could say, "No. I haven't even graduated yet. Why would I get married right now?"

We had explained our word, ungirlfriend, and all my mom had said was, and I quote, "Oh. That sounds nice."

Later that night, I'd overheard her talking to my dad. He didn't sound angry. They were arguing—but in a bewildered sort of way. "But do you understand it?"

"No! We'll figure it out!"

"I tried to look it up," he said. "I even asked Twitter. No one knows what that means. How are we supposed to support her if we don't know what it is?"

"You didn't see her face. This is important to her. This cannot be like last time. That's your daughter—she's just like you and she's only going to give us so many chances. She has to feel like she can come to us or she'll stop doing it." She huffed. "I just want her to have a better relationship with us than I did with my parents."

"I know, honey. I know." He sighed. "If this is what she feels like she needs, then that's it. The end. We'll ask questions and figure it out later."

Parents messed up, but could learn from their mistakes, too. They just needed a chance.

So did Kara.

And I wasn't ready to give up on her.

Instead of going through the Winter Wonderland Books front door, I used the back steps and let myself in.

"Hello," I called. "It's Winnie."

No answer. Junie worked at a bank a couple of towns over, so I knew she wouldn't have been home. I had assumed Kara's parents would be downstairs and she would be up here. Crossing the kitchen, I went down the first few steps and peeked over the banister.

"You're actually working?"

Kara looked up, not even remotely surprised. "Took you long enough. I saw you skulking around the building on the security camera."

"I do not skulk." I walked down the rest of the stairs and then toward the front counter. "And you could have said something."

"You could have come through the front door."

"Fair." I held up the plastic bag and posters. "I wanted to surprise you."

"With?"

"I thought we could make new vision boards for the dorm." I sat the supplies down. "I even went to the library to find a *National Geographic* magazine that had pictures of Iceland."

That earned me a smile. Iceland—her dream country. Kara wanted to move there even if it was only for six months and take me along for the ride. She began to pick through the bag, grabbing the markers and stickers she wanted.

"Do you want to make them down here?"

"Yeah. My parents went out to lunch and threatened to kick me out of the kitchen for a week if I didn't stay put and on duty while they were gone."

We cleared off the far corner, closest to the back of the store. Part of the reason Kara flew the coop so often? The bookstore didn't really have a steady stream of customers on a daily basis. It did pretty well overall. They held events, did special and online orders, and obviously knew every customer who did eventually come in by name and could find *the* book for them, whatever it was. Winter Wonderland Books was a beloved Haven Central staple.

I sat across from her. We positioned our boards side by side.

"What should we do?" she asked. "College? Career updates? Or just general life stuff?"

A decent-sized chunk of our relationship revolved around goal setting. At first, Kara being so sure about her future freaked me the hell out. Made me feel stupid, lazy, and inadequate. My girl was a little intense. A lot intense. But her certainty had also been infectious.

I wanted to be on her level.

Honestly, I didn't know what I wanted out of life beyond not letting the entirety of my existence flop. Being with Kara helped me realize I could reach for more.

I had decided to major in hospitality in college because I loved working in Goldeen's so much. My little brother had the potential to become a head chef. My ungirlfriend baked liked she'd been born to do it. I knew a sign when I saw one.

The idea of starting my own family-centric restaurant or bed-and-breakfast might be so outlandish that the universe would laugh at me for the next thousand years. I might not ever be able to make it happen. The point, though, was to dream, to believe, to try. And to trust and support each other.

"I think we're overdue for a life check-in. Let's do that."

Kara eyed me for a moment before sighing and picking up a dark green marker.

We needed to at least poke the beast sleeping between us before our relationship devolved into a toxic, radioactive cesspool of hurt and misunderstanding.

If she wasn't willing to work through this, the proper way, then—well, that wasn't something I could make her do. But I would be clear that it was something that I wanted to do. I needed her to know that. Whether it worked out or not, telling my truth, opening that door for her, would be my bottom line. I refused to compromise on that.

In bright blue marker, the same color as the stone in my ring, I wrote *Remember: Life is messy and imperfect. It's okay if you are, too.*

I looked at Kara, who had been watching me write my heading.

"Nobody expects you to be perfect," she said.

"It's just a reminder." I shifted on the stool and cleared my throat. "It's okay to make mistakes even if they hurt people you care about."

Kara turned away, looking off to the side and twirling a piece of hair around her finger.

"Sometimes all you have to do is just *apologize* and it can make a world of reassuring difference."

She began to sort through the stickers, landing on a baking-themed one with pink-and-white anthropomorphic cupcakes. "I panicked. It was a mistake," she said quietly.

"Definitely allowed to make those." I nodded and waited until impatience won. "And?"

"And what? I don't know what you want me to say? That I'm sorry? That I'll never do it again?"

"That would be helpful."

"I don't know if that's true."

My heart skipped a beat as my stomach dropped to my feet. "What?"

"I don't want to talk about this." She dropped the stickers and stood up, her stool scraping against the floor.

"But I do. You can't just say something like that and walk away!"

"I don't want to talk about it because I can't. I'm still trying to figure this out and you trying to push me isn't helping. It's just going to make me say the wrong thing and make it worse." Kara stood a few feet away from me with more pain than I had ever seen in her eyes. "I think you should leave."

"Kara, come on, don't be like this." What was happening to us? "Just talk to me."

"I can't do this." She shook her head. "I want to be alone. Go."

Twenty-Six

I hate this."

It'd basically become a ritual for me to loudly complain about going jogging. Oh, I'd finish all right, but Sam needed to *know* how much I detested every step.

"We've barely started. Give it time." Sam moved into the next stretching position she wanted us to copy.

"You said the same thing about studying Spanish and I almost failed."

"But you didn't." She shook her arms out at her sides. "Whenever I need to laugh, I think about the shocked look on Ms. Flores's face when you aced the oral during finals. Hamstrings."

"Adrenaline, fear, and coffee pumped full of espresso will do that. I swear my soul ascended to a higher plane of existence. I probably could've spoken Mandarin in that state."

"Calves. The mind has a way of tricking you into thinking you can't do something, but your body has the capacity to surprise you. Muscle memory and all that."

"For the record, not that anyone asked, I also hate this."

Winston's eyes were barely open. He must have stayed up late watching something.

Sam on the other hand, bright and full of sunshine, placed her hands on her hips in a frustrated huff. "Then why are you here?"

"Because she's here." He pointed at me. "I go where she goes."

"Like a cute little shadow."

"I may be cute, but I am not little and I am not a shadow. You don't get to say stuff like that to me."

"I didn't mean it like that."

"Says the high-yellow girl."

"Don't do that." I stood between them, hands out to keep them apart.

"She called me a shadow."

"You know what I meant. You're like a duckling sometimes, that's all."

"I am also not a duck. Or any kind of nonhuman animal."

"Okay." Sam laughed. "I'm clearly not going to win today."

"No. You won't. But you will stop trying to make fun of me for wanting to spend time with my sister or I will give no quarter."

"No quarter?" That had to be a movie reference. And a way for me to steer the conversation toward me before they really started fighting. "Ooh! *Pirates of the Caribbean?*"

"That was one acceptable answer."

"My God, y'all are weird," Sam said.

"And you're an only child," Winston threw back at her.

"*Look.*" I glared at them. "Let's just be chill and get this done. I'm stressed enough without you two going at it."

"He started it."

"Jesus, you both make me feel middle-aged. Stop making me be the voice of reason! I don't want to! It's gross and above my paltry pay grade."

Winston smirked, turning his head to the side.

Sam offered her hand to him. "Truce."

"For now." He crossed his arms over his chest.

"Anyway." Sam rolled her eyes. "Same rules as always: follow my pace, not my body. Breathe in through your nose, out through your mouth, keep Mabel closer to the water."

At the sound of her name, Mabel gave a reassuring bark as if she understood.

Sam hit the timer and we set off.

Five. Six. Five.

Walk. Jog. Walk.

The first four minutes of speed walking practically flew by. The one-minute warning sounded again and that same surge of adrenaline and slight fear hit me. Six minutes.

Everything about my body became hyperfocused in those six minutes. The feel of my knees bending, the impact of my feet hitting the ground, the tightness in my lungs, the way parts of me moved around my muscles and bone, the sound of my skin—I knew my body, but also didn't.

I'd seen running ads for years. Gorgeous models, slick with sweat, controlling their breathing as they sprinted effortlessly like gazelles. The skin on their stomachs moved, their tiny thighs and sculpted calves jiggled because that's what bodies did. But I'd never seen someone who looked like me move that way. It was different, exaggerated; it was more, but it was still okay.

Extreme weight-loss shows were the work of the devil because at the core, they'd been built upon a foundation of shame and the constant need to embarrass the contestants. No one went on those shows happy and bubbly: "Hi, I'm Contestant Three, my life is super awesome and I'm here to learn how to lift weights because it seems really great!" No, it was always, "My weight controls my life. I'm at rock bottom. Please exploit and verbally abuse me until I lose hundreds of pounds, and if I don't, have me sit down and continue to talk about my struggles for the world to hear and judge me."

And those shows only showed the positive side of working out. All of the grunts and straining and skin-slapping sounds covered by motivational music and voice-overs. Fat people working out wasn't allowed to be real. It had to be aesthetic and motivational. The contestants never talked about the way their bodies felt until they'd gotten lighter. Everyone wanted the inspirational journey and the result.

I wanted to know I wasn't alone. That feeling kind of sick was normal. That feeling sore and weird and self-conscious was all a part of the process. That I could learn new ways to move in my body as is, without having or wanting to drastically change my appearance.

The beeping sound brought me back out of my thoughts. Six minutes. Done. I slowed to a walking pace, chest aching and breathing hard, but I'd jogged the whole thing without stopping. I smiled, happy and proud, but it didn't last.

Wheezing.

Winston was *wheezing*. He knelt on the ground, one hand clutching his chest, eyes wide and frightened as strained air whistled in and out of him. "Can't"—gasp—"breathe"—gasp—"Winnie"—gasp—"help"—gasp—"Winnie."

Help.

~

The little bell above Goldeen's door chimed.

Footsteps padded across the floor.

I could move, but also couldn't. I cared but also really, really didn't. I shouldn't have been there.

Every few seconds, I lost control of my body. An involuntary deep breath shuddered through me—the kind of breathy hiccup someone made when they'd been crying for too long.

I twisted a straw wrapper around my fingers.

"Winnie."

I closed my eyes against the sound of his voice. Real life wanted to pierce through the protective bubble I'd created for myself, filling it up with hurt to wallow in.

But it was also a voice I wanted to hear. A voice that made my heartbeat speed up from the sluggish thump of devastation.

Dallas.

His hand hovered in the air, hesitating near my shoulder, trapped between wanting to touch me and knowing that he shouldn't.

Reality snapped back into focus when I looked at his face. "Hey. Uh, sorry." I licked my dry lips. "Do you want to sit or, um—"

"I'm fine." He placed a plastic container full of cookies on the podium. "My mom sent these for Winston."

"Oh. Cool. Thanks. He loves cookies. He loves any kind of food, actually." I tried to smile—it sort of felt like one. My cheeks rose. My lips pulled. I showed my teeth. "He's like a human garbage disposal."

"Is he okay?"

"Yeah. Yeah. He, um. I mean, I'm sure you heard. He has asthma. We didn't know and now we do."

"Are you okay?"

"Yeah. Yeah. I mean, it's not like I had the attack."

"But you were there. It must have been scary."

"Yeah." I could barely hear myself. "Yeah."

"Do you want to talk about it?"

"Hmm? What? No. There's nothing to talk about. He's fine. He has an inhaler now, is probably going to be tired for a bit, and has some follow-up appointments with our regular doctor, so he has to fly home. That's all. Everything's fine."

"That's really great. But I meant you. Do you want to talk about what happened? I know how much he means to you."

Everyone did. Find one of us and the other wouldn't be far behind. Something raw ripped open inside of me again. "He was there because of me. I agreed to do that stupid jogging plan because Sam wanted it, and Granny wanted it, and he went because of me. Because he goes where I go, and if he hadn't, today wouldn't have happened."

"That's not your fault."

"It is. He's been saying it since we started. His chest hurt. His back hurt. He didn't feel good after we were done and would be tired all day. Dr. Skinner said those were all symptoms. Winston kept telling us he was having a hard time and we ignored him. Sam thought he was only complaining because I was complaining. No one thought to take him seriously because of the way I was acting and how much he copies me."

"No offense, but your cousin's kind of an asshole for suggesting that."

"But she's right." I wiped my eyes before the tears had a chance to even think about falling. "I was so scared. *Scared* isn't even the right word because the right word doesn't exist. I have never felt like that in my entire life. I don't even know how to describe it. He couldn't breathe and he kept wasting the air that was getting in to say my name and I just—I didn't know what to do. I didn't know how to help him. And his eyes—he—he looked at me like he knew I couldn't fix it, but I fix everything. Not Sam. Me. I'm his big sister. I'm supposed to take care of him. I should've known something was wrong. That's my job and I didn't and he knew it."

"She isn't right, Winnie." He moved closer to me, placing his arms around me in a way—one hand on the podium, the other on the back of my chair. He had nice hands. I'd never thought about them before.

Long fingers, clean short nails, smooth skin, and bluish-green veins making random, interesting lines down to his arm.

I wished he would hug me.

"I don't know him that well, but I do know that y'all make everyone jealous. We all want to be as close as you two. I don't even have any siblings and I want it."

"I didn't even want him." I sob-laughed. "I never told anyone this—I don't even think Sam knows. A couple of months after he was born, I tried to give him away to my neighbor. I went to their house, rang the bell, ran back to my house, picked him up out of his bassinet, and went back to the neighbors. According to my mom, I said, 'I don't want him,' and tried to give him up."

"You didn't."

"I did and my mom whooped my ass. Like, I still remember it. But after that, everything was different. Something in me changed. I was Winston's Big Sister. Through and through. I made my mom teach me how to make his bottles and change his diapers. When he started walking, I held his hand and brought him with me everywhere. I remember crying on my first day of school because my mom wouldn't let him stay with me. He's such a big part of my life. Without him—I don't even want to know what would be left. There might be nothing."

"I don't think that's true. I can't say that I understand. Thinking like that doesn't exactly sound healthy, but if that's how you feel then it's valid."

"Valid?"

"Yeah. My mom uses that word. I like it. Whatever you feel might not be good or positive, but you experience it, so it's real and it matters."

"I'm not obsessed with him or something. I'm his sister. It's—I don't know how to explain it. It's just something that I take seriously.

It means a lot to me. Being his sister. It's very specific—a very specific kind of love. I don't think that's a bad thing."

"I'm not saying it is."

"But people do. Like it's weird or something that we like to spend time together and hang out and talk. We're family and we like each other. I don't get why people always try to twist that into something ugly."

"Now, that? I understand. People are assholes. They project the way they see things onto you, and you're supposed to change to make them happy. They only want to see what they want to see, no matter who it hurts."

❧

My dad had warned me about bursting into Winston's room unannounced. "He's not a baby anymore. He needs his privacy. How would you feel if he did that to you?"

I still did it anyway. There wasn't a single thing he could do to make me cringe. I've changed his diapers. I've nursed him back to health through *unbelievable* bouts of food poisoning. I've seen it all. I mean, *he* might get embarrassed, but I never would. Besides, I knew he wouldn't ask my parents any questions about certain . . . things. Someone had to be there for him.

We could both live to be over one hundred years old, and he'd always be my precious baby brother who needed me.

Winston had turned off all the lights in his room, even the little night-light that cast sheer rainbow shadows on the walls. He wasn't afraid of the dark, but couldn't sleep in total darkness. He was awake.

"Hey?"

"Yeah?" He rasped and my heart stuttered. His throat was fine. He shouldn't have sounded like that.

"You okay? Do you need anything?"

I listened hard, absorbing the silence for any sign that he was mad or didn't want to talk or wanted to be left alone. I'd retreat with quickness if he needed space from me. I owed him that much.

He moved, sheets rustling. "Want to watch a movie with me?" His laptop screen flared to life on his bed.

"Yeah." Halfway in the room, I started crying again. "Anytime."

Twenty-/even

After dropping Winston off at the airport, I abandoned ship.
I packed a bag, canceled on the Royal Engagement for
that night, called in sick for the third time ever at Goldeen's,
and all but ran to casa de Alviar for an emergency sleepover with
Kara.

Her room had gone from posters of four nondescript white boys
and two brown boys—clearly thrown in so their makers wouldn't
seem racist—whom she called her small sons who "deserved so
much better," to tapestries of spooky-looking forests and misty
ocean waves, hanging fairy lights, candles, and shelves for days lined
with cookbooks and big-headed toy figurines.

Only one photo of the boy band had survived the overhaul. Kara
had framed it.

"Do you even still listen to them anymore?" I placed it back on
the nightstand next to her side of the bed.

"Of course. I don't love them and nearly lost my life to obsession
because of their sheer overwhelming hotness."

Last time I checked her music library, there'd been a definite spike in new singers who had a penchant for sounding like soulful frogs.

"How is he?"

I flopped face-first on the bed.

"That bad?" She laughed because she knew, same as I did, that he truly was okay.

He had wanted to go home. The revelation, *the betrayal* that he and Sam never really wanted to come to Haven Central in the first place had been nagging at me.

My parents were just as bad as I was, if not worse, ready and willing to spoil him rotten. He'd start sending me pictures soon, no doubt, of him and *our* parents having fun together. Without me. Movie dates and beach boardwalk runs for games and they'd buy him hamburgers, ice cream, and taffy by the pound—nope, I wasn't jealous at all.

He'd probably do something cheesy like tag every picture he posted online #whereintheworldiswinniesandiego.

"I ruined his summer."

"Nope." Kara rubbed my back in slow firm circles. "We should do something fun."

"First Starlight. Now asthma. Who knows what I'll unintentionally do next?"

"At least it won't be on purpose."

I glared at her and she beeped my nose.

"All I'm saying is life happens. Murphy's Law plus you finagling yourself into situations where you don't belong."

"I refuse to give you that pun point."

"Winston would have."

"*Rude.*" Flipping onto my side to face her, I propped myself up on my elbow.

"Hey, someone has to treat you normally to make you feel better. You will not get a single drip-drop of sympathy from me."

"But whyyyyyy?"

"Because you're being sad for no reason. It wasn't your fault. Winston is fine. You are fine but you won't let yourself be."

"I can beat myself up if I want to."

"Not on my watch." She leaned forward, copper curls framing her face. "All you've done since you've been here is work at Goldeen's, fight with your granny, literally run yourself ragged in the mornings, and gallivant around being the Misty Summer Queen."

"We do not *gallivant*."

"The Winnie I know is always smiling. She screech-laughs from the depths of her soul, worries about everyone else and what she can do to make them happy *only if* it benefits her later, and recharges her batteries by sitting in the sun because she's a celestial goddess. I haven't seen her in a while. I miss her."

"Me too."

"All of that stuff has been for or because of someone else. What do you really want?"

"To spend time with you." I sighed. "And Dallas. I like him."

Kara seemed to blink in slow motion before turning away.

Sometimes when I looked at Kara, reality turned into a dream. Everything went fuzzy and softened just like that moment right between being asleep and awake when I would open my eyes and stare at the ceiling, unmoving, unthinking, just breathing and waiting.

Nothing seemed impossible in that surreal state.

I sat up, inching as close to her as I could. Her hands in mine, foreheads touching, I whispered, "Can we talk about it yet?"

She kept her eyes down. I wanted to make her laugh.

"*Hurry.* If we stay like this for much longer, my body heat will start fogging up your glasses."

Her nose scrunched. The laughter I'd earned was mostly exhaled air. "I love you too much. That's my problem." She blew out another huff of air, shoulders sagging. "I love you too much. I wanted you all to myself when that wasn't what we agreed on. That's something that I have to deal with, but I'm sorry. You've always been all-in with me, and I just thought if someone else came along, that would change."

"You asked me what I really wanted. At first, it was just a chance. And then I wanted more. I want him. I'm sorry if that hurts you. I don't want it to. I wish it didn't, but I never hid this side of me from you."

"That part doesn't *hurt*. That's not it. I'm scared. I don't want to lose you to him. It never works out for people like me. I want to be with you. I want you to be in my life forever. But I can't feel the way everyone expects me to."

"I only expect you to be yourself."

"I want to believe that. I do. I just—I can't compete with someone like him."

Compete? There was no *competing*. "Instead of doing what you did, you could have said, 'Hey, Dallas is asking about you and it's making me really uncomfortable. Can we please talk?' The Kara who didn't do that? I don't know her. I don't *like* her. And if that's how you really feel, we need to talk about it now."

"I know I can't give you everything you want, so you're going to find it with someone else and then there'll be this shifting. I'll have to step back because you're dating someone. What I have to offer isn't good enough. I'm not good enough. What right do I have to ask for forever?"

"You have that right with me because I gave it to you. You can ask for that because I say you can, because I want it too. I feel like what you're trying to say is you don't trust me to not abandon you for someone else."

"I didn't—that's not what I meant."

"Yeah. I think it is." I tried to keep my voice flat. That hurt so, so much. Like someone decided to punch me in the face and then didn't stop doing it. "What have I ever done to make you think that?"

"The Wine Tasting."

"Before that. Be honest."

"Nothing. I guess I kind of always thought it would eventually happen. And then it did."

"We're going to mess up. Both of us. My parents have been together forever and they go to counseling. If they need to talk to someone, then it's okay if we fall apart, too. As long as we both want to keep going, we can find a way. It's always been *in addition to* for me. Always."

"For you. What if it's not for him? Or whoever comes next? Don't they get a say? What if they say they don't want me because I'm not—because they don't understand? What if they make you choose?"

"If they're not cool with us, then what's the point of them?" I meant every single syllable of that.

Kara grinned, smug and happy. "I love it when you're like this. So fierce. So unyielding. I chose well." Now there was the Kara I knew. "I'll come to your next Royal Engagement. If the offer is still open."

Relief flooded through me. I knew it. I *knew* that had been it. Forcing myself to wait and let her figure that out on her own had been the right move. It took her a while and it scared me and pushed me to be the ungirlfriend I knew she needed but didn't think I could be.

She did it. I did it.

We did it.

~

FAM-BAM-MAJAMA

Winnie: Hey did he make it there
okay? I keep calling ...

Mom: He's here. Everything is fine. We love you.

Winnie: I'm too paranoid. I need a secret
code that only we would know so I know
that someone didn't kidnap you all.

Mom: Winnie. My child. My first born.
Pride of my soul. Blood in my heart.

Winnie: OKAY I BELIEVE IT'S YOU I'M GLAD
HE MADE IT GOING TO BED BYEEEEEE

Mom: Your accuser wishes to remain
anonymous. Where are my earrings?

Winnie: Earrings? What earrings? I
don't know anything about earrings.

Mom: The ones that are missing. The ones you took.

Mom: Gold studs. Amethyst stones.
Sunflower pattern. Sound familiar?

Winnie: Oh. Those.

Winnie: Yeah, those are here. Perfectly safe.

Winnie: I was going to ask to borrow
them but I ran out of time

Mom: ... Sam took them didn't she?

Winnie: NO!

Mom: Winfrey Diane.

Winnie: Okay. Maybe.

Momma-da-vida

Winnie: I need advice. Help?

Mom: I'm relaxing in the garden with the birds so I've got some time. Do you need to call me?

Winnie: Sam is with me. I don't want her to hear.

Mom: Go for it.

Winnie: It's about Dallas. The guy I told you about who volunteered to be king with me.

Mom: Ooh! Yes! You still haven't sent me a picture. Is he cute? He sounds cute and like a nice young man who likes to buy my daughter flowers

Winnie: It's also about Kara.

Mom: WHAT'S WRONG WITH KARA?

Winnie: Nothing! We're working through it.

Winnie: She's really worried that he won't like her because of something she did and I can't be with someone who doesn't accept Kara but I really like him mom. A lot.

Winnie: I'm trying to prep myself for disappointment.

Mom: I see. Have you asked him out yet?

Winnie: NO. I'm not doing that.

Mom: Why not? I asked your dad and look what happened: Marriage! Babies! 85% life-fulfillment!

Winnie: 85!?

Mom: There's still some things I want to do once I'm retired

Winnie: Oh. Okay. Just making sure lol

Mom: My advice is the same as always. Be direct.

Ask. Get your answers and then give it time to play
out naturally. What will be, will be, my love.

                                       Winnie: Time sounds stupid

Mom: Winnie.

                            Winnie: I mean, time sounds boring

                        Winnie: I need answers now. Like a get rich
quick, harebrained scheme that will cut all of
the this is where you learn a lesson corners
for me. I need solutions! I need results!

Mom: You need to calm down lol

Mom: I know it feels like the world is going to end
but what you and Kara have isn't new, sweetie. Lots
of people are in relationships similar to yours

Mom: I know because I've researched :)

Mom: But it's scary because you're young and this is
your first time for everything, right? You don't have any
experiences to match with what's happening to guide you

Mom: I think everything will be okay. You just
have to live through it first which is the hard part I
know but I think you'll find that it'll be worth it

Twenty-Eight

"Sam is sixteen." Eyes open and dry as sand, I stared at the alarm blaring across the room. Yesterday with Kara had been *wonderful.* The second I stepped back into this apartment, the brilliance of the day got leached from me. "She's sixteen. That means something."

But did it really?

Sam, two years younger than me and two years older than Winston, who had an asthma attack two days ago and left me, couldn't be bothered to think that maybe I needed a break from jogging with her at that place.

After everything I'd done for Sam—constantly protecting her from Winston, always making sure she's okay and smiling and happy, taking the fall when she did shit wrong like *stealing* from my mom, jogging every morning even though I *hate* it—she couldn't even be bothered to ask me if I was okay. My heart *ached* for her on an hourly basis. I worried about her to the point of stressing myself out until I got stomachaches. And yet?

A simple text—*hey, are you up for this today?*—would have been stellar. Actually, it would have been the absolute bare minimum of concern Sam could show. She could have thought to give me the option of backing out without making me seem like a bad person for abandoning our "thing" since Winston was gone.

I rolled onto my back, blowing all of the air out of my lungs, and then checked Twitter to make sure the world hadn't burned down while I slept. Half asleep with blurry vision, I always checked in with the internet like we were in a relationship. A one-sided, abusive relationship, but hey. The state of the world made it that way.

Dallas had sent me a text. I curled into a ball after a surprise heart palpitation. Dallas, the non-texter, had actually sent me something.

(Arthur) DALLAS

Dallas: Have a good day

In spite of all the crappy feelings fumbling around inside of me, I smiled so big my cheeks began to hurt. I couldn't bring myself to skip two nights of work in a row, so I had called him. He showed up not even ten minutes later to keep me company during the Midnight Oil.

We talked. I cried because I couldn't help it. He listened.

And he'd given me another present.

"Here," he had said. "I brought this for you. I think you'll like it. There's also a movie, but it's kind of trash."

"Thanks." I'd taken the paperback book from him, old and battered with the spine falling apart. "Did you get it from a used bookstore?"

"No. It's mine. One of my favorites." He had turned slightly red.

Whatever I said back to him had to be brief and to the point because he might not reply. If he didn't, I'd be stuck thinking about what his non-response did or didn't mean all day. "You too" sounded dismissive. "Thank you" was a given. I typed and deleted a few more times before settling on:

Winnie: I'll call you later

"You gonna turn that off?" Granny stood in the doorway.

I locked my phone screen. "I thought about it. But then I figured if I got used to the sound, my body would stop responding to it. Exposure therapy for the lazy person's soul."

Granny made her usual wordless objections, sounds I'd heard my whole life. "You're not lazy." The alarm stopped. Moments later, the bed shifted as she sat down.

"He's fine, Winnie."

I curled around Granny, resting my head in her lap. "I know."

Whenever I used to get upset, we'd sit like this.

When kids outside teased me for being fat and that word still hurt; when I punched those same kids in the face one by one and cried after because I thought I would go to hell because Jesus was disappointed in me for fighting; when Sam stayed home one summer and kissed my crush—a boy whose name I couldn't even remember, but my heart was broken and betrayed; when I got a low score on the summer PSAT prep course and test I took in Misty with Kara; when I figured out I might like girls, too, and thought I was going to hell again—Granny had been there for all of that and more.

This summer had been hell on our relationship. But at the start, if someone had asked me, I would have wanted Granny with me all the time. It always bugged me when my friends treated their grandparents like ATMs or Santa Claus. Granny helped raise me, too. I wanted us to stop fighting and be able to spend the little bit of summer we had left together being happy.

"Maybe you should go home for a bit."

I sat up so fast I almost hit my head on the top bunk. "You're kicking me out!?"

"No." She touched the side of my face, thumb rubbing my cheek. "I'm sending you where you want to be."

"I want to be here. Summer equals Goldeen's. That's the way it works. Who's going to cover my shifts?"

Granny raised an eyebrow. "My diner is open and does just fine for the nine months when you aren't here. My business doesn't stop when you leave, Winnie." She tugged on my chin, then rested her hand in her lap.

"But—" I opened my mouth and closed it. "But—you're on stay-cation. Goldeen's needs me."

"What is that? And what makes you think I'm on it, whatever it is?"

"I'm here so you can take a break and not have to worry about the diner."

Granny's whole body reacted—sucked in a breath, blinked at me, shook her head, turned away, pressed her lips together as she exhaled.

"You're enjoying your summer off, aren't you?" I asked. "You got to start that painting class, take piano lessons like you always wanted; you've been to concerts and renaissance fairs and pirate festivals with the other grannies, and you're going on a cruise with Mr. Livingston—"

"Mind your business."

"I am! You're always telling me that I'm too serious and I need to have fun and, well, so do you. You've worked hard your whole life! You deserve a break more than me."

"I made you a co-assistant manager because you earned it. Because I thought the experience would be good for you. It's sure as hell not because I need you to replace me." She wagged her finger and shook her head—the holy double play of an upset elder. "I don't know why you're in such a rush to be grown. You're eighteen. You need to start acting like it." She stood up, fussing with the tie on her robe. "If you want to stay here, I'm changing your shifts. No more mornings or deliveries. You work five thirty to two a.m., half hour meal break. Sundays and Mondays off from now on."

"*What?*" I looked up at her, nearly frozen in shock. "That's not fair!"

"It is fair. Even if it wasn't, it's my business. I make the schedule."

"But—"

"I don't want to hear it," she said. "Be mad all you want. It's for your own good. You'll see."

⌒

Some days, good days were an impossible thing. I got dressed and drove to the park because I had to get out of that house. Breathing the same air as Granny made me punchy.

I'd mostly always used my words, but every now and then I thought hitting something would make me feel better. Running sucked, but kickboxing might be worth looking into.

"Good morning." Sam smiled—happy but trying to scale it back to a tolerable level that didn't give a rainbow a run for its money.

"Bad morning."

Her smiled disappeared. "That's an option."

Winston had collapsed right there, right next to that patch of shrubbery. We had to half drag him to the car. If I closed my eyes, I could see it. When I opened them, he was still there, fading away. Dying.

He could have died.

The sameness of the scene felt offensive. The geese. Mabel happy as ever. The stagnant water. Sam and her seemingly endless supply of Technicolor workout clothes. I was supposed to walk and run past that spot like nothing ever happened, to honor me and Sam's "thing."

Five. Seven. Five.

Walk. Jog. Walk.

Rage powered me through the entire seven minutes. Around minute four, my knee decided to *twinge* hard enough to make me have to hop the next few steps. Sam had called it that, ordering me to push through. I had wanted to push her into the pond for a hot second. That seemed to be enough to appease the Knee Gods, because mine relaxed after that.

And if one more goose pretended to charge at me, I'd seriously start reconsidering my punting policy.

In the car, Sam tugged on her seat belt. "You feeling okay?" Mabel's head appeared between us. "I've been worried about you. After what happened."

Now she worried. None of her concern had appeared that morning.

"He's fine. Everything's fine." I started the car.

"I know." She chewed on her thumbnail. "He wasn't supposed to be there anyway. It was supposed to be our time. Whenever it's just supposed to be me and you, here he comes."

"Feel free to stop saying things that are going to make me get mad at you."

"What?" In the corner of my eye, her wide eyes stared at me.

"He's my brother. So what if he tagged along? What is your problem?"

"I don't have a problem." She shook her head, lowering it like she always did when confrontation came for her. "I don't. I'm sorry."

"What are you sorry for? Do you even know what you did? Or are you just apologizing because you think that's going to make things better?"

I could feel her shrinking beside me, retreating like a snail into its shell.

"Did you even think about me at all this morning? How I would feel going to that pond after what happened?"

No yelling. No counting. I'd probably unconsciously developed this neutral nonthreatening level of rage exclusively for her.

Well.

I'm sure the steering wheel had an opinion about that nonthreatening claim. I shook out my hands quickly and placed them back. There'd be two-hand driving at all times with me behind the wheel.

"Oh." She held her hands together, squeezing them. They changed colors—white-tinged red from effort. She called it caramel-skin problems.

"Yeah, *oh*. He could've died. Why would I want to go back there so soon? At all?"

"I didn't think about it like that. To me—" Sam paused. "Can I say something, too?"

"That's how conversations work."

"Okay. I wasn't sure. Thanks." She grimaced, wringing her hands tighter. "I was scared, too, but the doctor said he was fine. He said he was fine. You said he was fine. Everything was fine. You kept saying it, so I thought—I didn't realize you were lying."

She picked up on more than I'd given her credit for. "I wasn't lying. Not on purpose. I was trying to convince myself. Like if I said it enough, it would be okay for me to believe it was true."

"You do that a lot. Sometimes I can't tell the difference."

This was exactly why I worried for Sam so much. Why I always stuck my neck out for her. She wouldn't have admitted that to anyone else. Her M.O. involved shrinking and wilting until she could figure out the least painful way to escape. She didn't let people see this side of her.

"You can ask me. If you get confused, just ask. Otherwise, I'll just assume you don't care about me."

"Of course I care about you! You're like my favorite person ever." She looked out the window. "But I feel like I already annoy you all the time."

"Well, not *all* the time." I smiled as she said it, but Sam's reflected face crumpled in the window. "Sorry. I didn't mean that. I was kidding."

"And I feel like sometimes you don't like me as much as you like Winston."

"That's stupid. I love you both."

"I didn't say you didn't love us. I said I think you don't *like* me. I know a lot of people don't." She was trying so hard not to cry. Mabel whined, nudging her—she didn't like it either. "It's not the same thing."

"We have different interests that don't really overlap, but that doesn't mean I don't like you. Having stuff in common isn't the only reason you can like someone."

"I know that. I just wanted us to spend time together before you moved away, and I wanted to help you and Granny get along again because all you two do is fight now. I know you're upset about *that*."

My little cousin was an actual sweetheart. A meddling sweetheart, but she meant well and I swear to God sometimes it felt like no one else could see it but me. She'd never do anything to intentionally hurt me. I knew that. This summer had just warped everything I knew to be true into unrecognizable monsters trying to eat me alive.

"You're my little sister. You know that right? I'm always going to look out for you. Whether you annoy me or not, that's never going to change." I poked her in the cheek, holding my finger there for five seconds before putting my hand back on the wheel. "I'm not sorry that I don't like running. I'm willing to do it while we're here, but once we go back, I'm done."

"I know."

"But *we're* not done. We have time to figure out a new thing for us. Maybe kickboxing?"

Her eyes lit up. "I've always wanted to try that!"

"Find a class and we'll go for however many sessions we can before I move. And then we'll find something we can do long-distance, too, okay?"

"You promise?"

"Yep."

She smiled at me. "Do you really hate running?"

"I do. But I think it's really cool how dedicated you are to it. I'm not sorry for complaining so much. You're not getting that out of me. But you're a pretty good instructor. You should look into getting a part-time job doing that instead of babysitting all the time."

Sam's smile had reached high-beam status. "Well, you're a pretty good baby runner. I'm sorry it made you so miserable."

"Guess I'm still waiting for those endorphins to kick in." I felt a distinct pang of hurt and guilt. Winston wasn't there, but his joke lived on.

Twenty-Nine

'd been in bed for a whole ten minutes before tiny plinking noises made my imagination act up. Something kept hitting the window.

How I'd even heard the noise over Sam's snores was beyond me. She kept right on trying to blow a hole in the roof with her powerful snoring. I got out of bed, darting for the wall, and placed my back against it. Sly as a fox with no common sense, I tried to peek through the curtains without being seen.

A fire-red helmet glowed in the moonlight. I lifted the window and hush-yelled, "What are you doing!?"

Dallas replied louder than what was safe, "Sorry I'm late. I had to wait for my mom to fall asleep before sneaking out of the house."

"Late? Late for what? What's happening?" I gripped the windowsill for dear life. Did we have some weird three a.m. Royal Engagement I'd forgotten about? Some Haven-sanctioned sleepover we had to go to?

"I want to spend time with you." He held up a bright orange sparkly helmet that matched his. "Please?"

"It's almost three o'clock in the morning!"

"It's summer. Time doesn't exist." He pointed to the left and said, "Meet me at the door," running off before I could disagree.

"This is not happening." I changed into a dress.

"He must be drunk." I shoved myself into a pair of leggings.

"I'm going back to bed." I grabbed a pair of socks and peeked into the hallway.

Granny's closed bedroom door meant nothing. The woman had supersonic hearing. Forget sneaking out of the house—one wrong step, one creak, one second of the refrigerator interior's hum would have her out in the hall, rollers in her hair, velvet bathrobe and all, asking me what the hell I was doing.

I stood flush with the wall. Standing on my tiptoes, I slid along, feet as close to the baseboard, where it was less likely to groan, as I could manage. Lips pressed together, I held my breath, quickly inhaling and exhaling every five seconds.

Slide.

Slide.

Slide.

Granny would kill me if I snuck out. But. Dallas had come to see me in one of the most iconic and romantic ways possible. How many shows and movies and books had people showing up and crawling through their crush's window?

It was a Moment.

My Moment, and I didn't want it to be ruined. Or shared.

Maybe he didn't mean for it to be romantic, but that didn't mean I couldn't imagine it that way. Until I had definitive, rock-solid proof of disinterest, this crush of mine that I had denied for so long would live on.

Hallway down, the kitchen was the next obstacle. The back door's hinges didn't make noise. No alarm system. The floor, though? The linoleum squeaked on certain soft spots that rotated with the sole intention of getting me caught. No clear way across it.

Dallas's shadow bounced impatiently behind the curtained window.

I was 100 percent making the wrong choice. No denying that. An illogical and dangerous wrong choice.

Staying on my tiptoes, I crept forward, one step at a time, pausing to let my weight balance before moving again.

Creep.

Creep.

Creep.

The wicker doormat under my feet sans Granny's eyes boring holes into my back brought sweet, rough relief. After putting on my shoes, I braced one hand against the door and turned the knob with the other. The door opened barely a crack before Dallas's smiling face filled it.

"Hi!"

"Hush yourself! My God." I rushed out, closing the door behind me with care.

"Why so jumpy?"

"I don't want to get in trouble."

"That only happens if you get caught. Come on." Sneaking out must have been something he did regularly.

At home, my nonnegotiable curfew stayed in full effect no matter how old I got. Sunset, then streetlights, ten p.m., eleven p.m. Midnight. No exceptions. Sneaking out was impossible because of our alarm system, not that I'd ever wanted to.

"Where are we going?"

"I have a surprise for you."

"Is it murder? I've seen TV movies on Lifetime that start like this."

Dallas grinned and handed me the orange helmet. "Definitely not murder."

"And this surprise couldn't wait four hours?"

"It's time sensitive." His eyes were clear and bright, smile easy as sunrise.

"What is it?"

"Something you want." He stepped closer, taking my hand.

The cool, post-midnight air did nothing for my skin, burning hot enough to sear the next unwanted hole in the ozone layer. His palms and fingers felt clammy—like he was nervous.

"I don't know." Eye contact. So much eye contact. "If my granny wakes up and I'm gone—that might be the end of me."

"I won't keep you out too late. Or early." He shuffled closer to me.

The apartment had a decent-sized porch ringed by a metal banister. We stood near the top step with plenty of room around us, and yet he stood unnecessarily close. His thumb rubbed along the back of my hand in slow, lazy circles, daring me with an inviting gaze to defy logic, forget the rules, and run away for the rest of the night.

"Okay. But we have to be quick."

We slinked down the stairs, Dallas snorting with suppressed laughter every time the wood creaked. The second we hit the pavement, we took off running toward the front of the building.

"Really, if it's murder, you can just tell me."

"It's not murder."

"Okay, it's really dark. The murder vibes are really high right now."

He squeezed my hand. "Trust me."

"You are truly asking for a lot tonight."

We exited Goldeen's parking lot, running a few more feet until we reached a black-with-dark-red-trim motorcycle.

"You have a motorcycle, too. Of course you do."

"I don't actually have a car. The one I usually drive here is my mom's. This is mine." He tilted the bike and swung one leg over, positioning himself on the seat. "Hop on."

"I am *not* hopping any goddamn where."

"We're just going up the road. A quick little trip, there and back."

"Why are you doing this to me? Think of my blood pressure!"

He held out his hand.

This was my Moment after all. Would I live in it or reject it?

Remember that time I snuck out my house, almost *got on a motorcycle with my crush to go to a surprise he'd planned specifically for me? Good almost times.*

"Is that thing safe? You have your license, right?"

"Yes and yes."

I sighed. Closing my eyes, I put the helmet on. My braids made it a tight fit, but it wasn't uncomfortable. "This better be worth it or I will never trust you again." Once settled on the bike behind him, he showed me where to put my feet. "Where do I put my hands?"

"Around me. Lean forward." He guided me into position. "Not quite so tight." He laughed. "I still need to breathe."

I adjusted my grip. That familiar mint-and-soap smell woke up my crush butterflies. "This is terrifying. You realize that, right?"

"I think the word you're looking for is *exhilarating*." The bike roared to life. That explained why he had parked so far from the diner.

Not even thinking about the Wrath of Granny could stop me from screeching as we thundered away. "Too fast! Too fast! OH MY GOD!" I squeezed him tighter—I could feel him laughing as I buried my face into his neck.

He tapped my hands a few times. His thumb rubbed my right wrist. And then he let go. Before I even had time to get used to riding on the bike, we rolled to a stop. I opened one eye as I lifted my head from my ridiculously ineffective hiding spot.

"The park? A picnic? I wanted to go on a picnic in the park?"

A large gingham blanket had been set up underneath the massive willow tree. Haven Central had voted to wind fairy lights around the trunk and attach hundreds of hanging ones to the branches. Usually, the lights were turned off by now, but they shone, twinkling in the summer moonlight.

Dallas removed his helmet and looked at me over his shoulder. "Did you really think *I* would make it that easy?"

He helped me dismount the bike and kept holding my hand as we sat down on the blanket facing each other.

"Now what?"

"Now you tell me?" He smiled biting his lip. "How's your brother?"

"He's okay."

"And everyone else?"

I laughed softly. "You're so cute. Inquiring about my loved ones."

"If they're important to you, I'd like to know how they are."

"And you couldn't just call me and ask that? I would've answered in the safety of my bathroom so I didn't wake up Sam."

"Nope. Because you don't see your face right now. You didn't see it when you opened the window or when you opened the door. You didn't see your smile when we ran down the stairs and across the parking lot. This was as much for you as it was for me because—"

"—we want the same thing."

He kissed the back of my hand.

Everything was happening, speeding up and dragging us along with so much going unsaid. Asking felt like it would break the spell. I wanted to know for sure, but part of me was strangely content. Not saying it out loud didn't make these moments, these monumental baby steps, less real.

The first step to coming to terms with a serious crush is admitting you have one. It was never a simple, "*Oh dear. I appear to have a crush. How quaint.*" It was "*JESUS NO HOW DID THIS HAPPEN I ABSOLUTELY DO NOT*" kind of denial. Explosions and heart eyes and awkward stuttering and throat clearing. Bad, irrational decisions and hormones and condoms in back seats and empty houses. It was awful and wonderful and it caught me off guard every time.

None of that was happening with Dallas anymore. Now that we were friends, everything felt different. It was a slow, insidious kind of feeling that made me stare into space, imagining his face, his smile. I thought about his skin, his nimble fingers and callused palms, thought of myself thinking about him. Thought of how it came from seemingly nowhere but had been building this whole time. How he had crawled into my head and refused to leave, occupying space that wasn't his to have.

I wasn't sure what to do next. Last time, I had told Kara out loud. Everything had worked, but lightning wasn't supposed to strike twice. This didn't feel like how it felt with her.

Different, yet familiar at the same time, and just as confusing.

I loved Kara more than I loved anyone else. Even still, the way I felt never crossed that intangible romantic line. I didn't crave her the way I did with Dallas. The way I wanted him to touch me felt different from what I wanted from Kara. Equally intense but not the same.

Sometimes when I tried to hold those thoughts in my head side by side, they looked identical, but I knew they weren't.

"It's not just me." I crawled across the blanket to sit next to him instead. "Kara told me what she did. We're working through that now, but we're still together."

"I figured."

Feeling bold, I rested my head on his shoulder. His fingers grazed my forehead as he pushed back the braids that had fallen over my face. I closed my eyes, imprinting that touch to memory.

"It has to be both of us. That's still where I'm at."

He was quiet for so long, I thought I'd lost him. "What would," he began, unsure, "what would I have to do? I want you, not her. I'm not interested in her at all."

I raised my head to look at him, fear and worry slashing through me. "Not even as a friend?"

He shook his head. "I'm sure you see something I don't, but no."

"Would you be willing to get to know her?"

"No offense, but I probably know her better than you do."

I sat up, trying to rein in a sudden flash of anger. "She made a mistake."

"When people show you who they are, you should believe them."

"If I can forgive her, couldn't you at least try?"

"I don't see why she would have anything to do with us in the first place."

"It's the other way around actually. She comes first. If we're not together, me and you"—I couldn't believe I fixed my mouth to say those words—"then she comes first."

"And if we are?"

We stared at each other. He wanted to be with me. I hadn't missed that, but I couldn't just say yes and lie to him. "Then it has to be equal. I've never done *anything* like this before. I only knew that I might want to someday, so I'm winging it. I just know I don't want to be one way with you and then another with her. I want us all to get along. You don't have to *date* her, but I can't be with someone who doesn't want to at least try being her friend."

I didn't know how to make him understand. I couldn't force him to give her a second chance. All of my hopes began to crumble into ash because it wasn't going to work.

He looked away first. "Looks like you're the one asking for a lot tonight."

Kara (Kara Kara Kara Kara) Chameleon

Kara: You are cordially invited to
dumpling night at my house
Kara: My mom wants me to tell you that
she would really like to see you

                                    Winnie: Just your mom?

Kara: And me. Always me.

                                        Winnie: Sure.

        Winnie: I'm going to say something. I don't
know if I mean it or if I'm just sad and getting
my feelings out. I want to talk about it later.

Kara: Okay. I'm ready. I'm here for you.

        Winnie: I'm not mad about what you did
anymore. But I still feel like you betrayed
me because you messed up something
that could have been really good for
me that I wanted /on purpose/

        Winnie: I really like Dallas.
And he likes me too.

        Winnie: But he doesn't want
anything to do with you now.

        Winnie: I'm not choosing you or him
because there isn't a choice to be made.
I'm just upset so if I'm not my usual
self at dinner, that's why. I'm sad.

        Winnie: I'm allowed to be sad about this.

Kara: I never told you this but during the pearl
diving competition, he helped me. Underwater. He
found the pearl necklace and gave it to me.

Kara: He could've won at any time. At first I
thought he helped me as payback to humiliate
me later. That's why I kicked him.

Kara: I think he did it because he wanted to make it fair.
He likes you and he knows you like me so he wanted
to try to make you happy by giving me a chance.

Winnie: THIS IS MAKING ME
FEEL WORSE STOP

Winnie: He gave you an extra
minute too. He waited the full three
minutes you wanted damn it

Kara: I don't know if I can fix this for you. I'm sorry.

Thirty

S am didn't show up.

    I waited almost fifteen minutes, sweating in the sun, grimacing against the funk, ready to go, before texting her.

SA(RU)M(ON)

Sam: SORRY!

Sam: The Hernandez family had an emergency at 4 am and called me in!

Sam: I thought they'd be back by now but no sign of them

Sam: Can't leave the kids.

> **Winnie:** Soooooo you couldn't text me and say that?

Sam: I figured when I didn't send my usual morning reminders you'd guess something was up since you don't want to run anyway

I groaned, kicking a rock back toward the parking lot. The geese had already assumed the position. One of them bared its teeth— that weren't really teeth but looked a whole lot like teeth—and serrated tongue at me. Those things had to be some genetic experiment. Some mad scientist out there gave them the body of a goose, the mind-set of a hippo, and the teeth and bloodlust of a piranha, and then dumped them in Misty Haven because they kept attacking their creators, who loved the homicidal things too much to euthanize them.

They seemed to have an extra murderous slant to them today. No Mabel the Doggyguard—they'd probably attack me the second I set foot on the path.

No one would know or care if I skipped today.

Each session, I had jogged one more minute than the previous session. I memorized how to control my breathing and keep my stride steady. But who would egg me on when I was seven minutes deep and swearing up a storm when I wanted to stop? Who would tell me jokes to distract me? Who would sing while running backward?

Going at it alone seemed even worse than doing it in general.

I set the alarms on my phone. "All right, geese." *Jesus*, they were already watching me. "I've been nothing but respectful of you. So just let me do my run, don't start none, won't be none." I walked toward the trail.

A goose leaped out of the water, another charged at me *while flapping*, and a chorus of *HONKS* serenaded me as I ran back to the car screaming, "PLEASE DON'T MURDER MEEEEEEEEEEEEEE!"

Safe inside, clutching the steering wheel, I tried to catch my breath. "If God wanted me to run today, he wouldn't have let the Devil Birds win."

"It **is** not **funny!** Those things are horrifying!" I should have known Dallas would laugh. Why did I even bother to tell him?

Kara had laughed, too. Her nonstop *LOLOLOLOLOLOLOL* and *LMAOOOOOOOOOOO* texts didn't stop until I threatened to block her number.

Dallas *continued* to laugh as he capped off the bottle he'd filled and set it to the side. He reached across the table to start in on my bottles. The boy had some kind of ketchup-bottle-refilling supernatural ability. I'd been doing this for years, could do it in my sleep, but he was faster than me.

I finished my bottle but didn't start a new one. Instead, I pushed all of mine toward him without making eye contact. "You haven't bought anything yet. Work off your debt."

"As you wish."

I totally recognized that quote and did the most dramatic thing ever: *sighed*, resting my chin on my hand. I'd expected things to be awkward between us, exposing my total lack of romantic dating experience and just how much I still had to learn about him.

Fact: Dallas had all but asked me to be his girlfriend and I turned him down because of my commitment with Kara.

I have never hated myself so much in my life. In a summer of bad decisions, that felt like it had to be the worst one yet. I wanted to say yes, throw my arms around him, kiss him, and finally, *finally* touch his hair, because those beautiful curls had started to grow back.

But my brain and my heart had reached an agreement. I definitely did the right thing, but *fuck*. And worse, I had no idea what to expect from him.

Would we only see each other during Royal Engagements?

Would he stop calling and telling me he just wanted to hear my voice?

Was he upset? With me?

Did he want to stop being friends?

And then he'd showed up, unannounced, to keep me company.

"I'm glad you're here."

"Are you?" I loved that cheeky grin of his.

"This feels gross but I'm going to say it in the spirit of whatever this is." I tried to keep my tone light and kind of playful, copying an aloof, flirty vibe I'd seen in a movie once. "I thought you wouldn't want to talk to me anymore because of the other night."

He topped off the last ketchup bottle and sat back with a shrug. "You don't live here. Even if you did, we're going to different colleges in August anyway. Things can stay how they are."

Oh. I hadn't even thought of that, what would happen when summer ended. I'd gotten so used to Kara I guess I thought it could have been the same for us. We didn't have to end when the seasons changed.

I'm not saying we would have had to promise each other forever and a day or anything like that, but we could've at least *tried*.

I think that might have been a big difference between us.

He wanted a summer fling. I wanted some effort.

"Is that okay?" he asked.

"It might be better that way. Less pressure." I didn't sound nearly as disappointed as I felt, because he was still there. Still looking at me with an expression that made my heart feel safe and my knees weak.

I might always want more with him, but he was still in my life.

"Yeah. Better." Bittersweet looked agonizingly beautiful on him.

My phone buzzed. Winston. "Do you want to re-meet my brother?"

"I already know him?" He sounded unsure.

"No, you know *of* him. Winston hides himself really well." I smiled, grateful for the subject change into something I could be happy about. "He's on a steroid inhaler for a bit and it's keeping him up at night. We're going to watch a movie."

I slid out of the booth, running back to my podium to grab my backpack. Returning to the table, I set up my laptop against the window, between us.

"What do you mean he hides?"

"I mean exactly what I said. He only lets you see what he wants you to. Whatever you think you know about him is guaranteed to be a minimum of eighty percent wrong."

"I'm strangely intrigued."

Winston had already logged on. When we joined, the smile that he used only for me faded with the quickness.

"I didn't agree to this." He spoke directly to me.

"Winston, this is Dallas. Dallas, this is my brother."

Dallas gave a little wave. "Hey."

"No." Even though he swore it never happened, Winston slipped up and fell into jealousy every now and again.

"It's fine. What are we watching?" I asked Winston.

"*Lord of the Rings.*"

"I'm not sitting through a six-hour movie."

"It's three movies. We can just watch the first one."

"*Elves*, though."

"And hobbits."

"I have a strong dislike for this one," I said to loop Dallas in. "I read an essay that said orcs were supposed to represent Black people. Ruined the whole thing for me."

"Yeah." Dallas grimaced. "That's what people say."

"You don't think so?" Winston challenged.

"Fantasy is my favorite genre. I'm used to side-eyeing a lot as a defense mechanism. Otherwise, I feel like I'd never read or watch anything. I see it, I get mad, and if it's not too egregious, I keep it moving."

"Egregious. Wow."

"Do you like books, too, or just movies?" Dallas asked Winston.

"Mostly movies."

I pressed play. Through the opening credits about the history of the world and a ring, I watched Winston reluctantly continue the conversation he pretended he didn't want to have with Dallas.

"I do wish there were more Black people in mainstream fantasy. There's some, and it's good when it's by us, but there should be more. And they can't be stereotypes or the only one to ever exist in the whole universe."

"Definitely."

A maniacal smile appeared on my face. Not that either of them saw it. Everything was going way smoother than I'd planned.

"I'm so *tired* of Black people being slaves there, too," Dallas continued. "That's hard to read, you know? Obvious reasoning aside, it's impossible to disconnect and just enjoy the story after that because I start thinking, what if the writer is secretly racist and I'm supporting them without knowing it? It just sits there in the back of my mind the entire time."

"Yeah. Exactly," Winston agreed.

"And would it kill writers to include literally anyone else? Jesus. I will never understand that one. America is huge, but only white and maybe Black people get to exist in our media? It's fantasy! They can literally do whatever they want. But no."

"He can stay." Winston looked at me. Not a thinly disguised insult or mocking smile in sight.

That had to be a record. One conversation and Dallas had earned a spot in Winston's peripheral vision. For scale, that's where Sam and Kara lived, too.

"I figured you'd like him."

I winked at Dallas. His resulting confused-happy face made me laugh.

All the lights cut off in the diner.

I jumped up, panicked, and sat in the booth on my knees. *Ow*—my thigh muscles pulled taut enough to hurt and the tabletop cut into my side, but I didn't have time to worry about that. Darkness covered the parking lot, too.

"The power went out. Shit." Besides the moon, the stars, and my laptop, the only other light came from Dallas's phone. He'd turned on his flashlight. "Oh, smart. Good thinking."

"Are you okay?" Winston asked at the same time Dallas asked, "What do you do when this happens?"

I answered Dallas. "Nothing. It's never happened before." I left the booth, almost running for the front door. The ring of keys clinked against one another as I inserted the right one with shaking hands.

"Do you need help?" Dallas stood next to the booth, phone aimed in my direction. The light cast an eerie glow on his face—he looked like he'd walked straight out of the scene where the storyteller in the friend group sets the stage and atmosphere in a dark room.

Meanwhile, my breathing sounded like I'd just run away from a serial killer who was hiding in the dark, trying to be quiet when I saw their feet walking toward me. I would never make fun of those scenes again. "I'm not allowed to close early, that's one of Granny's rules. Goldeen's never closes early."

I fumbled with my phone, struggling to turn on my flashlight.

Dallas touched my arm—I gasped, a scream lodging in my throat.

"Hey, calm down. Why are you so jumpy? It's just a power outage."

Winston and his love of horror movies had thoroughly wrecked any possibility of me having any semblance of emotional stability in scary situations. My brain leaped from *Oh, the lights are out, hmm, strange* to *SOMEONE CUT THE POWER AND THEY'RE GOING TO MURDER ME.*

"I'm not. I'm not." My flashlight clicked on. Just a power outage.

Sure. Okay. That's what the guy usually said before getting stabbed in the throat. "Walk me to the back? I should check all of the doors."

Confession: I may have been the tiniest bit afraid of total and complete darkness, but hey, wasn't everyone? An acceptable and primal fear. I knew every inch of Goldeen's like the back of my hand. In the dark, every inch of it was an enemy capable of concealing anything.

Dallas aimed the light at our path. He stayed with me as we hustled to the side door—already locked—and the back door—locked as well. I exhaled.

"Any other doors?" He held the light so it lit my face without blinding me.

"No, just those three."

"Winnie. Breathe. It's okay."

"I'm just really on edge right now. I'm not made for these kinds of situations—and look, look at my hands. I'm flapping! I'm going to break out in hives."

"I promise everything is fine. Come here." Dallas opened his arms and I walked right on in. He rubbed my back while I laid my head on his shoulder, and *then* I realized we were *hugging*. We'd held hands a lot before, but this was our first hug. "I'm sorry but this is the most adorable thing ever."

I whined into his shoulder. Warm and solid, he smelled like laundry detergent, not some super-overpowering cologne. Safe. Familiar. Like everything might be okay.

Did he press his cheek against the side of my forehead? I had less than half a second to wonder before he said, dangerously close to my ear, "Do you think we should do anything else?"

My beating-too-fast heart hit the turbo button. Thank God he couldn't see my face, because I'm sure I looked like one of those tiny nocturnal mammals with the huge eyes. "Umm."

"Umm?" He laughed—standing so close to his chest, it felt like quiet, rolling thunder.

I knew you didn't have to date someone to kiss them. Is that what he meant? Obviously, I was down. Obviously. Yep. And bonus points for him asking first. "Do? Like what?" Lifting my head, I tried to find his eyes in the darkness.

"The windows? You can't really see out, but maybe we should close the blinds. Also, Winston's out there."

OH.

He meant the diner.

Right.

The diner.

Not kissing.

The diner.

Great, now I'd be stuck thinking about kissing him.

He placed his hands on my shoulders and took a step back. "I'll go close the blinds. You wait here. I'll call when it's safe." Not waiting, he started to walk away.

"No, not okay." My hand shot out and found his as if it were always meant to. "We stay together. Splitting up means people die in horror movies." I clutched his bicep with my phone in hand, standing so close to him I probably made his shadow jealous.

The front door looked the same—dark and terrible. Nothing outside the windows moved.

"Stay behind the counter. I'll be quick."

It physically pained me to let him go. Somehow, I survived.

"Where's my sister?" Winston asked.

"I'm here!" Dallas placed the laptop on the counter. "It's fine. The power's out."

"You all right?"

I watched Dallas move from booth to booth, letting the blinds down and turning them to the closed position. "I think so."

"Do you want me to wait with you?"

I looked away and at Dallas again.

"Never mind. I'm going. Talk to you later."

Oops. "I'll message you."

Dallas doubled back, stood with me behind the counter again. "Let's sit here." He started to kneel.

"Wait." I walked to the end of the counter to get a few towels stored under it for spills and such. I laid them on the ground to sit on.

"Okay, so I'm not supposed to close early. I have broken a lot of rules this summer, but not that one. We're not closed. The doors are just locked. If someone comes, they can knock, and I'll politely explain that the power is out and I can't serve them."

"Sounds good."

"She can't get mad at me for this. There's no way this is my fault."

When he held one of my hands in both of his, I held my breath. Not sure why. Everything sort of closed up. But not my eyes. Those definitely widened, searching for him again. It wasn't fair. I needed to see him to read him. I had to be sure I wasn't jumping the gun again.

"Do you fight with your parents a lot, too?"

"No. Before this summer, I never really fought with Granny either. Something's just off lately."

"Tell me about your parents? I can't believe they never come here."

"I don't think my dad would mind visiting, but my mom is a hard no. She absolutely refuses." I tilted my head back, staring at nothing. "My dad is huge. A giant, burly Black man with a beard. Do you know who Kimbo Slice is? He's built like him except way bigger and kind of jolly. When he laughs it's always this deep, rumbly chuckle that makes you laugh just from hearing it. He's *really* funny, too. Once during dinner he made Sam pee on herself from laughing too hard."

"I don't think she'd want me to know that."

"Too late. And my mom is an undiscovered supermodel. Seriously. She's Winston's height—how I ended up so short, I'll never know—and the literal definition of svelte. You know how some people are considered conventionally beautiful solely based on the fact they have a quote-unquote 'perfect' body even though really they're like a total Monet? My mom isn't like that. Her face is out-of-this-world beautiful. But the best part about her? She's super smart, just brilliant when it comes to academic stuff. People shouldn't be allowed to be beautiful and smart and talented, because it breaks reality and pisses people off. She's going for tenure at her university next year and she's worried she's not going to get it because of discrimination disguised as a bullshit technicality. If that happens, I will personally set their offices on fire."

"Wow."

"Yeah. I wish I were exaggerating, but my parents are almost perfect. It's a lot to live up to sometimes, but I know, *I know*, that even if I can't? They'll love me anyway because that's just the kind of people they are."

"That explains a lot."

It seemed like he had said that to himself, so I didn't say anything else. We fell into a natural silence, and it didn't take long before that feeling of wanting began to claw at me again.

"And it's just you and Winston?"

"And Sam. She's my cousin but we all live in the same house. Her dad, too." I leaned to the side, resting my head on his shoulder. "I feel like I ruined their summer. Sam told me that they only come here because I want to be here, and Winston confirmed it. I kind of made it up to her already, but I need to do something extra special for Winston."

He never asked for much. He liked movies—had subscriptions to all kinds of streaming services thanks to my parents. He wasn't really into clothes or music. Not a big reader either. What could I—

Oh. My. God.

I knew what to do. The idea struck me like a runaway train. I might die during and probably for sure after, but oh my God.

Winston would *love* it.

"I've been thinking," Dallas said. "Would you like to re-meet my parents?"

I blinked, attention immediately shifting back to Dallas. I wish he could've seen the huge smile on my face. Ever since I'd snuck out of the house with him, I'd had this theory that he collected my smiles and facial expressions. Like his brain took a snapshot and filed it away so he'd always remember me.

"I would love to."

Thirty-One

my shoulders tensed. I heard my name begin to ripple through the small crowd in Merry's town hall. I'd walked in alone, filled out my registration forms, was given a number, and then was told where to wait to be called.

No one knew I'd gone there. Not Granny or Kara or Sam or Dallas or Winston.

By the time it was over, everyone would know, because nothing would stop me from getting Winston featured on Sana Starlight's show.

Granny could lump my silent treatment/punishment for this in with sort of closing early during the blackout. Once the news hit, she'd probably try to find a way to blame me for a blackout caused by a downed power line, too.

Everything would work out. Eventually. She might be mad for longer than average, but we'd get through it. One of my mom's favorite things to say was, "That's how love works. Among many other things, it means forgiveness."

I expected the place to be empty. The taping was coming up soon, so I figured everyone who had wanted to audition, already had. I had a short wait, maybe five minutes, before they called my name.

Up the walk and through a red door, straight to a small room with cameras and lighting set up. I knew that. I knew they would be there and no, I was not about to throw up. At all. Nope.

What did an embolism feel like? A pain thumped in my chest. It moved from time to time—my chest, my gut, the backs of my eyes—always pulsating and reminding me I was uncomfortably alive with *feelings*. I would have paid good money to be put into a medically induced coma rather than be interviewed.

Winston.

I had the strength to keep calm and sell our story just like Kara had outlined.

For Winston.

I also knew what the producers and casting assistant saw when I walked in. People's faces betrayed their initial snap judgments all the time. The lifted eyebrows, gradual widening of their eyes, the dismissive slight eye roll. Some tried to be less rude, clearing their throats before looking away. I could recognize it all with ease.

Pretty or not, I was still Black, fat, and a girl who didn't have a naturally nice demeanor. Three strikes and I'd lucked into the ultimate social misfortune of scaring people just by existing.

"Please have a seat." A man in a black snapback pointed to the chair in the middle of the room.

"It's a fairly simple process," a different man with a clipboard said. "I ask a question, you answer. If you mess up, take a moment to compose yourself and begin again. It'll all be edited later. I'll be using the stock questions we provided at the time of your registration, but I'll also follow the ebb and flow of the interview. Any questions?" I shook my head and he continued, "Excellent. Please state your name, your town, and which competition you'll be entering."

"My name is Winnie Woodson." They never said I had to look at the camera. If I didn't have to look at it, I'd be fine. Maybe. I concentrated on staying calm and keeping my voice shaking-free. "I'm from Misty Haven and I'm signing my younger brother, Winston, up for the savory category."

"You won't be competing?"

"No. He's a culinary genius but also fourteen. I turned eighteen in May." *Genius.* Damn, I shouldn't have said that.

"That's nice of you. We have a father-daughter team already signed up with the same story," one said. "She was too young to enter so her dad—passionately—convinced us to give her a chance."

"Why don't you tell us a bit about why he wants to enter and why you've decided to help him," the other asked.

Deep breath. Sit up straight. Smize. Adjust your tone. Watch your cadence. Emphasize with your hands. This is for Winston.

"Honestly, it's absolutely a family affair. My grandmother, Geraldine, owns and runs Goldeen's Diner in Misty Haven. I've spent every summer here since she bought and restored it fifteen years ago. Owning her own restaurant had been her dream since she was my age in the fifties and now it's my dream, too. Growing up in Goldeen's had a profound effect on me. I'm all set to attend college in the fall to begin my degree in Hospitality and Business Management. I love the sense of community here, connecting with customers, our staff is like family, coming up with new menu items, and such. My grandmother would have entered but she didn't think she'd have the time—summer is our busiest season—but my brother wouldn't stop talking about it, so I decided to help him. Team Win-Win."

Kara had been *right*. Both the producer and the casting agent exchanged *Looks* while I spoke, quickly jotting down notes on their clipboards, tilting them so the other could see. No more jaded, bored expressions. Their eyes sparkled with interest.

"Very good. Tell us a little about your brother. Is he here, too?"

"Unfortunately, no. He's working his shift at Goldeen's." I laughed for effect. Little white lies never hurt anyone. "We're really dedicated. I mean, he's fourteen but wakes up every day at nine a.m. for his shift without fail. He prefers the kitchen, where he's apprenticing under our head cook, Aaron, and learning more about cooking, food handling, safety, and how to craft an irresistible and complementary menu. Other than that, he's really passionate about film and movies. He has a gift for quoting perfect one-liners exactly at the right moment and makes me watch awful horror movies that give me awful nightmares. But I love him, so I watch them." I rolled my eyes playfully. "We're really close. I totally spoil him rotten. Always have, always will."

"You must really love your brother."

"Not to be dramatic, but I'd risk my life for him."

Which was exactly what I had just done.

❧

Kara (Kara Kara Kara Kara) Chameleon

Kara: YOU

Kara: DID

Kara: WHAT

> **Winnie:** I did it for Winston!

Kara: It's like you WANT me to jump through this phone and attack you

Kara: GOD how am I supposed to keep you safe!? She knows where I live!!

Thirty-Two

I stood in front of the drive-in screen alone. Okay, not *alone* alone. Dallas stood at my side. The gentle, reassuring pressure of his hand lay across my lower back.

Mostly to keep me from running away.

"Hi. Some of you may know me. Or all. I don't know, I feel like my name gets around more than I would like anyway. I'm Winnie. I work at my granny's diner, Goldeen's, and I get to wear this nifty crown for the summer but am also being forced to do a lot of not-so-nifty things. Well, some of it's nifty. Not all of it. This is not nifty. This is terrifying."

A smattering of polite laughter rolled through the crowd. Some people sat in the trunks of their cars or the flatbeds of their SUVs, others posted up on the roof of their cars, but most had sprawled out on blankets.

Dallas whispered in my ear, "Roll back on the *nifty* usage. You're doing fine." Before I'd started he'd given me a few public-speaking pointers to help me along, and I'd rightly blown him off. Comedic politician-speak wouldn't work for me. I had to be myself—nervous rambling and all—or there wasn't any point to this exercise.

I was doing this for me.

My life-endangering audition taught me something. If I could talk on camera/stand in front of crowds in a tiara/do a choreographed dance and lip sync/wear a goddess dress to a pool for someone else's benefit, I could do it for me, too.

Correction: I could *try* to do it for me, too.

I appreciated his hand, though. Like a five-finger weighted security blanket to keep me warm and calm.

"Since he, Dallas, usually does all the talking when we come to these things, I thought I would try it tonight. Clearly mistakes were made." I laughed at myself, staring at my feet, and the crowd continued to humor me, laughing along.

The sun had gone down a few hours ago. I couldn't tell if I was sweating because of nerves or the residual summer heat mucking up the air. It helped that I couldn't see any individual faces other than the cluster of kids up front sitting with Sam, who kept giving me a thumbs-up any time I glanced in her direction. How she could wrangle more than three kids at one time was pure magic and worth a metric ton of money. Her playdate parties were rarer than leprechauns, capped at twelve, and parents fell over themselves to get a spot.

"But Dallas is really great and supportive and nice—he's a genuinely nice person. I don't know if any of you have ever tried internet dating, but that's super rare and hard to find, so, uh, thanks for the hookup." I shot a finger gun at the audience, clicking my tongue.

Sam dropped her head in her hands, shaking it back and forth, but when she looked up again, her smile was so wide it gave me an immediate shot of confidence.

"My queen, ladies, gentlemen, and gentlethems," Dallas said.

Someone in the crowd shouted, "WOO! YEAH!"

"For the record: I don't call him 'my king.' That's not a thing that happens."

"We're working on it."

"No, we're not."

"Fine. We're not. That was a lie." Dallas pouted for a second. "But I have been trying to come up with a nickname for her because 'my queen' is so formal and we're definitely past that stage. Problem is, Winnie is just so cute on its own. Maybe we should hold a contest. Let the kids pick." He nodded at the cluster in the front row, who immediately began cheering.

"No, no." I smiled, trying not to let my annoyance show. "Not doing that."

"Sorry, kids. Queen Winnie is just no fun. Oh!" He looked at me, surprised. "Queen Winnie. *Queenie.* That's a good one, right?"

The kids did what kids do and started chanting, "Queenie! Queenie! Queenie!"

I looked Dallas dead in the eye. "Why are you like this?"

He shrugged, grinning at me.

"Settle down, settle down," Sam whispered in a kind, firm voice. Eventually, they all quieted.

I let loose a long-suffering sigh. "I think we've taken up more time than we were allotted. I hope you enjoy the movie."

Dallas held out his hand for me to take, which I did. The crowd clapped as we walked away—I darted back to the center. "Oh, and please start locking your doors at night. It's really weird and unsafe that no one does that here."

Small-town life made people gullible. Made them more trusting and more likely to be a mark. During Drive-In Movie Night last year, Winston convinced Ms. Irene to let him play *The Strangers* for their own good, and not even that could change their minds. "It's just a movie," she had said. "That wouldn't happen here, Winnie. Stop."

You can lead a zombie to a school, but you can't make them think. Someone had to protect them.

"Queenie." Dallas maneuvered me away—playfully lifting our joined arms in the air and using my surprise as momentum to spin me around into a tight embrace. "Sorry about that," he said to the crowd. "Enjoy!"

I ducked and twisted around, turning his embrace against him, holding him at his sides from behind. "No one can call me Queenie! I mean it!"

Kara stood next to our blanket, clapping as we approached our spot, in a quiet corner of the park, just to the left of the screen. "Beautiful! Just beautiful! Did y'all write that beforehand?" She had wanted to sit up close.

"No. He didn't want to sound stiff."

"That's not what I said."

"Well, it doesn't matter. That bit at the end? Winnie totally stole the show, as expected. I'm. So. Proud. Of. You." I let her hold on to my cheeks. "*Woo woo woo.*"

"Mmkay. How long are you going to be like this?"

"I'm done." She dropped her hands, turning to Dallas. "I'm not really a beat around the bush kind of girl, you know. If I'm ready and I have something to say, I say it, so I'm going to say it. She likes you."

I sputtered. "O-okay!?"

"It's true. She does. We both know it, and I shouldn't have stood in the way of that. If it means anything to you, I'm sorry, and I hope someday you can forgive me."

He shoved his hands in his pockets. "Okay."

Oh shit.

"She likes a lot of people because that's her thing. But once she cares about you? You're in for life. I, on the other hand, do not care. At any given time, outside of my family, I like two to three people tops. I will tolerate up to an additional five."

"Sounds reasonable," Dallas said without a hint of emotion. I knew this would happen. When I told him she wanted to come tonight, he had gotten this strange look on his face and said, "If you want her there," and then shrugged. *Shrugged.* The unaffected kiss of death.

"But then everything changed when the Winnie Nation attacked. I super aggressively wanted to be her friend. I needed to. I had no choice. I was obsessed and honestly still am."

"You don't say."

This just wasn't going to go well *at all*, was it?

"When you're like me, you get used to losing friends," she said matter-of-factly. "I'm used to losing friends. The second they start dating someone is the second I start to disappear from their lives. And it's like, cool, I get it. Sure, I'll totally cry myself to sleep every night because no one thinks friendship is as important as I do, not that they care. But her"—she grabbed me into a bear hug, squeezing extra hard—"No. Not her. This is *different.* She's my *ungirlfriend.* I did something I shouldn't have because I didn't know how to express what I was feeling. I don't think that makes me a bad person. It makes me human. I'm allowed to make mistakes."

"Yes, you are," I affirmed. "Everyone is."

"You don't have to accept my apology," Kara continued. "I don't need you to forgive me to learn from this and move on. That part is up to you. I can't tell you how to feel. But if you even think to fix your mouth to say the words 'it's me or Kara' to try to manipulate her into choosing, I will go full-on Mrs. Lovett from *Sweeney Todd* on you."

"*Sweeney Todd?*"

"Look it up. Respect my boundaries and time with Winnie, and

I'll respect yours. She has good taste in people, so if she sees something in you, I'm willing to see it, too. No, I want to see it. We should be friends in our own right. Not just because we have Winnie in common. I understand if you don't want to or if you think you can't trust me, but I'd like to work towards earning that from you."

That was a wild ride, from start to finish. Only Kara could flip from *I will murder you and bake you into my pies* to *Let's be friends, okay?* Holding grudges truly was not in her. I kissed her cheek because I could, and she ducked her head to the side, smiling.

"See?" I said to him. "That's how we're able to make it work."

He didn't know it, but that was a near-perfect demonstration of what being an ungirlfriend meant. No secrets, no hiding, and constant communication. Kara had found her way again—being honest, faults and all.

And I was so damn proud.

Dallas looked at us. He focused on us as a whole, the way we stood together, united. And then our eyes met. "I don't really like texting." He shrugged. "But Winnie says you do, so I guess we could start there?"

Kara gave me an extra squeeze. "But you don't like it. I don't want you to do something you don't want to do. That's not how friendship works."

"Yeah, but I like reading. Send me book recs? Tell me stories? Send me recipes? I love cookies, by the way. Fully willing to be your taste tester."

"See?" I gave Kara a light headbutt. "Told you he was great."

"I guess he's all right." She let go of me, crossing her arms over her chest. "For a boy anyway."

I rolled my eyes. She's as bad as Winston sometimes.

"Thanks? Do you not have guy friends?"

"I prefer girls. Less drama and way less hostility. Until they leave me, anyway."

"From what I can tell, it seems like their loss."

"*See?*"

"Yes, I see. Calm down." She glared at me. "Now you."

"Don't be mad."

"I'm very mad."

"Side note," I said to Dallas, "she's also very motherly."

"And this one is determined to get herself killed."

"Don't bring him into this!"

"Maybe we should sit," Dallas said. "Get some snacks for you two and some background information for me."

"Done."

I'd seen the potluck table when we first arrived. Appetizers had been pushed to the front: deviled eggs, a veggie and cheese platter. The smoky tang of charred meat and barbecue sauce became more distinct the more dishes showed up—ribs, turkey wings, hot and mild links. Grilled corn on the cob, baked beans, and salad for sides. A giant pot of spaghetti and meatballs. For dessert, there were two pies, apple and sweet potato; a cake covered in chocolate frosting, most likely yellow cake because it was always yellow cake; and a regretfully watery peach cobbler.

Kara had already raided it, mixing the food she picked with the standard movie snacks she'd brought from home: popcorn, candy, and soda. She sat across from me, next to Dallas, who was between us, forming a tight triangle.

Interesting.

"You know about the Starlight competition, right?" Kara asked. Dallas nodded and she continued, filling him in on how she had entered and how me asking to enter didn't go as planned.

"My granny doesn't really tolerate talking back."

"Asking why you can't enter is talking back?"

"It can be."

Kara continued, explaining about how Winston wanted to enter, why Granny had said no again, and that she was seriously worried about my future on this Earth.

"She went behind all of our backs and not only entered the contest, but thanks to whatever she said during her interview, they're going to feature Winston. This level of defiance is unheard of. We can't even guess what's going to happen when Granny finds out. Didn't she tell you no like *four* times?"

"I had to do it. I don't care. If it's for Winston, I'll do whatever. Like I'll die if I don't. Die. Just wither and die." I grabbed a can of soda and popped a straw in after opening it. "It's my job. I'm supposed to take care of everyone, make sure they're happy, do everything I can to make sure they're living their best life, overthrow corrupt governments, and save the world."

"Um, nope," Kara said.

"Yes. Yes. It's what I do. That's who I am."

"Wow." Dallas laughed.

"What?"

"I've never seen you like this. You always seem so on top of things and kind of serious but in a playful way. This is different. You're different."

"Not really. I'm always like this. Desperate. Frantic. Emotional," I said with a twinge of disgust. "I just don't show it to the general public. Welcome to my inner circle, by the way."

"Maybe you should. It's cute."

I ducked away, trying to hide my face while pretending to sip my soda.

He leaned toward me. "It's very cute."

"Iheardyouthefirsttime."

"Damn near adorable."

"Enough. Okay. Let me live."

"Hey, hey!" Kara snapped her fingers. "No distracting her with compliments. We're supposed to be a combination of concerned, stern, and partially angry here."

The screen reflected a blast of white light as the movie started. Bass pounded through the speakers while the production company's bumper played. Respectful silence surrounded us—Kara got in one last squinty-eyed look at me before turning away.

"I wish Winston was here," I said sometime later to no one in particular. "He loves this movie."

When it was over, Sam stopped by to say hi before leading her little ducklings away for the night. Kara yawned dramatically before locking eyes with me. "You should probably sleep at my house tonight."

"That seems wise."

"Do you want to come over? You can't spend the night, but my dad won't mind if you visit."

"Me?" Dallas looked as shocked as I felt.

"I'm *trying* okay?" Kara's cheeks flushed.

"Hey, Winnie!" A girl approached our blanket. My brain wanted to call her May but wasn't sure if that was 100 percent correct. "How are you?"

"Fine." I'd definitely seen her around town—her long, black curly hair; chubby face; and blue eyes were a hard combination to miss. But I really couldn't figure out precisely who she was.

"Did Sam leave already?" May asked. "I wanted to ask her something."

"Oh. Yeah, she did. You just missed her."

She continued to stand there waiting for something, chewing on her bottom lip. "So she's like helping you with—stuff—right? It looks like it's working." Her eyes flicked to Dallas. "Could we maybe talk in private?"

"I don't think so," Kara interrupted. "I feel like I know what you're about to say, and you better not."

May blanched. "It's just I saw her up there before the movie, with him, and she seemed so different, so I thought . . ." She trailed off.

"Wait, what did I do?" Dallas asked.

"Oh no." The light bulb didn't just click on. It shone so bright it shattered. With more kindness than I thought I possessed, I said, "Look, I'm sorry, but I can't help you with this. There's literally nothing to talk about because whatever you're thinking isn't what's happening."

She didn't look convinced. "Could you just—if you could give Sam my number and ask her to text me?" Her eyes pleaded with me to understand. "It's my mom. She made me come over here."

"Okay. Sure."

I refused to watch her leave. I didn't want to see her go back to her family. I didn't even want to remember the last five minutes.

"I think I missed something," Dallas said.

"Yeah, you did. Keep on missing it," Kara said.

"Except I'm not stupid." He frowned. "I got most of the pieces. Sam. May and her mom. Winnie. The jogging. I get it. I just don't see how I fit into it."

"Because you like her." Kara sighed. "And they think you shouldn't."

"I know about that," he admitted. "What does that have to do with Sam and Winnie?"

I seemed so different. With him.

My confidence, my ability to be in front of crowds without visibly and slowly dying while my stomach tried to turn itself inside out wasn't because of him. I did that. I was learning to conquer my fear on my own because I was ready. He had helped me up there just like any friend would, but that's not what any of them saw.

Dallas was teaching me how to put myself out there.

Dallas was making me better.

Dallas was my everything now.

Dallas was the reason I was jogging—I had to make myself worthy to stand beside him.

Bullshit. All of that was *mine*.

"You know," I said, voice harsh. That girl was breaking my heart and I hated it. "I am really tired of people thinking I have low self-esteem and don't love myself just because they think I'm too big and don't deserve to be happy."

A voice in the back of my mind wailed bloody murder. I'd just called myself big in front of Dallas. The voice hissed that I should be ashamed, that girls never talked about their weight in front of boys and now he would never fall in love with me because boys didn't want fat girls who stayed fat. They didn't like the ones that never planned to diet, that never planned to look good for them the way they wanted and deserved. I would never be arm candy. They would never be proud to be seen with me. Never. Never. Never.

That voice could shut the entire fuck up.

Deep breath in and out.

"Sam wanted to run, so we are. Sam doesn't have a brother like Winston or a partner like Kara. She cries at night because she thinks nobody really likes her. People use her because she has money. She worries everyone thinks she's annoying."

"Well, she is," Kara said. "But still very loveable."

"Sam has me. I'm running with Sam for Sam. No different than how I entered the contest for Winston." I looked at Kara. "Or worked at the grocery store with you and gave you all of my paychecks so you could get that mixer thing. And I think I do those things for me, too, because I want to be able to say I did it.

"Not bragging like I'm a better person because I give more, but I view it like me saying I was able to talk to producers without having a panic attack or 'Hey, remember that time I ran a mile without stopping? That was pretty dope.' They're my accomplishments, too. I just want to experience my life, my way." I stared at the blank screen while I spoke—and then promptly had the life scared out of me when I turned to Dallas. "Why are you looking at me like that?"

"Like what?"

"That." I gestured in his general direction as if that were good enough and in no way a nonsensical answer. "You're doing a thing with your eyeballs."

"A very obvious thing," Kara said.

"Am I? I'm not sure what you mean." He began to smile, all of his teeth showing.

"You better be careful," Kara warned, while standing. She stretched on her tiptoes, hands reaching above her head. "That one will have you throwing yourself in front of vans skidding across ice to save her life." She dropped into a squat, eye level with him. "And that's just the start of it."

~

SA(RU)M(ON)

Sam: Hey um Granny is looking for you.

Sam: She says you're not answering your phone.

Sam: You really messed up this time. I don't think I've ever seen her this mad.

Sam: I think what you did was really cool. But um.

Sam: Maybe you could stay with Kara
tonight? I don't think you can be here.
Sam: I could try to talk to her? See if
I can get her to calm down?
Sam: I'll let you know when the coast is clear. If it ever is.
Sam: Um, Winnie?

> **Winnie:** Yep. I'm at Kara's. I'm off
> work tomorrow and I'm going to the
> Christmas in July party with Dallas so
> maybe I could come back after that?

Sam: Um.

FAM-BAM-MAJAMA

Mom: You know the rules. When I call, you answer.
If you miss my call, you return it immediately.
Mom: Where are you? With Kara? Dallas?
Mom: Answer your phone.
Dad: I can see you read that. Don't play with me.

WINSTON (Zeddemore)

Winston: Dude, what did you do? They won't tell me
Winston: Does Sam know? Don't
make me ask her PLEASE
Winston: WHY DOES EVERYONE KNOW BUT ME

Momma-da-vida

Mom: I'm not mad, sweetie.

Mom: I don't like this. Stop hiding from me.

Mom: Please just talk to me.

WINSTON (Zeddemore)

Winston: ASDFGHJKLNVIPAFLJDANF

Winston: !!!

Winston: I GOT AN EMAIL FROM SANA STARLIGHT

Winston: IS THAT WHAT YOU DID THAT'S WHAT YOU DID ISN'T IT YOU GOT ME ON THE SHOW??????????

Winston: I LOVE YOU SO FUCKING MUCH

FAM-BAM-MAJAMA

Winston: NO ONE IS ALLOWED TO YELL AT WINNIE FOR THIS

Winston: THAT IS ALL.

Winston: NO PUNISHMENTS EITHER!

Dad: Boy, you better relax off that caps lock

Thirty-Three

"You can't ignore them forever." Kara kissed my forehead.

"I'm not ignoring. I'm monitoring. Checking for tone and vibes." I put on my smuggest big-sister smile. "Winston loves me."

"Of course he does. Don't be wimpy. Call your mama." She walked on her knees to the edge of the bed. "Taking a shower. Miss Jepson wants us there by ten!"

She left me alone in her room with the boy-band photo staring at me. I used to know their names; she talked about them enough that it was impossible not to absorb some of their bio data through osmosis, but the little one with the hair swoop looked like the type who would never ignore his mom.

"Fine."

He was yelling at me with his pretty eyes.

If I had to do it, I'd take the long route, dialing the number manually. My mom's number was one of the few I had memorized. She made me do it for emergencies. My uncle called it "old-school style," back when everyone's brains were "basically meaty phone books full of numbers."

Three rings. "Hi, Mom."

She sighed.

〜

One frantic afternoon spent with Kara and Miss Jepson later, I arrived at Dallas's house. Walking up the drive, I smoothed down the skirt of my dress. Red wasn't really my color, but Miss Jepson had worked a Christmas Miracle.

Kara explained the idea—Mrs. Claus: Teenage Dream. Ready to flirt it up before old Saint Nick locked her down. Back when she had a first name, probably stayed out too late, went on kissing sprees, and had hobbies other than baking and elf-wrangling.

My new dress had the perfect cut, fold, and amount of material to create a fantastic flare shape when I twirled, and the hem hit the exact spot on my thighs where I liked my dresses to end. She also added a white faux-fur hem around the bottom of the dress, at the waist, and around the neckline; fashioned a pair of silent jingle-bell bangles for my shoes and wrists; and created a hooded white shoulder cape out of material that could double as fresh snow. Meanwhile, Kara had helped put my braids in rollers and dip them in boiling water to make the curls stay in place once dry.

I looked good. Felt good and pretty and happy.

And considering I was basically in the witness protection program until Granny calmed down, that was saying something. Plot twist: my parents weren't even upset about it, which I think really pissed Granny off. For once they had taken my side and were excited for Winston to compete.

Oh, but I was still in trouble for not returning their calls. No way they'd let that slide.

Dallas stood on his front porch. He kept wiping at his forehead and flushed cheeks but broke into a huge heart-stopping smile when he saw me.

"Aren't you hot?" The black dress shirt, black slacks, and red-and-gold vest combo had to be cooking his organs.

"I'm a single bead of sweat away from dehydration."

I snickered.

"But my mom is happy. So." He gave me a once-over, smile growing impossibly wider. "You look great and surprisingly on theme."

"Miss Jepson."

"Ah." He held out the crook of his elbow. "Shall we?"

"A gentleman. I like it. How befitting for a girl in a cape."

I'd been to his house dozens of times for deliveries. I could walk the path from his driveway, through the garage or the front door to the kitchen with my eyes closed. Now I'd finally get to see the rest of his house.

We unlinked arms as we rounded the first corner. I slowed down, but he kept pace a few steps ahead, clearly giving me time to marvel at all of the pictures on the walls. The kitchen had zero personality. There were showrooms in model houses that had more flavor. I guess I thought the rest of the house would be like that, too—sterile with no traces of the people who lived there.

Row after row of pictures showed the three Meyers in front of beaches, majestic cliffs, and hilly green mountains covered in mist; dinners at huge banquet tables full of laughing and smiling people; his mom with her arms outstretched on a grand stage in front of a packed house and a microphone; Dallas in every kind of sports uniform you'd imagine; his dad in his college football uniform and several of him once he'd gone pro. I tried to look at each picture, but there were too many to notice as we kept walking.

The trophy case was a different story.

"Oh, come on. Really?" I gestured at the huge glass case trimmed

in gold metal. It had been split into three sections—pictures, tro-
phies, rings, awards, and plaques for each of them.

"My parents are a proud people."

I made a noise in the back of my throat. "I guess I would be, too,
if I had all this."

"It doesn't mean anything."

"Um, yeah, it does. You earned this stuff. It's cool. Showy as hell,
but still cool."

He leaned against the wall facing me.

"My grandpa played baseball. My dad played football. My mom's
side of the family is full of athletes, too. I was literally born to be
good at sports. The only reason why I have all these things in the
first place is because collective *someones* decided my type of physical-
ity is worth rewarding. I could probably win music awards, too, if I
wanted."

"You cannot sing. No. It's too much. Begone, you foul, talented
demon."

"I'm lucky and I'm naturally good at a bunch of stuff."

It kind of bothered me how much he had downplayed his accomplishments like that. I didn't care about sports, but it was impossible not to notice how the cheerleaders were always the first ones at
school, how the football team practiced late into the night, how the
track and field team would sweat to death in the sun every day.

"Being naturally good doesn't mean you don't work hard at being
successful. Dedication isn't necessarily something you're born with."

Dallas held out his hand. "Come on."

After passing under a pointed archway and walking down a short
hallway, the backyard came into view. The enormous backyard with a
giant white tent in the center of it. Most of the houses in Merry had
plots of land but not that massive.

"Jesus, did you buy the house behind you and tear it down?" Fake snow coated the ground and a snow machine blew featherlight sparkly confetti into the air.

"It's still there. And technically mine."

"Your parents gave you a house?"

"More like a cottage. I use my room in the main house more often."

"The main house." I snorted. "Just so you know, I like you, but I also hate you. Don't take it personally."

"I never do."

Right before we entered the tent, Dallas gave my hand a tight squeeze and then let go. I knew that meant *thank you*. Technically, this wasn't a Royal Engagement.

It was his mom's birthday party.

A band played music while people danced. I recognized the song, something by Glenn Miller, because in a movie a character holding vinyl records called out to her sister and said it was Glenn Miller and then the same song played.

The wooden floor had been placed over the grass and an uncovered block of it took up the center of the tent. A few brave souls danced, but most of the partygoers sat in groups of six to eight at round tables that surrounded said dance floor or stood mingling with whoever crossed their path. The food had been set up in a U shape along the sides of the tent, and waiters in tuxedos walked around with drink trays balanced on their flat palms.

I shivered. "Not complaining, but a penguin could survive in here. How is it so cold?" If I had a choice, cold was the way to go. You can only get so naked before you run out of cool-down options.

"Air-conditioning units. Six of them." He placed a hand on my lower back. We walked to the left toward the food tables.

"How cute. Melting snowman cookies. So sad and yet hunger-inducing." Everything on the food tables looked delicious and none of it could be trusted.

Dallas pointed toward a small table. The red tablecloth didn't match the others. The placement seemed a little off, too, as if it had been squashed in at the last minute. "This is the Winnie-approved food table. Everything on it is gluten-free."

I stared at him in surprise.

"I called Kara. She gave me most of these desserts, and I sent my dad to the store to buy the rest of what she recommended."

Kara was the kind of person you'd wait for forever if she asked you to. Straight from epic poems with devoted ladies-in-waiting and befuddled knights left on hills to rot forever cursing and revering her name. "You ever just love someone so much it makes you want to die in the most dramatic way possible for them?"

"That was some solid hyperbole."

I dragged myself out of my Kara-reverie. "Hyper—what now?"

"Dad." Dallas snapped to attention, shoulders back and chin raised. Interesting.

His dad, Rob, wore slacks and a plain dress shirt. Not a single jingle bell or candy cane to be found anywhere on him.

"Miss Winnie." There was a thing with my name that only older Black people did. I was always *Miss Winnie*.

"Sir." And being called that automatically made *sir* and *ma'am* jump out.

"I hear you're off to college soon. That's quite an achievement. Your grandmother must be thrilled."

"Thank you." Granny was also a fiery ball of rage on the hunt for me, but she was still proud! Probably!

"Well. It was nice to see you again, Miss Winnie. Dallas, be sure to help your mother with anything she needs."

"Right." His dad left as swiftly as he had arrived.

"He seems nice and very chatty."

Dallas nodded. "Um, I should also probably warn you." He looked around the room. "I tried to make the rounds before you got here, but I didn't get to say hi to all of my relatives. They're probably going to come say something to me at some point."

"It's a party. I'll just duck out and hide somewhere until you're done. Over there somewhere. There's punch." I gazed up at him, teasing smile out in full force. "I *love* party punch."

"That's not very date-like."

"Date?" But we weren't wearing our crowns! It wasn't a public event! Did he mean a *real* date? "This is a non-royalty date?"

He nodded. "And this is my aunt."

Before I could stick my foot in my mouth, Dallas said hello to a white lady in a white dress and white hat covered in feathers. She air-kissed both of his cheeks, fawned over how tall he'd gotten, and admonished him for not calling her more. Yep. Definitely family. Only thing missing were the humiliating cheek pinches.

"And where is Lacey?" She glanced at me in confusion.

"We broke up. It was mutual."

Another glance at me and slight crinkle of her forehead later, she said, "Oh, that's too bad."

"It's not. This is my queen, Winnie."

Surprise crawled across his aunt's face in slow motion, morphing into confusion before relaxing. "Oh, of course! Right! Your mom told me about that. Something your lovely little town does. I'm glad you two were able to become friends. I mean, I'm assuming you're *just* friends."

That feathered freak had the nerve to look relieved.

"Actually, there's no 'just' about it. I don't quantify people I care about that way."

Dallas's soft laugh made me float for half a second. "It was good to see you. We're going to get some punch."

If only it had been that easy. On the way to the glass punch bowl with a freaky yet adorable ice statue of an elf inside it, lined by frosted goblets, someone stopped Dallas every thirty seconds to say hi, catch up on this, that, and the other.

And he introduced me as his queen, every single time.

"Hello, my darling!" Dallas's mom appeared in a cloud of snow-flakes. Literally. Two little kids followed behind her, giggling as they threw handfuls of paper confetti snowflakes into the air around her. She planted a huge kiss on Dallas's cheek, rubbing her lipstick off with her thumb after. "Are you having a good time? WINNIE!"

She let him go, reaching and pulling me into the mommiest, most spiced-rum-scented hug to ever exist. "Look how grown up you are," she said. "I feel like I haven't seen you in ages. Did your grandmother come?"

"Unfortunately, she and the other grannies in town had concert tickets for tonight that they'd bought months ago." I only knew that because Sam had told me and thought it might improve Granny's mood enough for the goddess magic to work later that night.

"And how are you? Ready for college?"

"Ready-ish."

"I understand. Dallas has been the same way. It's just so good to see you." Another hug. "He talks about you *constantly*."

"*Mom.*"

That quick, flat outburst almost made me laugh.

"What? It's true"—she looked at me with a conspiratorial twinkle in her eye—"he does."

Dallas stared at her. If I had to put words to it, I'd guess he was silently screaming.

"And he made us *promise* to leave you alone. We came to all of your events."

"Wait, seriously?"

"Mom. Please."

"Forced by my own son, whom I love more than life itself, to hide in the shadows like some commoner. Anyway." She made a drunken twirl of her hand. "I expect a dance later, young man. Winnie, you let me know if he misbehaves, yes?"

"Sure."

Once she and her pint-sized entourage left, Dallas said, "Not a word. She's drunk and having a good time."

"I gathered as much, thanks."

"I don't talk about you all the time."

"Uh-huh. Why are you so obsessed with me?"

For an answer, Dallas only looked at me and sighed.

⌒

After more mingling, a few spins around the dance floor, and eating some Winnie-approved snacks that mightily impressed Dallas, he asked me to follow him outside, where I was rudely reminded that it wasn't a chilly seventy degrees outside.

"No, let's go back inside. I want to be one with my inner penguin."

"It's not far."

I gasped. "Are you taking me to your cottage in the woods?"

"Maybe."

Said cottage was at the end of a stone path lined with flowers. Inside, someone, probably his mom, had filled it with soft blues and soothing yellows. Couches surrounded a TV, and behind them was a nearly full bookcase built into the wall. I ran my hand along the spines. "No dust. Hmm."

"Bathroom"—he pointed to the left—"bedrooms"—he pointed to the right—"kitchen"—straight ahead.

"Still hate you." I read the book titles one by one. "Aha!" I held up the sequel to the book he had loaned me. "Can I?"

"Sure."

I did a little happy dance. "Iorek is officially my favorite talking bear. I love him more than Bear *and* Winnie the Pooh. He defeated my own alter ego, which is saying something. You have no idea how hard it was to stop myself from buying the box set I found online."

"Why didn't you?"

"Because I wanted to borrow your copy. I loved reading all your little notes. Did you mark this one up, too?" I flipped through the first few pages.

He leaned against the back of the couch. "I just sort of fell in love with books this year and didn't question it."

"Nice." I left the bookshelf and leaned next to him.

"I tried to change my major to English and publishing, but my parents flipped out. *'How are you going to support yourself!?'*" He laughed.

"Wild guess here, but you have an athletic scholarship, right? Basketball? Football?"

"Yeah. It ended up being basketball. But I can choose any major I want to study. My knees won't last forever. It would be supremely stupid to bet my entire future on them."

"Are you undeclared then?"

He shook his head. "Pharmacology and drug development. Minoring in English literature."

"Wow! Holy—are you for real?"

"Don't sound so shocked. You might wound my indestructible pride."

"Sorry." I tried to laugh off my embarrassment. "I just never thought of you as that kind of smart. I mean, I'm not saying I thought you were stupid or anything. That just sounds really intense."

"I'm sure it will be." He shrugged.

We stood there for a while, together and not speaking. Looking through the book was a cheat. I wanted to say more, but the nervous twitchy feeling in my chest wouldn't let me. Almost like someone had flipped a switch, the tension in the room began to press down on me. Gravity had it out for us. Each minute that passed, we leaned closer together. His arm touched mine. My head tilted toward his. Our hands inevitably found each other.

Mint lip balm. A couple of false starts. Melting into softness. A rapid beating heart. That's what first kisses were made of.

"I like you, Dallas."

"I like you, too."

"I *like* you," I insisted. "And I don't know how far that goes because it hasn't stopped yet."

He stood up straight, that perfect crooked smile out in full force, and held out his hand.

I took it. "And thank you for giving Kara a chance."

"Technically, I'm giving *you* a chance. I'm willing to try this because I like you. If being with you means accepting her, too, then that's what I'll do." The intensity burning in his eyes made my breath hitch. Sometimes, when Dallas looked at me, I'd swear he could see the entire history of my soul if he wanted to. "I don't know if this will work. I don't trust her and I don't know if I'll ever truly like her. But I like you and I know exactly how far that goes. I can't give you up." He shook his head. "That's why I volunteered. I had to know. Because I tried, and I couldn't. I can't."

"*Good.*" I laughed, unable to control my smile. It felt too big and too gummy, because I was so damn happy. "Because I don't want you to."

~

SA(RU)M(ON)

Sam: You can come back!
Sam: I don't think it's a trick either!
Sam: But you're gonna need to be on your best behavior!
Sam: Are you picking Winston up from the airport this week?
Sam: Winnie?
Sam: Helloooooo?

Winnie: Goddess <3333

Sam: <3333333

Thirty-Four

ehold!" Kara shouted from the front. "I have retrieved and safely delivered the crowned Prince of Zamunda!"

Gripping a bucket full of water in my hands, I shouted, "Great! Perfect! Come help!" through the kitchen window. Moving as fast as I could to avoid unwanted slippage, I hurried to the sink and dumped the water out.

"What's going on?" Winston asked. He appeared in the doorway just as I positioned myself in front of one of the more furious leaks, catching the water with a bucket.

"Holy shit!" Kara's jaw couldn't drop any further if she were a starving anaconda.

The dishwasher decided to make a deal with a demon and was currently in the throes of possession. Water sprayed around the sides of the door, bubbles seeped out and onto the floor. Layla tried to keep it from spreading deeper into the kitchen with towels, sponges, and a mop. Meanwhile, Aaron struggled to find the right valve to shut it off.

If it wasn't fire, it was water. Next a sinkhole would swallow the kitchen whole and the air conditioner would give up the ghost. Where was the Avatar when you needed him?

Winston gave himself a running start before sliding clean through a patch of bubbles with amazing balance to help Aaron.

Hand clutching the edge of the metal rim, he bent his knees, ducked his head, and crawled/slingshotted himself under the sink. In a crab position, he kicked a blue lever once, twice, again—and the water shut off, dishwasher groaning to a halt.

"Praise Jesus." Layla let the mop fall to the floor. She wasn't quite soaked from head to toe. More like from the waist down, like she'd been wading through a river.

I asked, "Where did you learn to slide like that? I would've busted my head wide open."

Winston stood up, giving Aaron a smug look. I couldn't help it—I all but ran and gave him the tightest hug my arms had ever given.

Aaron crossed his arms over his chest. "I'm a chef, not a plumber."

"But it's *your* kitchen." Winston rested his chin on top of my head. "Is the sink not a part of it?"

"JR handles it."

"Speaking of," Layla said, "I'll call and see if he can come in early." Her shoes *squished* as she walked. "Welcome back, sweetie."

"I'll call Frank." I reluctantly let go. Ovens, dishwashers—basically the same thing. Right? No? "And then I'll get this cleaned up."

"We'll help," Kara said. "Right, Winston?"

He had the nerve to give her a shifty-eyed no.

"Boy, if you don't grab a mop." I threw a towel at him.

"Fine, okay, I'll help. Jeez." He pouted and spoke with a mocking voice, "Everyone *loves* scrubbing day."

"Ooh! I know that one!" Kara exclaimed.

Silent and crabby, Aaron began picking up the soaked towels and took them upstairs to be washed. I headed to the office alone to get the cordless phone.

We weren't able to get all of the water up until JR arrived with a special vacuum to finish the job. Somehow, Goldeen's only had to stay closed for two hours. Granny was away negotiating contracts—I hadn't seen her since I'd gotten back. I had the feeling she didn't exactly want to see me.

Kara and Winston had ditched me to go shopping, which if I'm being honest, felt weird as hell. But the contest was coming, I had a shift, and they needed to prepare. It made sense for them to go together.

"Winnie." Layla came into the kitchen as I was supervising Frank fixing the leak. "The party at table four would like to speak to the manager."

I sucked in a breath, lips pulled back over my teeth. "What's up?"

"They are unhappy with the quality of their meal."

"They can send it back."

"Now, if only there were anything left to send back." Layla presented the check with a flourish. "That woman could make a saint hesitate. Good luck, darling."

I sighed, taking the ticket and marching out to the table. A woman with freckles sat with someone equally as freckled with the same coloring and hair. Mother and son, most likely, but Thing One and Thing Two made me happier. Both of their plates looked as if they'd been scraped, sopped, and licked clean. "Can I help you with anything?"

"We're waiting for the manager."

I plastered on my best customer-service smile. The one that said friendly and approachable but also terribly shy. "Hi, I'm Winnie. I'm the co-assistant manager here at Goldeen's. How can I help you?"

"Aren't you a little *young* to be a manager?"

That *"young"* had a tone. Almost as if that wasn't the word Thing One had wanted to use.

"My name tag says otherwise."

"Well. I'm sorry to have to say this, but this food just was not good. The lettuce in my salad was wilted, the eggs tasted like they'd been frozen, the dressing was too tangy, and my son's omelet was dry and his potatoes were burnt."

Dear God, I hoped Aaron wasn't listening. If he walked out here, his very presence would give Thing One a heart attack. Or she'd try to give him her number, and I would be forced to suffer through secondhand embarrassment.

"The only reason why we came here was because it is so highly rated on Yelp," Thing One continued.

Ah, Yelp. People seemed to think service staff lived in fear of one-star ratings on review sites, considering how often ornery customers mentioned it during complaints. What they didn't know? Kara used to regularly monitor Goldeen's online reputation and refuted all one-star claims.

"And the only reason we ate it was because after driving all night, we were both starving."

"I see. That's unfortunate that your meal was less than satisfactory. What can I do to make this right for you?" *One . . . two . . . three . . .*

"I don't think we should have to pay for this. It's the least you could do."

"I see." Oh, she was a bold one. Usually, when I danced with scammers, they pussyfooted around, asking for a free meal by implying I should be the one to offer it. "I'm afraid I can't do that." *Four . . . five . . . six . . .*

"Excuse me?"

"You heard me."

Thing Two laughed.

"We have a policy for these types of—situations. Our waitstaff is trained to check in on customers twice during a meal to ensure our guests have a pleasant dining experience. Shortly after the food has been delivered and again when the food is nearly gone. At either of those times, did you tell her the lettuce was limp, the eggs were frozen, the dressing was tangy, the omelet was dry, or the potatoes were burnt?"

Thing One's gaze skidded sideways around the half-full diner. I had seen that look enough to know exactly what Thing One wanted to happen. "No," she said, raising her voice. "I told you we were hungry. We didn't want to wait for another order."

A few heads turned.

"Okay." Damage control: acknowledge and compensate; keep my voice quiet and confidential, using the same tone I would if a customer's card had been declined. "That's fair. I can understand that."

Thing One found some chill and sunk back in her seat, a half-smile creeping out. "Thank you—"

"I can offer you a twenty-percent discount on your bill."

"I want to speak to your supervisor." Thing One had reached shouty levels, as expected.

"I don't have one."

"Fine," she ground out. "I want to speak to the owner."

I intertwined my fingers, holding my hands in front of me. *Seven . . . eight . . . nine . . .* "Hi, my name is Winnie. I'm the owner's granddaughter here at Goldeen's, and she left me in charge. How can I assist you?"

"That is *not* funny."

"No one is laughing. Except your son." I shrugged. "This is my family's diner. And I'm going to ask that you lower your voice. Other customers are trying to enjoy their meals."

"This is ridiculous." She began to gather her things. "I refuse to discuss this with a child, and I'm not paying for a shitty meal. Let's go."

"Oh, I think you will." *Ten.* "Because that's how business works. You entered my establishment, received wonderful service from my staff, ate my cook's food that I can personally guarantee was perfect in every way, and are now attempting to leave without paying. That is considered theft. I am well within my rights to call the sheriff to have both you and your son arrested."

Thing One's mouth hung open like a Venus flytrap. "You would call the police over twenty dollars?"

"You're the one causing a fuss over twenty dollars, so yeah, sure." I would never. All I needed was for this woman to *think* that I would. "Aaron! Call Sheriff Mills, please?"

"You can't treat customers like this!"

"Says who? *The customer is always right* is not a law; it's a courtesy that people like you have abused." I placed the ticket down on the table. "Now will that be cash, debit, or credit? We don't accept checks."

Thing Two sighed, loud and pained as if his soul were suffering a thousand emotional deaths and he needed to journal out some bad poetry. "Jesus, Mom. Just fucking pay. It's not even that serious."

He—he cussed at his mom!? And she didn't reach across the table and smack him into the next time zone? These people were something else.

"Language, Philip," Thing One snapped. Huffy and frowning, she retrieved her wallet and threw a card onto the table.

I didn't touch it. "I need to see your ID."

Thing One flipped open her wallet.

"Sorry, but I can't see the state hologram. I'm going to need you to take it out and place it on top of the card you threw."

"No."

"Then I can't accept this as payment."

Aaron, right on time, appeared behind me. I didn't have to turn around—I felt him there, having my back. "Sheriff says he's five minutes out."

"Finally, an *adult*!" Thing One said, dismissing me with a wave of her hand. Again, that *"adult"* had the same tone as before. "I don't know what your hiring process is, but you might want to consider changing it. This *girl* is so disrespectful and out of line—"

"Why are you complaining to me?" Aaron nodded to me. "She's the boss. If you'll excuse me, I have more dry omelets to make."

Thing One screamed inside of her mouth and threw down twenty-one dollars. A whole nine cents left for Layla's tip. With Philip in tow, she left the diner, complaining loudly at no one in particular, probably just wanting to be heard.

At the register, I cashed out the ticket. "I really was going to give her twenty percent off. The change must be your tip."

"Oh, sweetie, you don't have to do that!" Layla said.

"I didn't. She did." I rubbed my eyes. "Granny is going to be so mad at me when she finds out."

Resigned to my fate, I walked back over to the main floor. "Excuse me, everyone. I apologize for that scene with that customer, but it's the principle of the matter, and that lady was just wrong. To make up for it, free coffee, pastries, and donuts on the house for everyone. As many as you can eat or want to take with you. And if you can't have those, come see me and we'll work something else out. Thank you, please enjoy your meals."

It started slow, like in the movies. One person began to clap before the entire diner joined in cheering for me in support.

~

SA(RU)M(ON)

Sam: WHAT PART OF BEST BEHAVIOR
DID YOU NOT UNDERSTAND

Thirty-Five

Sometimes, a girl's gotta vary it up. Instead of fleeing to Kara's house, I sent her an *Update: I'm dead. Again.* message, and *crashed at cottage.*

Dallas set down the sodas and snacks his mom had sent over with impressive timing. I had showed up not even ten minutes ago. "Being a hostess is kind of her thing. She stays ready."

We settled onto the couch. I checked my phone one last time. Radio silence from Sam made me paranoid. It was the definition of Not Good™. After putting my phone back in my purse, I tucked into a corner of the couch.

"How are you feeling?"

"Crappy." I rubbed my eyes, pushing down until bright lights appeared.

"But this is what happens with you two, right? You fight, she gets mad, you apologize or don't, and then it gets glossed over. It'll be fine."

It felt good to drag my hands down my face, pulling on my skin. "It's not just that." The other reason I hadn't gone to Kara? As much as she tried, as much as I loved her, I don't think she'd be able to relate to how I was feeling. "Do you ever think that it doesn't matter what you do; people are always only going to see you one way?"

"Yeah. Every day of my life."

"Don't be dramatic. That's my job."

"I'm not. I know exactly what you mean." He looked at me, straight-faced. "One of the things I like most about you is that you're always the same Winnie no matter who you talk to. You don't care about other people's opinions."

"Who told you that lie?" I laughed. "I can admit I'm slightly ahead on the self-worth curve, but I still care. To the point of panic sometimes."

"But you don't hide yourself. There isn't a separate Winnie in there caught between two worlds. You're always you. For better or for worse." Dallas shook his head.

"I don't hide. But." The words were there. All I had to do was say them.

My rage and sorrow and happiness had digestible requirements placed on them. Stay calm. Don't get angry. Never let them see you cry. I hated that so, so much.

Only two people tried to understand, my mom and Kara, but they ended up on different ends of the same messed-up spectrum. My mom wanted to find the cause and destroy the root, to talk through my feelings calmly and with purpose. Kara would let me burn everything to the ground so we could dance together in front of the flames, screw the consequences.

And neither of those worked. Too soft, too hard, either way I ended up a target. Bullies would come for me. Public judgment would come for me (and leave Kara out of it).

I wasn't ever allowed to be my full self.

He waited for me to continue. No pressure. No pretense. Only his usual patient expression waiting and wanting to hear what I had to say. "It's like I'm *dimmed*."

His eyebrows raised in surprise and he blinked a few times. "Really? I would've never guessed that, because you don't feel that way to me. Everything about you has always been so overwhelming and *so vibrant*, but in a good way, if that makes sense? You're impossible to ignore—at least for me anyway."

"That makes me happy." I said it without a smile even though I inherently knew those words would stay with me for a very long time. "It's not *always* like that, though. I wish I was allowed to tell someone how I felt without having to make it palatable."

"*Oh*, okay. I get it, I get it." He nodded. "The way people perceive you affects how real you get to be? I understand that. Definitely. Perception is everything in my family. I have to be perfect and presentable all the time."

"I don't think you *have* to be. For me, I don't feel afraid to make mistakes." My parents had a lot to do with that. They gave me the security to fall down and a hand to help me back up again.

"I do. Wanna know why I broke up with Lacey? I was driving, and we got pulled over. She had an open bottle of vodka in my car. I still don't know how she cried her way out of us getting in trouble, but she did. Sheriff Mills didn't charge us. He told my parents, though." He didn't look sad or upset. Just resigned in an *it is what it is* kind of way. "My dad flipped the fuck out over it. He said being light skinned and talented wouldn't save me. None of the shit I had accomplished mattered at all to them or their guns."

I sucked in a sharp breath.

It would never stop flooring me how honest he always was with me.

"All it takes is one time," he continued. "One mistake and everything my parents worked for will disappear. One case of mistaken identity and I'll get falsely accused if I'm in the wrong place at the wrong time. One mistake and the police will shoot me. I don't ever not think about those things."

Dread sunk into my bones. We'd been born into this, trapped in a game of half-life and certain death, and it might never change. Not in our lifetime or the next.

A sniffle. I didn't mean to let it out, but the little bastard escaped.

"And here I was thinking that that woman had just hurt my feelings."

"Don't cry." He wiped my tears away. "That counts. It's looks a bit different for you, yeah, but it's still just as hard and terrible. You don't deserve that shit."

"Neither do you."

Dallas leaned forward and I closed my eyes. He kissed both of my cheeks and my eyelids. My forehead and nose. My mouth.

"I'm glad you came here," he whispered. "To me."

Thirty-Six

Five. Ten. Five.

Walk. Jog. Walk.

Purgatory was a ten-minute jog when the air decided it wanted to try catching on fire. A heat wave had rolled through Haven Central and refused to leave. At seven a.m. it had nearly reached eighty degrees. The sun had forsaken me, but another cosmic entity up there still liked me.

The cool water had felt marvelous on my cramped muscles and tired feet. Bath bomb, bubbles, and a book. I'd been truly blessed.

"Winnie, get in here."

I barely finished drying off and getting dressed when Granny yelled for me. I looked out the door. "Yes?"

"Downstairs, my office, five minutes."

Just when I'd thought it was safe to go back into the water.

WINSTON (Zeddemore)

Winnie: I am in such deep shit that not even
my bath bomb could make the smell go away

Winston: That's what happens when you play
the game The Customer Is Not Always Right

Winnie: In my defense, she deserved it.

Winston: YIKES that's even worse.

Winnie: . . . I know

Winston: Punishment?

Winnie: Not sure. She's been hardcore avoiding me but now she wants
me downstairs in five minutes.

Winston: Godspeed. May the angels
have mercy on your temper

Winnie: My life, it crumbles
like ivory towers of old

There wasn't much to Granny's diner office. A desk and chair; file cabinets; framed business-related things like her license, safety inspection certificates, her first dollar from her first sale, a picture of the family standing in front of Goldeen's on opening day, and the like.

Granny sat across from me, writing on a triplicate paper—the kind that had a white, yellow, and pink copy. I only knew what those were because of my time in Goldeen's and never thought I'd see one of those forms with my name on it.

"You're writing me up!?"

"You're an employee. I'm dissatisfied with your performance."

"But I'm your granddaughter?"

"Did you sign a hiring agreement?"

"Yeah."

"Do you work here?"

"Yeah."

"Do you receive a paycheck?"

"Yes."

"The second you put on that uniform, you agree to do what's asked of you by your employer. I agreed to hire you. I signed your hiring agreement. I sign your paychecks. This is my diner, Winnie. Not yours. When you are working here, you do as I say, not what you want. Is that clear?" She turned the paper around and slammed a pen on top of it. "Read it and sign."

I read it.

"I'm supposed to write my side of it. Am I allowed to do that or is this going to be a continued dictatorship? Because I did the right thing. She had no business acting like that and thinking she could get away with it. So what if I was rude to her? She was rude first. You didn't hear the way she talked to me. You didn't see the way she looked at me."

"I don't need to see it. I already know."

"So if you *know*, then I was just supposed to roll over, take it, and be nice? That's ridiculous."

Granny kept her eyes on the desk, chest visibly rising as she breathed in and out. "I shouldn't have to tell you what happens when white people feel threatened."

Thing One hadn't been the first to try to skip out on a ticket, and had been relatively calm compared to the more scandalous incidents. Others had complained, whined, and tried to use their tears to get me to bend. They'd scanned the diner, too, searching for someone to come help them, to take their side, even though they were obviously in the wrong.

It wasn't fair that Thing One and Two had eaten all the food that

Layla served with a smile, that Aaron worked hard to make, that Granny worked to secure contracts for, that the farmhands picked and delivered, that farmers grew and raised—and had tried to refuse to pay for it.

Everything was connected. How did they not see that? Did they think it just came from nowhere? Sprang into existence as soon as the words left their mouths like magic?

"I would have done that to anyone. She was wrong. I don't care that she was white."

"But she was. That's the point."

I tapped my bent knees.

"They don't know you like how we know you. They don't see you right. They might never," Granny said gently.

Barely eighteen, and there I was, the angry Black *woman* bullying people again, but inferior enough to be called *"girl"* even after I'd told Thing One my name.

"It's not about a stolen meal or an unpaid ticket. In some cases, it's better to just give 'em what they want. It's not worth it," Granny said. "If you want to own a business, these are things you need to think about. Not just white people, but men of all colors, too. They won't respect you. They won't listen unless you make them, but only if you do it in the ways they want you to make yourself heard."

I signed the paper. The room felt too hot, the walls too close, my temper high and feelings bruised. I needed air and to calm down. I just needed to *go*.

"I know it might feel like I'm being hard on you, but I need you to listen to me," she said. "Which you never seem to do. You're going to tell Winston that you were wrong and that he has to drop out of that contest. Set a good example for him like you should be doing."

If I had any fight left, that might have crushed it out of me. "He's not entered as Goldeen's. It's just Winston."

"I know. And I'm *telling* you to drop out because I told you no."

"That's not good enough. Tell me *why*."

I didn't want to talk about it. I didn't want to fight.

I thought of the way Winston's face lit up like a Christmas tree when he showed me the recipe he'd chosen, the way he had hugged me so hard he lifted me off the ground—he had even kissed me on the cheek. My wonderful and stoic brother, who stood stock-still anytime anyone hugged him, voluntarily gave me a kiss. A whole two seconds later he said, "She can be mad all she wants. She doesn't believe in me anyway."

Anger and sadness mixed together and made me forget how to see reason.

This thing that I had given him wasn't mine to take away. A part of me hated her for thinking she could force me to.

Something cold and broken shredded its way through a very specific spot in my heart. I loved Granny. I did. But this last stretch of growing pains had fractured our relationship forever.

"I don't have to explain myself to you, child. You do what I say. Period."

"What is wrong with you? Why are you like this?"

"Who in the hell do you think you're hollering at?"

I didn't even realize I had yelled at her. It just happened. I pressed my lips together but didn't break eye contact.

Her entire face morphed into someone I didn't recognize—harsh and pinched, barely hiding its disgust. "Just nasty and disrespectful like you ain't got no goddamn sense."

My mouth all but opened on its own. "Like you're any better? You're always trying to control us. What about what we want? You never listen to anything we say unless we agree with you."

"I don't have to listen to you. This is my house. If you don't like it, you can get out."

A scoff jumped out of me, loud enough to echo around her office. "You always do that. That's your perfect solution for everything. The second someone disagrees with you or steps out of line you kick them out."

The strongest sense of déjà vu rocked through my entire being. We'd been here before. Over and over and over, and we'd be here again.

Granny had told me no. I had disobeyed on purpose. Clear-cut and dry, I was in the wrong. But I had assumed she'd get over it after a prolonged silent treatment. I would apologize and take my punishment, whatever it was, like I always had. She'd talk to me again on her terms. We'd move on like it never happened. That was the standard. That was our reality.

My hands shook as I realized I only had two choices: accept this awful and unchanging cycle or stand up for what I believed in.

Granny would never give me a reason why.

I believed in Winston and that Granny would never change.

"You know what? If you don't want me here, I don't *ever* have to come back." Regret tasted bitter in my mouth as I stood up. "And my brother is entering that contest if he wants to, and there's nothing you can do about it because *I* say so."

I whirled around, and my fury returned, seething in my ear to *leave*.

"Winnie!" she shouted behind me. "Get back in here."

Taking the steps two at a time, I ran up the familiar stairs, not stopping until I reached my room.

Her room. Her house. Her rules.

What did I do? *What did I just do?*

Covering my face with my hands, I breathed through the gaps in my fingers, too fast and burning on the way in and out. The tightness in my chest wrapped around my heartbeat—it thrummed in my ears and pulsed in my fingertips.

What was I going to do? Where would I go?

Packing. I had to pack.

My mom had bought me a new suitcase set for college. I had brought the largest one with me to Haven Central. A hardshell, bright green with silver stars, it clattered to the floor after I unzipped it, falling open in front of the dresser. Yanking the drawer open, I pulled all my stuff out and threw it inside of my suitcase, not bothering to be neat. Fueled by frantic energy, I did the same for the closet and the desk and the bed. Clothes. Shoes. Bras. Panties. Laptop. Chargers. Anything and everything that was mine. I ran to the bathroom to grab my toiletries and shoved those in, too.

"What are you doing?" Winston stood in the doorway, gaping at me.

"Packing." Disorganized and bursting, my suitcase refused to close until I lay on the lid.

"Yeah, I can see that. Why?"

"Because she kicked me out."

"Yeah, but she always does that."

"And today she did it for the last time." He didn't need to know the details. His focus needed to be on winning the contest, not his sister fighting for him. And myself. "I'm going to Kara's."

Winston blinked at me in surprise. A small, proud smile quirked at his lips. "I'm coming with you—"

"No. Stay here." With both hands, I tugged my suitcase into an upright position, wheeling it to the door. "I don't need Mom and Dad mad at both of us."

"Like I care about that. I'm not staying here without you."

"You are. Just until I get this figured out." I hugged him. "Keep an eye on Sam for me."

Thirty-/even

"'m fine."

White powdery patches and dark red smears in straight lines covered Kara's blue and white gingham apron. "You are not fine."

"False." I rolled my suitcase into the corner of Kara's room. "I'm peachy keen, jelly bean."

"Don't use cutesy quotes with me." She watched as I passed her to sit on the bed, crossing her arms, pursing her lips, and finally huffing at my continued silence. "So you just left? You fought and you left?"

"Also false." I concentrated on the floor, eyebrows up to stop myself from blinking. "She lectured. She demanded. I called her out. She kicked me out. I left."

"With your suitcase, though? What the hell happened?"

I loved how everyone kept being so shocked that I had left for good. As if they'd all become so used to this cycle of shit that their first thought revolved around me overreacting and taking this too far.

"She wanted me to tell Winston he couldn't enter the contest. She wanted me to make him drop out."

Kara's jaw dropped. "*Why?*"

I shook my head and shrugged and threw up my hands—a trifecta of *I don't know*. "Her reasoning was literally 'because I said no.' The usual."

"I'd ask if you were joking, but I know you're serious. I cannot *believe*."

"I'm tired. I'm so *tired* of her acting like that and threatening me." I ran my hands through my braids, tugging on them before lacing my fingers together on top of my head. *Breathe*. In and out. Eyes closed, I tried that again. My left leg had begun to bounce involuntarily. "I don't understand how she can keep making somebody feel unwanted and expect them to stick around. She always kicks me out when she doesn't want to deal with me, and I always wait her out and come back, but that stuff sticks to you after a while, you know?"

The bed shifted next to me. I opened my eyes to find Kara's concerned face, open and waiting for me to continue. She rubbed my back from shoulder to shoulder. "It's okay," she said. "Tell me."

Tears began to bead in my eyes, ready to crest over, but I wiped them away before they could fall. I hated how hurt I felt. My anger had abandoned me and left me with this unbearable pain in my face and jaw and throat, left me shaking and raw.

"She tried to send me home after Winston had his asthma attack," I admitted. "She said it was for me, but now I think she just wanted me gone but didn't want to come right out and say it."

"I don't—" Kara began, but stopped. Her brows lowered into straight lines as she stared at me. I'd known her long enough to guess her initial reaction would have been *I don't think that's true*. But that would have been a lie, and we didn't lie to each other. "Yeah. I can see how everything together would make you think that. I see it."

"But?" I wanted to be wrong. That one word was saturated in the hope that Kara saw something else, too.

"I got nothing." A sigh. A headshake. "I mean, I know she loves you." The oven timer beeped in the kitchen. Kara's gaze darted to the doorway and then back to me. "My tarts are ready. Okay, um, hang on. I'll be right back."

Breathe. I wished I could believe in anything but the truth. Instead of trying to find and talk to me, because anyone who had known me for longer than ten seconds could correctly assume I'd run straight to Kara, Granny was probably calling my parents to make them feel bad for how I turned out.

They'd call me any second.

"You know what?" I asked no one at all. Reaching into my pocket, I took out my phone. She answered on the first ring. "Mom?"

"Where are you?" Her voice came through clear but with a slight hollowness around it. Speakerphone. My dad was listening.

"Kara's. Before you say anything, I want to tell you myself for once."

Silence for six torturous heartbeats and then, "Okay. I'm listening."

The knots curling in my stomach loosened. Wonderful as my mom was, this almost never happened. When confronted, I never lied about the things I'd done. Downplayed? Oh, yeah. One hundred percent. But not lie.

I also never fessed up first, or at least tried to.

Taking my time, I told her what happened from the beginning, starting with when Granny had pushed me in Dr. Skinner's office, how she had yelled at me and kicked me out because of what happened. That tied into the diet, how she tried to control and monitor what I ate, and how she refused to listen to me when I tried to explain how she was making me feel.

I jumped ahead then, mentioning the silent treatments before talking about the woman in Goldeen's who tried to make me feel like I was beneath her and worthless, why I stood up for myself and Goldeen's honor.

Kara returned, sitting next to me, wordlessly holding my hand while I talked about my last conversation with Granny—how unfair it felt to be written up, how helpless and ignored I felt as I sat there, how confused and angry I was when she changed the subject to Winston. My resulting anger. How fast I had packed. How unloved I began to feel. How disposable.

All of it poured out of me in a cathartic rush. It was like a curtain lifting to let the sunlight in to expose all of the dark corners I had avoided out of fear. My perfect summer in Goldeen's with my granny had been tainted by disappointment and betrayal and hurt. There'd always been a balance before with Granny—maybe more good than bad. Or maybe I had convinced myself that was the case.

"Oh, sweetheart. I'm so sorry."

Hearing those words, the pain from the lump in my throat lessened, relaxed to become tears I desperately wanted to cry but held on to.

My mom continued, "I think it's time for you to come home."

Without thinking, my gaze shifted to Kara, whose eyes were wet with unshed tears, too. She wasn't a crier either, but if I lost it, so would she. I'd see her again in just a few weeks, but I didn't want to leave her yet.

Dallas. I didn't want to stop spending time with him. Our late nights in the diner, our Royal Engagements, the phone calls—it had been so special to me. It was never going to last forever, but it also wasn't supposed to end so soon.

Winston. *God*, would he even be allowed to compete if I wasn't here? And even if he could, I *wanted* to be there for it. Front row and center with Dallas and Sam, cheering for him and Kara. His first big moment doing something he loved in a competition he wanted to be in.

"I don't want to," I whispered.

My mom sighed. "I know, but I want you to. I don't want to make you. I want you to agree to do this for me."

"Why?"

"Because I want my daughter here with me. I want you home."

I thought back to the few times my mom had kicked me out, too. Fifteen minutes tops later, she apologized and asked me to forgive her. "Sometimes, I feel like I'll never escape how I was raised," she had told me. "My mom did that to me, too—threatened to kick me out, take away the safety and shelter she provided me with when I talked back or was acting 'too fast.' I want to be better than her. I want to learn to be better than what I was taught. I try so hard, but those words always jump out of me when I'm angry with you. I don't mean them. I *never* mean them."

My mom wanted me home. She wanted *me*. Realizing that, believing in that truth almost made me say yes.

"I'm sorry she made you feel so terrible," my mom continued. "I'm sorry I can't make any of that go away. Your granny is— difficult." She paused. "I don't get along with her for a reason, and I'm not going to get into why, but she's had a hard life. I'm not saying that to excuse what she's done to you or take her side in this. When people have certain—experiences—that they're unable to deal with, they can start to lash out at everyone else, even their loved ones. Sometimes, especially their loved ones."

"That doesn't make any sense."

"It still happens, sweetie. I'm sorry you had to learn that lesson."

Kara placed her head on my shoulder. I didn't know if she could hear my mom, but I heard her sniffle as she squeezed my hand.

"I know I'm not like the best kid ever, but why would she say that about Winston? He's never done anything wrong. Why would she try to make me do that?"

"Because you didn't listen to her. Because your dad and I were fine with Winston being in that contest; she thinks we spoil you, which is ridiculous."

I laughed in disbelief, joking, "But you wouldn't even get me that pony I wanted."

Kara chuckled, too, vibrating against my shoulder.

"Your granny can't see the difference between us encouraging you to be your own person and letting you run wild. To be clear, I don't like what you did. She told you the answer was no and you went against that."

"I know."

"But. I understand why you did it because I understand *you* and it was such a Winnie thing to do. I couldn't be mad at you for wanting to do something nice for your brother. Not once I saw how happy you'd made him. I just couldn't. I can't." She laughed, breathy and resigned. "Maybe I am an enabler."

"Did she call you that?"

"No. Your dad did."

"Are you mad at me, too?" I asked him. He'd been silent this whole time, but I knew he was there. They'd always liked to talk to me together.

"I don't think 'mad' is the right word," my mom said. "Hold on."

The line went silent, but the call didn't drop. She muted me. While I waited, I said to Kara, "You don't have to stay. Finish baking."

"I'm okay. Unless you want me to go?"

I didn't. My mom and her infallible mom magic had made me feel better. Having Kara at my side made me feel best.

"Winnie." He said my name in a flat monotone.

"Hi, Dad."

"You're coming home."

Deep breath. In and out. "Can I at least stay for the contest? If Kara's parents let me stay here, I mean. I'm not going back to Granny's."

"They will," Kara whispered.

"I should tell you no." My dad never sighed—he was more of the grumbling type. "You're a good kid, and I love you. But you need to stop testing my patience, Winnie. You truly do."

"I'm sorry." This was harder on him than it was for my mom. He couldn't stay neutral, but he also couldn't take a side. I wanted him to be on mine, though. I would never ask, but I still wanted it anyway.

"You don't have a malicious bone in your body," he said. "Everything you do, right *and* wrong, comes straight from your heart. I gotta learn how to remember that. That's on me, not you." Another grumble. That one turned into a reluctant growl. "And that's on my mom, too. She swears up and down you do it to torture her. I know that's not true, but no matter what I say, she's gonna believe what she wants, and that's all there is to it."

I wanted to tell him thank you. Surprise had made the ache in my jaw come back, and I couldn't move my mouth to form the words. I had never heard my dad say anything like that about me. That's exactly how I felt inside. I called myself evil and supervillain all the time not because I wanted to hurt people, but because I would do anything for them. My moral compass was messed up because it ran on unconditional love. To be seen, really seen by my dad of all people, made my heart feel like it would explode.

"You're leaving the same night of that contest," he said, words nearly blending together from speaking so fast. "Your butt will be on that plane, in your seat, no excuses. Is that clear?"

"Yeah." My voice broke around the word, feeling finally cracking open like a dropped egg, tears splattering on my cheeks. "Thank you. For everything."

Thirty-Eight

I f the Haven Central masses knew about my falling out with Granny and shacking up with Kara as a result, no one had said anything to my face.

Dallas and I had just finished our latest Royal Engagement, a little event called *Haven Central Toastmasters*. Five minutes in, I called shenanigans for false advertisement—it had nothing to do with bread.

That joke had made Dallas laugh. Let it never be said that I didn't own my cheesiness.

For our portion, we had to talk about how being Haven Summer Royalty had impacted our public speaking skills. Unsurprisingly, I had a lot to say.

"Where to?" Dallas asked as we left the town hall together. I would always love seeing him in his crown. It twinkled in the growing nighttime, reflecting the lights from the lampposts. His curls stuck out around the bottom, forced down and brushing the tips of his ears. "Do you need to take a nap before your shift tonight?"

He hadn't mentioned anything about my disappearing act either, but that didn't mean he didn't know.

"Actually, no." I turned right, leading him toward Winter Wonderland Books. The heat wasn't nearly as intense as it had been when the meeting began—bearable but still sweat-inducing.

"Ah." He regarded me out of the corner of his eye, saying nothing else.

"Jerk." The worried half-smile gave him dead away. "You could've said something."

"Or I could've waited for you to bring it up like the gentleman that I am."

I tossed a playful glare in his direction before scrunching my nose and smiling. It was easy to do that, pretending like a bomb hadn't gone off inside of me. Everything was fine. My parents weren't angry. Winston was happy. But there I was feeling hollowed out and desolate. Lost. Nothing felt right. If I spent too much time alone, the emptiness would start speaking to me, telling me to just *call her*, to *go there*, to *make it right*.

"I'm sure you've heard the gist of it," I told him. "We fought. I lost. Life goes on."

"And you're okay?"

"Not particularly."

Dallas wrapped an arm around my shoulder. I leaned into him, curving an arm around his waist, and we walked together. Was it creepy to want to bottle his scent? I'd never been a scent-based person, but every now and again, one would hit my nose exactly the right way. Miss Jepson and her lemons always made me feel relaxed. Kara always smelled like vanilla—not the perfume kind, the baking extract one—and made me feel like cloud nine was a real place.

My parents simply smelled like home. It was the only scent I was never able to describe perfectly.

With Dallas, at first, I didn't think it was more than detergent on his clothes mixed with his natural scent. I could always ask him what kind he used, but I knew it wouldn't be the same. God help me if I ever got near his pillows.

Yep. Creepy.

Reaching up, I took off my crown, so I didn't accidentally stab him with it and snuggled closer.

"Do you want to talk about it?" he asked.

"I don't. I'm tired of being sad and talking about it." I wanted to be sad in solitude. I'd earned these punishing feelings. It wasn't right to shove them off on other people. "Talking about it isn't going to change anything."

"Got it." He kissed the top of my forehead.

"No, don't do that." I cringed. "I'm sweating."

"Ehh, it's fine." He grinned at me as I pouted up at him. "I'm going to kiss you if you keep looking at me like that."

"Okay." I willed my pouting to intensify.

Dallas laughed, enthusiastic enough for me to feel it through his chest. He leaned down and kissed me twice quickly and lingered on a third. Fun fact: walking and kissing at the same time wasn't as easy as movies made it seem. I'd fall on my face before I pulled away, though. I had zero shame when it came to kissing him.

We didn't have an official title yet. My best guess was we had landed somewhere in between summer fling and full-on dating. Sort of a wholehearted test run while we grew more familiar with each other—mainly, while he tried to get used to Kara.

Once we arrived at the bookstore, I showed him the not-so-super-secret alleyway we used to enter in the back.

"You're staying with Kara for the rest of the summer, then?"

"Not exactly." I climbed the steps and looked back over my shoulder. "Come up. You are expected, my dear gentleman."

Dallas stayed at the bottom of the stairs. "I don't know about this." He rubbed the back of his neck. "I know I said I would try, and I am, but this is *her house*. Maybe we could go somewhere a little less uncomfortable for me?"

"Oh." I hurried back down, stopping on the bottom step. "It's not just Kara. Winston and Sam are there, too. We're going to hang out, and I thought you could join us. I'm sorry, I should've asked first."

"That would be helpful." Not a hint of a smile could be found anywhere on his face. "It would give me time to prepare not to be an asshole on purpose."

"You're not."

"I *can* be when I don't like someone." He blew out a frustrated huff of air. "I appreciate what she said at the drive-in, but it's not that easy for me. I want to believe her because you do. I just don't see it. And I know the only way to see it is to be around her, which I really don't want to do, but I want to be around you so I have to deal with it and this is a little stressful for me because I don't want it to turn into some big unnecessary thing. I want it to work. My brain won't shut up long enough to let that happen."

My smile had to have been criminal. Like, I'd just pulled off a major bank heist and was on my way to a country that didn't extradite to the US. "I'm so happy to hear you say that." I couldn't help it—I did a little celebratory getting-away-with-a-felony shimmy.

"Okay? I don't—I didn't—what?"

I sent up a special shout-out to whoever came up with the idea of stairs, because from where I stood, Dallas and I were the same height. I reached out, took his face in my hands and kissed him. Never one to disappoint, he kissed me back, warm hands resting on my waist, and I let my fingers find and twist in the curls at the base of his neck.

"Because of this," I said, coming up for air. His cheeks had flushed slightly, and he stared at me, looking happy, but confused. "*You*. I love this stuff. You being honest with me about how you're feeling so we can tackle it head-on."

The most wonderfully perplexed grin spread across his face. "But whenever you're honest with me, you say it's gross."

"Have I said that to you lately?"

He thought about it. "I don't think so?"

"That means I trust you. Well, I *want* to trust you." I rubbed my nose against his quickly. "I feel like—like I knew you'd fit in with us because I thought you were looking for the same thing we had. I tell her everything. There's nothing I can't trust her with. I don't hesitate to get naked and bare my soul to her."

"Metaphorically?" he joked.

"Stop." I laughed. "I'm serious. That first night when you came to the diner, you said you thought I could be someone who could understand you. For me, this is that." I lowered my voice, looking into his eyes. "This is how that starts."

"Yeah." He blinked too hard, gaze landing downward on my lips, but he didn't kiss me. "Whenever we talked it was so weird because we were always on the same wavelength. No matter what you said, I just understood." He rolled his eyes. "When my mom said I talked about you all the time, that's what she meant. I was trying to figure this out, and I asked because I'm stupid and like pain and being embarrassed. She came up with the *wavelength* thing."

When he spoke, it was almost a whisper, low and rushed, as if he only wanted the words to exist between us. They weren't for anyone else. They were ours.

I tried to match him in that. "I'm only like that with Kara. The fact that I want to feel that way about you really means something to me. I'm not talking about romance and dating, although for the record, I definitely, *definitely* want that with you." I paused to let him know I was serious. If I could, I would have made the word GIRLFRIEND flash in my eyes. "I'm talking about a genuine connection with another person. Something meaningful and lasting."

He bit his lip, pulling back slightly. "You are—intense."

"I'm aware. I have very high expectations and refuse to settle."

"Jesus, help me, but I am *so* into it." He laughed, looking away from me but smiling. "Wow. How did you end up like this? You're going to ruin me."

"Or we could be ridiculously happy together. It could go either way, really. The fun part is finding out which one will win."

"Okay." He exhaled nodding and then kissed me. "This made me feel better. In the future, I would still like a Kara-warning. But I'm good for right now. Let's go."

Upstairs, I used the spare key I'd been given. "Shoes off." I pointed to the shoe rack and then led him to Kara's room. "Knock, knock."

"Took you long enough," Winston said, sitting at the foot of Kara's bed, while Kara and Sam sat at the top.

"Hi, Dallas," Sam chirped.

Kara waved. "Welcome to my house. This is my room. Please enjoy your stay."

"Why are you talking like that?" Winston asked.

"I don't know." She *hmphed*, staring at the bedspread. "I don't know."

"Uh, thanks for inviting me." Dallas stiffened at my side, reaching for my hand.

Yeah, no. This awkwardness wasn't going to fly. "Okay!" I snapped my fingers. "This feels weird, and I don't like it! So, let's skip all of this tension and fake it till we make it, cool beans?"

"Works for me." Sam slumped in relief.

"Me too," Winston said.

"Absolutely me three," Kara said.

We all looked at Dallas expectantly. I squeezed his hand, cheesing at him.

"Uh, me four?"

I shot him with a finger gun. "That's the spirit! Let's do this."

"Thank God. You two need to learn how to *actually* whisper. We could hear you outside." Winston hopped off the bed, rushing past us—but not before giving me a quick, painless flick on the arm. "I'm getting snacks."

"I'll get the drinks!" Sam began to rush after him. "We listened at the kitchen window. Sorry!"

"Of course." I sighed, pinching the bridge of my nose. Kara hadn't moved when I looked up. "We good?"

"I'm good." She looked at Dallas.

"I'm—getting there."

She stood up, smiling at us. "I'll take it."

To my surprise and utter delight, he smiled back at her. God, I wanted to kiss his face off.

"So, what's the plan?" he asked.

"Movie night," Kara answered. "It's kind of a thing with us."

"I've heard." He turned to me. "More *Lord of the Rings*?"

"Not on your life." I lugged a stack of extra blankets and pillows from the closet, dropping them on the bed.

"Blanket fort?" Dallas asked.

"No, but that's such a good idea. Why have we never done that?"

"Because Winston would probably say something like, '*Ew, no.*'"

"What am I saying?" Winston returned holding a giant bowl of popcorn in each hand and a bag of chips under each arm.

"Do you want to build a blanket fort?"

"Ew. No."

Dallas laughed.

Once Sam came back, we piled onto the bed. Kara took her usual spot on the left side while I sat next to her, immediately wrapping myself into a blanket cocoon—everything covered except for my face. Dallas sat next to me on my other side, knees up, arms wrapped around his legs. Sam squeezed herself in between Kara and me. And Winston, after making a pillow barrier to protect himself from our feet, draped himself across the entirety of the foot of the bed.

"What should we watch?" Sam asked, working the remote.

"Oh, I've meant to ask," Dallas said to me. "Have you seen *The Matrix*?"

"No, she hasn't," Winston said. "And it embarrasses me on a daily basis."

"I like sci-fi even less than horror," I said. "I kind of refuse to watch it."

"Interesting," Dallas said. "I really think you'd like this one. It's a trilogy. Unfortunately, the sequels aren't as good as the first, but in their defense, the first movie was a pretty tough act to follow. Also, it's a mixture of sci-fi, dystopia, and while not quite fantasy in the elves sense, it has a prophecy at the center, which is a bit like a fairy tale. There are a few romances and lots of women, Black and brown people."

"As main characters?"

"Yes."

"Do they die?"

"Some people die, yeah, but it's pretty balanced."

"I am intrigued." I looked at Winston. "See, if you had pitched it like that, I would have watched it years ago."

Winston's vicious stare threatened to shred Dallas to pieces telepathically.

Kara cackled, but said, "*Winston, no!*" She kept laughing as she held him by the cheeks and physically made him look away. "Winnie, you should be ashamed of yourself."

"Only a little bit." I winked at Dallas.

I didn't remember falling asleep. Wrapped up in my blanket cocoon, I had nursed the smallest swallow of soda and ate popcorn without my hands. The movie had played—noticeably not *The Matrix* because Winston's petty streak showed up to the party—the room had quieted minus the obligatory quoting and laughter, and I let myself relax. I didn't think about Granny or leaving Haven Central early and having to tell Dallas about it. By the third movie, I had felt myself nodding off but couldn't place the exact moment I passed out.

I inhaled deeply, stretching until my feet hit Winston's pillow barrier. He slept like the dead—quiet and unmoving with one arm draped over his eyes. Sam snored next to me, covering up Kara's mumble-sleep talking.

Someone had turned off the TV and the lights. Outside, the moon shone. The familiar scene made me feel even warmer inside, making me want to close my eyes again and drift back to sleep. I rolled over, ready to snuggle down for an epic sleep, but ended up looking Dallas right in the eyes.

"You're awake."

"I should probably leave, but I heard someone put the alarm on a while ago."

I laughed into my blankets to muffle the sound. "You could've woken me up."

"Nah." He grinned at me.

I narrowed my eyes at him. "Were you watching me sleep?"

"Not on your life."

"Come on. I'll escort you off the premises." Carefully, we got off the bed and tiptoed out of the room, down the hall, and to the kitchen. While he put his shoes on, I disarmed the alarm—the code was Junie and Kara's birth dates—and walked him outside.

"Are Sam and Winston staying here, too?"

I shook my head, closing the door behind me. "I'm the lone

outcast. Banished to book-filled pastures." I stared at my feet as I said, "I can't stay." Now was as good a time as any to break the news.

"Stay where?"

"Here. My parents are making me go home."

"When?"

"After the Starlight competition. The same night."

"That's so soon." The way he sounded, surprised and upset, almost made me look at him. He didn't want me to go. It was almost enough.

"Yep."

"What did you two even fight about? You said she kicked you out because of the thing with Skinner and you went back."

Arms crossed, I sat on the top step watching the stars for a quiet moment until Dallas sat next to me. I gave him the CliffsNotes version of what had happened, limiting it to the parts about Winston and the Starlight competition.

"That's messed up."

"I don't get why she just wouldn't tell me. She's always had this attitude about explaining herself. Like being an elder automatically gives you the right to be unfair, no questions allowed to be asked. More than anything, I think I just want to know why. I just keep thinking about it. There has to be a reason. Some kind of deeper meaning."

"Or you just need one to exist." He placed a hand on my knee. "I think your granny having a reason gives you permission to forgive her. You'd be able to say sorry and mean it. You two could move on, business as usual."

Did I want to forgive Granny? She would never say sorry to me. That absolutely wasn't happening. But I said it to her all the time. I guess it was a bit of an unspoken rule between us. One apology was enough to mend us, and it always had to be mine. But this time . . . there was nothing. I couldn't see anything good behind her tyranny. And no one could explain it to me.

"I want you to stay. I want more time with you," Dallas admitted. "But not if it has to happen like that."

I placed my hand on top of his.

Thirty-Nine

O nce upon a time and six mayors ago, Haven Central sent out a request to the farmers in the area for an event idea to attract tourists in the summer. The residents would make and sell their best recipes using the produce provided by the farmers—they'd have food contests and a mini-carnival. That first year, two acceptance letters had been sent out instead of one:

To a corn farm about two miles west.

To a cherry farm three miles east.

It's been cherries and corn galore ever since at the M&M Carnival.

Summer had finally decided to chill out. The sky remained clear and even though the sun shone like it had lost its mind, a strange breeze had appeared out of nowhere. Just windy enough to make the sunlight bearable, but not so windy that it kicked up the dirt into dust devils at the fairgrounds.

I couldn't count on one hand how many Daisy Dukes and flip-flops I'd seen already. Mr. Gatling's shorts were so short they might as well have been underwear. But Dallas and I had chosen to lean further into our supposed fate, dressing up to stand out even more.

If we had to pose in pictures, say hi to everyone, and be stared at all day, we agreed we'd look damn good the entire time.

Dallas's royal-blue suit looked marvelous on him. He kept it casual and unbuttoned, showing off a cornflower-blue-and-white polka-dot dress shirt, which also had the first few buttons open. His white socks and dark shoes completed his look, bringing it all together in one enviable package topped with his crown.

Today would be the last day we'd be required to wear our crowns. Couldn't really be a Misty Summer Queen if you had a nine p.m. flight home with no plans to ever come back.

Strangely, I didn't feel sad about it. Everything was kind of—muted now. Kara thought I had overloaded and my brain decided to make me feel numb instead of feeling anything. Sometimes, things happened exactly how they were supposed to.

Granny was never going to accept me. Never going to be willing to see the real me and be proud. I had accepted her, all of her kindness and faults, and loved her anyway. I guess I wasn't worthy of the same kind of effort.

When people showed me who they were, I was going to start believing them.

I decided to keep on pushing my luck and wore white. A final trip back to Miss Jepson's resulted in her simple white summer dress being layered with rainbow tulle until it puffed out like a tutu. We fashioned a belt out of shimmery purple ribbon and converted an old, rich purple suit coat into a perfectly fitted blazer with three-quarter-length sleeves *and pockets*.

Our first Royal Order of Business was meeting with Rush, who begged for a few photos in front of the carnival's entrance. He followed us around after that, like paparazzi who were paid per shot but couldn't get to close, always right in the corner of my eye snapping photos. I didn't let myself worry about that. Rush meant well, and whatever happened in the photos, all I cared about was that I looked like I was having a good time.

We judged two contests early in the morning. One for artwork that would be put on display in the town hall and a second for dog swimming, which was a bit weird but fun.

By midday, we shuffled over to the large barn. The smell of hay and dirt and God knew what else was inescapable, but the sheer number and variety of *rabbits* had made my entire day. Since we weren't qualified to judge the animals, we'd been put in charge of handing out ribbons, pinning them to cages and owners, and posing for pictures. Chickens, pigs, cows, ducks—there were even chinchillas and dwarf hamsters. All the reptiles had been relegated to a corner. Dallas made me take a picture holding a baby alligator on my lap. I threatened to never forgive him. He laughed at me, the jerk.

After that, we'd been set free to wander around as we pleased. The carnival had come alive by then, packed with people and the smells of cotton candy, popcorn, and giant pickles. Dallas played games and won gigantic stuffed animals for me. The only rides we rode were with littles, who wanted to wear our crowns and share seats with us, and refused to stop calling me Queenie.

When we finally got hungry, we found a quiet place to eat— sweet-cream cherry turnovers for him and a roasted sweet corn on the cob drizzled in honey and sprinkled with Parmigiano-Reggiano cheese for me—and sat together in private.

Dallas asked, "Do you want to fall in love with me?"

That was an absolute spit-take moment. If I had been drinking, it would have shot straight out of my mouth and left me sputtering in a dumbstruck state of *ohmygod*.

"Is there a reason why you're asking me that?"

"Because this is the end. You're leaving me. Legend has it that we're supposed to fall in love by the end of our reign. So, do you love me?"

Jesus Christ, how in the hell was he so confident? How could he just bald-faced *ask* something like that without turning red, without smiling to hide his embarrassment or stuttering? He waited for an answer, watching me like a hawk ready to go in for the kill.

"I didn't know you believed in the divine matchmaking."

"I don't." He scoffed. "If I'm going to be with someone, I'm going to pick them. I get to decide who I fall in love with. Not some unofficial beauty pageant pretending it's not a popularity contest."

"Aww, you remembered." I scrunched my nose at him.

"But the thing is, I did pick you."

Jesus, just when I thought it was safe! He had me trapped and I schooled my face as best as I could, but any second I'd give myself dead away. "Are you in love with me?"

"No." He kissed my cheek and his mouth lingered near my ear. "But I'm not ready to say good-bye."

"Then don't." I laughed—it sounded high-pitched and reedy, the epitome of nervous. "I'm, uh, pretty good at the whole long-distance thing. I even come with references."

He laughed, too, his forehead against my temple. "Kara."

"It's a lot of work and it can be really hard at times."

"Do you think we could be happy like that, though? Does thinking about it feel like it'll be worth it to you?"

"Why don't we take it one day at a time? You call me. We talk about our day. You tell me you wanted to hear my voice. I tell you a ridiculous story that you aren't sure is one-hundred-percent true. And when we get tired, we can make a bet about who hangs up first. First one to fall asleep loses. When that stops being fun, then it won't be worth it anymore, I think."

"Let's change one thing. If I fall, you fall, and vice versa."

"Asleep?"

"Sure."

Kissing Dallas still felt like an impossible snatch of surreal happiness in an unkind reality.

～

My last day in Misty Haven was turning out to be a good one, and I got to spend it holding Dallas's hand the entire day. We'd been so busy I almost didn't have time to worry about Winston. Almost.

At four p.m. we headed to the tent where the filming would take place. Kara had saved us seats, front row center. "I'm not nervous. I don't get nervous." She said that seven times in a row. "I win."

"Do you want to sit down?" Dallas offered, already beginning to stand. "Not saying you're nervous or anything, but you're kind of shaking. A lot."

"Okay, I'm not supposed to tell you," she said, voice a frenzied whisper. She squatted down in front of us. "We're top five. Both of us."

"*What?*" My jaw dropped.

"*Keep your voice down!*" Kara looked around and then pulled Dallas and me into another tight triangle. "Winston's still inside. They filmed the preliminary round in the auditorium and they're going to announce the winners here. I saw the list. One of the judges wasn't paying attention and I. Saw. The. List."

"Oh my God." I covered my mouth with my hands. "Ohmygodohmygodohmygod. Have you told him?"

"No. I didn't want to freak him out or steal that moment from him, you know?"

"I can't believe it. Well, no, of course I can. Top five is *amazing.*"

"Am I late?" Sam asked.

"No," Dallas said as Kara shot up like a rocket. "Right on time."

"I should go back inside. I think they want to get a shot of us walking out." Kara hurried away, arms wrapped around herself.

I ran after her, reaching for her arm. "Hey."

"Yeah?"

"I love you and I'm proud of you no matter what."

"I know."

"And thank you."

She looked confused. "For what?"

I wrapped her in the tightest hug I could manage. She stopped shaking, slumping against me, head resting on my shoulder. "Just for being you. It's you and me. You know that, right?"

She nodded, pulling back and taking a deep breath. "You and me. Always."

"She okay?" Sam asked as I sat down next to her.

"She doesn't get nervous. She wins."

"Right." Sam laughed but abruptly became serious. "You should know that Granny's here."

"Here? Really? At the contest she wanted nothing to do with, how interesting."

"Yeah, I don't get it either."

The truth was, I didn't want to get it. Part of me wanted to apologize again. Part of me just didn't care. Outgrowing people was a thing that happened. Sometimes those people were family members who maybe hadn't treated you all that well.

Walking away, even though it felt painful, felt valid, too. Sometimes love just wasn't enough.

Before long, twenty contestants lined the stage and the cameras started rolling. Winston stood next to Kara in a bright yellow shirt with beautiful black lettering on the front:

Win-Win Creations

Oh.

I started crying *immediately*.

"They're filming you." Dallas draped an arm across my shoulders, pulling me closer. I turned to face him quickly, long enough to wipe my eyes before looking at the stage again. I blew out an unsteady breath, and oh God I was *such* a wreck.

Winston smiled at me and gave a tiny wave. He was just so *pleased* with himself, I could have died a proud sister right then and there. I had made the right choice. Every fight, every act of defiance, every single time I kept pushing for what I knew was the right thing made everything that had happened that summer absolutely worth it. Nothing would ever make me regret choosing to put Winston first.

Sana Starlight strolled onto the stage, microphone in hand. She looked the same in person as she did on TV—bright blue eyes that could be seen from space, perfectly golden and hair-sprayed blond hair, a giant smile with too many teeth that somehow worked with her sun-kissed tan skin. She greeted the crowd, moving quickly through her rehearsed speech.

If this woman didn't announce the names soon, I'd explode. My legs wouldn't stop bouncing. Dallas held both of my hands in one of his to keep me from flapping them. He stayed close to me, probably closer than he needed to be, but I would never complain. Our minutes were numbered.

"Are we ready for our top five contestants?" Sana called. My heart rate skyrocketed. "Just as a reminder, from this group of five there will be two first-place winners, one for each category, and from those two a grand-prize winner will be selected. Any questions?" She winked at the camera. "If I call your name, please step forward to the white line."

Kara's name came second, and even though I knew Kara would never lie to me, with each passing name I couldn't help but think: What if she was wrong? What if it's not him?

Winston Woodson. Contestant number 215. Grilled pork tenderloin with cherry salsa. Top five.

I exhaled, tilting my head back. Laughing, crying, and praying to any God that would listen, I begged, *please, please let him have this.*

The applause for Winston outshone all of the other contestants. People got up out of their seats, stomped their feet, hooted, hollered, and whistled for him. They congratulated me and Sam, crowded around us, wanting to be a part of something truly special in the making. They all felt it. This was extraordinary. Winston was so young and already extraordinary.

I don't know what made me turn my head, but I did. Granny stood with Mr. Livingston on the edge of the tent. Watching me. Not Winston or Sana or the stage. Just me.

At the end of every summer, I left Misty Haven aching to come back as soon as possible because I thought it had always felt like home. It had never been the town.

It had been my granny. I came here because it's where she wanted to be. Along the way I'd found Kara, then Dallas, and when I left here this year, I'd be taking them with me. But not Granny.

In the fall I'd start college with Kara, email my parents every day to annoy them into remembering how much I loved them, make plans to have Sam and Winston come visit me, and stay up too late talking on the phone with Dallas. I'd go to class and learn all the things, get a part-time job, and explore my new city every chance I could.

I didn't have a space for her. I didn't know if I even had the will to make space. My heart broke with the truth of it. We were done. Maybe not forever. Maybe not even a week.

A bittersweet good-bye and a necessary one.

"Well," Sana said, voice slightly raised to get the crowd's attention. "It seems there is a clear crowd favorite."

Winston, usually so stoic and surly, beamed on that stage. He belonged there.

"And now for our winners." Sana waved a red envelope.

And in a handful of moments, everything came crashing down.

Kara's gluten-free ultimate brownie waffles version 7.0 won first place in the sweet category, but she didn't win the grand prize.

Winston had won second place, losing to Colin's smothered chicken fried steak.

I knew I had cameras trained on me, so I didn't react at all. I kept my eyes on Winston, holding on to that unstoppable feeling of pride I had for him.

"Before we wrap up," Sana began, "I have one last thing to say. I lied."

Confused murmurs rippled through the crowd.

"I said there would be two first-place winners and one grand-prize winner, which was true, but it wasn't the whole truth," she said. "One of the reasons I created this show was in hopes of finding and rewarding undiscovered talent. It's not just a spotlight on the towns we select, but also the people within it. *Small Town Spotlight with Sana Starlight*'s biggest secret, never announced to the press, is the existence of ten scholarships to be awarded to young people who demonstrate unparalleled potential.

"I'll be honest, I didn't think we'd find someone quite so soon, and when I found out how old this contestant was, I demanded to see the cooking footage to ensure they didn't have any assistance while creating their dish."

It was Kara or Winston. It had to be. Everyone else was older.

I couldn't breathe.

"I am proud to present the very first Sana Starlight Culinary Scholarship to"—she paused, walking toward the top five—"Winston Woodson." She grabbed his hands and raised his arm in the air in triumph.

I didn't remember running onstage, but the footage I watched later didn't lie. Me, in a tutu dress and crown, hugging my brother for dear life, who held me just as tight. Kara, Sam, and Dallas right next to us.

Forty

Kara volunteered to drive me to the airport. Dallas volunteered
to go along for the ride. In between was me, emotional from
Winston's victory and desperate to not have to say good-bye.
She pulled into Goldeen's front parking lot and parked off to the
side. "So do we go in? Should I honk?"

"I'll message him." Winston had decided to leave with me. Sam
would stay another two weeks to fulfill her babysitting obligations
because she didn't want to disappoint her families.

"It's really packed tonight." Dallas gestured toward Goldeen's.

"It usually is after the carnival. People mostly come in for drinks
and to sit and talk. Deonna's is probably super crowded right now."
Inside I could see Layla and Victoria taking orders. I think JR zoomed
by the podium on his way to the kitchen. "I hope there's enough
staff to cover the floor."

It's like Granny had said: Goldeen's existed just fine for the nine
months that I wasn't there. The neon sign, *Goldeen's* written in perfect looping cursive, turned on at sundown every night. Its doors
opened and closed on time, people ate its delicious food, the staff

worked their shifts and took care of any mishaps like fires and flooding.

Goldeen's didn't need me.

"Why are you crying?" Dallas's hands flew to my face, catching my tears. "What's wrong?"

"*What?*" Kara whipped around in the driver's seat.

"I don't know. My eyes just started leaking," I wailed, pushing his hands away and covering my face. But I did know. Saying it out loud would make things worse. Goldeen's didn't need me. Granny didn't need me. "I'm fine. Everything's fine. Just had a moment. That's all."

Kara handed me a small pack of tissues. "You're allowed to be sad about this."

"I know."

"She'll come around."

"Maybe."

Kara reached out, placing a hand on my knee, and squeezed. Dallas wrapped his arm around my shoulder.

"This is weird and amazingly comforting." I blew my nose.

"We love you. So." She thought about it. "Well, *I* love you. I can't speak for him. Oh, here they come."

Winston and Sam walked toward us while talking to each other. I got out of the car, walking around it to open the trunk. "You got everything?"

"Yep." Winston put his suitcase in the trunk. "Shotgun?"

"Yeah, you're with me," Kara called through the rolled-down window. "You can't touch my music."

"You have the worst taste." He rolled his eyes. "If I have to listen to one more girl croak about post–high school ennui—"

"What review did you steal that line from?" I laughed.

"Don't insult my music!"

"I'll do whatever I want. Try and stop me." Winston opened the door, sitting inside. "I was *this* close to winning, and I just started cooking two years ago. Imagine—"

Sam tugged on my jacket, drawing my attention.

I smiled at her. "Are you going to be okay?"

"My dad thinks it's a good idea for me to stay to keep her company." Sam nodded. "I know you probably don't want to hear this, but she's upset, too. Are you going to say good-bye?"

I looked at Goldeen's. My gaze drifted to the right corner, to the apartment upstairs.

During the Sana Starlight contest, when I saw her, when she looked at me, I felt in my soul she was waiting for me to apologize. She was waiting for me to ask to come home.

In my heart, I knew she would've said yes.

In my heart, I knew I couldn't let myself ask.

All my life people have told me that I take after her—we had the same temper, same eyes, same stubborn streak, same dream, same ability to hold grudges to the point of absurdity. But I wasn't her.

I was Winnie. Until she recognized that, our unsaid good-byes would always live between us.

"Nope." I gave Sam a hug, holding on for so long she started laughing.

"It's only two weeks! I'll see you soon."

"But I'm gonna miss you so much." I pretended to cry, overexaggerating my whines. She loved it. When I finally let go, I stood back, placing my hands on her shoulders. "Message me if you need me?"

"I will."

"Or if you want to just talk?"

"I will."

"Or if—"

"Let's gooooo." Winston hung out of the window, already in the car. "Save that for when you leave for college."

"Or I could just do it twice."

"Whatever."

"All right," I said to Sam. "I love you, Goddess."

"Love you, too."

Back in the car, I put on my seat belt. Dallas grabbed my hand the second the seat belt clicked, as if he'd been waiting. Ridiculous.

I loved it.

I kissed the back of his hand and then held it to my chest. Our impending airport good-bye would be temporary, resetting every time I answered the phone when he called.

"Are we ready?" Kara asked. I would see her every day once we started college. No good-byes there either.

"Ready."

I waved at Sam as we drove away, at Goldeen's and all of the people inside who couldn't see me, at the tiny apartment in the right corner, and at the sign as we passed it:

THANK YOU FOR VISITING MISTY HAVEN! WE HOPE TO SEE YOU SOON!

Acknowledgments

And so, here we are again.

I wish I had a hilarious and insightful micro-story to cram in here about the creation of this book, but I don't. Not really. When my debut novel came out (ha!), I promised myself I would learn how to be more present online. You know, make friends, network, and market *LTAL* like an entrepreneur with a felony-proof Ponzi scheme in my back pocket. I lied. I failed. You still can't really find me anywhere. Reply to emails (on time)? Reply to tweets and be engaging? Post *Candid yet Photogenic Selfie Attempt* #72 on Instagram? *Me!?*

It's just not realistic. But I do see and appreciate you all.

My first thank-you belongs to Readers—those who've read *LTAL* and/or my Wattpad books. Those who've shared my work with their friends or posted about it online. Those who've taken the time to write wonderful and heartfelt letters and emails that made me cry at two in the morning. And those who've never said a word to me or anyone else about the comfort and hope they found through Alice's story. I was able to keep going this year and not give up on everything because of you all.

Right beside readers, thank you to librarians, booksellers, teachers, bloggers, and vloggers who've read and ordered my books, pushed them into the hands of those readers, and hyped my work to their colleagues and on their platforms. There are copies of *LTAL* all over the world in bookstores and airports and libraries—*libraries!* One of my biggest dreams I thought would never happen. Y'all did that, and my gratitude is unyielding and eternal. Hopefully one day, my brain will find some chill, and I'll be able to talk to you.

To the Swoon Reads/MacKids Books team: thank you for giving me a job and believing I could do it successfully. I like being employed. It's kind of cool. Jean, Lauren, Kat, and Emily, all of the editors, Swoonterns, assistants, designers, sales and marketing teams, and everyone whose name I don't know yet but will in the future. And a super extra-special thank you to Liz Dresner, who has designed both of my Swoon covers with care and compassion.

Thank you to everyone who made 2018 memorable and enjoyable in the face of a gross amount of pain and anguish, particularly:

Tuna & Jonghyun—I will never, ever forget you.

Mom, Dad, Teasha, Mikee, and the rest of my family

Sarah, Nikkiee & Nes, Allie & Nia

SHINee & Shawols

Kevin M., Jason A. & Megan B.

Alysha D'Souza & Samantha Pennington

Ariel Klontz, Jandra Sutton, Mikaela Bender

Leah & Julia

Mariah, Ali, Moriah, Peyton, Jordan, Ariana, Liz, Kelly, Rachel

The Electric Eighteens

Becky Albertalli, Julie Murphy, Amy Spalding, Rebekah Weatherspoon & their books

Lydia & Alex & Vicky & Shani & Kristen & Cat & Lillie & Jessika & Aiden & Katy & Kim & Olivia H. & Tiana & Nikki & Karole & L.E. & Maggie & Tiffany & Kristy & Jennifer & Kate & Melinda & Olivia W. & Dee & Danielle & Jenn & Shannon & Shana & Hanna & Samantha & Prerna & Bethany & Caitlin & Natalie & Danika & Devon & Jen & Sandy—you know why <3

And lastly, Anna & Macy for saving my literary bacon time and time again. I'd be lost without you.

My blanket thank-you for this time is for anyone who was ever kind to me, especially when I was less than nice to them.

Until next time,

Claire <3

FEELING BOOKISH?

Turn the page for some

Swoonworthy EXTRAS

A Letter to My Main Character
upon the Occasion of Her Book Birthday

Dear Winnie:

It's your birthday today. Welcome to the world! After a year of working on a book that wasn't yours about a girl named Sunny, I realized she and Imani didn't belong in Misty Haven at Goldeen's. So . . . I started over with the same setting, and then you showed up.

We spent our first month together yelling at each other.

Me: "Stop being so stubborn and do what I say!"

You: "I'm NOT Sunny! Get over it!"

We spent our second month together reaching a compromise: You wanted to narrate.

You: "Let me do it."

I had a flashback of how chaotic Alice in *LTAL* was as a narrator and got shook for a second.

Me: "Absolutely not."

You: "Good thing I'm not giving you a choice."

You took my third-person-POV draft and set it on fire.

We spent our third month together researching movies and recipes, crafting accessible references and perfect puns, and sliding in some of our inside jokes. This was also the month you quietly told me you were queer and about the fight you had with your parents about it. You told me about Kara, who you love with your whole heart, and about Dallas, who you thought you might want to love someday.

We spent our fourth month digging into the emotional core of the book. Going on dates with Dallas, writing the fights you had with Kara and with Granny, carving into how terrible and insidious racial microaggressions truly are, and trying to figure out why we were okay with being fat when everyone else hated us so much because of it. I can't believe how much we cried lol.

We spent the rest of our time together fighting to edit and polish this story into something worth reading. *IIMYH* is a messy, quiet book about a life without plot but with lots of purpose and love. You filled your pages with how wonderful you are, how much you care, your sense of justice, your offbeat humor and joy, and your boundless confidence. You live how you want, and that's the story you told. I wish I could have placed you in something stronger, but I know you'll just say, "Shut up. I'm exactly where I'm supposed to be, loser." Then you'll smile and say, "I got your back if you got mine."

And I do. Always. Happy birthday, Winnie.

Love, Claire ♥

AN INTERVIEW

between author Claire Kann and
her editor, Kat Brzozowski

Kat Brzozowski (KB): I love hearing about how stories begin. What was the starting point for this story? Do you usually start with a character? A scene? A setting?

Claire Kann (CK): Usually my stories begin with plot. Once I have that, I wait for the right characters to show up. The plot for *IIMYH* went through three different sets of characters and their circumstances before I settled down with Winnie and her people. The setting, Goldeen's Diner, was the only thing to remain the same.

KB: What were the challenges of writing your second book? What was easier this time around?

CK: Everything was a challenge haha! For a long time, I didn't have a clear vision of the story's heart, which threw my usual writing process out of whack. I don't think I've ever cried over a book more while writing it. However, being a challenge wasn't necessarily a bad thing, because I also learned a lot about myself in the process—who I am as a writer and who I want to be as a human.

KB: If you were going to spend one day with one of the characters from this book, who would you choose and what would you do?

CK: Winston! I know I shouldn't have favorites, but I love him the best (probably because his character was inspired by my little brother *shhh*!). I would take him to Universal Studios theme park and on studio tours in Hollywood, since he loves film so much. Maybe even a tour of USC if we could swing it.

KB: Set in local diner Goldeen's, this book made me *really* hungry for diner food. What's your standard diner order? Mine is scrambled eggs, sausage, and toast.

CK: I love the basics, too (minus the toast, because I'm gluten intolerant lol)! I usually order eggs over easy on top of crispy hash browns with a side of bacon. And coffee, of course.

KB: How did writing this book influence your process for writing your third book, *The Marvelous*?

CK: It wouldn't be an exaggeration to say *The Marvelous* exists in its current form because of how I felt while creating *IIMYH*. There was a lot of pressure (real *and* imagined) to deliver a certain type of young-adult contemporary story to follow up *Let's Talk About Love*. I bowed to that pressure telling me how I should write as opposed to believing in myself and trusting my instincts. A story can exist without pain. A story can exist without struggle. A story doesn't have to make readers sad or scream while throwing a book across the room.

When I started drafting my third book, I made some promises to myself: *You have to have fun. You have to create a story that brings you joy. You have to challenge yourself to be better than you were yesterday.* I decided to choose happiness (pun intended) and refused to look back.

I decided to become a writer after a series of interesting events—almost like I was being guided toward my path. Was there a moment, event, or a particular book you read that made you want to become an editor? How long have you been an editor?

KB: I've been an editor since 2009. I've always loved reading. I used to try to push the limits at my local library for how many books you could check out at one time, and I remember having stacks of books on my bed when I was a child. I didn't think about working in publishing until I was in college and a family member gave me a great opportunity to intern at her literary agency. Seeing how agents and editors can really shape a book

made me want to be an editor, and I love that I get to work on projects I am passionate about!

CK: I still vividly remember getting the offer email from you for my debut. What was the first book you ever acquired? Why did you select it?

KB: The first book I ever acquired was an adult mystery, *Blood Orange* by Karen Keskinen. I'd met Karen at a writer's conference in San Diego—the first one I'd ever gone to!—and saw so many things I loved in her story. I can tell right away when I want to acquire a manuscript (meaning, select it for publication) if I start thinking about all the ways I would edit it! That means I can see the potential in the story. *Blood Orange* drew me in with a really dynamic protagonist and an interesting setting (Santa Barbara).

CK: Receiving editorial feedback is an important part of my writing process. I need opinions! I'm an indecisive Libra! Can you describe your editing style? What do you focus on first when tackling a new manuscript?

KB: Some editors love big-picture edits, some editors love line edits, and I am definitely in the latter camp! Even when I'm reading a first draft, I find it hard not to comment on certain sentences I love or ones that aren't working for me. I do try to start big (characters, plot points, voice) and work my way down to the details; I've learned the hard way that it doesn't make a lot of sense to line edit a scene in a first draft because it may just get cut by the second!

CK: I'm a perpetual hobbyist, always trying to improve my writing by experiencing and learning new things. What skill unrelated to editing has helped you most in your job?

KB: I am *definitely* a people person and find it easy to connect with other people quickly, and that's been an asset to me in this job! I find the social aspects of my job, both with my colleagues and my authors and their agents, to be incredibly rewarding. I feel lucky that I get to work with so many people I like, and this job has given me the opportunity to meet and connect with so many interesting people.

CK: What is something people wouldn't necessarily know about editing as a profession?

KB: Oh boy, where do I start? :) I'm asked by friends often to correct their grammar, and I am definitely not that kind of editor; that's what a copyeditor does, and they are *really* good at it! Someone asked me recently if I read all day, which is another common misconception; there's definitely a lot of reading in this job, but most of the work isn't reading, sadly. Being an editor involves managing a lot of moving parts, and while we certainly get to edit, that's just one slice of our job's pie! And now I want pie . . .

A spectacular mansion, a life-changing cash prize,
and a reclusive heiress await in Claire Kann's next novel.

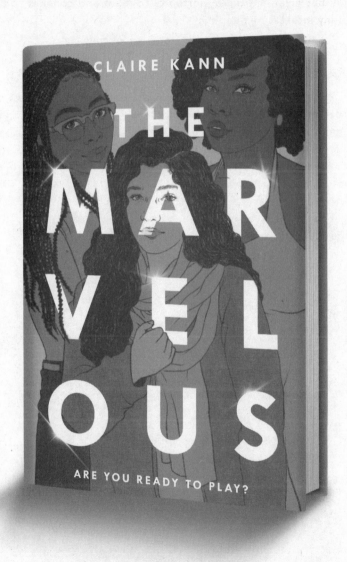

Turn the page for an excerpt.

Goldspiracy Forums

Transcript #947
Original <u>Golden Rule diary entry</u> by Jewel Van Hanen
March 14, Year Three
💬 Transcribed by **SilentStar**

Hi. Hello. I've been gone for a while, I know.

[sighs]

I needed to take some time to think about what I was doing here. What my goals were. How close I had gotten to achieving them before I began to grow complacent with the status quo.

A couple of days away from Golden Rule to clear my head turned into weeks turned into months, and now here we are one year later.

[pauses]

I created Golden Rule to be an escape—a safe place to revel in the minutiae and greatness of real life, not hide from it while hoping for something better. A place for authenticity and kindness and support. A place to plan and grow, to figure out what your best life would look like, and how to get there. A place for stories. Yours and mine.

This app saved me, and I know it saved a lot of you too. It organically grew into something so beautiful I almost couldn't believe it. Everything Golden Rule became absolutely exceeded my wildest dreams. I genuinely thought moving beyond the screen, inviting some of you to my estate for Golden Weekend, was the natural next step.

There is always a price for getting everything you want.

[audio distortion/unacknowledged by subtitles]

While I was away, my app continued to thrive and evolve without me. A few new users broke engagement records that were never supposed to exist. Golden Rule stopped being a community and became a glorified popularity contest.

While I was away, I spent a lot of time thinking about the nature of expectations. Our lives follow patterns. We seek the familiar, and our brains make sense of it. It transforms what we see into something recognizable and digestible, even if that's not what it really is. It's comforting to know how something will go, how it will end. Everybody loves watching a train wreck because it's a guaranteed release. You see it coming, and then you see it burning.

[audio distortion/unacknowledged by subtitles]

I wasn't ever going to come back.

And then a very precious bespectacled beauty said to me, "Are you really going to leave without saying goodbye? You? Jewel Van Hanen?"

Me. Jewel Van Hanen.

[pauses and smiles]

Did you know today is White Day? Shall I give you chocolates, or would you like something much, much sweeter?

[pauses]

One more time. One more group. One more Golden Weekend. I will follow four users for three very different reasons.

Additional Video Notes by **SilentStar**

Jewel is sitting close to the camera. Torso completely in frame. Background is the Pink Room and appears to be unremarkable. Audio distortion appears at 00:02:47 and 00:03:20. No clues present in autogenerated or user-corrected subtitles. The video also appears to be edited, as several jump cuts are present throughout. Since Jewel is known for filming in one take, this is cause for documentation. Replies were disabled on the video.

SilentStar

After school, Luna sat alone under her favorite tree on the front lawn, eating the rest of her lunch while waiting for her ride home.

And then she started choking.

Her mouth opened and closed like a fish gasping on land. She blinked in disbelief, eyes watering as she pulled at her collar. Air could get in, whistling past the lump of mush bulging in her throat, and luckily, it was just enough to keep her alive. She took a final breath, clenched her core muscles, pushed on her diaphragm, and coughed like her life depended on it. Because it did. She spit the food out into a napkin and collapsed on the grass next to her phone.

Really, eating and reading were two activities that Luna had no business doing at the same time. The girl simply was not built for that kind of multitasking. But in her defense? The gaspworthy news was *probably* worth dying for.

Jewel Van Hanen had finally returned to Golden Rule.

Everyone had speculated and wondered, but Luna *believed*.

She took a moment to relish the feeling of breathing. The crisp fading-winter air smelled like pine needles and felt just as sharp in her lungs. Sunlight streamed through the leaves, making shadows on her hands. The wind fluttered softly through her hair. She had half a mind to make a new video for Golden Rule and title it something like *Resurrection in Green* in honor of not choking to death and Jewel's return.

Videos on Golden Rule were technically called diary entries, and Luna's always kept her face in frame—the app wouldn't record otherwise—but she never spoke. Her silence got filled by the roaring wind on blustering days, the panging echoes of emptiness when her sister left her alone on weekends, the cacophony of her loud classmates, and the like. Crickets at the park were her costars on good days, as were the sounds of speeding cars while she stood on a bridge on bad days.

True to her screen name, Luna was *the* SilentStar of Golden Rule and one of the Founders of the Goldspiracy Forums.

A steady thrum of too much bass peeled around the corner. Luna rolled over, smiling as she packed up her stuff, and ran for the sidewalk.

Alex always drove like a getaway driver fleeing the scene of a bank heist—with a car full of money, riding the hubristic high of making it out alive. He'd never been late, never missed a day, and never slowed down in front of her school, choosing instead to come to a tire-screeching halt. Inside the car, Luna immediately turned back to her phone. The forum had gone feral with excitement when Jewel had announced Golden Weekend X—the tenth time she would host the event. And as promised, she had followed three of the four users:

JadeTheBabe
BelleLow
StreetcarBouvier

One. More. Spot. Left.

Luna could *not* let herself think about that because if she did, she would get her hopes up, and once they were up, they'd be inevitably shot down when she wasn't chosen. So, instead, she concentrated on her work.

The Goldspiracy was *real*—Luna had coined the term after figuring out *everything* Jewel did in the app had purpose. Her idol was also a low-key genius, planting clues and Easter eggs in all her videos, essentially challenging the community to figure them out without ever acknowledging any of it. Sometimes Jewel even roped in Olive, her bestie, and Ethan, her brother, by hiding clues in *their* videos too.

Most of her challenges could be solved with an internet search or two and strung together to create a message, but that wasn't the hard part. What stumped most was discovering the meaning *behind* the message using the Easter eggs.

No one on the Goldspiracy Forums was better at interpreting Jewel than SilentStar.

Alex cleared his throat, drawing Luna back into real life. She looked up, noticing for the first time that he hadn't sped off the way he normally did. The car idled, engine vibrating under her feet.

"Moon Princess," he said.

"Alex." She gave him her full attention, turning her phone face-down in her lap.

"Notice anything different about me?"

"No?"

"No? Nothing at all?" He lifted his chin, looking down his nose at her.

She assessed him quickly. Hair: same reddish-brown. Face: frustratingly smooth and blemish-free. Eyes: a little red for a likely reason Luna refused to even consider because she didn't want to think Alex would do that to her. Private school uniform: pressed and starchy.

The silence stretched between them. Nothing to say, nothing to add. She knew what he wanted, but held back . . .

"Nothing. At. All." Alex turned his head to the side—ah!

"You pierced your ear!"

A gold stud stood out beautifully against his dusky skin tone. "Ears," he said, showing her the other one. "I've been thinking about stretching. Gotta start small. What do you think? Do they look good?"

He checked his reflection in the rearview mirror for probably the umpteenth time.

Luna didn't feel one way or the other about it but liked that they seemed to make him happy. "Yeah. Sure."

"Yeah? Sure?" He scoffed as he put the car in drive. "Just recklessly breaking my heart, as always."

She laughed, shaking her head at him. "Your heart or your ego?"

"Same difference with me." He gave her the sly smile that could brighten the most terrible of days.

Alex claimed the honor of being the third person Luna had met after moving in with Tasha—her half sister from their dad's first marriage. He attended an elite private school on scholarship—sports and academic because he was amazing—but they lived in the same apartment complex. His mom, Cynthia, had volunteered him to be Luna's school chauffeur. If it bothered him, he never showed it.

"Did you skip school to get that done?" she asked.

"Hmmm?"

"You didn't have them this morning?"

"What?"

"Uh-huh. Your mom's going to kick you out." She grinned at him before looking at her phone again. Her smile didn't last, fading as she watched the number of her notifications continue to climb. Luna's mentions were in absolute shambles—inbox bursting with messages asking her thoughts, and she'd been tagged in literally hundreds of posts. The other Goldspiracy Founders were no different, speculating in their private chat and yelling for her to respond in all caps.

"*Threaten* to kick me out," he said. "There's a very loving difference in there."

They didn't live far from her school—about a twenty-minute drive. Alex pulled into their parking lot, finding a space in between their respective apartments. Painted a drab cream color with mellow brown accents, they weren't much to look at it. The interior of her apartment was even plainer—a tiny two-bedroom, one-bathroom apartment that cost more than it was worth, and yet the price went up every year.

Tasha had done her best to decorate with what she could find at thrift stores. The result was a mishmash of colors and styles that clashed horribly but still felt cozy. She loved pictures, filling the walls with a growing collage of prints of her friends, their family, and most important, her and Luna together. Selfies, stills from videos, the experimental portraits shot for fun at a park one day—almost every photo they had ever taken together eventually ended up on the wall.

When Luna's mom had decided she didn't want to be a mom anymore, Tasha had said, "Look, I don't know how to be anybody's parent, but I think I can be a guardian. I can do that." Two weeks later, twelve-year-old Luna had moved in with her half sister, who was a whole ten years older.

And it had changed Luna's whole life.

As usual, Tasha was at work or school or both and had left a note on the fridge.

Warm up one of the frozen lasagnas for dinner.
It'll take about an hour to cook. Home by eleven ♥

Luna folded the paper in half, sticking it in her pocket for safekeeping until she could put it in her journal with the other notes she'd saved, and then, messaged Tasha.

Luna: HOME!!!!! OH AND
JEWEL'S BACK! AHHHH!!!

**Check out more books
chosen for publication
by readers like you.**

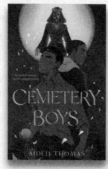